Bird in the Cage

RONALD JAY ALVAREZ

Published by RWS PRODUCTIONS, 2024.

BIRD IN THE CAGE

First edition. July 6, 2024.

Copyright © 2024 RONALD JAY ALVAREZ.

ISBN: 979-8227903327

Written by RONALD JAY ALVAREZ.

Also by RONALD JAY ALVAREZ

Detective Toni Santiago
Pilgrimage to Ruin

Standalone
Bird in the Cage

Watch for more at https://ipprobe.global/about-ron/.

Table of Contents

CHAPTER 1 | Tuesday, May 9 1

CHAPTER 2 | Wednesday, May 10 17

CHAPTER 3 | Thursday, May 11 34

CHAPTER 4 | Friday, May 12 36

CHAPTER 5 | Saturday, May 13 44

CHAPTER 6 | Sunday, May 14 47

CHAPTER 7 | Monday, May 15 51

CHAPTER 8 | Tuesday, May 16 82

CHAPTER 9 | Wednesday, May 17 95

CHAPTER 10 | Thursday, May 18 135

CHAPTER 11 | Friday, May 19 158

CHAPTER 12 | Saturday, May 20 168

CHAPTER 13 | Sunday, May 21 181

CHAPTER 14 | Monday, May 22 185

CHAPTER 15 | Tuesday, May 23 203

CHAPTER 16 | Wednesday, May 24 224

CHAPTER 17 | Thursday, May 25 255

CHAPTER 18 | Friday, May 26 299

CHAPTER 19 | Saturday, May 27 305

CHAPTER 20 | Sunday, May 28 326

CHAPTER 21 | Wednesday, June 7 – | Saturday, June 10 327

CHAPTER 22 | Sunday, June 11 329

CHAPTER 23 | Monday, June 12 330

CHAPTER 24 | Wednesday, June 14 336

CHAPTER 25 | Friday, June 16 337

THE END 339

Dedicated to the memory of my father, Octavio "Joe" Alvarez, a retired NYPD officer and WWII veteran, whose legacy of bravery and integrity has shaped my path.

And to my fellow FBI National Academy Associates around the world and all the men and women of U.S. and global law enforcement, past and present, thank you for your sacrifice and service.

CHAPTER 1
Tuesday, May 9

At about 8:30 a.m., NYPD Lieutenant Maximo "Max" Valentin was sitting in a department car alongside a few of his fellow Joint NYPD/DEA Task Force detectives and agents when his iPhone rang.

They had just executed a search and seizure warrant on an entire five-story building on West Twenty-Seventh Street that was being used for drug labs to mix the precursors to create fentanyl—exclusive distributors originating from the Xhinghi Chemical Company in Macau, China. It was a 24/7 operation. Fentanyl production did not have a time zone.

The owner of the building leased a floor to each of the New York drug gangs to operate their respective labs. Of course, the owner would plead ignorance, claiming no knowledge of the activities taking place on his property and should not be held liable, but the courts were finding "willful blindness" an affront.

Max and his team arrested not only the various gang members, seized all the fentanyl, paperwork, computers, and cell phones, but they took control of the owner's building as well.

"How you doing, Max? It's Eddie V," Lieutenant Ed Vance said.

"Hey, Ed, what's cooking? Everything good?"

"Yeah, all good."

"Sarah and the boys, grandkids?"

"They're all good, thanks," Vance said. "Maya and the twins?"

"Yeah, they're good too," Max said. "Why you out so early? Don't you still work ten to six? You got something?"

"Fresh homicide."

"Ah, huh."

"Listen, so, the feds are stealing you from the drug task force to join a new IP strike force?"

Max Valentin didn't answer right away. "Ahh, sorry, Ed, what are you talking about? Did you say IP—Intellectual Property? IP Strike Force?"

A couple years earlier, when Max was in the Nineteenth Precinct on the Upper East Side of Manhattan—they had assigned him as the nineteenth detective squad executive officer. Ed Vance was the commanding officer of the squad and had been for the previous eleven years.

As the executive officer, Max was the second in command, the second whip. Ed was the first whip. Vance had broken Max in as a detective supervisor.

"*Si, senor*. You didn't see the orders? I just saw the notification on my phone," Vance said and read the message, "'Effective immediately: Lieutenant Maximo Valentin, NYPD/DEA Task Force transferred to the NYPD/FBI IP Strike Force.'"

Max was silent for a couple of seconds, slowly shaking his head.

"You there, Max?"

"Yeah, I'm here, Ed. Thanks for letting me know. I'll call headquarters later, talk to Joe Mulkern. Find out what's going on."

Mulkern was the administrative lieutenant for the NYPD Chief of Detectives Office.

"Yeah, right. Joe can give you the inside scoop on that."

"So, where's the homicide, Ed? Sounds like you're over by FDR Drive somewhere. I can hear the traffic."

"Good ears. I'm on the Roosevelt Island tram."

"The Roosevelt Island tram," Max repeated. "On the tram itself?"

"*Correctomundo.*"

"What's it look like?"

"Male/Asian in his early forties. ME figures stabbed right through his jacket into his kidney. Not much blood. Ice pick maybe. The booth guy said two Asians in twenties or thirties in casual dress, short and taller, raced off the tram and down the stairs and gone. Shorter guy had paint on his face and neck."

"Tattoo?"

"Probably."

"What then?"

"Tall guy walked off with a black business bag. Then the booth guy is alerted by a couple of British tourists about the vic. Booth guy gets on the tram, thought he was asleep, gave him a shake, he toppled over, called 911," Vance said. "Just found out the DOA is the chairperson of the chemistry department at the Brooklyn Institute of Technology—BIT."

"No kidding," Max said. "Chemistry professor?"

"Yeah."

"What's his name?"

"John Xu," Vance said. "Doctor John Xu."

"Huh. Two Asians take out an Asian chemistry professor. Doesn't exactly sound like your random mugging gone bad."

"No, it doesn't. It's got that targeted feel. Did he owe big bucks to somebody? A gambling problem? Is it a cultural thing? Like he refused to let his daughter marry the guy she had in mind, and the guy took him out? Who knows?"

"Right, Ed," Max said "CCTV?"

"Yeah, we're going to find out. You know how it is. It's hit and miss what's working. If it's not a sensitive location, it's never a guarantee," Vance said. "Oh, listen, there's a retirement racket for

Chief Harnett on Wednesday, up in the Bronx—Castle Harbor. Why don't you try to make it? It'll be good to see you and I know Harnett always thought real highly of you."

"Chief Harnett, no kidding," Max said. "He's putting in his papers. Good for him. Damn good boss."

"You're right. A real gentleman. He just hit forty-one years on the job, and sixty-three."

"Ahh, mandatory retirement. I'll try to make it."

"Listen, Max, got to go. The press is starting to show. I'll text you the retirement flyer when I get back to the office."

"Okay, Ed. If nothing comes up, see you Wednesday."

"Sounds good."

ABOUT EIGHT HOURS LATER, Max's team finished vouchering all the property as arrest evidence. The magnitude of this takedown required a massive tractor trailer to empty the five-story building of not only the drugs, electronics, and paperwork, but all the machines that mixed the lethal precursor chemicals to create enough fentanyl to kill millions of Americans—delivered to the drug gangs' courtesy of the Xhinghi Chinese Chemical Manufacturing Company.

After one of Max's detectives pulled the front door to the building shut, she plastered a yellow "DO NOT CROSS" sticker across the front entrance, "AUTHORITY: NYPD/DEA TASK FORCE."

He then signed the arrest reports for his detectives and agents to take the eleven prisoners down to the federal Manhattan Correctional Center on Park Row; then got on the phone to the NYPD office of the chief of detectives.

The phone was picked up on the second ring.

"Chief of Detectives Office, Lieutenant Mulkern."

"Joe, it's Max Valentin. What's going on?"

"Hey, Max, you saw the transfer order?"

"Yeah, what's up?" Max asked. "I don't want to work in any IP task force or strike force, whatever it's called."

"What can I tell you, Max? The chief had a meeting late last night at Twenty-six Federal Plaza with the FBI assistant director. She needed a boss to assign to this new strike force. Your name came up, plus you got the FBI National Academy cred."

Max shook his head. "So, I don't even get asked if I want to work that strike force. There's plenty of bosses in the detective bureau that would jump at the chance. We're doing good work with the DEA. We've got a couple major fentanyl cases breaking, not to mention the takedown we did this morning."

"The chief wants somebody with the IP experience to work in the strike force. She opened your personnel folder, remembered you worked on our Trademark Enforcement Unit—counterfeiting squad—when you were a detective before you became a boss."

"Yeaaaaaah."

"And you have—are you kidding me, Max? You have a master's in intellectual property law from a university in Italy. What the hell?"

"Huh, yeah, yeah," Max said, feeling his face get a little red. "Something that caught my interest a couple years ago. I knew that was going to bite me on the ass one day."

Mulkern let out a laugh. "Well, it caught the chief's interest, too. Listen, upside is you can pick two investigators to work with you directly."

"What do you mean?" Max asked. "Pull detectives from our DEA group? I can't do that. They'll need them to keep working our pending fentanyl cases."

"Yeah, right, but, no, you can also pick federal agents if you know any you want to work with. The FBI boss gave the okay on that."

"Is that right?" Max said and paused for a moment.

"That's the word."

There was a long silence.

"Can I see the chief, Joe?" Max asked.

"Sure. When are you getting back?"

"Twenty minutes."

WHEN MAX WALKED INTO the front office for the chief of detectives, Lieutenant Mulkern stood up, knocked on the door of Chief Delia Mannix and opened it.

"Come on in, Max, grab a seat," Mannix said. "How's your sister and the twins?"

"They're good, chief, thank you for asking."

"So, Joe gave you the details. You have to see Special Agent in Charge, Dick Roach," Mannix said. "He oversees their Computer and IP Crimes Section."

Max paused for just a second before speaking.

"Chief, I appreciate your recommending me to work in that strike force, but we're doing important drug enforcement work. That's really where my recent enforcement experience is, as you know. We're giving those Chinese fentanyl manufacturers a really hard time dumping their poison on us."

"I know, Max," Mannix said. "And that was an outstanding takedown and seizure you and your squad did this morning."

"Thanks, Chief," Max said. "I guess this new strike force will branch out to trade secrets theft cases, which is terrific, but I don't have any enforcement experience with those types of cases. Any squad commander in the detective bureau could learn how to work those types of cases as quickly as I could."

"Maybe so, Max. But I noticed you picked up a graduate degree in IP recently. Very good," Mannix said. "You must've picked up some knowledge about trade secrets theft and how the Chinese are robbing us blind..."

"Yes, Chief, but..."

"What was the subject of your master's thesis?"

Max paused with the recognition that their talk would now end. "Chinese Strategies to Steal Western Trade Secrets."

Chief Mannix looked at Max with a smile and with open palms and arms that communicated, *C'mon, man.*

"But. Chief, you know what I'm working on."

"I want you to do this."

Max stayed silent and looked at the chief as she gave him an almost undetectable nod. Max knew in that moment there was no rescinding his transfer to that federal IP strike force. And Max knew she was absolutely being fair in asking him to do this. Not that she had to ask. She could assign Max to any detective squad in the city.

He would always be grateful to Chief Mannix for transferring him to the NYPD/DEA Strike Force when he was still a sergeant in the Nineteenth Precinct Detective Squad and his brother-in-law died from exposure to fentanyl. Both his immediate boss then, Lieutenant Ed Vance, and the chief understood what it meant for him and his family.

MAX'S BROTHER-IN-LAW, a dedicated ER nurse at Jacobi Hospital in the Bronx, faced a tragic incident that shaped Max's focus. During a high-pressure response to a fentanyl overdose, Max's brother-in-law found himself without a mask. In a moment of urgency, he inhaled fentanyl particles as they stripped the victim, leading to a sudden cardiac arrest that killed him. This heart-wrenching event hit his sister and him hard.

Upon his transfer to the NYPD/DEA Task Force, Max and his team embarked on an arduous journey of investigation. They recognized the need to curb the rampant fentanyl crises, which was claiming countless lives across the city. Their approach involved heartfelt interviews with the families of over two dozen overdose victims. Those grieving families, willing to do whatever they could to combat the epidemic, handed over their loved ones' iPhones.

With the digital trail provided by the families, Max's team meticulously analyzed the data to identify the last calls made from the victims' phones. This breakthrough led them to trace the distribution network backward, eventually exposing a chilling connection. The NYC fentanyl dealer turned and disclosed ties to the infamous Mexican Sinaloa cartel—formerly led by the life-imprisoned drug lord, "El Chapo."

Max and his team formed an alliance with Mexican law enforcement. Their shared goal: to unravel the intricate web woven by the cartel. This pursuit took them to Mexico, where they navigated through shadows and whispers to gather vital intelligence. In a pivotal turn of events, Max's team successfully turned a Sinaloa operative, extracting critical information about the cartel's far-reaching global connections.

Among the revelations provided by the operative was an obvious link to China. This connection pointed straight to the heart of the fentanyl epidemic: Mr. Fentanyl's operation in Macau. The investigation, now spanning borders, catapulted into a new phase, uncovering the threads that tied together the intricate world of international drug trafficking.

NOW, SHE WAS ASKING him to take an assignment he was not looking for.

"Max, you have the FBI Academy cred, too," Mannix said. "You got along well with the FBI down there, didn't you, and you've worked with the FBI on a number of cases on our Trademark Enforcement Squad and with the DEA Task Force, I'm sure?"

"I did, Chief," Max said, and knew it was not a good time to explain the difference between being treated with genuine hospitality by the FBI instructors down in Quantico during his three months of training and working on cases with individual FBI street agents. But working in an FBI strike force meant he would be under the thumb of FBI administrators, and that dynamic could be a whole different story. And Max knew the chief knew that, too.

"And I've been told you've kept up your Mandarin fluency," Mannix said with a bit of a wider smile. "You're the lieutenant for the job."

"Yes, ma'am," Max immediately replied.

"Good, I don't have to tell you how important this IP trade secrets theft business is," Mannix said. "I know you'll give it all you got."

"I will, Chief."

MAX HAD A GOOD IDEA of what was behind the establishment of the new NYPD/FBI IP Crimes Strike Force.

A couple of years earlier, the U.S. Department of Justice had established the China Initiative to counter the persistent theft of U.S. trade secrets from U.S. universities and private industry by Communist China-connected actors.

Although the current U.S. administration dropped the title "China Initiative," they are no less committed to taking down state-directed Chinese IP thieves.

The entire U.S. Department of Justice—including its ninety-four United States attorneys—had been directed to identify trade secrets theft cases. And the number one target was obvious: China. China was into everything.

Not until his assignment to the NYPD Trademark Enforcement Squad years before did Max learn China drove about eighty-five percent of the counterfeit products that flooded the globe. The massive seizures of counterfeit goods from warehouses, tractor trailers, public storage facilities that flowed in from air, sea and land originated in China.

It ran into billions of dollars in lost revenue to the brands every year—the rightful IP rights holders. And, China, as the "world's factory" for legitimate and illegitimate goods, the Chinese could and would counterfeit anything. If it existed, the Chinese counterfeited it: clothing, jewelry, footwear, electronics, computer software, medications. You name a popular brand; no doubt the Chinese counterfeited it.

But not only would they counterfeit it, but, often, if a particular Chinese manufacturer was the authorized manufacturer of a brand's product, the manufacturer would not only produce enough of the brand's product to meet the client's production requirements but would produce extra to sell on the black market for themselves.

Until then Max did not have any genuine sense of how deep the Chinese state was into stealing Western trade secrets from any entity that did research and development in any conceivable area.

He didn't know that China had their own initiative, an initiative in which they intended to catch up and overtake the U.S. in technological advancement by all means necessary, which, included, stealing it.

That's when he learned that if the Chinese could not discover it, and could not reverse engineer what others discovered, they would steal it. And there was no limit to the lengths they would go to do just that.

In law enforcement circles the Chinese theft strategy was referred to as the three Rs:

Rob. Replicate. Replace.

Rob the American company of its intellectual property.

Replicate the technology; and

Replace the American company in the Chinese market and, one day, in the global market.

Max learned the thieves would receive financial incentives and status promotions from the Chinese state. The Chinese state supported them in using the stolen information in their own company to compete with the U.S. company that spent millions in R & D.

That's when he explored master's programs that focused on intellectual property law and protection and stumbled onto the low residency master's IP law program at Turin University that only required his living in Italy for six weeks between his first and second year of study. He'd saved up enough vacation days to take the six weeks without the department even noticing.

Max despised trade secrets thieves. It just cut through him. After others had invested millions of dollars and worked for hours, days, months, and years, inch-by-inch, sweating, and bleeding, jotting something down, developing it, then discarding it because it just wasn't there yet, starting again, and again, and again, to create something, create anything that was original, that was innovative, that often led down countless dead ends, countless hours lost, countless hours of lost sleep, the hard slog, before the idea, the invention, the music, the vaccine, the novel, had reached full clarity, that someone, some entity or some government would swoop in and just take it without having earned it—

That disturbed him. That disturbed him badly.

"DID JOE MENTION YOU can pick two investigators who can go into the strike force with you?" Mannix asked.

"He did, Chief," Max said. "I don't want to pull any of our detectives from the DEA Task Force, Chief, but I do know a Homeland Security agent, FBI agent, and a senior analyst with the U.S. Marshals Service I've worked with before that it would be great to work with again."

"If you're requesting them, they must be damn solid people."

"They are, Chief."

"I'll let the FBI assistant director know," Mannix said. "He'll make the arrangements."

"Thank you."

"All right," Mannix stood up. And Max stood up.

"You don't have to keep me up to date on the play-by-play. I'll leave it to your judgment if there comes a time you need to let me know something in particular."

"Yes, ma'am."

"So, we're good?"

"Yes, ma'am," Max said. "I'll walk right over and introduce myself."

"Good."

Max headed for the door. Just as he was about to turn the knob, Chief Mannix spoke up again, "Max, an unusual incident happened in the South China Sea when you were on vacation last month."

"Is that right?"

"Yeah, apparently that Chinese fentanyl manufacturer—you know the one—was kidnapped from his home in Macau and there was a big chase with the Chinese Coast Guard and the speedboat allegedly holding the fentanyl guy."

"Oh," Max said as he tried to keep a neutral expression. "That's interesting. Did they rescue the bad guy?"

"They did," Mannix said. "But the kidnappers got away. Nobody knows who they were."

"Oh," Max said. "That's really something. Well, I hope everyone sees their day in court soon."

"Yeah, me too," Mannix said, with a nod and just a glimmer of a grin. "Okay, be careful out there."

"Yes ma'am, will do," Max said with a determined nod and moved to let himself out.

"That fentanyl creep is still in China?" Mannix asked. "Isn't he?"

"He is, Chief," Max replied, closed the door behind him and thought, *he better stay in China.*

"YOU'RE VALENTIN?" ROACH asked Max as they escorted him into the impressive office of the Special Agent in Charge of the New York FBI Division, Computer and IP Crimes Section, at 26 Federal Plaza.

Roach was in his early fifties, clean-shaven and bald. Looked like Mr. Clean except for the missing muscular build. It seemed to Max the gym hadn't seen Roach in quite some time.

"I am."

Roach did not look away from the Mac on his desk, giving Max the opportunity to take in the cherry wood theme of the office.

Max always appreciated the interior decorating theme of the federal law enforcement community, whether it was the federal courts, prosecutors' offices, or offices of federal agents. All of their offices had the cherry wood theme. What was it about cherry wood, he often wondered, that made you feel the authority of the legal process? The wood communicated sincerity, seriousness, integrity, depth, the real deal.

Offices of the police department maintained a gunmetal gray decorating theme. And it didn't matter if it was the local precinct or the multitude of offices at One Police Plaza. (Except for the police commissioner's office; deputy commissioners and the various chiefs with one-to-four stars on their collar.) The desks were gunmetal; the chairs were gunmetal; the file cabinets were gunmetal—the impact wood versus gunmetal had on its employees and the citizens who had occasion to visit was undeniable.

"So, what's your background?" Roach finally asked as he continued to tap away on his computer.

"My background is I'm an NYPD lieutenant. What's yours?" Max asked and looked at Roach until he turned away from his computer to look up at him.

"If you're going to be supervising one of my teams, I need to know your background."

"Mr. Roach, I'm not applying for a job. The chief of detectives of my department assigned me to this strike force," Max said. "I assume you know that up to today I was a supervisor in the NYPD/DEA Task Force and a few years back I worked in my department's Trademark Enforcement Unit."

Roach looked down at his desk and opened a folder which apparently contained Max's CV. "Yeah, okay, I see that."

Max remained silent and finally took a seat, even though Roach hadn't made the offer.

"Look, Valentin," Roach said and finally looked directly at Max. "I'm going to be straight with you?"

"Good," Max said, and leaned back.

"This wasn't my idea."

"It wasn't mine either," Max said. "But I figure at least our aim is the same: to catch IP thieves."

"Yeah, okay, well, I think strike and task forces are a waste of time. Police departments have their way of working and we have our way of working. I think it's a colossal waste of time to combine the two," Roach said. "It's the politically correct thing to do, but it's not effective."

Max took that in for an extra minute before replying.

"They're not a waste of time, in my experience, Mr. Roach," Max said. "But I agree cops pick up some unique skills and develop some different instincts."

"A lot of bad habits, I would say."

"And FBI agents don't have any bad habits?"

Silence.

"Look," Max continued, "it's been working out in the NYPD/DEA Task Force with good results and other NYPD/FBI task forces have been working out as far as I know—like Bank Robbery and Joint Terrorism—I guess they've learned how to work together and get the job done."

"Yeah, well, we'll see," Roach said. "Anyway, the bottom line is my boss wants this IP Strike Force, and your department has agreed to be part of it. So, we're stuck with each other, at least for a while. Just remember, in this strike force, you're acting as an FBI agent, not a cop."

Max stiffened and held Roach's eyes.

"I'm a cop. And that's the way my head works," Max said, then relaxed. "But I know who I'd officially represent in this job. And I'll do the job in good faith."

Silence.

"I see you want to bring in two ex-cops to work with you?"

"That's right," Max said. "Sam Ashe and Teresa Tan. And Parth Mehta. He's an analyst with the marshals. You know them?"

Roach did not reply.

Max found it a pleasure working with Tan and Ashe; they both grew up in big cities and worked as cops in those cities before going federal.

Teresa Tan in San Francisco and Sam Ashe in Chicago, respectively. And they'd both graduated number one, ironically, in their respective police academies. Teresa Tan was the first Chinese American to graduate first in her class at the San Francisco Police Academy, and Sam Ashe was the first African American to graduate number one at the Chicago Police Academy. They were both a class act.

"All right. See the agent outside. He'll show you the office you'll be using," Roach said and turned back to his computer screen.

After Max saw his office on the twenty-third floor, he then took a slow walk back to One Police Plaza to let them know he'd introduced himself to Special Agent in Charge Dick Roach. He would keep the tone of their exchange to himself.

One final thought Max had about the furniture experience of the police department versus the feds: It may screech and scrape its way into your senses, so everyone feels a perpetual state of doom—criminals, civilians, even cops. But the feds presented an image that was unfair. The feds presented an image of order when they were about to throw you into Dante's inferno. At least when you entered a police facility, you knew the inferno could not be far.

CHAPTER 2
Wednesday, May 10

The next day Max was walking across the plaza to the entrance of the federal building with his backpack across one shoulder as he was trying to balance a tray of Dunkin coffees and a box of muffins. He stayed away from the donuts. Not that muffins were better. He never checked the calorie count and ingredients of muffins, they just seemed healthier to him.

"Hey, Max, hold up."

Max turned back to the voice. It was Sam Ashe.

"Hey, Sam," Max said, and stopped until Sam could catch up to him. "Great to see you again."

He'd met FBI Special Agent Sam Ashe years before when Max was a detective in the NYPD Trademarks Enforcement Squad. He'd received a tip about a digital crime gang that had taken over millions of website domains to carry out their criminal enterprise. Max reached out to the FBI because they had the digital forensic range to take on that volume. The FBI connected him with Sam Ashe.

The investigation led to the seizure of over one million domains, and over three million erroneous e-commerce links that appeared on social media sites and third-party marketplaces involved in selling counterfeit goods, including pharmaceuticals and pirated films. It was a cooperative effort with countries from all around the world, including Europol and Interpol, respectively.

"Likewise, Max. You need a hand with that?" Ashe asked, reaching out for Max to hand him either the coffees or the muffins. Max handed him the muffins, and they could now shake hands.

"Thanks, Sam. I wasn't sure I was going to make it."

"No problem," Ashe said, as they kept moving to the string of doors that permitted entrance into 26 Federal Plaza, and drifted to the far door on the left, the 'Employees Only' entrance. "Thanks for inviting me into this strike force. I was getting bleary-eyed staring at blue screens tracking bogus domains."

"Great to have you aboard."

"You read about the homicide on the Roosevelt Island tram?"

"I did. Yeah, in fact, I was on the phone with the Nineteenth Squad commander when he was on the scene."

"Oh, yeah? Interesting, huh," Ashe said. "Chemistry professor."

"For sure," Max said, then told Ashe what Ed Vance had told him about the British tourists noticing two Asians racing off the cable car, and that it looked like an ice pick had been used. "No blood. Professional. I want to get ahold of the tram CCTV footage."

"I'd like to see that myself," Ashe said. "Parth Mehta can work on that."

Max was delighted to have Parth Mehta now working with them on the strike force too.

Mehta was one of those senior U.S. Marshals Service analysts who made one immediately recognize what made the U.S. Marshals Service what it was today. When Max was in the NYPD Trademark Enforcement Squad, his friend, Assistant U.S. attorney Jack Hunt had asked Mehta to put together a case analysis report for one of Max's transnational counterfeit cases for trial. Mehta's analysis knocked Max's socks off.

He had a PhD from Georgetown University in Applied Intelligence and had been with the marshals service for seven years.

He was an expert in risk assessment, intelligence operations, and analytical techniques.

"Terrific," Max said.

TERESA TAN STRUTTED into Max's office while he and Ashe were talking.

"Hey, Max, Sam!" Tan said and gave them each a handshake and a bear hug. "I missed you guys. Thanks for calling me in on this, Max."

"You kidding? I'm delighted you guys could jump on board."

"Absolutely," Tan said, and Ashe nodded.

WHEN MAX WAS A DETECTIVE in the Trademark Enforcement Squad, the NYPD Vehicle Accident Investigation Squad referred a case in which the brakes on an ambulance gave out. The ambulance smashed into the Christopher Columbus monument at Columbus Circle in Central Park. The two medics and the sixty-nine-year-old retired schoolteacher—heart attack case—they were rushing to St. Luke's Roosevelt died on the scene.

The Accident Investigation Squad suspected the brakes were counterfeit. Max and his squad took over the investigation.

They started with the results of the lab analysis from the brand manufacturer of the brake pads that confirmed the brake pads were fake.

The investigation established that a Ford dealer that serviced the ambulance unknowingly purchased the brake pads from a shell company pretending to be the Wisconsin manufacturer.

Going undercover as a representative of the Ford dealer, Teresa Tan purchased more counterfeit brake pads from the bogus

Wisconsin manufacturer who they subsequently arrested and who gave up his third-party shipper and actual manufacturer of the counterfeit pads in Hubei, China.

Max and the NYPD Trademarks Enforcement Squad then took the unusual step of retaining an international risk advisory private investigation firm based in China, knowing that Chinese authorities would not conduct a thorough investigation. Max would need to give Chinese authorities a complete case before they would take any action.

The CEO of the risk advisory and PI firm was Max's friend. Max had collaborated on various projects with the CEO when Max was in Marine Corps intelligence and assigned to various diplomatic posts in China.

His friend embedded an undercover in the counterfeit factory who secured a job and got copies of fake shipping invoices and several fake brake pad samples.

Max then officially delivered all this information to the Chinese Ministry of Public Security through the U.S. State Department for further action. With the comprehensive case investigation, the Hubei Public Security division executed a raid on the manufacturer's factory, where nine people were arrested and over 100,000 fake brake pads were allegedly seized by Chinese authorities.

Except, the owner of the factory had not been arrested.

The Hubei counterfeit brakes manufacturer was a protected member of the Chinese Communist Party. The CCP, and, in fact, subsidized the counterfeit manufacturing plant.

"GRAB A COFFEE AND A muffin, guys."

"Thanks, a lot," Tan said and moved toward the coffee table in Max's office and grabbed a muffin. Ashe grabbed a coffee.

"So, we know Communist Chinese trade secrets thieves will be our main focus, right?"

"No doubt," Ashe said, and Tan nodded.

Max adjusted himself in the small sofa in his office while Tan got comfortable behind his desk and Ashe grabbed another seat. "So, we know that the Chinese use spies like every other country on the planet to get government secrets, including us. But what makes China different?"

"They don't just go after another country's government secrets," Tan said.

"Right. Like the Chinese hack a couple years ago of personnel management records by the hundreds of thousands," Ashe said, "they pulled records on thousands and thousands of federal employees. Home addresses, dates of birth, financial status, family tree, parents, children. Critical information for an adversary nation state to have. To pick out those U.S. federal employees they want to bribe or just get the inside track on."

Max said, "Right, as the assistant attorney general recently mentioned, the Chinese have weaponized data. They target troves of data." Max pulled out his iPhone and read a quote from the attorney general's statement:

"'This leads me to the second threat: the weaponization of data. Personal data is the fuel for our adversaries' surveillance and intelligence states. Whether through traditional or corporate espionage, our adversaries are targeting troves of data.'"

"That nails it," Tan said. "And the Chinese state doesn't just go after personal data and government secrets of an adversary, but the trade secrets of private industry in that country."

"And turn the secrets over to their state-controlled companies," Ashe said.

Tan added, "And they use nontraditional collectors to get the trade secrets they want. Employees of U.S. companies, R & D institutions…"

"Right," Max said. "So, how do they get nontraditional collectors to collect?"

"They either get them on board with their theft program before they arrive here, like through the Thousand Talents recruitment program," Tan said, "or they look for what makes them vulnerable while they're here."

"Right," Max said. "We know that U.S. companies are turning down more and more candidates out of concern about being robbed blind of their R & D, so, we know they've been reaching out to risk management investigation firms to do enhanced background screening of the candidates to see if they can detect indicators that would show if those candidates can be leveraged to steal."

Ashe said, "Born in a foreign country, naturalized U.S. citizen or foreign national on a work or student visa, strong roots with the motherland…"

Tan jumped in, "And they're not partial to gender—male or female, married or single, with or without children, of almost any age. Often a group effort, such as a husband-and-wife team."

Ashe jumped back in, "Like last year, a Chinese scientist at a pharma company in Pennsylvania downloads company trade secrets, emails it to her twin sister in China, also a scientist, and the twins conspire with another ethnic Chinese husband and wife scientist team, at another American-based pharma company here that also stole trade secrets and sent it back to the scientist twin here who then sends it to her twin in China. And where do the twins set up their shell company to facilitate their IP theft enterprise?"

"Here in the U.S. no less," Tan said.

Ashe nodded. "Exactly. They set up a company in Delaware to coordinate with the twin sister who had set up a pharma company in China, not to mention the twins' brother, another scientist in Switzerland, steals that company's IP from there to help set up a lab in China and market the data they stole from the U.S. and Swiss company."

"That crew got a patent for the U.S. research in China, didn't they?" Max asked.

"Yeah. A real family IP crime team," Ashe continued. "Background screening. That's what that's all about. The company the thieves set up in Delaware even had the word 'pharma' embedded in their name. And the scientist's name is recorded on the Delaware corporation's site for the world to see," Ashe said. "These pharma companies—and not just pharma—need to do periodic background screens of their employees, especially those working on heavy R & D."

Tan said, "The pharma company she worked for and stole from could've done a simple name check that would've shown she had a company of her own."

Ashe added. "Exactly. Instead of her being able to steal for years, she would've popped up on their radar during a biyearly screening."

"How about this recent indictment of that Google AI thief," Max said. "Allegedly steals over 500 AI files, transfers them over to Apple Notes then converts the data into a PDF and sends it to his personal account."

"Slick attempt to evade digital detection," Ashe said. "Then he goes to China with Google trade secrets that he pitches to investors that he says only need to be replicated."

Max shook her head. "Not only that, to keep Google from noticing he wasn't at work, he gave his ID to another Google employee to swipe him in which led Google to think he was at the U.S. Google facility, but he was actually in China right at that time giving his pitch to investors as a Google insider."

"And it's not just China," Tan said. "Russia, Iran, and North Korea are in the game, too."

"Right, except China steals more trade secrets from us than all the other countries combined according to the FBI director," Max said.

"True enough. The Bureau currently has over two thousand active Chinese-connected theft or espionage cases now," Ashe said. "And we pick up another case every ten hours."

Max's personal iPhone buzzed. "I got to take this, guys. It's my sister."

Tan and Ashe drifted out of Max's office.

"Hey, Maya, how was the ER last night?"

"The usual trauma flow, a few gunshot victims. You know how it is," Maya said. "Everything okay with you?"

"Yeah. Just wrapped up shooting the breeze with my colleagues. Everything okay?"

"Got a call from Ben's teacher yesterday. Apparently, all the kids in his class have to come up with a science project to work on. The teacher gave them a week to come up with an idea."

"Okay."

"So, instead of coming up with his own idea, Ben copied another kid's and submitted it as his own idea."

Max shook his head. His eight-year-old nephew was already practicing the art of stealing trade secrets.

"Did Ben tell you about it?"

"No, first I'm hearing about it."

Max could not help feeling a burst of affection for his nephew over the stress he must be experiencing that drove him to steal a classmate's idea. "Well, that's not good."

"No, it's not. I wish he'd told me about it. I could've helped him try to come up with something of his own."

"Want me to talk to him, Maya, and help him come up with something?"

"Would you, Max?"

"You bet," Max said. "I'll tell you what. How about I take Ben out to miniature golf over at City Island on Saturday. See if we can come up with something as we putt a few balls."

"Would you, Max? Thank you so much."

"Absolutely," Max said. "I'll pick him up at eleven. But I'll text you when I'm on the way. Sound good?"

"Thanks, Max."

"LISTEN TO THIS," TAN said and marched back into Max's office. Her gait always looked to Max like she was attacking the floor. Ashe drifted back in too.

"Listen to what?" Max asked, with a smile over Tan's eager office entry as he settled back and took a sip of coffee.

Tan smiled back and mumbled, "There's an immigration program for graduate foreign students who graduated and majored in a science or technology field, engineering or math, to be given a two-year extension to stay here in the U.S. if they have a job lined up."

"Yeah, I've heard about that program, Teresa," Max said. "Optional something…"

"Right, Optional Practical Training Program," Tan said. "So, ICE just found out that about two thousand six hundred Chinese foreign graduates who are here in the U.S. and allegedly working—"

Ashe interjected, "Just to be clear, not current students, but graduates who are now working here with that extension?"

"Yep. Two thousand six hundred that have graduated with a master's or more and are here working for a U.S. company," Tan said. "Except the company they claim to work for doesn't exist."

Max took that in for a moment. "Shell company?" he asked.

Tan nodded. "And the foreign graduates are not even trying to hide that they're employed by the shell. A bunch of them are on LinkedIn, claiming to be employed by the shell."

"Not trying to hide it because they think we don't know it's a shell. So, they feel safe," Max said, thinking out loud. "Interesting."

"Probably," Tan said, took a bite from her corn muffin, and with a full mouth continued, "And until recently, we didn't know."

"How's Homeland working it?" Max asked.

"They're doing a takedown early the day after tomorrow of the whole twenty-six hundred. It's going to be coordinated from the Homeland command center in Virginia. We've been invited down by my Homeland boss to watch it."

"The whole twenty-six hundred?" Max asked with wide eyes.

"Yep," Tan said.

"Arlington?" Ashe asked.

"Yep," Tan said. "We can fly down tomorrow afternoon. They'll put us up. And we can watch it all Friday in the a.m."

Max was in deep thought.

"There might be a case or two to pull from that crowd," Max said.

Ashe said, "Yeah, yeah. It's worth a look."

"Who does the shell come back to?" Max asked.

"Female and male Chinese names," Tan said.

"First and last?" Max asked.

"Yep."

"Immigration have anything on them?" Ashe asked.

"Negative," Tan said. "They don't exist. Fictitious all the way."

"Male and female names," Max repeated. "Corporation? LLC?"

"LLC," Tan said.

"Delaware?" Max asked.

Tan nodded.

"It's always Delaware," Ashe blurted.

"Names but missing in action," Tan said. "No photos. Names on the LLC docs but don't come back to any real people. IDs used to register were bogus. Homeland is still digging."

Max nodded. "All right. I'd like to hear if they come up with anything more on those two principals. What's the shell's name?"

"Tech Dragon."

"A front for a tech start-up. Interesting," Max said and paused. "What if these two thousand six hundred—through the enhanced background screening—were rejected for a U.S. position they feel qualified for? I mean, if they'd landed a U.S. position, why go into the shell? No need. Right?"

"Right," Tan said, and Ashe nodded.

"So, they get rejected for whatever reason—red flag concerns the U.S. company—"

"Red flag?" Tan asked with a grin. "Pun intended?"

Max shook his head and smiled. "No, but what do they feel after being rejected by the American company?"

"Resentment," Tan said.

"Right. We all know the one thing that drives so many trade secrets thieves, whether foreign or domestic, is resentment," Ashe said. "If they're in companies and feel that the company or organization doesn't appreciate their talent or contributions, or they're rejected outright—like this twenty-six hundred maybe—they're more prone to steal for their birth country."

"And the Chinese recognize that vulnerability, so when a recent rejected graduate finds out through the grapevine that there's a shell company that will employ them on paper," Max said, "to extend they stay in the states—"

"The CCP targets them," Tan interjected.

"Exactly, but it has to be conditional, right?" Max said. "On the condition that Chinese security services will support them as they float around for two years and see where they land and what they come up with."

"Darn interesting theory, Max," Ashe said.

"You know," Tan said. "That lines up precisely with the acronym used to explain the motivation of trade secrets spies."

"Right. Spies are driven by money, ideology, compromise, or ego—M-I-C-E," Max said.

Ashe stood up from the sofa and walked over to get another coffee. "So, there's twenty-six hundred ethnic Chinese graduates out there cruising the States who are not actually employed, but pretending to be employed by this shell?"

"Yep," Tan said.

Ashe said rhetorically, "I wonder how they're spending their days."

"Good question," Max said, and stood up too. "We should find out."

THAT EVENING, MAX STEPPED into the bar of the packed Castle Harbor Restaurant in the Bronx. Packed with detectives and bosses, male and female, three rows deep. From across the bar, he heard his name called out.

"Max Valentin. What are you drinking?"

Max looked across the sea of detectives to the other side of the bar. It was Chief Harnett himself.

"Hey, Chief," Max shouted. "Scotch and water, thanks."

Max worked his way through the crowd. When he got to the end of the bar, Harnett handed Max his drink.

"There you go. Thanks for coming."

It went without saying that since Harnett was the man being honored, he did not need to wait in line for any drinks. But it was more than that. He was paying for the party. It was an NYPD custom that the retiree paid for his or her own retirement racket. And everyone else just passed on the word of where and when.

"You bet, Chief," Max said. "Wouldn't miss it."

"Thanks, Max," Harnett said. "So, I saw you just got grabbed for that new FBI strike force."

"Yeah," Max said. "Wasn't looking for it, but that's how it landed."

"That's good, Max," Harnett said. "You're the right man for the job. You'll do us proud. Show those Bureau kids how it's done." Harnett let out a good-natured laugh and gave Max a pat on the arm. "Enjoy your drink. Chow will be served in the dining room in about fifteen."

"Thanks, Chief," Max said. They shook hands and Harnett went off to continue mingling.

After shooting the breeze with a few other Manhattan detectives Max worked with over the years, everyone headed into the dining room area.

As soon as Max walked in, he scanned the room for Ed Vance. There were about twenty circular tables with white paper tablecloths that seated eight at each. As he took in the room from one end to the other, he saw the hand of Ed Vance shoot high in the air at Max like he was a referee spotting a ball on the football field. Max nodded at Vance who pointed down to the seat he was saving for him.

VANCE WAS HOLDING COURT. His table filled with several of his Nineteenth Squad detectives. A real mosaic of the city of New York: Males and females in their thirties, forties fifties, bald and full heads of hair, gray and black, white, Black, Latino, gay, and straight.

After Max shook hands all around with the other detectives, all of whom he'd worked with directly when he was in the Nineteenth

Squad, plus one or two he knew but who came to the squad after he'd moved onto the NYPD/DEA Task Force. After a little banter, shaking a few hands and catching up, the food was served.

Castle Harbor Restaurant had one menu: pork loin, potatoes, and a vegetable. There wasn't any choice, but there was all you could eat, and it was delicious, so nobody complained. Another thing about that quintessential location for NYPD retirement and promotion parties was that those simple, delicious meals were all served on paper plates and bowls.

"How's that tram homicide looking, Ed?' Max asked. "You got CCTV?"

"Still waiting. Should have something by Friday. Still not sure if it was a robbery or something else."

"Your guys talk to his school?" Max asked. "Was he into anything deep?"

"He was on the staff of the department of chemistry and chemical biology; specialized in nanoscience. One of their senior researchers."

"Huh. Nanoscience. That's serious research. Nanoscience research is working on a material that can replace silicon."

"Is that right?" Vance said. "Well, maybe this case has a trade secrets theft angle for you. You know, maybe this chemistry professor was doing some important research that he wouldn't give up. Could be a good reason to kill."

Max nodded and couldn't help smiling. Lieutenant Ed Vance—twenty-eight years in the police department—never handled a trade secrets theft case in his entire career. But you don't spend that many years as a detective squad commander in a global city like New York and not get really proficient at picking up the scent of things.

Like every New York City cop, he read the *New York Post* and *Daily News*, but he also reads the *New York Times* and the *Wall Street*

Journal. New York was a global city. Vance would always say, "'Can't get the global view on things from the *New York Post*.'" But what Ed Vance also read regularly (and Max was one of the few people who knew) was *The Economist* and *Foreign Affairs*—not to mention the MBA he picked up from St. John's University.

"Could be, Ed," Max said. "What about the autopsy and tox report?"

"Cause of death was a combination of a punctured kidney, consistent with an ice pick-like instrument, his forearms broken in two. That did not satisfy the bad guys, so they somehow poured poison down his throat—fried his internal organs."

"What?" Max asked with narrowed eyes. "Poison?"

"Yeah. Somebody wanted to leave a message that wouldn't be missed."

"Looks that way," Max said and thought, *that's a lot of special attention for a chemistry professor.*

As soon as Max had that thought, he felt a hand touch his back; he turned and looked up at a stunning Latina.

"Hey, guys," the female said to the group with a big smile. Standing there was retired First Grade Detective Sophia Morales.

Ed Vance and everyone at the table gave Morales an energized greeting. A cacophony of "Hey, Sophie!"

"Sophie!" Max said too, stood up right away, and they hugged each other. "What are you doing here? What a surprise."

Max and Sophie had come on the job together and worked as rookies in uniform at an East Harlem precinct right out of the academy to start then the precinct Street Narcotics Unit, plainclothes Anti-Crime Unit, and then finally the precinct Robbery Unit before they moved on to other investigative NYPD assignments.

"How's retirement?"

"Good, Max, good. I got my PI license. Working with another retired detective who has his own PI firm in midtown."

"Good for you, Sophie," Max said. "Grab a seat."

After more of the usual catch-up conversation, she asked, "You still working with the DEA, Max?"

"No, just got transferred to a new one. Focused on intellectual property crime. Federal IP Strike Force. Big national push. Trying to stop the Chinese from sucking us dry."

"Ah huh, no kidding. I've been reading about that," Morales said, and then leaned into Max and whispered, "Listen. Let me run something by you on the Q.T."

"Okay." Max leaned in too.

"We'd been asked to do a surveillance on a Chinese PhD student attending the Schimmel Center on Roosevelt Island."

Max nodded. "Ah, huh? Why?"

"Client claims to be the head of a university science department in China and that the student stole some proprietary research they'd been working on and brought it to the U.S. without permission," Morales said. "They said they've sued him in China for restitution, but the targeted student has been evading them."

"What university?

"Tongji University."

"The client just wants him followed around?" Max asked. "That's it?"

"Yeah, just follow him around when he leaves the Schimmel Center and whoever he's with, and report back to them. The client said that they just want to know who he's been meeting with. Said they want to find the best time to approach him off campus."

"You verify the professor's ID in China."

"He's on the university website?"

"What about the lawsuit? You see any paper on that?"

"Yep. It was all in Mandarin, but we had it translated," Morales said. "It appears legit."

"Maybe. The Chinese wouldn't have a problem creating legit looking docs to further a bogus operation," Max said. "You guys meet the client face-to-face?"

"No," Morales said. "Email, texts, and the phone."

"Is there a lawyer here in the U.S. representing the client?"

"Negative," Morales said. "That's why we turned it down. The retired detective who owns the PI firm. He's been in the business for over twenty years. He won't touch any investigation coming from China, Iran, or Russia without a reputable attorney here in the States attached to it."

"That's smart," Max said. "Student's name?"

"Name on the lawsuit docs is Wei Ming."

"You confirm a student by that name at Schimmel?"

"No, never did. No need since we weren't going to run with it."

"The Chinese professor's name?"

"Zhang Kan."

CHAPTER 3
Thursday, May 11

It was a little past four p.m. when Max and his team—Ashe and Tan—jumped on a Homeland Security jet and fastened their seat belts for the thirty-minute ride down to Arlington, Virginia.

"What the hell is it about Delaware and bogus companies?" Ashe blurted with wide-open hands.

Tan jumped in, "Yeah, even Trump's fixer lawyer, Michael Cohen, established a bogus company in Delaware to pay off Stormy Daniels."

Max shook his head and squinted his eyes shut for a couple of moments as if he'd gotten a sudden migraine.

"By the way. I went to a retirement racket last night for a chief I used to work for and ran into the Nineteenth Squad Commander, Ed Vance."

"Yeah, Max," Tan said. "Sam mentioned he's got the tram homicide, right? How's it looking?"

"The deceased was not only a chemistry lecturer," Max said, "he was a senior nanoscience researcher at the university."

"That's big," Ashe blurted. "Nanotechnology is close to replacing silicon."

"And silicon is the prime material in microchips, right?" Tan asked.

"It certainly is, Teresa," Ashe said.

"And he just got the autopsy and tox reports," Max said. "Cause of death punctured with ice pick-like instrument."

"Sounds like a street thug robbery," Tan said.

"Yeah, maybe, except his arms were broken too."

"So, the professor put up a fight," Tan interjected.

Max continued, "And he was poisoned."

"What?" Ashe and Tan said, both with wide and intense eyes.

Now Max nodded.

Ashe finally spoke up, "That's assassination stuff."

"Yeah," Tan said.

Max nodded again.

A TYPICAL BLACK-GOVERNMENT SUV was waiting for them and dropped them at a Marriott in Crystal City.

CHAPTER 4
Friday, May 12

The following morning at six a.m., Teresa Tan escorted Max and Sam Ashe to her home turf, Homeland Security Headquarters in Arlington, Virginia. As soon as they entered the lobby, Tan introduced Max and Ashe to the Homeland Security Investigations, Assistant Director in Charge, Renee Fox.

"Thanks for inviting us in, Director Fox," Max said, shaking the assistant director's hand.

Fox was a lean, five-foot-two, no-nonsense woman in her fifties with intelligent, focused eyes and short hair. She reminded Max of his third-grade schoolteacher, Miss Grossfeld. Miss Grossfeld was as kind and attentive as any teacher in the South Bronx could be. Just don't give her any shit. Max liked Fox immediately.

"No problem at all," Fox said with a warm smile. "I'm delighted you guys could come down for this."

"We appreciate it," Max said, "And thanks very much for lending Teresa to us. She's a star."

Fox pulled Tan in with a hearty hug. "She is a star and we're very proud of her."

Max could see Tan was blushing a bit as she acquiesced to Fox's embrace.

"Thank you, ma'am," Tan said. "Working with Max and Sam is a pleasure. They're the real best. The real stars."

Fox smiled and waved them to follow her. "Okay, let me tell you what we're doing today."

They trailed Fox down the long florescent-lit corridor to the command center as she explained.

"We're going to take down twenty-six hundred of the Chinese nationals that used that shell company, Tech Dragon, as their place of employment," Fox said over her back to them. "We have arrest and search warrants for each of them. Since the day we learned about the visa fraud, we were working our case, worked on pinning down the location of each."

"That's massive," Max said. "Twenty-six hundred. What percentage of the group were you able to nail down?"

"About ninety-eight percent," Fox said. "With twenty-six hundred folks to track, there's always a few that move around a bit more than others. You get their last known location but may not be the location at this exact point in time."

"Right, of course. But even if you have most of their locations, how the heck can you take down that many at one time?" Ashe asked.

Max could see Ashe was as intrigued as he was and said, "I guess they're all on a no-fly list."

"Right. If you pick them up at different times, the word would get out and they'll be scurrying to JFK," Ashe said.

"They are on a no-fly list, but you're right. The challenge was deciding how to pick them all up without spooking the others," Fox said. "Of course, at first, we thought to maybe have Immigration contact them to come in for some routine matter, but that would definitely spook them. So, we came up with a plan to invite them all in at the same time. But not for an immigration matter—for a job."

Max took that in with a smile. "A job?"

Fox smiled back. "That's right. We're using a company that's not up and running yet, but actively inviting candidates in for interviews. We arranged with the company to invite them for an interview, too. Today is that day."

"Twenty-six hundred?" Ashe blurted.

Fox nodded and opened the door to the command center as they followed her in.

The command center had state-of-the-art screens from one end of the center to the other, covering one-eighty degrees, like a Sensurround movie theater. Max estimated there were about 200 analysts, ten rows deep, with headsets and mouthpieces strung across the half-moon desks in front of the sweeping screen. To Max, it looked like a video game competition on steroids.

"Yep, we've invited them all in for a job interview and we used LinkedIn to do it."

"Ahh, this is too much fun," Ashe said, shaking his head in appreciation.

Fox continued. "Using the same LinkedIn profiles they claimed to be gainfully employed—the Tech Dragon shell—to invite them in for an interview."

A beaming Teresa Tan jumped in. "Isn't this damn ironic?" she said, looking up at Max and Ashe. "Through their same bogus profile on LinkedIn, they're being invited in for a bogus job opportunity."

"Smart to not use the contact info Immigration had on them," Ashe said.

"Exactly. We didn't want to use contact info. They'd wonder how our recruiting tech company got that information," Fox said. "But inviting them for a job interview on LinkedIn fits right in."

"This is ironic," Max said. "China is notorious for using LinkedIn to manipulate whoever their targeting in the U.S."

"Indeed," Fox said.

"This is great," Ashe said, still smiling.

"We reached out to a tech company that had recently built a new facility, already had it filled with furniture, computers, the works," Fox said. "So, we approached them, asked if we could use their company's name and the physical location for one day before their employees trickle in."

"The company's still not up and running; just their team preparing the place," Max said. "And they agreed?"

Fox nodded.

"Too cool," Ashe said.

"They didn't even want a dime for our one day of use," Fox said. "The site is over three hundred thousand square feet: about the size of six football fields. Plenty of space to process interviews and arrests of twenty-six hundred."

"What kind of tech company?" Max asked.

"If you want to hear something even more ironic, it's a Taiwanese semiconductor chip company that built a fab... a fabrication plant in Arizona."

"A fab," Max repeated. "What's the name of the company?"

"ESM," Fox said. "Essential Semiconductor Manufacturing."

"Taiwanese company," Max shook his head in admiration. "Damn interesting. And they were willing to help?"

Fox continued, "Yeah, we explained the whole situation to them about the twenty-six hundred Chinese nationals who are pretending to be employed by a Chinese state-sponsored shell company and they were actually excited to assist. Couldn't do enough to help us out."

"How about this," Ashe said. "This is really something."

"So, now it's filled with Homeland Security agents awaiting the twenty-six hundred," Fox said.

"Did you find out anything more about the principals registered to the LLC, Director?" Max asked. "Chinese names, male and female, I understand."

"Not yet. Still just the names. Xu Nan and Fang Yang," Fox said. "They're a mystery for now. No immigration records, and we put their names into N-DEx, but no hits."

"I see," Max said, pensively.

The National Data Exchange System, otherwise known as N-DEx was the law enforcement database for most other active federal investigations, so various federal agencies wouldn't crash into each other.

"So, we're focused on the twenty-six hundred," Fox said.

"We can follow up on those two principals," Max said.

"Really? That's great. Appreciate it," Fox said. "As you can see, we're swamped with this phase right now."

"Pleasure. We're just up and running. Gives us something to do," Max said. "We'll let you know what we come up with."

"Excellent," Fox said, and pointed to several long tables with missile-size coffee urns lined up. "There's coffee, bagels, donuts over there. Make yourselves comfortable. The first group of interviewees should arrive soon."

Fox drifted off to work.

MAX, TAN AND ASHE TOOK a seat at the Arlington command center, got comfortable with their bagel and coffee, and waited for the operation to begin.

The section of the massive Arizona facility to be used for the interviews was consumed with hidden HSI cameras and audio recording equipment. It was impressive. Every inch of the facility was being recorded.

Max, Teresa Tan, and Sam Ashe watched the operation unfold on the multiple screens. They watched the cars pull into the massive parking lot, watched the candidates ease out of their vehicles, some carrying briefcases, other backpacks. Uber cars pulled up on the facility's driveway to the front sliding doors. The men wore suits, collared shirts, some wearing ties; the women were attired in skirts, blouses, and pants suits. It looked like they were all arriving for a professional convention. Then, after being escorted past the lobby check-in to the interior, the cameras showed them being brought into offices. It was carried out with ballet precision.

Homeland had scheduled 300 interviews at fifteen-minute intervals. So, the first 300 were scheduled to arrive at nine a.m., sign in at the lobby, then be escorted through to an office where other agents would be there to search and identify them. Then brought to another holding area until the end of the day and the 2,600 were in custody. Someone would eventually interview them all right, but not for a tech company job.

The interior design of the tech company they were using is just what you would expect, four floors, over twenty elevators, at different corners of the space, with a lot of sliding glass doors to offices, conference rooms, with living room-like lounge areas scattered throughout the facility including two theaters that each had the seating capacity of over 2,000.

The ritual was consistent. The escort-agent brought each target into one office with the sliding doors, where another HSI agent was waiting, the sliding door was closed, and they were informed of the true reason they were invited in. A brief identification interview and body search began.

Agents then exhaustively interviewed them concerning their activities while living in the U.S. under false pretenses; their interaction with their Chinese Tech Dragon principals; what the principals expected them to do, and what they, in fact, did. Finally, photographed, fingerprinted, DNA samples taken and logged into the U.S. Law enforcement database for Chinese foreign agents.

Then escorted to one of the two theaters. Males in one; females placed in the other, to spend their day until the end of the operation in the evening at which point 100 Immigration buses would arrive and transport the twenty-six hundred to the Immigration facility where they would remain until their return to mainland China, or, if there was probable cause to believe they'd committed a crime beyond visa fraud, they would be kept and eventually charged.

For those who wished to request asylum, the U.S. government would offer them due process which included a hearing before an administrative judge. Immigration would then execute the decision of the hearing officer, which, in most cases, meant their eventual return to Communist China. Requesting asylum was often a ruse ethnic Chinese spies would use to extend their espionage work in the U.S.

So, the message was crystal clear: if you remain in the United States under false pretenses, we will escort you out, and not be invited or permitted back.

Max, Tan, and Ashe watched and listened to many of the interviews.

Although there was some intelligence to be gathered from the twenty-six hundred, the targets refused to say much.

But there was one common denominator. They were all associated with Chinese organizations in American universities professing to assist ethnic Chinese students in networking with American private industry. These university organizations were front groups for the CCP's influence and interference operations routinely coordinated by China's Ministry of State Security.

Beyond that, Max did not hear the one key piece of information he was hoping to hear. He was curious whether one or more of the twenty-six hundred had met with the principals of the shell company face-to-face. They had not. Or so they said.

Unfortunately, their pseudo employment with Tech Dragon was all done electronically. No direct contact with Fang Yang or Xu Nan, the recorded owners of Tech Dragon.

Max would coordinate a loose follow-up on Tech Dragon and the two principals.

Late that evening as Max, Tan, and Ashe walked back to the SUV standing by to get them back to the Homeland jet and return to New York, Max mentioned what his retired detective buddy (now a PI) Sophie Morales told him about being approached by a Chinese university science head to put a Schimmel PhD student under surveillance.

"Now, that's a switch," Ashe said.

Tan blurted with wide eyes. "This Chinese university guy, Professor Zhang Kan, claims the Schimmel student stole trade secrets from China?"

Max nodded. "Let's find out if Schimmel has a student named Wei Ming, and what we can find out about Professor Zhang Kan on Monday."

CHAPTER 5
Saturday, May 13

"Nice putt, Ben," Max said as they walked to the next hole. "So, your mom told me you've had some trouble coming up with your own idea for a science project?"

Ben was about to putt the ball at the seventh hole and froze. He didn't look up at Max but didn't hit the ball either for a few seconds, then said, "I don't have any science ideas, Uncle Max," still without looking up or away from the ball.

"Did you tell the teacher that?"

"No."

"Well, next time, let the teacher know you're having trouble coming up with an idea," Max said. "What's most important is that you tell your teacher or your mom or me that you're having trouble with something. Never feel ashamed about asking for help. It takes courage to ask for help."

Ben looked up at Max, "Yes, Uncle Max."

"Okay, good," Max said. "Why don't you putt the ball now?"

Max then did the same.

Ben was closer to the hole, so he took his second shot, and it went right in.

"That's great, Ben. That was one under par for that hole. Excellent."

Ben broke a grin.

As Max putted his second shot and missed the hole, he asked, "So what are some of the science project ideas your classmates are trying?"

Max watched Ben look up in thought before answering.

"One kid is trying to find out if something can float."

"Okay, that's interesting. What else?"

"Another kid wants to find out the strength of a bridge."

"Ah, huh, okay."

As Max was about to take his third shot, Ben pulled out a small bag of pretzels Max had bought for him to snack on as they played the eighteen holes.

Ben put his hand in the bag, pulled out a pretzel, and it dropped to the ground. Without hesitation, Ben bent down to pick it up, was about to put it in his mouth and said, "Five-second rule."

"Don't eat that," Max said, and Ben froze again. "Five-second rule?"

"Yes, Uncle Max. If something falls to the ground and stays there for less than five seconds, it's okay to pick it up and eat it."

Max tried not to smile at the stuff kids come up with.

"Where did you learn that?"

"The kids in school."

Then the light went on for Max and prayed the light would go on for his nephew.

"Is that true?"

Ben stood there with the small pretzel in his hand looking up at his Uncle Max, then looked at the pretzel, then looked back up at Max.

"I don't know, Uncle Max," Ben said and looked back down at the pretzel. "Maybe I can try to find out if it is true. Maybe I can find out for my science project," he said with a glow in his face and eyes like he'd just discovered gold.

"Why not?" Max said.

Ben then walked to the trash can outside the hole and threw the pretzel in, looked at Max and said, "I will wait until I find out."

CHAPTER 6
Sunday, May 14

It was about 9:30 a.m. when Max returned to his East Eighty-Fifth Street apartment after having gone for a run through Central Park. It was one of his favorite routes. A nice easy jog from York Avenue, west on Eighty-Fifth Street, south on Fifth Avenue passing the Metropolitan Museum of Art, and into the park at Seventy-Second Street, by the Bethesda Fountain, south on the West Drive, to Central Park South and up the East Drive up to the Ninetieth Street reservoir, once around, and back to his block.

It wasn't as demanding as the FBI National Academy ten-mile yellow brick road run, which required jumping over walls, going through and around obstacles and mud and some repelling, but it did the job.

Max finished his run on the East River promenade over by Gracie Mansion, the New York City Mayor's residence, walked it off, and checked his iPhone for messages. All quiet.

Max then punched in Sophie Morales's number.

"Hey, Maximo," Morales answered. That was often how his former partner would call out to him over the years.

"Hey, Sophie," Max said with a laugh. "Great catching up with you at Harnett's retirement racket the other night. And thanks again for the heads-up on that student."

"You got something!" Morales eagerly asked.

"Can't say, Sophie," Max said with appreciation for her intuition.

"Huh," Morales said with a chuckle. "Understood. But let me ask you something. I've been doing some reading on Chinese spy strategies since we got approached by that Chinese university rep. What are your thoughts on why the Chinese use students to steal? Not that that is a surprise to me. But they have professional spies like every country does to get what they want? We have spies too, right?"

"Right. The basic difference between what the Chinese do and what we do is that we do not conduct espionage to support private companies in the U.S. We conduct espionage, as every country does, to gather information about their government and military."

"Right."

"But the Chinese gather not just traditional espionage but steal trade secrets of U.S. companies to give Chinese companies a competitive advantage. And Chinese companies are not independent of the Chinese Communist Party. Chinese companies are hermitically sealed to the state. By law, Chinese citizens and companies must make their private and proprietary data available to the state."

"Yeah, like TikTok being owned by the Chinese ByteDance outfit that's hit the news big time."

"Yeah, exactly. They have a calculating, persistent, patient, and multi-layered approach to getting what they want. Our view is that they have turned trade secrets theft into an art form," Max said. "They use nontraditional collectors to do their spying for them."

"Nontraditional collectors, huh? I read something about that recently, too," Morales said. "It was about Chinese tourists claiming they got lost and landed on our military bases, or conveniently found scuba diving around our rocket launch sites down in Florida."

"That's how they operate."

"The article said they give the excuse that they were only looking for a McDonald's that happens to be on an army base or a hotel they had reservations for on another military base."

"That's it. The Chinese often press their citizens with no formal training from their intelligence services, like those Chinese tourists, or they use ethnic Chinese living, working, and studying here to steal. The FBI had an analyst who came up with something called the 'thousand grains of sand' theory.'"

"Thousand, what?"

"'Thousand Grains of Sand.' An FBI analyst came up with this back in the nineties: If a beach were the target, meaning the grains of sand of that beach had value, so were a trade secret, the Russians would send a submarine to that country's shore, send a scuba team in, get handfuls of sand, and leave. We, the U.S., would use satellites to analyze the grains of sand on the beach and figure out its composition that way. The Chinese would send a thousand tourists to the beach, and each pick up one grain of sand."

"Oh, man, what a creepy image that is."

"This is also called the vacuum cleaner approach. The sheer number of Chinese gathering bits and pieces of information and delivered to the Chinese state over time; they put the thousand grains together and eventually arrive at the inside information they are looking for."

"Wow, crazy."

"Except, more recent analysis shows that the Chinese Ministry of State Security has always been much more organized about it than that by working through Chinese state-controlled community organizations throughout the world," Max said. "What is called United Front influence and intimidation operations?" Max was thinking about Alex Joske, that Australian Chinese espionage analyst's comments he'd recently heard on YouTube.

"Darn interesting, Max."

"It is," Max said, and started to walk to his building. "Listen, I just got back from a run and need to jump in the shower. Thanks again for that heads-up, Sophie."

"You got it. Good luck, partner."
"Thanks, Sophie."

CHAPTER 7
Monday, May 15

It was about seven in the morning when Max, Tan, Ashe, and Mehta convened in one of the operational command centers at 26Federal Plaza. The command center was about the size of a classroom, with two rows of desks strictly dedicated to a particular team's operation, with about eight different screens spread across a wall that wrapped around half of the room with amphitheater seating for observers.

"So, what's the deal with that shell company—Tech Dragon—and those two names?" Max asked. "When did they open up for business?"

"Two years ago," Tan said, as Parth Mehta pulled up the Delaware LLC registration papers for Tech Dragon on the big screen. "As we knew, Xu Nan and Fang Yang are named as the principals."

"Any background on them yet?" Max asked.

"Not yet," Mehta said. "For the time being, they're ghosts."

"What's the story on the address?" Max asked. "Actual office location or bogus?"

"Bogus, Max," Mehta said, and pulled up a simple Google photograph of the address of the business according to the incorporation documents. "It's the address to a UPS store in Wilmington. And the suite number noted in the documents is a mailbox number."

The UPS store was secreted in a strip mall between a liquor store and a jewelry store, with a line of parking spaces directly in front of the storefronts and another line of parking spaces next to the main road.

"Any cameras inside the store?" Max asked.

Ashe jumped in, "I reached out to the Wilmington resident agent. They sent an agent out to the UPS store and talked to the manager. I spoke to her a few minutes ago. Negative. No cameras, but the manager told the agent that either a middle-aged male or elderly female Asian stopped by for their mail about once a year. Never much mail at all."

"Most likely the principals," Mehta said.

"Yeah, probably picking up routine follow-up renewal notices from the Delaware Division of Corporations," Ashe said. "Since that's the only address they have on record."

"Did he say when somebody stopped by last?" Max asked.

"As it turns out the manager said the Asian female happened to stop by the end of last week."

"Great," Max said. "Any CCTV in the parking lot?"

"The agent didn't say," Ashe said. "She had to race out the door on a bank robbery while we were talking. Soon as she finishes writing it up, she'll get it to us."

"Good," Max said. "Anything on the alleged Schimmel PhD student with the name we got?"

"Yep," Mehta said. "According to student records, there's a Wei Ming in his third and final year at Schimmel."

"What's he studying?" Max asked.

"Quantum science."

"Quantum science? Quantum computing, that's big," Ashe said. "What current classical computers would take a billion years to calculate..."

Tan blurted, "Billion?"

"That's right, what present-day computers would take a billion years to solve, quantum computers would solve in a week or a month," Ashe nodded. "Center for Strategic and International Studies, CSIS, put out an interesting YouTube video with the assistant director for U.S. Quantum Information Science."

"That's true," Max added. "It's important work. The CEO of Google said what would take ten thousand years for today's super computers to crack today's cryptography, quantum computing can get the job done in seconds."

"Are you kidding?" Tan asked.

Mehta shook his head. "No. And a bunch of universities and private outfits are all working on it. China has put billons into it. And Congress passed a Quantum Development Initiative a few years ago."

Max added, "China claims to have created a quantum computer that is a hundred trillion times faster than any current digital computer."

"That's what they say," Ashe said.

Max nodded and pulled his Kindle from his backpack. "Here's a quote from David Sanger's Book, *The Perfect Weapon*. It's all about cyber warfare. 'They [China and Russia] look at quantum computers and see technology that could break any form of encryption and perhaps get into the command-and-control systems of America's nuclear arsenal.'"

"There it is," Ashe said.

"Yep," Max said and asked Mehta, "Anything on Zhang Kan?"

"Preliminary is there is a professor with that name attached to that university in China," Mehta answered.

"But, as my ex-partner said, since the PIs never met the client face-to-face, it could be him or it could be somebody using his name and profile," Max said.

"Right," Tan said, and the others agreed.

"Any other Chinese nationals in the quantum program?" Max asked.

"Yes," Mehta replied. "Zhao Hua. He's a first-year student."

Tan jumped in, "Does he live in the same building as this Wei Ming student?"

"He lives on Roosevelt Island, too, but not in the same building," Mehta said.

"Okay. Let me talk to Roach. Let him know what we're looking at," Max said.

"Hey, Max. Before you see, Roach," Tan said, "Parth has CCTV on the tram homicide."

"No kidding, let's see it," Max said. "Roosevelt Island Authority, pull it for you?"

"No," Mehta said. "As it turns out, Immigration had both sides of the East River camera'd up on their own."

"Excellent," Max said. "I'm sure they didn't say why."

"Right. Wouldn't say," Mehta said. "It didn't come from them."

"Got it," Max said and grabbed a seat.

Parth Mehta pulled up the CCTV video taken at both Roosevelt Island and Manhattan sides of the Roosevelt Island Tramway and put it up on the big screen of the command center. It was a direct view of each of the platforms, which captured the point of entry and exit onto each cable car as well as the interior of the car.

Max, Tan, and Ashe looked up at the big screen like they were watching a high-wire act. There were two Asian men standing on one of the two platforms—one platform for getting on, and the other platform, on the opposite side, for getting off.

They stood apart from each other, the shorter one was wearing black jeans, a black polo shirt, and a black wool cap, the other was in dark green pants, and a white polo shirt. Both were clean-shaven, the taller one appeared to be in his early thirties, the shorter one, early twenties, and appeared to have a tattoo on the left side of his face. Neither was carrying a briefcase. One appeared to be reading from an iPad, the other was looking at his iPhone or Android. Then, suddenly, the taller one looked in the staircase's direction and nodded at the shorter one—not one word appeared to have been exchanged between them.

Soon after that subtle communication, Dr. John Xu came into view, walked past the other two Asians, seeming not to take any notice, and stepped right up to the sliding doors to the tram, just as the cable car was pulling in.

"The doc timed that right," Tan said. "Knew the schedule."

Max nodded.

When the sliding doors opened on the opposite side of the tram from where the doctor and the two other Asians were standing, it let off three people. One middle-aged male, with long gray hair, and two student-looking types, Max thought, with backpacks and that depleted look of infinite hours of research and study in front of a computer. Or crack addicts.

The sliding doors then opened on the side where they were standing, and Dr. Xu was the first to step on, went directly to the unoccupied bench, the taller Asian got on after him and sat on the bench on the opposite end of the cable car, and the tattooed one held on to the center pole. Their electronic devices consumed all three, or so it seemed. The doors to the cable car slid closed, and the car lifted at a forty-five-degree angle until it was out of CCTV view.

Parth then started the CCTV video on the Manhattan side.

The British tourists were standing on the platform, two adults and two kids, apparently having a conversation. There was no audio. As the cable car lowered down into the shoot, you can see the tall and shorter Asian standing upright in front of the two sliding doors, like portraits in a frame. As soon as the doors slid open, the taller one dashed out first, almost knocking the boy down, followed by the shorter one. Neither looked back.

The taller one was carrying the briefcase Dr. Xu had been carrying when he'd gotten on.

They then watched the young British boy get on first and look back at his father and say something, at which point the father walked closer to the bench where Dr. Xu appeared to be asleep. The father opened his arms wide and waved his wife and kids to get off the tram, then approached the controller in the booth who entered the cable car, appeared to say a few words to Dr. Xu, who was unresponsive, shook him, at which point Xu tumbled to the cable car floor. The wife appeared to scream, put her two hands to her mouth, then pulled her kids further away from the car down the stretch of the platform.

"Great footage of these killers," Tan said when the video ended.

Max nodded and hit the cell number for Ed Vance on his iPhone.

A voice suddenly crashed into Max's eardrum. "Vance."

"Eddie, it's Max."

"Yeah, hey, Max, what's up?"

"We have CCTV on your tram homicide."

"No kidding," Vance said. "You get it from the Rosie Island authority? We've been waiting on it."

"Negative."

Silence.

Vance spoke up, "Thanks, Max."

Ed Vance had been around more than long enough to know not to ask twice.

"I'll stop by the precinct a little later. We'll get a copy onto a flash drive for you."

"Great, Max. Thanks. See you later."

MAX KNOCKED ON THE door. "You got a minute," he said to Roach, who was staring into the Mac on his desk.

Roach nodded once without looking away from the Mac.

"We're following up on the principals attached to the shell company that supposedly employed that group of Asian graduates."

"Why?" Roach asked, without looking away from his computer.

"Homeland was overwhelmed with processing the twenty-six hundred, so I offered to take that off their hands. Following up on the principals," Max said. "Plus, I want to know who they are. Maybe we can pull a case from what we find out about them."

Roach looked up at Max. "We don't take things off other agencies' hands," Roach said. "It was Homeland's operation. You should've let them follow up on it. We have enough to do here."

"Mr. Roach, we're not working on anything yet," Max said. "It seems like a good opportunity. There could be an IP angle we can follow up on. The likelihood is the twenty-six hundred attached themselves to that bogus Chinese company understanding that when they land a job, they will steal IP for the Chinese."

"You don't know that."

"No, not for a fact, not yet," Max said. "But that's a theory that's worth following up on, plus it's possible the shell is associated with the Chinese state."

"You don't know that either."

"No, that's why I think it's worth taking a few steps to check it out. The principals don't have any verifiable ID. Just names on a Delaware LLC."

"I don't want the strike force going off on tangents."

"It's not a tangent."

"Yeah, we'll see."

Max paused.

"You want me to give it back to Homeland?"

"Too late for that," Roach said, and turned back to his computer.

Max paused again. "All right," he continued, "I got a tip from a retired detective now a PI, somebody claiming to be a Chinese university official reached out to her firm to follow a student at the Schimmel Center on Roosevelt Island. The client said the student stole IP from their university in China and they want it back. The PIs turned it down."

"Good."

"We did a quick check on the student," Max said. "Turns out he's in their Quantum Science PhD program, and there's a professor with the same name attached to the mentioned Chinese university. Tongji University."

"Don't waste the strike force's time."

"Don't waste the strike force's time?" Max repeated and stood there looking down at Roach's back, wondering how any investigator worth his salt wouldn't be interested.

Roach still did not turn, and a few seconds passed.

"Yeah, okay," Max said and shook his head. "Anyway, Parth got the CCTV on the Roosevelt Island tram homicide. Both ends with video of the professor and two other Asians getting on the tram on the Roosevelt Island, and the professor left dead when it arrived on the Manhattan side."

"Why do we care?"

"Because we haven't picked up a case yet," Max said. "And it turns out the dead professor was doing nanoscience research."

"Who says?"

"The Nineteenth Precinct Squad commander. His detectives interviewed administration at the Brooklyn Institute of Technology—the murdered professor's school—BIT," Max said. "His murder could have some relationship to his research."

"You don't know that either, Valentin, do you?" Roach said without raising his face from his Mac.

"No," Max said and remained silent, taking Roach in.

So much of Max's experience came through trusting his instincts. Using some imagination. Learning not to dismiss something outright because there wasn't enough yet. Ed Vance reminded him and his detectives repeatedly, *Don't dismiss something just because there isn't yet enough. Follow up on your gut. There may not be any there-there that time, but if you develop that persistent follow-up and imagination muscle, you're going to nail it sometimes. So, check it out.*

"All right, well, it's good for us to have and a good break for the Nineteenth Precinct detectives."

"What do you mean?" Roach finally pulled his face out of his Mac again and looked up.

"I gave the Nineteenth Squad a call to see what they had and to let them know we have CCTV for them."

"How'd Mehta get the CCTV?"

"Not from Roosevelt Island cameras."

"From U.S. Intelligence?"

"You have to ask Mehta."

Silence.

"Why'd you tell the locals we had it?"

The locals. So fucking condescending. Like the NYPD was in Mayberry RFD.

Max took a moment for his blood pressure to drop.

"Because they have a murder investigation, and we have video of the likely killers, which is important, and they may come up with more information that will be important for us," Max said. "I just told you they already gave me a heads-up on his nanoscience research, plus they gave me the results of the tox and autopsy report. The deceased professor punctured with an ice pick, both arms broken, and he was poisoned."

"You shouldn't have done that."

"So, because the source of the CCTV is not from the Roosevelt Island Authority, but from another source, we can't share it."

"That's right."

"Even though it's footage the detectives will get anyway?"

"That's right."

"For crying out loud, I told the squad commander I'd head up there to give them a copy."

"Don't."

Max was silent.

"Listen, Valentin," Roach continued, "now that we have it, we have to hold on to it in case it turns into something for us. It could have national security implications. We can't get local detectives involved. Too sensitive."

"But we have nothing. You know that," Max said, raising his voice a bit more than he planned to. "And they have an active homicide investigation."

"We'll give them what we can after we're sure we don't need it."

"So, an NYPD detective squad is handling a fresh murder investigation, and we have video of the possible killers roaming the streets of New York City, and we're not going to share that with them because it may jeopardize something that doesn't exist?"

"That's right," Roach said. "Let them get it themselves."

"Wow," Max said and couldn't help shaking his head again. "So, I have to tell the squad commander that the video I told him we have, and would share with him, is suddenly not available?"

"That's the way it is."

"This sucks," Max said. "They're going to develop more information that will help us. What if they decide to keep it to themselves?"

"We'll get all their reports," Roach said. "They won't hold anything back from us."

"With all due respect, Mr. Roach, that's nonsense," Max said. "There's a lot between the lines of any investigation that never makes it into a report."

"That's the way it is."

This was the crap he expected from the FBI. What was all this hype at the FBI Academy about cooperation between federal and local law enforcement? What was all the hype that since the tragedy of 9/11 we were one big happy law enforcement family? *What bullshit,* Max thought. He recognized there was no need to share every detail of each other's investigation. It was always on a need-to-know basis, but when they have information that would directly help a city PD with a murder investigation, how can a fed hold back?

And that was an odd difference between U.S. military intelligence and the FBI, too. When Max was in marine corps intelligence, it wasn't unusual for local, state, federal, or European law enforcement like Interpol or Europol to send a query for information. Military intelligence was always willing to pass it on under one condition: it didn't come from them.

Law enforcement understood that, and would not use it in court, but the intel provided leads they could follow up on and build independent and/or corroborating evidence to advance their investigation.

What also disturbed Max was that for Roach, there was not even room for discussion. His position was simple. When our non-existent case is done, we'll see what we can do for the locals. And that is an institutional thing, an agency cultural thing. And that was something Roach didn't pick up on his own. He picked that up over his twenty-five years of exclusive FBI experience. All take, and we'll give if it suits us.

Except Max recognized it wasn't just the FBI culture, per se. Special Agent in Charge Dick Roach had probably been in administrative/internal affairs positions in the FBI most, if not all, of his career. He was never a field agent for any length of time. And Max had seen similar rising stars, so to speak, in the NYPD. Police officers who tested well on promotional exams but never made an arrest or worked a case and were suddenly captains overseeing your investigation. They'd never gained the sixth sense of working the gray of investigations in good faith.

Roach spoke as if he could read Max's thoughts. "Remember something, Lieutenant Valentin," he said. "When you agreed to accept an assignment with an FBI strike force, you no longer work for the NYPD. I told you that. You're not a cop. You work for the FBI. In your present capacity, you're an FBI agent. Your responsibility is to protect the integrity of FBI investigations or leads."

"The direct deposit into my checking account spells, 'N-Y-P-D.'"

WHEN MAX RETURNED TO his office, Tan, Ashe, and Mehta were each wearing concerned expressions.

"Max," Mehta said. "SAC Roach just directed me to not give you the Roosevelt Tram CCTV video."

Max nodded and remained silent for a moment and shook his head.

"What the hell was that all about?" Tan asked.

"Walk me to the elevator," Max said to Tan and Ashe, then looked at Mehta. "Thanks, Parth, if anything urgent comes up, give me a shout."

Max pushed the button and turned to look at them.

"Roach thinks we're wasting our time with the twenty-six hundred, the dead chemistry professor, the Schimmel student and the Chinese client who wanted the student tailed," Max said. "And doesn't want me to take us on tangents."

Tan and Ashe were speechless for a couple of seconds.

"This isn't a tangent," Tan said. "The dead professor's a nanoscientist for crying out loud."

"And there's a Chinese university official who wants an ethnic Chinese student at a U.S. university studying quantum science put under surveillance," Ashe said. "He didn't express any curiosity?"

Max shook his head.

"Wow," Tan said.

"It didn't grab him," Max said. "You ever work with him before, Sam?"

"Not directly," Ashe said. "Word is he spent six months as a field agent then went the administrative and internal inspections route at headquarters."

"Of course," Max said. "He said now that we have the CCTV, we have to make sure it doesn't jeopardize any national security investigation down the road."

"Wow, what is he, mental or something?" Tan said. "That's bizarre. We have nothing active yet."

"Exactly," Ashe added.

"That's my view too, but he doesn't see it that way," Max said. "At least not yet."

"Well, that's bullshit," Tan said. "The detectives have already filled us in on the autopsy and tox report."

"This is strange," Ashe added. "They're working a homicide for crying out loud."

"I feel the same way," Max said. "Anyway, I'm going to play it his way for now. I'm only going to tell the squad commander what I saw on the CCTV. Nothing in writing or video. But if I get a sense that not having the CCTV jeopardizes their case, then I'll do what I have to do, but we're not there yet. I just want you both to know that."

Tan and Ashe nodded with appreciation for what Max was saying.

AS SOON AS MAX ENTERED the Nineteenth Precinct station house, he noticed Desk Sergeant Mike Regan booking two handcuffed prisoners who towered over the arresting officer—a petite female uniformed cop—holding them like she was standing between two Roman columns.

The sergeant noticed Max. "Hey Loo, long time, how's it going?"

"Good, Mike," Max stopped. "You look busy."

"Always open for new business."

"I see that."

Sergeant Regan was the middle linebacker for the NYPD football team, and Max never missed a game.

"Lieutenant Vance upstairs?"

"Sure is," Regan said and thumbed up to the ceiling.

"How's the team shaping up for next season?" Max asked, as he kept moving.

"Great. We're going to crush those fire-eaters one more time." Regan said. "They're going to have to dispatch their 'super pumpers' to slow us down."

"Outstanding."

NYPD vs. FDNY was the most important game of the season for both teams.

"HEY MAX," VANCE SAID with a broad smile, looking over the shoulders of two detectives he was talking to when Max approached his second-floor office door.

The handful of male and female detectives facing Lieutenant Vance looked back and greeted him, "How you doing, Loo?"

As big as the NYPD was, with about 35,000 active-duty police officers and bosses, the Detective Bureau was about ten percent of that number. The number of ranking officers in the bureau was about one percent of that, so it wasn't unusual for detectives to know a boss even if they'd never worked on the same squad or a case together. The boss may not know an individual detective, but that was understood. They were all in the NYPD Detective Bureau and greeted each other, anyway.

"How you doing, guys?" Max said. "Sorry to interrupt."

"We just wrapped up," Vance said, and gave the detectives the nod that they'd finish up after he talked to Max.

"Good, Loo," the detectives said and stepped out.

"Grab a seat," Vance said, and pointed to one of the gunmetal chairs in the office. "What's the CCTV look like? Two male Asians?"

Max confirmed the description of the Asian males who got on the tram with the deceased Dr. Xu, and got off the tram, leaving Dr. Xu behind.

"You have it on a flash drive?" Vance asked.

Max looked at Ed Vance with raised eyebrows and didn't answer.

They looked at each other for a few long moments, then Vance leaned back slowly, his chair delivering a long, irritating squeak, interlaced his hands behind his head like he was going to take some sun, and grinned.

"The feds won't let you show it to us?" Vance asked with those twenty-eight years of detective experience etched into his face.

The only thing Max could do was an almost imperceptible shake of his head.

Vance nodded. "Don't worry about it, Max. I'll follow up with Roosevelt Tram people and get it ourselves. I appreciate your telling me what you saw. At least it corroborates what the Brits told us about the two Asians, and we're not chasing a couple of invisible gangbangers from the South Bronx who were miraculously secreted on that evening tram and made the professor their prey."

"I'm sorry about this, Ed."

"Don't sweat it," Vance said again. "One thing about this business, the pendulum swings one way one day and swings another way another day.

"Maybe reach out to Chief Manley, Ed."

"Exactly, I'll give Kieran a call. See if he can help us out."

Max nodded.

The director of public safety for Roosevelt Island Operating Corporation was former NYPD Deputy Chief Kieran Manley. The chief had been the special operations lieutenant when Max was assigned as a rookie to his first precinct command in East Harlem.

After one year on patrol, they assigned Max to a plainclothes anti-crime unit where he'd developed a reputation as a gun-collar man. Max had gained the skill for recognizing subtle movements a bad guy would make—unwittingly—that would broadcast he was carrying a gun: adjusting his belt in front, slipping his hand into the back of his pants, leaning to side of his waist as if the gun weighed him down.

Max almost felt sorry for gun-carrying bad guys. They made it too easy and were at a disadvantage. It wasn't acceptable for a bad guy to carry a gun in a holster like a cop: part of their mystique was they didn't use holsters. It wasn't in fashion. The problem with that strategy was un-holstered guns were not very secure in a waistband. Un-holstered guns tended to float around in a waistband, which required more and more adjusting. They might as well have had a neon sign circulating around their foreheads that announced: Search Me, Search Me, Search Me. The former chief loved Max: fewer guns on the street, fewer shooting victims, fewer homicides.

"Listen, you'll appreciate this, a short precinct jurisdiction quiz for you," Vance said. "So, the body of the deceased is discovered on the tram on the Manhattan side, but which precinct catches the case?"

Max couldn't help breaking into a grin. It was going to be another Vance exercise in presenting a what-if scenario to train a younger detective supervisor.

Vance continued, "The Seventeenth Precinct and our precinct, as you know, are divided by the Fifty-Ninth Street Ed Koch Bridge, right? If the body was discovered on East Fifty-Ninth —on the street itself..."

"If it's on the south side of the street, the Seventeenth catches it, north side, the Nineteenth catches it."

"But the body wasn't discovered on the street..."

Max nodded. "Nineteenth gets it because the tram travels on the north side of Fifty-Ninth Street and the bridge."

"Right you are," Vance said, with a big smile. "But what if the medical examiner determines that the body expired while the tram was suspended over the East River? Who catches it then?"

Max raised his chin in acknowledgment and nodded. "Now it gets dicey."

"It does, doesn't it," Vance said. "This is the first homicide on the tram itself, by the way."

"Hmm."

"Let me help you out," Vance said. "How would we assign a floater?"

"If the floater is traveling north or south in the river until it gets caught up in something and gets stuck, whichever precinct shore it is closest to takes the case," Max said. "If it doesn't stop until a harbor unit catches up to it and fishes it out, it's the precinct shore harbor brings the body to. The closest shore."

"Very good. So, how would you size up this tram homicide?"

"All right, this is how I see it," Max started, "The 114th Precinct in Queens handles Roosevelt Island to the halfway point of the East River, heading west back toward Manhattan. The Nineteenth covers up to the halfway point of the river heading east."

"Okay, so if the ME says the deceased expired on the tram closer to Roosevelt Island than Manhattan Island..."

"The one-fourteen catches it," Max said. "So, you're telling me that if the ME makes that call, you're going to drop the homicide on the one-fourteen."

"Not right away," Vance said. "If we make a collar and clear it, we'll keep the stat, but if we don't, then, yes, I'm going to pull out the ME report and dump it on the one-fourteen. Let them hold the open homicide."

"This is one macabre conversation, Ed."

Vance opened his arms wide and with an equally wide smile said, "Like Hyman Roth said in *The Godfather II*, 'This is the business we have chosen.'"

All Max could think, at that moment, was how much he would miss Ed Vance when he pulled the plug.

WHEN MAX GOT BACK TO 26 Federal Plaza, he dropped into the small sofa in his office. He was still in no way ready to sit behind that cherry wood desk and hoped he never would.

Teresa Tan strutted in right behind him and said, "We got something here."

Max looked up.

"Looks like we have somebody who wants to give us something on trade secrets and wrote it in Braille," Tan said. "Just came in from 'main justice.' Time to break our cherry."

"Braille?"

"And DOJ put a query through personnel to see if we had a Braille transcriber. And you know what?"

Max waited.

"Sam's name came up. How ironic is that? Our first case and Sam's name comes up as a Braille transcriber," Tan said. "It's meant to be."

Max smiled and nodded.

Just at that moment, Sam walked in, sipping on a cup of coffee.

"So, you know how to read Braille?" Max asked.

"Ah, yeah," Sam replied with squinted eyes and a grin. "Why do you ask?"

"We just received a doc from main justice that was written in Braille," Tan jumped in. "What the heck, Sam. How the heck do you read Braille?"

"Ah huh, I see. Well, yeah, it's true," Sam said, clearly enjoying Tan's surprise. "I did some volunteer work a couple years back for an organization for the blind. St. Anthony's Society for the Blind, on West Sixty-First Street."

"Yeah, I've driven by the place," Tan nodded with a wide, curious grin.

"Decided to take the Braille transcriber course on the side," Ashe said. "National Federation of Blind runs it."

"On the side," Tan said. "Awesome."

"Give him the doc, Teresa."

Tan handed it to Ashe and said, "How about you read this to us?"

Tan then grabbed the seat behind Max's desk, stretched her black jean attired, athletic legs, with stylish women's combat boots, onto the corner, crossed them, interlaced her hands onto her stomach, twiddling her thumbs, like she was an unruly teenager in the principal's office.

Ashe remained standing and read the transcription out loud slowly.

"My name is Wei Ming..."

"What?" Max said and sat up straight.

"Yeah, whoa," Tan said too.

"Wei Ming," Ashe repeated. "The name your ex-partner gave you."

"Yeah, the one who the Chinese university guy wanted put under surveillance," Tan said.

"Sounds like it," Max nodded.

"Whoa, yeah," Tan said

Ashe continued to read the Braille message. "I am a third year PhD graduate student at Manhattan University, Schimmel Science Center, on Roosevelt Island, New York City."

"That's him," Tan blurted. "That's the same student."

Ashe continued. "'I fear Chinese state representatives have contacted me. I fear they want me to give information about our current research. I have family in China. I need help. I will help you if you help me protect my family. You must assume, as I have, that I am being observed and monitored. This is my mobile and email address. But please do not communicate with me in this way unless you have the capacity to encrypt your communication to me.'

"'I have enclosed an English alphabet to correspond with Tai Chi. I do Tai Chi on the river every day at seven a.m. I can give you brief messages that way when necessary. And you can do the same perhaps on a boat that pauses opposite Roosevelt Island, or with long-range signals from the Manhattan side of the river or suggest another way to communicate. I will pay attention to a boat if you contact me in such a fashion. Hang a red cloth somewhere on the outside of the boat, so I know it is you. I don't know what else to suggest. Please help.'"

Max and his team were quiet for a few moments after Ashe finished reading the Braille letter.

"So, what have we got?" Ashe said rhetorically. "The student thinks Chinese authorities have approached him to steal. Or is he an IP thief, as the Tongji University rep told your friend?"

Max nodded. "Something we got to find out."

The letter intrigued Max, and why the student sent it the way he did. He imagined that if the student were not a Chinese IP thief, but a legitimate victim of Chinese pressure to steal U.S. university research, that the student knew if he didn't cooperate with the Chinese, his only option would be to contact U.S. law enforcement. The student may have thought briefly about notifying school administration. Many of the heavy R & D graduate universities had already been lectured about being approached by persons inquiring about their research.

They would've been told of the presentations the FBI had given school administration about students and professors stealing research and passing it on to representatives of other countries.

"Let me see the envelope it came in," Max said to Tan, who then handed it to him.

Max took a long look at the New York, New York postmarked envelope.

U.S. Department of Justice

Washington, D.C.

He had to trust the U.S. mail the student must've thought. He would secrete a note to the U.S. Department of Justice. He would not look up the address on any electronic device. He probably didn't know an address could be found in a phone book; Max figured. The student had probably never seen a phone book in his life, wouldn't know where to look. Come to think of it, Max wasn't sure where he could find a phone book himself—a library, perhaps?

The student wisely must've thought—No Electronic Fingerprints. He took a stab at the "Washington, D.C." address. How far off would he be? But not even a ZIP code. Max admired all the precautions the student took. He had to trust that the United States Postal Service would get it to U.S. authorities, to the United States Department of Justice. And it worked.

Max looked up from the envelope, gently waving it, and said, "If he's legit, and not a Chinese university IP thief, it looks like we may have a PhD student researcher maybe approached by Chinese state reps to steal here. A Chinese national on a student visa."

"He's trying to minimize exposure," Ashe said. "And he didn't want to send the information electronically. Smart move."

Max nodded.

"This is brilliant," Tan blurted, as she looked over the student's use of the Tai Chi alphabet to communicate.

"You know, Tai Chi, Teresa?" Max asked.

"I do," Tan said, dropped her legs to the floor, stood up, and did a slow, swirling move with her arms and legs. "It's a cultural thing. You should try it."

Ashe let out a roaring laugh.

Tan gave Max a wink. "But what he did here is really smart. There are twenty-eight movements in Tai Chi. He noted that each of the movements corresponds to a letter in the English alphabet, except..."

Ashe jumped in, "Except there's twenty-six letters in the English alphabet."

"Right," Tan said and continued to give a demonstration using the informant's corresponding use of the Tai Chi alphabet with the English alphabet.

"The first and last movement in Tai Chi is the starting and closing movements, so he left those out. The twenty-six letters in the English alphabet correspond perfectly. You see, the first movement in Tai Chi is called Parting the Wild Horse's Mane." Tan slowly thrusted her hand out and took one step forward, then did it another two times. "That's the letter A. The letter B is White Crane Spreads Its Wings," and Tan brought her arms up slowly and brought them down like she was flying.

"The letter C is called Brush Knee Push and you do that three times," Tan said, and pretended to push a door open with one hand and her other hand brushing her knee.

"The letter D movement is Playing the Guitar," Tan said and made a motion that looked like she was reaching out to shake someone's hand, then brought her hand back as she bent her knees. "And it goes like that throughout the alphabet."

"That's terrific, Teresa," Max said, his eyes open wide, genuinely impressed. "Fabulous."

"You know, Max, we may need a FISA warrant to screen his email and mobile number," Ashe said. "See if we can pick up third-party monitoring. Maybe catch who's reached out to him."

"We may not, at least not right away," Max said. "The student is bringing us in. He may give us permission to sweep his electronics."

Ashe nodded. "Good point."

"I'll give Jack Hunt a call and run it by him."

Hunt was one of two AUSAs assigned to prosecute IP cases out of the New York City federal prosecutor's office, and one of over fifty assistant United States attorneys assigned to the elite computer hacking and intellectual property prosecutor network under the umbrella of the Department of Justice, Computer Crime and Intellectual Property Section (CCIPS).

And now, going forward, all the cases developed with Teresa Tan and Sam Ashe they'd bring to AUSA Hunt. Max had complete confidence and trust in Jack Hunt.

Max continued, "We know the student is working on quantum research, but let's do a complete background on him now: photo, family, education, affiliations, the total package. And by the way, we're going on a boat ride tomorrow at zero-seven-hundred."

"Seven a.m.?" Tan asked with a squint, then said, "You know, Max, this letter could be bogus."

"Not likely it's bogus, with that Chinese university official looking to put him under surveillance," Max said.

"True," Ashe said.

"But if it is, we'll find out on the river tomorrow morning," Max said. "We'll give it a look."

Ashe and Tan nodded.

"Okay, let's get going," Max said, and stood up. "Learn that Tai Chi alphabet, Teresa. Practice communicating that way. We'll do a river-cruise-by just to signal we got his message, if he's out there. We won't stop, just a drive by. I doubt we'll be able to communicate anything more to him or him to us, but I think he'll get the meaning."

"Okay," Tan said. "I'll start working on the background."

"Good," Max said. "Sam, try to find out if you can if he's a registered member of the Communist Party. Not that that's a deal breaker. Even if he is, he may not have had much of a choice. But it'll be important to have for the record."

Ashe nodded and gave Max a knuckle pump and headed out the door. "Let's rumble."

Max could not help breaking a smile. He rarely saw Sam Ashe express any emotion.

"Good. I'll give Hunt a call and walk over to see him," Max said. "By the way, you guys have a red something or other to hang outside the boat?"

"I'll come up with something," Tan said, and Max's team marched out.

Max stepped over to the window of his twenty-third-floor office that displayed a clear-day panoramic view from the Hudson River all the way to the East River and everything in between, including the United States Attorney's Office for the Southern District of New York. Exactly where he was about to visit.

WHEN HE STEPPED OUT of 26 Federal Plaza into that sunny and breezy early May rush hour afternoon, he knew he'd have to give himself a few extra minutes to get there. If he'd been taking the six-block walk to the United States Attorney's Office for the Southern District at One St. Andrew's Plaza a couple hours later, say about 7:30, it would've taken him ten minutes flat. But on a bright weekday late afternoon, while folks were diligently executing their escape from their respective city, state, federal, and commercial offices, it could take him thirty. The clutter on the sidewalks reminded him of Beijing.

Max had worked with Jack Hunt on a few cases that were developed when he was in the NYPD Trademarks Enforcement Squad. Each of the cases had a wide transnational component. Max could've presented the cases to the Manhattan District Attorney's Office, but in his view, a prosecution under certain federal statutes could sometimes be more effective.

Like a Nike counterfeiter/entrepreneur who started with the very original idea of paying the homeless as "runners" to stand on line to receive the latest super limited Nike sneaker edition, which he would then sell online at a huge profit.

No problem so far. But, when demand exceeded his inventory, he succumbed to arranging with counterfeit manufacturers in China to recreate thousands and thousands of fake sneakers, which eventually led to the Trademark Enforcement Squad and the prosecution skills of Assistant United States Attorney (AUSA) Jack Hunt.

The Nike counterfeit/entrepreneur was convicted of counterfeiting and money laundering to the tune of over $15 million.

AFTER MAX PRESENTED his Strike Force credentials bypassing the metal detector at the U.S. attorney's office, he jumped onto the elevator up to the office of AUSA Jack Hunt.

"Hey, Jack."

"Hey, Max! Grab a seat," Hunt said as he came from around his desk and pointed at the small sofa with a coffee table in front of it. "Coffee, bottle of water?"

"No, I'm fine, thanks," Max said as he stepped into Hunt's office. "Thanks for seeing me right away."

"Not at all. I wasn't going anywhere anytime soon. Just working on a sentence recommendation for a Chinese national working as an engineer at a U.S. company. His routine was to conveniently take photographs of his employer's trade secrets displayed on his employer-issued laptop with his personal iPhone."

Max shook his head.

"And this crook used steganography to hide the photos of the stolen IP inside the file of an innocent-looking photograph," Hunt said. "He embedded the images of the trade secrets into the digital photograph of a butterfly."

"Steganography," Max repeated. "Relentless."

"Sure is."

"How's Delores and the kids?"

"Oh, they're good, Max. Yeah, good, ahh, Lucia just made her school's soccer team."

"She must be fast."

"Damn fast," Hunt said with a laugh. "Conan is dazzling us with the gymnastic moves he learned in school this spring, and Josh is going through Harry Potter books like he's preparing for the entrance test to the Hogwarts School of Witchcraft and Wizardry."

"That's great, that's just great," Max said. "Talented kids."

"Yeah, thanks, buddy," Hunt said. "So, what about you? When are you going to commit to a beautiful *señorita* and create some *bambinos*?"

Max opened his hands in resignation. "What can I say?"

"Speaking of beautiful *senoritas,* what happened with that beauty in her last year of law school you brought to our Christmas party last year?" Hunt asked with a huge smile.

"What can I say? She was very busy, and so was I, so it just faded away," Max said. "Too busy, plus, you know, my sister and her twins. They need the regular visits from Uncle Max."

"Right, of course," Hunt said. "How old are they now?"

"Seven. And they're doing great. They go to public school. Jessica's a chess prodigy and Benjamin is learning how to play the piano. He has a real good ear. And my sister has assigned me to teach them the catechism," Max said. "I just read with them from their workbooks."

"The catechism, ahh, that's great," Hunt said. "So, how's your first week in an FBI strike force?"

"I like the cherry wood furniture," Max said, with raised eyebrows and wide eyes like an emoji, and looked around Hunt's cherry wood office ambience. "You don't see as much in DEA satellite offices."

Hunt let out a howl.

"So, what do you have?" Hunt asked and grabbed one of the two chairs in front of his desk, turned it to the coffee table, cracked a bottle of Poland Spring, took a swig, then leaned down, elbows on knees.

Max pulled out the transcription of the Wei Ming letter, placed the envelope on the coffee table and read the transcription Ashe had written up in its entirety. After Max finished, Hunt leaned back slowly.

"Interesting," Hunt said, and took another long pull from his bottle of water.

"We just got it," Max said. "We're doing a background screen on the student, for starters. We got a student by that name at the Schimmel Center. But we don't know if the writer is one in the same. Teresa and Sam are working on that right now. In the meantime..."

"You thinking FISA warrant?"

"If you think we need it," Max said. "We'll write it up to go through the FBI field office chain, office of general counsel, before coming through you guys, as usual, but I wanted to get your thoughts on it first since you'll be prosecuting the case if it goes all the way."

Hunt nodded. "This'll be a different FISA request. Assuming he is who he says he is, it's not as if we discovered that he's working for the Chinese and we're looking for permission to monitor his electronics and put him under surveillance."

"Right, that would be a no-brainer request to the FISA court, I would think."

"Exactly. In that case, it's cut and dry. He's acting as a foreign agent in the U.S. colluding with a foreign government," Hunt said. "You would need it before any electronic monitoring."

"But in this case, he's giving us permission and wants to cooperate with us," Max said. "He's a foreign national who claims a foreign intelligence service on U.S. soil has approached him."

"Right, so you may not need a FISA warrant right now..."

"... that's what we were thinking."

"Right. Once you confirm the informant's existence, you need his permission to monitor his electronics. I'll prepare a document for him to sign. You need to communicate with him face-to-face. And if he gives you permission to monitor his electronics, we don't need a FISA."

"Okay, so jumping ahead, let's say we confirm his ID, and he is who he says he is, and he gives us permission, and we sweep his devices and come up with some connection to the person or persons who are trying to get to him and that turn out to have a connection to a Chinese state entity."

"Will you need a warrant to monitor those other numbers?"

"Yes?"

"Yes, you'll then need a FISA then," Hunt said. "And to search their devices if you get your hands on them."

"Especially if they're connected to China's intelligence services?"

"Yes, absolutely," Hunt said. "But it doesn't need to be any state intel service. The FISA will allow electronic surveillance of all persons connected with this investigation, whether they're a government/state intel service or not."

"Right. Okay. One other thing, Jack," Max said, then went onto explain the request for PIs to put the Schimmel student under surveillance by the alleged Chinese university official.

"No kidding."

"Yeah, the PIs turned it down, but it's something to keep in mind if this informant turns out to be the real thing. The question we'll have to answer is..."

"... whether he stole from the Chinese or the Chinese just used the thing about stealing IP from a Chinese university as a reason for the PIs to tail him around," Hunt said.

"Yeah, exactly. Which is typical for the Chinese. They come up with some bogus reason to harass the Chinese diaspora living, working, or studying here legally to do their bidding."

"Exactly," Hunt said, with a huge, curious smile. "Keep me posted."

"Will do. Let me get on it," Max said, and stood up, but then noticed a yellow covered paperback sitting on Hunt's desk titled, *Spies and Lies: How China's Greatest Covert Operations Fooled the World* by Alex Joske.

Max lifted it up and leafed through it. "Alex Joske. He's that Australian analyst. Came across him on YouTube."

"He sure is," Hunt said. "He takes a deep dive into how, essentially, the Chinese Communist Party has pulled the wool over our eyes for the last thirty years, convincing us and the West that they had every intention of embracing a few democratic values and be a little less authoritative."

"Yeah, that's what he said on YouTube, but I didn't have a chance to pick up his book," Max said. "He talked a lot about how the MSS has infiltrated and influenced government through the United Front Work Department."

"That's it. The book is a darn intriguing read."

"Oh, by the way, listen, we had an interesting weekend down at Homeland."

"Oh, yeah," Hunt said. "Arlington?"

Max nodded and gave him a briefing on the 2,600 graduates claiming to be employed by that shell company.

"Whoa, that is interesting," Hunt said. "You know what U.S. attorney's office is working it?"

"No, but we offered to take the background investigation of the two principals off Homeland's hands since they were swamped with the twenty-six hundred," Max said. "We have names from Delaware corporation records, but no IDs yet."

"Interesting. What's the shell's name?"

"Tech Dragon."

"And the principals?"

"Xu Nan and Fang Wang."

"Huh, interesting," Hunt said. "Maybe Immigration's just going to handle them administratively and deport them."

"Don't know."

"Huh. Interesting," Hunt said and looked up and away in thought, not having sat down yet. Max smiled as he watched Hunt drift away. He'd seen that look before.

"All right, so no FISA application yet," Max said. "We need to get his permission to sweep his electronics, see who it connects with, see if what he gives us connects with Chinese intel. Got it. I am out of here. Thanks, Jack."

When Max got to Hunt's office door to let himself out, he turned back to him. "Oh, Jack, you hear about the homicide on the Roosevelt Island Tram?"

"Yeah, real shame, the press said first homicide on the tram. Said he was a chemistry professor."

"Right, he was a Chinese chemistry professor."

"Mugging?"

Max shook his head. "We got a copy of the tram CCTV. Two mature looking Asians got on the tram with him. The Asians raced off, and the deceased toppled over when it docked. Autopsy and tox report said he was likely stabbed with an ice pick, arms broken, and he was poisoned."

"Poisoned?" Hunt repeated.

"Yeah. His area of study was nanoscience."

"Nanoscience?" Hunt said with eyes open wide. "Really?"

"Name's John Xu."

"Huh."

"Okay, thanks," Max said and stepped out leaving Jack Hunt staring at his office door.

CHAPTER 8
Tuesday, May 16

The next morning Max Valentin, Teresa Tan, and Sam Ashe jumped onto a NY Waterway Ferry at 6:30 a.m. and took a slow ride down the East River to drift around Roosevelt Island, hoping they would see the informant. Max was grateful it was a cloudless and odorless morning.

The NY Waterway Ferry service made stops on East Ninetieth Street and the East River right under the nose of the Gracie Mansion, the mayor's residence, across the river to Astoria ferry landing, made a stop at Roosevelt Island, across to Long Island City, continued down the river to East Thirty-Fourth Street across the river to the Brooklyn Navy Yard and then swung back to the Wall Street Pier on the tip of Manhattan.

They'd developed more background information on the PhD student. It was fortunate that soon after the Justice Department's China Initiative announcement in November 2018, many research universities gave the FBI direct access to student and faculty database records of those connected with advanced research and development programs. Wei Ming's resume and educational history were accessible.

In addition, they had a record of his family history from Immigration. Homeland Security/Customs and Border Protection provided his travel history that included his semi-annual visits to China during his almost three years of PhD studies in the United

States. And he was not a registered member of the Chinese Communist Party according to U.S. government sources.

Tan yanked out a red cloth of some sort from her backpack like it was a flag.

"Where do you want the red thing?" Max asked, with a grin from ear to ear. "Is that a scarf?"

Teresa smiled from ear to ear too and wrapped the sash around her neck like Amelia Earhart. "It's my graduation sash from Stanford. Go Stanford Red!" she cheered, and marched up the aisle of the ferry, pumping her arms like a majorette in a marching band, giving them a rendition of the Stanford University fight song.

"Teresa Tan. Stanford Cardinal. That was great," Max said. "Stanford's in the Pac-12 conference, right?"

"Yep."

Max then looked at Sam, who had clapped in rhythm throughout Tan's performance. "Sam, Loyola's your alma mater. That's the Atlantic-10 conference, right?"

Sam nodded. "It is, yep."

"Let's hear your fight song, Sam." Tan gave Ashe a friendly punch in the arm. "Loyola. Your mascot's a wolf, right? Let's hear it Loyola Wolf?"

"Oh, no, no, not me," Ashe said with a hearty laugh. "Let me get your sash, Stanford Cardinal. Time to hang it outside."

"All right, Sam, another time," Tan said with a chuckle, and handed Sam the sash. "I better take another look over my Tai Chi alphabet and advance my interpreting skills."

Max went up onto the second level with the captain of the ferry. Ashe and Tan stayed on the main level facing west, sitting back on a long bench, as far away from the providentially tinted windows as possible. They all had earpieces in place to communicate with each other.

Tan had a set of binoculars, and Ashe had a tripod set up to videotape the potential informant as he did his exercise. Max had a set of binoculars as well and took a deep breath of the river as he felt and listened to the rumble of the engine and waves. The water was running upstream that morning.

They traveled down the East River at ten knots and about three city blocks from the Roosevelt Island shoreline when Max could see a figure approach the walkway opposite the informant's apartment building on the island wearing a sky-blue polo shirt and black gym pants.

"You see him?" Max asked.

"We got him," Ashe replied.

Max then directed the ferryboat captain to slow down more.

They could then all see that the informant appeared to recognize the red sash and started his Tai Chi routine.

"You getting this, Teresa?" Max said into the radio.

"Getting it," Tan promptly said, and recited,

"T - H - A - N - K -Y - O - U,

"F-O-R - C-O-M-I-N-G

"I -H-A-V-E -B-E-E-N -C-O-N-T-A-C-T-E-D -A-G-A-I-N

"P-L-E-A-S-E -H-E-L-P"

The informant ended the Tai Chi there and meandered back to his high-rise apartment building on the river.

"Okay, we can keep going," Max said to the ferryboat captain, and kept his narrowed eyes on the Roosevelt Island shoreline with a flash of excitement over where this initial contact would lead.

BY NOON, MAX, TAN, Ashe, Mehta, and Roach were sitting in the twelfth-floor conference room at 26 Federal Plaza. Max and his team were still in casual attire: an assortment of jeans, khakis, and polo shirts. Roach was in a suit and tie, sitting at the head of the long table like Vladimir Putin.

Ashe cut the lights and Parth Mehta dragged and clicked the mouse to his laptop. Projected up on the wall screen was a video of Wei Ming doing Tai Chi, as well as copies of some of the background screening records. After the presentation, Ashe threw the lights back on.

Max went over the FISA warrant issues. Everyone understood that once they met with the informant and he'd given them authorization to monitor his electronics, there was no need to apply for a warrant until they had confirmation that Wei Ming was dealing with Chinese agents.

"Now you have a proper case to work on, Valentin."

Max paused for an extra moment, taking Roach in. "Right," Max said. "So, we need to arrange a face-to-face with him."

"That's the tough part. We have to do it without giving it up to the Chinese," Ashe said. "They got to be watching him. PIs or not."

"Yeah, exactly," Tan said. "We have the Tai Chi deal going for the time being, but we can't rely on that for long. We're going to give him one of our encrypted phones and an email address, but we need to make face-to-face contact first."

"So, what are you thinking, Valentin?" Roach asked.

Max noticed how in all their exchanges, Roach always used Max's last name or didn't use his name at all. But would address Sam, Teresa, and Parth with their first names.

"We need somebody in the school to be an intermediary between him and us. Somebody already in his school. No electronic communications. Not yet," Max said. "We need to either identify somebody we can trust who can work with us inside and won't raise any suspicion if the Chinese are watching him or put somebody inside."

"The school won't approve that," said Roach. "We've done a lot of outreach at these research universities. We've gained their trust. They're starting to pay attention to who their students and teachers are in ways we haven't seen before."

"That's what this case needs," Max said.

"Valentin," Roach said. "Maintaining the trust of these institutions is critical to our future success."

"I understand that," Max said. "But I think we need to balance the potential enormity of how this could develop against the risk of ruffling a few school administrative feathers. If this was just about getting wind of a student or a professor receiving funds from the Chinese, I'd have no problem with letting the school know about it and letting them know what we're going to do about it, but this is different."

"It's not different, Valentin?" Roach said. "It's about trust."

Tan spoke up, "I think it's different too, Mr. Roach. There's a lot at stake here. If the informant can give us the recruiter and maybe we uncover other students or teachers who were also recruited, and cooperating with the Chinese, that would be an important case for us to make."

"I want to see if there's another student we can use. Somebody who's around the informant," Max said. "Look, remember the real truth here. And I don't want to be too damn direct about it, but these research institutions have been cooperating with law enforcement lately not just because they want to do the right thing, but because they receive public funds from the National Science Foundation or the National Institute of Health, and don't want to lose that funding. So, they don't have much of a choice."

Max and Roach faced each other in silence for an extra moment. Then Roach turned to Ashe. "What do you think, Sam?"

"I agree with Max," Ashe said. "We can start going through the student personnel records at the school and see if we can identify one who will work with us."

"And if we can't find somebody suitable, we can try to get somebody in there, an undercover," Tan said.

"Exactly, but even if neither of those options pan out, I still don't want to bring school administration into this until we have no other choice," Max said. "All right, Mr. Roach?"

Another awkward pause.

"Let me know who you come up with," Roach said and stood up. "That it?'

"Yes," Max said.

Roach left the conference room.

Mehta jumped on his laptop and pulled up the student records for every student in attendance at the Schimmel Center.

IT WAS ALMOST MIDNIGHT, and they were still in the office. Max, Tan, Ashe, and Mehta were working to identify the right student to approach.

They'd started with coffee and Ritz peanut butter crackers for lunch, from evening until 10:30 p.m. they'd worked their way through Chinese food: wonton soup, egg rolls, shrimp, and chicken lo mein, ribs, fried rice, and the fortune cookies, but by midnight they were back to water, coffee, and Ritz peanut butter crackers.

There was a certain profile they needed to stick with to avoid stumbling onto somebody who would jeopardize their investigation.

Here's what they felt they needed to direct their attention to:

• U.S. Citizens and/or countries with good diplomatic relations with the U.S.

• Electrical and computer engineering

• Preferably students in the same program as Wei Ming

• Even better, a student working directly with the same research professor as the informant

    • Quantum computing/semiconductor development

    • Female students

    • Has potent feelings against the theft of R & D

    • Objects to the Chinese communist system and the way they operate

According to the school student enrollment database, there were eight master's programs and four PhD programs at the Roosevelt Island campus, with a total enrollment of about 450 students. Any of the 450 would be in the same building as the informant for them to potentially work with. But it was an enormous building. Wei Ming's specific program—PhD in quantum science—had twenty-one students. Identifying a student in Wei Ming's program to work with, Max knew, would be ideal.

THEY'D REVIEWED THE preliminary personal backgrounds of each of the twenty-one quantum PhD candidates and their academic records.

Here's how it broke down:

- 6 U.S.
- 3 India
- 3 South Korea
- 2 China
- 2 Saudi Arabia
- 2 Japan
- 1 Taiwan
- 1 United Kingdom
- 1 Nepal

Of the twenty-one students, seven were in their third and final year in the program.

They then thought it ideal if the liaison was female, someone who could give the appearance of being the informant's girlfriend. Three were female:

- 1 India
- 1 South Korea
- 1 Taiwan

Of the three females, one was living in the same high-rise building on Roosevelt Island as the informant. It was the Taiwanese student whose name was Jia Li May. She was twenty-six years old, the daughter of a female justice with the supreme court of the Republic of China (Taiwan) and an American lawyer with an international law firm with offices in Taipei. She had received her BS from the Taipei University of Technology in Materials Science, her master's degree in electrical engineering at the University of North Carolina at Chapel Hill. She was bi-racial and had been a prima ballerina with the Taiwan Ballet Company.

If she helped, she could be ideal, Max thought. But he was not getting too far ahead of himself. He'd been around long enough to know that with potential benefits, there were often risks. And, more often than not, the risks do not raise their ugly heads until the moment of impact.

"She's beautiful," Mehta said.

Max nodded. Their reaction was based on only her student ID photo.

"And what a background," Ashe added. "This'll be a hard sell."

"We should try," Tan said. "Legal eagles raised her. Her father is American. She may jump at the opportunity. And she may have strong anti-mainland-China feelings."

"She may," Max said. "But it's cutting it close. She grew up in Taiwan. Some Taiwanese support mainland China."

"Except, she's a millennial," Mehta added.

"Which means she's almost certainly anti-mainland China," Tan said.

Max nodded. "Possibly."

"I don't think she'll go for it, Teresa," Ashe said, and tossed another peanut butter Ritz cracker in his mouth. "Sure, she has parents in legal, but she's not legal at all, and maybe she's anti-China, but she's a scientist. Why get involved in something so dicey if you don't have to?"

"She may see it as an opportunity to be of service to her country," Tan said.

"And she's in her last year of the program," Max said, just to hear himself say it.

"Yes," Mehta answered, "just like the informant. They've been in the program together for almost three years."

"They must know each other pretty well then," Tan said.

"I don't know," Ashe said. "We should take another look at some others. Maybe one of the Americans. No females, but it could be less risky for us."

Tan shook her head. "No. I think using an American will stand out more," Tan said, as they watched Mehta work his laptop, seeking all public information and social media he could find on the Taiwanese student beyond what was in the school's database.

"I agree," Max said.

"If they see American dudes overly interacting with our guy, it might spook the Chinese," Tan said, "think he's cooperating with us."

"All the Americans live off the island," Mehta said. "They live in Manhattan."

"Exactly, that won't work. She's in the same building," Tan said. "No, I think she's our girl."

"We need to do a fast assessment here," Max said.

And moving fast was about the last thing Max wanted to do. But they had no choice. The semester was wrapping up.

"And it has to be right," Ashe said. "If she's a mainland China sympathizer, we're toast."

Tan continued, "She can't be a sympathizer. Her mother's a Taiwanese supreme court justice for crying out loud, and her father's African American. Former marine lieutenant colonel assigned to the Staff Judge Advocates office in Hong Kong and Taiwan."

Mehta pulled up a YouTube video of a CBS *This Morning* program with a segment six years prior after her first performance in *Swan Lake*. She seemingly floated across the stage, the epitome of elegance; a perfectly proportioned five-eight.

In the profile piece, the narrator said, "To imagine that this now confident, stunning twenty-year-old was once a bullied kid..." Jia Li then told the interviewer, "Whenever the teacher told us to hold hands, other children thought my black skin would rub off on them, so they said, 'Don't touch her,'" she remembered. "Some kids wouldn't get in the pool with me, others threw garbage at me."

"Look at what she was up against," Tan said, and Mehta flipped his laptop around in Max and Ashe's direction and replayed the video, plus a few other articles and video about her.

Max and Ashe looked away from the laptop and back at Tan.

"Jia Li has got guts," Tan said, and thumped her chest with her fist as if she was a Roman gladiator. "Excelled in everything she did, top of her class despite those challenges, a prima ballerina by the time she graduated from college, never backed down from a challenge. She knew she would be ridiculed for pursuing ballet, and still went for it and reached the top. No doubt she did it to make a point. She was the Misty Copeland of Taiwan. Didn't need to put herself through that to advance her science education. She did it to prove to her fellow Taiwanese that she's here and not hiding from anything or anybody. No wilted flower. I think she's a formidable, beautiful, smart woman. I think she'll jump at the opportunity."

Max smiled and looked at Mehta. "Parth?"

"I wouldn't have thought so either, but Teresa's making strong points," Mehta replied, "I think as a scientist she'll have darn potent feelings about the theft of another's hard work and discoveries."

Max then looked at Ashe. "Sam?"

"If she wants to stick it to the Chinese, she could be ideal. She'll feel she has a real stake in resisting the Chinese for her country."

"All right. That's it then," Max said. "I'll let Roach know that's who we want to approach."

"He's going to ask how we plan to make the approach," Ashe said. "What do you think?"

"We have her mobile number and email address," Tan said.

"We don't want to reach out to her that way and take a chance she's already being monitored by the Chinese," Max said.

"Good point," Ashe said.

"Yeah. We have to think the Chinese would track an aspiring Taiwanese scientist studying quantum in the U.S.," Max said. "So, we can't take the chance."

Tan said, "Unless we run out of options and there's no other way to make contact."

"Which is not where we're at," Max said.

"Right," Ashe said.

"Another thing," Max added. "If we set it up where she appears to be a love interest of Wei Ming, then they'll definitely be looking at her to monitor her electronics."

"Yeah, for sure," Tan said.

"So, we don't want to play it that way after all," Max said. "She can help us exchange messages, but she shouldn't have any more contact with him than any other student in the program."

"So, if we get the green light from Roach, and she agrees to help us," Tan said. "We'll just use her as a discreet messenger between us and Wei Ming."

"Right," Max said. "We'll give her an encrypted mobile and email address after we meet with her anyway, just in case the Chinese have thrown out a wide net over all the students in the program."

Tan and Ashe nodded in agreement.

"So, we'll do a face-to-face for the first meet," Max continued. "We need to get eyes on her apartment building first thing tomorrow morning. Five a.m. She's a scientist, she's probably an early riser."

"I'll do it," Tan volunteered.

"I'll do it, with you, Teresa," Ashe said.

"No need. If Roach gives us the green light, I'll toss it to the *OJO* surveillance team tonight. You guys get some sleep," Max said. "Whoever they've got working early tomorrow morning can run with it. All they need to do is watch the building until she comes out and report her outdoor movements. Depending on what she does, we'll decide tomorrow how to approach her."

The FBI had the best surveillance operatives Max had ever watched at work, and he'd worked with a lot of good ones. They had invited Max to observe several FBI surveillance operations over the years. He came to think FBI surveillance teams were a bunch of magicians. Sometimes a case agent wanted to personally tail the target and not just rely on a surveillance report. But, even in those cases, *OJO* would be there to back the case agent up when the agent lost sight of their target. Even other FBI agents did not know what the *OJO* team members looked like or their names, and that's how the FBI liked it. They *were* magicians. Human drones. And Max always appreciated the handle FBI surveillance teams used, *"OJO,"* which is Spanish for the word, "Eye,"; pronounced "Oh-Ho."

"Sounds good," Tan said.

"Good, Max," Ashe said. Tan and Ashe grabbed their backpacks and started to leave. "What time you want us back tomorrow?" Tan asked.

"Ten-hundred."

"By the way, where's the second Chinese student living?" Max asked. "What's his name again?"

"Name is Zhao Hua," Ashe answered.

"Zhao Hua, right," Max repeated. "And this is his first year in the program?"

"Yes," Mehta said.

"Okay, see you guys in the morning."

IT WAS 12:45 A.M. WHEN Max shot a text off to Special Agent in Charge Dick Roach. Five minutes later Roach called him back. Max explained as Roach listened in silence, asked no follow-up questions, and gave Max and his team the green light to approach Jia Li May.

CHAPTER 9
Wednesday, May 17

At 7:55 a.m. Max was on the Q train down to 26 Federal Plaza from his East Eighty-Fifth Street and York Avenue apartment when he received a text from the surveillance team leader.

"Call when u can."

As soon as he came up into the rain from the Canal Street subway station, he stepped into the Bank of America ATM on the corner and returned the call.

"Max Valentin here."

"Hey, Max. This is *OJO*. We picked your girl up early, 6:05, out the door of her apartment building, went for a run south down to the tip of the island, stops to do about five minutes of stretching, then turns around and back to her apartment building by 6:45. She's dressed and out the door again at 7:25, walks to the Schimmel Center, goes through the front door at 7:37, and she hasn't been out since."

"Great, can you stay on her?'

"Sure, no problem. I'll keep you posted."

"Great, thanks, a lot," Max said. "It'll be great if she leaves and comes over the river to Manhattan. Better if we can approach her off the island."

"Got it, we'll let you know."

TERESA TAN AND SAM Ashe walked into Max's office at 9:25 a.m.

"*OJO* has Jia Li May at the Schimmel Center," Max said, then gave them all the details. "If she takes a run again tomorrow morning, that may be our opportunity to approach her. But we'll see if she takes a trip over the tram to Manhattan this afternoon or evening."

"Yeah," Tan said. "Doing this away from the Roosevelt Island would be better for us."

Max's iPhone rang. "Yes."

"Max, it's *OJO*. Your girl is heading to the tram. She's alone."

"Okay, good, good, we're going to head up there now. I'll give you a shout when we're in the area," Max said, and ended the call. "She's heading to the tram."

"Great," Ashe said, and shot out of the office. "I'll be in the car outside the garage exit."

Max shot out of the office with Teresa Tan and jumped on the elevator after giving Roach a heads-up by text.

Tan said, "It takes about five minutes before it goes over the river, then a few minutes to empty out, and for people to get to the street. We have a chance to catch her as she's coming off the tram."

"*OJO* will stay on her until they hear from us."

THE BLACK STRIKE FORCE SUV was running and waiting at the garage exit, with Sam Ashe behind the wheel. Max and Tan jumped in. Ashe whipped out and headed south down the Westside Highway, coming around the southernmost tip of Manhattan Island, and cruised up the FDR Drive, headed for the East Sixty-First Street exit on the left side of the highway, and shot west to Second Avenue.

Max received a text from the surveillance team, "Tram pulling in... she's on it."

"Perfect, the tram's pulling in," Max said, and texted the surveillance team that they would make the approach, but to keep the target under surveillance until Max advised to drop her. "Sam, go across Second Avenue, onto Sixtieth Street. Teresa, you jump out with me. We'll both approach her and invite her back to the car. But keep an eye out to see if she's meeting with anybody. We don't want to do this with company."

"Got it."

Max and Tan jumped out, stopped at the corner, and watched a stunning Jia Li May come down the Roosevelt Tram stairs, wearing a gray suede waist-length jacket, white blouse, black yoga pants, black heels, lugging a black LeFlore Paris backpack. She walked in Max and Tan's direction north on Second Avenue, seemingly to not take notice of them on the corner and made a left down Sixtieth Street where the SUV was parked. Tan and Max caught up to her from both sides, just passing Ashe parked in the SUV.

Max had his FBI strike force credentials in his hand. "Ms. May, I'm a United States federal agent. My name is Max Valentin," he said, and showed his credentials to her. She stopped cold with wide eyes, but no words. Max spoke up again, "And this is Agent Tan," as Tan pulled in front of her and showed her credentials with a warm smile.

Jia Li still did not say a word.

"Please don't be alarmed, you're not in any trouble," Max said. "But we would like to talk to you if you have a minute."

She remained silent, then said directly, "What is this about, sir?"

"We'd rather not talk in public. Our car is right over here," Max said and pointed over her shoulder to their SUV. "That's our vehicle. That's another federal agent behind the wheel. We can speak to you right there in the car."

Ashe partially leaned his head out, waved at her, and delivered a warm smile.

Max watched Jia Li swivel her head to look at the SUV, look back at him and Teresa Tan, then back to the SUV, then back to him and nodded, "Okay, but I have little time. I just wanted to purchase something at Bloomingdale's, and then I must return to my university. I attend the Schimmel Center on Roosevelt Island."

"Yes, we know, Ms. May," Max said. "This won't take long,"

Ashe and Tan were in the front seat. Max sat in the back with Jia Li. Passengers in the vehicle were not visible to passersby. The side windows of the SUV were tinted black.

"Ms. May. You're familiar with the problem of intellectual property theft," Max said. "The theft of trade secrets. Research and development secrets in particular?"

Jia Li looked at Max for an extra moment before answering, "Yes, of course. You don't think I…"

Max shook his head and waved his hand. "No, no. Not you. Just you know China has gone to extreme lengths to steal trade secrets from various universities here in the U.S. and other countries, including yours?"

"Yes, I do," Jia Li nodded. "And my university has instructed us to be leery of persons who inquire about our research and report it immediately to school administration if it occurs."

"Are you familiar with the Chinese state sponsored Thousand Talents Program?"

"Yes," Jia Li said. "My understanding is that they try to encourage students of science or scientists in private industry to return to China with what they have learned in university or in the company they work for in the United States or elsewhere."

"Yes. That's part of it," Max said. "But the other part it is that they want more than what was learned. They pay good money for them to return to China with stolen trade secrets and often offer prominent positions back in China upon their return. They incentivize trade secrets theft."

"I understand."

"Have they ever approached you?" Max asked.

Jia Li now shook her head. "No, at least, not that I am aware of."

"That's good to hear," Max said. "Well, it's happened to a fellow student in your school who has reached out to us for help."

Max was careful to not even divulge the student's gender and he would expect Tan and Ashe to follow suit.

"Really," she said, with a furrowed brow. "May I know who?"

"Not right now. But we want to share with you what has happened to the student," Max said. "Is that okay?"

"Yes, yes, of course."

"The student is a Chinese national on a student visa. Representatives of the Chinese government may have contacted the student to steal information about the school's scientific research," Max said. "The student brought it to our attention because the student doesn't want to cooperate with them. But there is a problem."

"Bird in the cage," Jia Li said.

"Excuse me," Max said.

"Bird in the cage. Yes, it derives from a Chinese folktale," Jia Li said. "If the student does not cooperate, there is apprehension for the student's family in China."

"Ah huh," Max said, intrigued by what Jia Li was describing.

"The student's family is considered the bird in the cage and the student is outside of the cage," Jia Li continued. "The folktale proceeds like this: If the caged bird is alive and singing, the strong person outside the cage is alive and singing too... But if the caged bird dies, the person outside the cage dies too."

It was quiet in the SUV as Max watched Jia Li look at Tan and Ashe, then back to him.

Max finally spoke up, "Yes, I see."

It struck him how living under the shadow of a superpower like China—as Taiwan has since 1949—someone like Jia Li would know how an authoritarian government operates. So completely unimaginable to someone coming of age in America.

"As long as the student's family is in the cage, the student's spirit is in the cage with his family," Jia Li said. "That is how China controls its citizens' behavior outside of China. He is risking much."

"That's right," Max said. "We admire his courage."

"It is terrible," Jia Li said. "I, too, admire my fellow student's courage. How can I help?"

Max paused before answering. This Taiwanese scientist beauty volunteered to help without even being asked. Was that a good or bad sign? Max wondered.

"We hoped you'd want to help. That's why we're here," Max said. "Ms. May, our problem is to find a way of communicating with him without the Chinese knowing about it. He may be under surveillance and the Chinese state, or their representatives could be monitoring his electronic devices."

"You want me to communicate with him for you?" Jia Li asked and twisted to look directly at Max. "To be a liaison?"

"Yes," Max said.

"I'll do it."

Max looked at Jia Li for a long moment.

"If you do this, if you work with us," Max said, "you cannot tell anybody."

"I understand."

Tan interjected, "We'll need you to sign a non-disclosure agreement as well."

"Do you have it with you?" Jia Li asked Tan.

"We do," Tan answered,

"Give it to me, I'll sign it now," she said, and put her hand out to her.

"Are you certain you want to do this?" Max asked. "You don't want to think it over?"

"No, nothing to think over," Jia Li said. "A fellow student is trying to do the proper thing, and he needs help, and you need help, so I will help. Give me what you need me to sign."

Max slipped a quick, intense glance at Tan, who nodded with a 'I knew she'd go for it' look. But this was going too easy for Max's taste. He was hesitant to direct Tan to give her the NDA to sign.

Even though he hadn't discussed it with his team, he still knew Tan, at some level, and Ashe for sure, were all thinking the same thing at that moment. It was a serious moment. Could they have stumbled upon somebody who is also working for the Chinese state? That what they were doing was giving an active Chinese agent the passkey into their case and the opportunity to be a double agent for the Chinese.

Jia Li broke the silence.

"With all due respect, do you understand what it means to me that a Chinese colleague has chosen to not give into communist China?"

"We know anti-mainland China feelings are very strong for some in Taiwan. We know China wants Taiwan to come under its control," Max said. "And many Taiwanese don't want any part of that."

"That is correct," Jia Li picked up from there. "We are a democracy. We elect our officials. The communist party does not select our representatives. They want us to do as Hong Kong has done. Live under a one country, two systems. But look at what's happening to Hong Kong today. Communist China has taken them over, and the youth of Hong Kong fought to prevent that. China has brought Hong Kong under the one country, one system form of government. And China was relentless in their pursuit to absorb Hong Kong and now, under their newly established security law, it makes it punishable for Hong Kong citizens to criticize communist China in any fashion."

"Yes, we are aware of the bounties placed on eight Hong Kong activists who have made it out of Hong Kong," Max said. "And the way China launched that massive military intimidation exercise by encircling Taiwan after the former speaker of our House of Representatives made a visit. Most of America is aware of your country's plight."

"Yes, and your new speaker met with our president. The United States supports my country and has recently sold millions of dollars in military equipment to us so that we can defend ourselves against a communist invasion." Jia Li said. "Such as F-16 fighter jets and other support equipment. And since Russia has invaded Ukraine, and Hamas has attacked Israel, that concern has only been heightened."

"We knew that, yes," Max said, "But isn't there an opposition party to the current president that wants to get closer to Beijing?"

"That is true," Jia Li said. "But they are an old party and do not have the support of most of my country. Their only hope of gaining support is to distance themselves from Beijing, which they have done. When my country's opposition party leader was elected, the Chinese president did not acknowledge it, which has been the custom for decades. In fact, the opposition party planned a visit to Beijing but had to cancel because their efforts to get closer to the communists outraged the Taiwanese people. We are the party for the present and future of Taiwan and do not want to be taken over. Absolutely not!"

Max and his team remained silent.

Jia Li continued, "Our elected president—elected by our people—has made it clear Taiwan is its own country, with its own elected officials, its own judiciary, its own military, and will never accept being a possession of communist China. I am a member of the Democratic Progressive Party, the party that wants the total independence for Taiwan."

"I see," Max said.

"So, please give me what you need me to sign. I want to help."

Max held Jia Li's eyes for several long seconds.

"Any objection to our giving you a polygraph test?" Max asked. "A lie detector test?"

"No, no, I do not, but how would you do that? When would you do that?"

"Right now, right here in this vehicle," Max said.

Jia Li answered without hesitation, "I would be happy to take your test."

With that, Ashe opened his MacBook laptop. Tan placed a harness-like device around Jia Li's chest and attached wires to her fingers.

Tan asked the questions, and Ashe monitored her reaction. Max knew very well that polygraphs were not entirely reliable, and therefore not admissible in court. But they weren't in court. They were trying to determine—within the time constraints they were under—if they should take a chance with Jia Li May.

Tan went through a list of questions she read from her phone. What is your name, date of birth, place of birth, parents' names, parents' occupations, where do you live, your education, what, where, and when? Then to the more sensitive questions:

"Have you ever been to mainland China or an authoritarian country?"

"I have not."

"Have your parents ever been to mainland China?"

"Yes."

"To your knowledge, have your parents ever worked for the Chinese state, Chinese Communist Party, or any Chinese entities state or private?"

"No, not to my knowledge."

"Do you have friends who are from mainland China?"

"I do."

"Are your friends, to your knowledge, directly working for the Chinese state?"

"Not to my knowledge."

"Are you an agent of the Chinese state?"

"I am not."

Ashe completed the analysis of the results and gave Max the thumbs-up.

Max took a few moments before he continued. "You still want to go forward with this?"

"Yes," Jia Li said, as Tan removed the wires and harness.

"All right, there's a couple other things we need you to understand. We don't believe that you'll be in any danger. But we can't guarantee your safety. We will give you a special phone and an email address with end-to-end encryption for you to communicate with us, we call it an ePhone," Max said. "And we will give you a bracelet to wear at all times, and some other devices that will keep us informed of your movements throughout the school or anywhere else, but even with that technology we sometimes cannot see you or communicate with you. Do you understand?"

"I do," Jia Li said, and put her hand out to Teresa Tan for the document to sign.

Max looked at Jia Li for a couple of extra moments, then at Tan, then at Ashe, and nodded.

After Jia Li signed the NDA, Ashe handed Max a black bag. Max placed it between himself and Jia Li on the backseat, unzipped it, and pulled out an ePhone and a fitness-tracker looking bracelet.

"This looks like a Fitbit," Jia Li said with a smile.

"Yes, it is, but much more," Max said. "It's capable of video and audio recording and has GPS monitoring. But we will not activate it until you've contacted our informant, and we are certain he will accept your being the liaison between us."

Jia Li nodded.

Max held up the bracelet and pointed out that the bracelet also had a red button on the side that could be pushed if she was in any danger.

"Please give me your wrist," Max asked.

"Either wrist?"

"Whichever you prefer."

She put her right wrist out and said, "I am left-handed."

Max put the bracelet around her wrist and when it clicked into place, they could not help looking up and into each other's eyes for a moment.

Something shifted inside of him.

"Okay," Max said, pulling away from her gaze, and handed her the ePhone. He also handed her a laptop. "When you open the laptop, there is already an encrypted email address you'll use to communicate with us. I'll receive every call, text message, or email you send. If I don't respond within three minutes to your text or email, it'll be forwarded to Agent Tan, and then Agent Ashe, and so on. We will promptly respond to you."

Jia Li nodded. "I understand."

Max then handed her a clip shaped like a dragonfly for her to wear on her outermost garment and said that it had a video and audio recording device as well, and explained that, as often as possible, especially when she was communicating with the informant directly, to clip it on her outermost garment.

"Again, all the devices I've given you are encrypted and will be continuously recording audio and video and GPS tracking, depending on the vantage point of each device. When you need privacy, all you need to do is hit this button on the bracelet on the same spot," Max said and pointed to a yellow button. "At that point, all recording capability will stop. The only thing that will not stop is GPS. We will always know where you are if you're wearing the bracelet. To start recording again, just hit the green button. We suggest you wear the Fitbit at all times during the investigation. It's waterproof."

Jia Li nodded again.

Ashe jumped in, "Now, what we need you to do is give some thought to the best way to give and receive notes from your fellow student without raising suspicions. For example, can you type the message we want you to give the student on your laptop and/or ePhone and just direct attention to it on the screen, if nobody else can see the screen?"

Tan said, "You must keep in mind that we don't know who else is watching him, Jia Li. There may be other students or faculty working for that government that are also monitoring the student's movements and interactions with others working for the Chinese."

"Exactly," Ashe said. "Is it the classroom, the lab, the library, the cafeteria? Would it be appropriate for the student to type on your laptop occasionally to give us a message?"

Max adjusted in his seat and said, "One key would be to not use any one location or way of interacting to exchange information regularly. You must mix it up. Do you understand?"

"I do."

"There may be times when we want to send the student an audio message. Think about how the student could listen to it," Tan said. "Maybe there'll be times in which you'll be sitting with that student in the cafeteria, for example, and you just hand the student your hands-free earpiece to listen as if it was part of your research, or, just sharing a funny video, but, in fact, we are sending an audio message."

"Yes," Jia Li said. "I will be as sensible and creative as I can be."

"Okay, good," Max said. "Now, when we're ready, we'll want you to just tell the student that you'll be the intermediary between the student and U.S. investigators, and that you will keep the investigators informed on the student's behalf and you will keep the student informed."

"I understand," Jia Li said, with complete focus. "May I now know who the student is?"

"Not yet," Max said. "Okay, we're done. Do we have any more questions for Ms. May?"

Tan and Ashe shook their heads.

"We'll be in touch, Ms. May," Max said. "Thank you."

"Please call me Jia Li."

"Okay, Jia Li," Max said and watched her put the equipment into her backpack.

She then turned back to Max, shook his hand, then Tan's and Ashe's. "It is good to meet you all."

She grabbed the door handle and jumped out like she was running toward a balance beam. Max watched her glide down East Sixtieth Street, dodging the other pedestrians toward Bloomingdale's.

Teresa Tan opened her laptop and they watched the surveillance video transmitting from the body camera being worn by *OJO's* surveillance operative tailing her.

"Don't flip on the Fitbit, but we can track the GPS on the ePhone she's now carrying," Max said. "*OJO* will do the rest. Let's see what she does."

AS SOON AS JIA LI GOT to the corner, the body camera caught just a glimpse of her back heading into Bloomingdale's, with the first door closing behind her. The female *OJO* operative darted across Third Avenue, making moves through traffic like she was a running back on a high school football field, causing intermittent screeching brakes to ricochet and a few car and truck horns to palm down on her back.

OJO yanked the first door, then the second door into Bloomingdale's which led right into the men's department and filmed Jia Li walk briskly through the jewelry, cosmetics, shoe departments, and a few others, but not only did she not stop but did not even look around at the abundance of merchandise, and directly exited the department store on Lexington Avenue.

"What?" Ashe said with exaggeration. "All that good stuff to buy or at least to peek at and suddenly no time to stop."

Max nodded and kept his eyes fixed on the bouncing *OJO* bodycam footage.

Jia Li went down the subway at Fifty-Ninth Street, jumped on the southbound number six train, got off at East Forty-Second Street, Grand Central Station, dashed up the stairs onto Park Avenue and walked west, dodging traffic at the Park and Madison Avenue intersections, not waiting for the green walk signs, and eventually pushed through the revolving door of One East Forty-Second Street—on the corner of Fifth Avenue—like she was a sumo wrestler pushing her opponent out of the ring.

OJO stood across from it, keeping it in view.

"Do a quick Google on that address, Teresa."

"On it," Tan said, then added, "Well. What do you know? It's a commercial building and the Taiwanese consulate happens to be located on the seventh floor."

"Ah, huh," Max said. He was relieved she hadn't raced to the Chinese consulate, but still disturbed she put off her urgent Bloomingdale's shopping trip to visit the Taiwanese consulate immediately following their conversation.

"So, what's her real story?" Max whispered under his breath.

The Schimmel Center PhD candidate dashed out of the consulate about ninety minutes later, jumped on the northbound

Third Avenue bus, got off at East Fifty-Ninth Street and headed back toward the Roosevelt Island tram.

"Time to find out," Max said and texted the *OJO* team leader so he could direct the surveillance operative to break it off.

"10-4," the *OJO* leader texted back immediately.

"I'll do this solo, guys," Max said. "We don't want to make her feel we're locking her up. I'll have my phone open so you can hear our conversation."

"Sounds good, Max," Tan said.

"Okay, Max," Ashe replied.

Max jumped out of their SUV, and followed Jia Li up the stairs, watched her slide her metro card through the turnstile and wait on the platform with a crowd of about ten others. Jia Li May had not noticed Max standing on the other edge of the crowd. When the tram docked and doors opened, before Jia Li could step on, Max slid up to her and whispered, "So what did you buy?"

Jia Li's head shot up and met Max's eyes. Her cheeks reddened, and eyes developed a flash of mist, but she did not speak for a moment or two.

The crowd flowed onto the cable car; Jia Li and Max remained on the platform.

"Oh, hello, hello," Jia Li said. "Oh, well, oh, they did not have what I searched for."

"Really, I'm sorry to hear that. It seemed very urgent when you jumped out of our vehicle."

"Oh, yes, well, it seemed so. What a coincidence to run into you again, sir?"

He nodded in appreciation for how she shifted the subject.

"Yes, well, as you know, we have a particular interest in who's coming and going from Roosevelt Island these days."

"Yes, yes, of course," Jia Li said, and blushed again.

"So, I thought you needed to get back to school right away and here we both are on this platform almost two hours later."

"Yes, well, I went for a walk."

"Did you happen to stop by One East Forty-Second Street?"

Jia Li was silent for several long moments as the tram ascended the cable without them toward Roosevelt Island. Then, her expression became serious, almost official.

"It's not what you think, Mr. Valentin."

"Why don't you tell me what I think?"

"May we talk someplace else?" she whispered.

"Here's fine. We're alone now," Max said. "I suggest you start talking before others arrive."

"This is a very delicate situation, Mr. Valentin."

"Agreed."

"We are in the same line of work."

"Are we?"

Jia Li looked around, letting a long breath out first, and said, "I am an agent with my country's National Security Bureau."

"What country is that?"

"Taiwan, of course."

"Sure, of course," Max said and looked at her for an extra second then looked up at the tram continuing to climb up the cable only feet from approaching the midpoint peak and said, "I'm listening."

"My role has been to monitor the movements and actions of the ethnic Chinese PhD students attending the Schimmel Center quantum program."

"Why?"

"To insure they do not steal."

"And the Taiwan NSB knows that and has authorized that?"

"Yes, of course."

"Do the Chinese know that?"

"They believe I am only another PhD student like the others," Jia Li said. "As far as we know."

Max held Jia Li's eyes for several long moments before speaking up again.

"Show me something."

Jia Li immediately understood, looked around apparently for any new arrivals and pulled her NSB credentials from somewhere deep inside her waistband, and handed it to Max. Max opened it.

The credentials had her passport-like photograph and in Mandarin read: Jia Li May, Special Security Agent, Republic of China, National Security Bureau.

"Nice of you to let us know," Max said, looked down on her again and handed her credentials back to her. "So much for signing a U.S. law enforcement non-disclosure agreement with so much enthusiasm."

"I am sorry."

"Does my government know what's going on?"

"They will."

"What does that mean?"

"My government is presently notifying your government's intelligence services that we would like to collaborate with you on your investigation," Jia Li said. "That's why I needed to report to my consulate immediately. To get my government's permission to work with you."

"I see," Max nodded with a sinking feeling. The case had only just begun, and he'd already invited the involvement of a foreign intelligence agency. It was not how he wanted to start.

"Why quantum students in particular? I know it's the way of the future. The speed at which it can figure out computer calculations, and so on?" Max asked. "But is there any reason they've embedded you in the quantum program?"

Jia Li nodded. "Sir, do you know what my country's most important scientific, technological contribution is to the world?"

"Semiconductors," Max said without hesitation. "Microchips."

"Correct, semiconductors," Jia Li said. "And semiconductors are in everything. From our coffee makers and refrigerators to our iPhones and computers. Including satellites, military defense technology and the United States space program, including China's. Chips are in everything."

"Yes, I know that," Max said. "And Taiwan is ahead of China in microchip manufacturing?"

"There is no comparison," Jia Li said. "We are the largest manufacturer of advanced semiconductors, yes, microchips in the world. We supply ninety percent of the world's most advanced chips, including to the United States and the West."

"What piece of the microchip pie does China have?"

"China possesses approximately six percent of the semiconductor world market," Jia Li answered. "But their acquisition of quantum could change all of that."

"Why?" Max asked. Then feeling the gravity of this development answered his own question. "The Chinese think they could speed up their semiconductor manufacturing capacity if they get their hands on quantum? Am I getting that right?"

"Yes, exactly."

He continued, "Because the speed of quantum could help them catch up and surpass semiconductor research and, by extension, manufacturing around the world. And if they did that, they would not need to depend on Taiwan for their chips. And maybe take over the market."

"Yes, but exceeding that, if communist China steals quantum research, they could supersede our technological and military capacity to defend ourselves against their potential aggression."

Max could feel another ripple of exhilaration go through his chest with what was at stake here. If China could catch up and overtake Taiwan's semiconductor manufacturing with the acquisition of quantum, they were surely going after quantum with the drive of a Mount Everest climber.

"So, stealing quantum is their fast track to taking over," Max said, as he continued to comprehend what was at stake. "Not to mention it sounds like microchips are a good reason for China to invade Taiwan, if they can't get quantum."

"Exactly, but one reason communist China hesitates to invade is because of the Silicon Shield."

"Silicon Shield?" Max asked.

"Yes. That an invasion of my country would disrupt the semiconductor supply chain for them as well as the rest of the world, which is clearly not acceptable to the United States and the West, or, for China itself," Jia Li said. Then she got a little more energized. "But if they have the most advanced microchips because of quantum, they will no longer be concerned about the Silicon Shield. The Silicon Shield will cease to exist. It will melt away."

"So, your theory is they need to steal quantum technology first, then they can fast track their semiconductor production, freeing them from dependence?" Max asked. "Which opens the option to take over the chip market and take/invade Taiwan one day."

"Yes, you have it. We have no trouble with innovative fair competition in advancing one's understanding of quantum and semiconductor science and increasing one's share of the market legitimately, just like the United States. But as you well know, communist China will steal, steal, steal, if that is what it takes to catch up and invade my country," Jia Li said. "And that's why I am here, to help make sure the Chinese do not steal."

"Pull out your credentials again," Max said, and pulled out his ePhone. "Open it and hold it against your chest and don't move."

Jia Li complied, and Max took a photo of her.

Max started to walk toward the staircase down to street level from the tram platform.

"Mr. Valentin," Jia Li called out to him.

Max turned.

"May I ask how you came to be waiting for me? I didn't notice anyone following me. And, as a trained NSB agent, I am very good at that."

"We're pretty good at it, too."

"Did you know I was withholding my true identity in some way?"

Max looked at Jia Li for a few extra moments, as people collected on the platform to catch the next tram across, walked back to her and whispered, "Your neck. In the car after the lie detector test, you held my eyes unusually long, as if you were trying to convince me of your sincerity. But it felt excessive. Not just a PhD student trying to be helpful. When you finally looked away from me, I noticed your carotid artery," Max gently touched her neck, "... was pulsating, an indicator of somebody who was not quite telling the truth."

Jia Li looked at Max with wide eyes.

"But we'd arranged for you to be tailed, pulsating neck or not."

Jia Li nodded. "Of course."

Max walked away and down the tram steps onto Second Avenue. He noticed she trembled when he touched her neck.

"WELL, THAT WAS ENLIGHTENING," Tan said with a smirk as Max jumped back into the SUV.

"Oh yeah," Max said. "Let's head down to Katz's and grab a sandwich. My treat."

"Sounds good," Tan said. I'm way overdue for a good pastrami on rye."

"Likewise," Ashe said and swung the SUV out and over to the FDR Drive, heading south for the Houston Street exit.

ON THEIR WAY DOWN, Max received a call from Ed Vance. Vance told him that the professor stabbed and poisoned on the tram and left dead had a tattoo on his right arm. Vance and his detectives thought it was a Chinese military tattoo.

"Huh," Max said. "Why do you guys think that?"

"The tattoo is embedded with the Great Wall of China."

"Huh," Max said again. "Can you send me a photo of it?"

"On the way."

"Thanks, Ed."

WALKING INTO KATZ'S Delicatessen was like going back to World Wars I and II New York City dining. As soon as you entered the narrow doorway, there were several things that engaged you simultaneously: the New York City old time deli smells of steamed corn beef, pastrami, mustard, knishes, franks, and sauerkraut.

An employee sitting on a highchair at the entrance handed you a ticket and pointed to one of about a dozen counterman standing behind a long glass partition who would cut and prepare your overstuffed sandwich, mark your ticket, and return it to you. The brown wood walls with hanging salamis attached in the background were like a balcony audience. There was a regiment of tables in two columns to one side that had stretched back about one half a city block for the last 130 years.

Max scanned the tables at the far end of the deli where their backs could be up against the wall. So far back, it looked like they were on a ship about to drift over the horizon.

Max and his team slid into the table and quietly took in the ambience of the place.

The waiter was there within seconds to take their order. No menus required. Pastrami on rye, side of potato salad, sour pickles and cream sodas, three times.

They waited for their sandwiches to arrive in silence—like a bunch of abbey monks.

In no time, their sandwiches landed. In synchronized fashion they each lifted the top piece of rye, squirted mustard on the pastrami, lined it up opposite their mouths like they were lining up their sights at the firearms range: breathe, relax, aim, sights, bite.

"Damn, this is good," Ashe mumbled with a full mouth. "I was hungry. Thanks."

They ate for a good ten minutes before Max spoke up. "So, she said she's an agent with Taiwan's NSB and the reason she didn't admit that to us when we spoke with her and gave her a lie detector test..."

"Yeah," Ashe moaned.

"... was that she needed to let her agency know we had approached her and get their permission to cooperate with us?" Max said. "Could you hear our conversation?'

"Yeah," Tan said. Sam nodded.

Max pulled out his ePhone with Jia Li's photo holding her credentials and handed it to Tan for them both to look at. Ashe leaned over and looked at the photo as Tan held Max's phone.

In the meantime, Max took another bite from his pastrami.

"Wow," Tan said, and passed his phone to Ashe. "I am sorry, guys. I didn't see this coming. I was feeling so right that she was a perfect fit."

"No apologies necessary at all, Teresa," Max said, waving his hand. "We all agreed it was the way to go."

"Interesting," Ashe said. "Damn interesting."

Max took a long swig through the straw in his can of cream soda.

"So, where do you think that leaves us?" Ashe asked. "She said her agency is notifying us officially with the request that she assist with our investigation."

"If she's now being straight with us," Max said, "I suspect when we get back to the office, Roach will have received the notification through channels."

"Well, we knew it was risky bringing somebody into our case without a thorough investigation," Tan said. "But what choice did we have? The clock is ticking fast on this case. The school year ends in no time. This is our shot to nail that Chinese operative."

"Exactly," Max agreed.

"Interesting discussion on how the theory that if China gets ahold of quantum, it will help to speed up their semiconductor production," Ashe said. "And that Silicon Shield business."

Max nodded.

"So much for the effectiveness of our lie detector test," Tan said, as they all got up to leave.

"Yeah," was all Max could say. "How do you guys feel about working with her now?"

"Good question," Tan said, paused, then continued, "She lied to us. How can we trust her? But what choice do we have now? The cat's out of the bag."

"The cat's not completely out of the bag. She still doesn't know who our informant is. But now she knows, and her NSB knows, a Chinese national who's being recruited by the Chinese to steal quantum research has contacted us. They'd have to work it—try to figure out who it is, follow up on it with or without us."

Ashe rubbed his face like he was trying to decide whether he needed a shave, then said, "It doesn't feel good, I have to admit. On the other hand, we should be grateful it went down this way. We may have approached the right person in more ways than one."

"I sure hope so," Tan said.

Ashe nodded. "Me too."

Max then looked down at the buzzed text on his ePhone. "It's Roach."

IT WAS A LITTLE AFTER two p.m. when Max, Tan, and Ashe got back down to the lower Manhattan—Jacob Javits, 26 Federal Plaza office building. They walked into Roach's office.

"So, your student selection turns out to be a Taiwanese NSB agent," Roach said as soon as they walked into his office without looking away from his Mac monitor.

"Looks that way," Max asked.

"Nice start, Valentin," Roach said and turned away from his Mac to face Max. "How'd this happen?"

"My fault," Tan said.

"It wasn't your fault, Teresa," Max said. "We made a team decision."

Max explained how they tailed her to the Taiwan consulate, then confronted her on the tram.

Ashe jumped in, "Lucky it turned out this way, Mr. Roach. We all know that's the way it goes down sometimes."

"It would've been very complicated if she turned out to be a Chinese agent," Roach said.

"For sure," Max said. "Except we're still not sure she isn't working for the Chinese."

Roach fixed his gaze on Max—as did Tan and Ashe—with wide, wondering eyes.

Max continued, "There's always a risk she is a Chinese agent, right, and Taiwan doesn't know it. But we have to go with what we know and take that chance."

After a moment of reflection, Tan slowly nodded. "Yeah, true."

"Agreed," Ashe said.

"Yeah, all right. So, Taiwan notified State, State notified Main Justice. Main Justice just notified the Bureau," Roach said. "Does she know who our informant is?"

"No, not yet," Max said.

"Let her know. The Taiwanese NSB is now officially working on this with you," Roach said and turned back to his Mac.

MAX, TAN, AND ASHE headed back up to the Manhattan side of the Roosevelt Island tram. Jia Li agreed to jump back over on the tram and meet with them again.

She was standing on the corner when they arrived. Max flung the door open, and she jumped in. They'd parked where they had approached Jia Li before. Under the tram on East Sixtieth Street.

Jia Li spoke first and swiveled her head from one to the other, meeting each of their eyes for a moment. "I am sincerely sorry for withholding my assignment with my country's security bureau from you. I knew I could not reveal my identity until I had the approval of my government, as much as I sincerely wanted to. I hope you can all forgive me and recognize that I will not withhold any further information as we proceed. I now have the full authorization of my government to cooperate with you fully. I hope you can forgive me."

"You're a bona fide PhD candidate," Max asked. "Everything we know about your educational background is true. Is that right?"

"Yes," Jia Li answered.

Tan jumped in, "So, you're a scientist that works espionage on the side. How's that work?"

Jia Li nodded. "They have educated me in the sciences since I was a tiny girl. In the middle of my high school studies, I entered an intelligence agents' program with the approval of my parents. In all my U.S. education, my role has been to act in the dual capacity as a student and intelligence agent."

"Have you had experience handling a Chinese recruitment operation?" Ashe asked.

"I have not," Jia Li admitted. "This is my first. But they have groomed me for this work for over ten years. I am ready."

Max nodded with the thought. *We'll see.*

There were a few moments of silence in the black SUV.

"My role is to cooperate with you fully," Jia Li emphasized. "My government said to assist you. I am under your direction, Mr. Valentin."

Max nodded and really hoped this would not bite them on the ass. When they thought she was only a student, any information he intended to pass on to her would only have been if absolutely needed. Now that he was directed to fully cooperate with her, they could not hold back much. Jia Li would know almost as much as they knew.

"It stings to be deceived that way," Max said, but then extended his hand to her. "But I doubt we would've acted differently if we had been in your shoes."

"Thank you," Jia Li said, shook Max's hand, then Tan's and Ashe's. "Thank you. I was shocked and delighted that you had approached me."

"Okay. Let's get on with it," Max said. "Yesterday's news."

"Thank you, sir," Jia Li said. "Thank you."

"Call me Max."

"Okay, sir," Jia Li said.

Max smiled. "Our informant's name is Wei Ming."

"Wei Ming!" she blurted with excitement. "Wei Ming!"

Max took in Jia Li's reaction. "Yes."

"Oh, my goodness, he is my friend," and overlapped her hands to her chest. "He is brilliant. He is my friend."

"Your friend?" Max said. "We know you've been in the same program together the whole time."

"Yes, more than classmates. We are friends. Yes, we started in this program three years ago together. We are two of only seven students in our final year of the program that have been together the entire three years."

"Okay," Max said again, and looked at Tan and Ashe, and back to Jia Li. "Does he know you're a Taiwanese agent?"

"No, no, he does not," Jia Li said. "Because we're friends, we communicate frequently. We frequently have meals together in the cafeteria. It is common for us to study together in the library. We sit together in the classroom. Naturally, we are both involved in the same project with Professor Kleinheidt. We spend a great deal of time together. I know about his family, he about my family."

Max took all that in for a few moments before he spoke up. "So, you're spending so much time with him it would not be unusual for you to continue spending time with him."

"Absolutely not. Our program is very intense. It requires our spending hours and hours in each other's company. And we have been doing this for three years. He has been to my apartment countless times, and I have been to his."

Max paused again to take in what she was saying. "I hope you don't mind my asking, this, Jia Li. Are you in a romantic relationship with Wei Ming?"

Jia Li shook her head. "No, no. Wei Ming. No," she said, then trailed off.

"Why'd you hesitate?" Max asked.

Jia Li looked at Max for another moment, looked at Tan and Ashe, then back to Max and said, "Wei Ming does not have a girlfriend. And to be more precise, I don't believe he likes girls. Or, I mean, not in that way."

"I see," Max said.

"But it is more than that. I don't believe he likes boys either," Jia Li said. "I think Wei is asexual. He is committed to his studies and his research. Completely devoted to it. We are together all the time, but I don't think people could think that we are boyfriend/girlfriend ever because we never hold hands. No romantic affection. Never. Professional affection and admiration, yes. Romantic affection, no."

Max took that in for another moment, holding her gaze. "You've been studying with him for almost three years now. You were monitoring him in your role as an NSB agent."

"Yes, of course," Jia Li said. "But I have witnessed no behavior that seemed suspicious or would indicate any thievery."

"That's good," Max said.

"May I ask how you learned of him?"

"The day before yesterday," Max said, "we received a note from him in Braille."

"Braille," she said with a smile. "His sister is blind. He learned Braille to teach her so she could go to school. He's very proud of her. She was one of only nine blind students in all of China who were permitted to take their national university entrance exam last summer."

"Really," Ashe blurted, obviously intrigued.

Max could not help feeling himself getting temporarily sidetracked too.

"Yes," Jia Li said to Ashe. "And that was nine blind students out of over ten million who took the examination."

"Nine blind students out of ten million?" Ashe repeated. "And she took the exam in Braille? I know Chinese characters are very difficult to transliterate into Braille."

"Sam is a Braille transcriber," Max said.

Jia Li nodded to Ashe with a big smile. "Yes, that is true. And she received a high enough score to be accepted to Nanjing University.

The same university Wei Ming graduated from before he continued his education in the United States."

"How about that," Ashe said, when Tan cleared her throat with a bit of exaggeration.

"Right, right, okay," Max said, and hurriedly pulled out the transcription of Wei Ming's note and handed it to Jia Li. "Did you know the Chinese had contacted him?"

"No, I did not know."

He watched her read Wei Ming's transcribed Braille note slowly, with complete focus. Max could imagine her working in a scientific setting, analyzing data, drawing conclusions, potential solutions radiating from her beautiful brown eyes.

Jia Li looked up. "Yes, he does Tai Chi every morning."

Max nodded. "We saw him yesterday morning from a boat, as he suggested, letting him know we received his note. He thanked us for coming, and, in Tai Chi, communicated that they had again contacted him and asked for our help."

Jia Li nodded. "You know, I believe I was with him when he was contacted. We were sitting in the cafeteria, and he was drinking a cup of tea when he looked at a text message. His hand started to quiver, and he started to perspire. I asked if he was well. He said he was, but clearly, he was not. But it did not occur to me that that could be the cause."

"Do you have any photographs of him?" Tan asked. "We have our river video and his school ID photo, passport and visa photos, but a few more in different outfits he wears wouldn't hurt."

"I do. I have some; several of just him inside and around the Schimmel Center, and several I took of him in Manhattan. We have visited many historical and cultural sites together since we arrived and took photographs. I can send them to you now if you desire."

"Yes, that would be great, but use the encrypted ePhone we gave you," Tan said, and pointed to her bag. "You have the photos on your personal iPhone."

"Yes."

"Transfer the photos from your phone to the encrypted phone," Tan said. "Then send the photos to our encrypted phone number."

Max asked. "Do you have photographs of you and him together?"

"I do."

"That would be helpful, too. It'll give us a sense of his height in relation to you," Max said.

"Yes, of course," Jia Li said. "I am several inches taller than him and if I wear heels, I am substantially taller than him."

"Good," Max said. "During this investigation, we'll have surveillance teams watching you both as often as possible when you're outdoors—for your safety."

Jia Li sent the photos to the encrypted mobile phone number.

Tan received the photos and thanked her.

Ashe jumped in, "We noticed that you both live in the same apartment building."

"Yes, the university owns many apartments in the building, and they offer students the opportunity to rent."

"According to our records, you're on the eighth floor and Wei Ming's on the twelfth," Ashe said.

"Yes, that is correct."

"Okay," Max said. "If he agrees, we'll want to do a sweep of his apartment for electronic devices, and we might as well do yours to be on the safe side. Is that okay?"

"A sweep," Jia Li said, and paused. "Yes, of course. But my agency routinely inspects my apartment for devices every week. Nothing has yet been discovered."

"That's good to hear," Max said. "But if you don't mind, since we'll be there to do Wei Ming's, we might as well do yours to be on the safe side."

"Of course."

"All right. Now, let me ask you something?" Max said. "You know about that professor who was killed on the tram last week?"

"Yes, of course," Jia Li said. "Professor John Xu. Very curious."

"You ever see him before?" Max asked.

"No, he did not look familiar."

"Your agency have anything on him?" Tan asked.

"Not beyond his university public profile."

"What about the other Chinese student? Zhao Hua," Ashe asked. "We know this was his first year. Any suspicions of what he's doing?"

"No, none that I have observed."

"Does he work closely with you and Wei Ming on research?" Max asked.

"No, no, not at all," Jia Li said. "Only Wei Ming and I are working on the most advanced quantum research with Professor Kleinheidt."

"What about the other final year students?" Max asked.

"Yes, yes, three American students, one from Japan, and one from the United Kingdom are also working with Professor Kleinheidt," Jia Li said. "But only Wei Ming and I are working on the most advanced research."

AS SOON AS MAX, TAN, and Ashe filed into Roach's office (he did not offer for them to sit down), Max's ePhone vibrated. Tan, Ashe, and Jia Li all now had the same encrypted, exclusive-for-case-use ePhones.

He pulled it out and silently read the first text message from Jia Li:

"He is delighted I am liaison... in tears... awaiting further instructions. Had long talk."

Max nodded at Tan and Ashe and looked at Roach. "Just got confirmation from Jia Li, the informant's happy that she's our liaison with him."

Tan and Ashe nodded.

Roach had no reaction.

Max said, "I want to speak to him right away. I'm going to ask her to let him know we'll stop by her apartment to do the interview tonight and have a tech sweep his apartment for electronic devices."

"Have the tech sweep hers too," Roach said.

"She said NSB does periodic sweeps of her apartment," Max said. "But she agreed to let us do it, anyway."

"Good. Did she have any information at all?" Roach asked. "Did he confide in her at all before today?"

"No," Max answered. "She had a sense he wasn't feeling good when he first got contacted, but she didn't know what it was about, and said he didn't discuss it with her."

Tan jumped in, "He will not want to tell us much of anything until we give him some assurance that we'll help protect his family. We think he's going to ask for our help to arrange for his family to be brought here."

"Oh, yeah?" Roach responded.

"I agree with Teresa," Max said. "He was up front about that in his Braille message. We may need to arrange visas for them to enter the U.S. in a hurry, finance their flights, and find them a safe place to live here when he brings it up again."

Roach remained mute for a couple of seconds. "That's a big investment of time and money and he hasn't given us anything yet."

"He told us the Chinese approached him and he reached out to us. We didn't find him." Max said. "Again, there's always a chance he's actually a Chinese agent that wants to take us for a ride to see how we handle him. But if he's legit, and we can take it all the way, will you authorize getting his family out of China?"

Roach was silent for a moment, then spoke up, "I want him to give us something first."

Max was silent for a couple of seconds. He couldn't blame Roach. They needed more before attempting an exfiltration of the informant's family.

"All right, I get it," Max said.

"Anything else?" Roach asked and turned back to his computer.

Max thought about letting him know about the appearance of a possible Chinese military tattoo stamped on the murdered professor but opted to wait until it was confirmed. And even then, he wondered if he would tell Roach at all.

"No," Max said, and headed to the door. "We're going to get on it."

Tan and Ashe followed Max out.

WHEN THEY GOT BACK to Max's office, they discussed when they wanted to do the sweep and interview Wei Ming. Max then sent Jia Li a text.

"We will visit 2nite. UR apt w/Wei Ming. expect us at 2:30 a.m. ok?"

Within minutes, he received a return text from Jia Li. "We will be ready."

Max and his team spoke with the techs. Since a sweep entailed recognizing vibrations coming from an audio device, video device, or both, inside a location, Max had to decide how to go about uncovering any devices inside Wei Ming's or Jia Li's apartments, so as not to activate any potentially Chinese-installed recording devices.

Tan said to the tech, "If we get you inside the apartments and there's recording devices secreted in the place, they'll be recording or videotaping you during the sweep. That won't be good."

"We can check from outside the apartment door and see what we pick up," the tech said. "If we get a spike from outside, we don't need to go in. But we can't tell you where the devices are located inside the apartment or whether they're video, audio, or both, unless we're inside and find them."

"That's all right," Max said. "We don't have to know where the devices are. We just want to know, for starters, if there're any devices inside."

"But if we do it in public, Max, in the hallway," Ashe said, "anybody coming out or going into their apartment will see what we're up to and could create problems for us."

"That's why we're doing it at two in the morning," Max said, then looked at the tech. "How long would you need to be outside the door to get a reading?"

"One to two minutes or so," the tech said.

"All right. You guys will stay downstairs. I'll go up with the techs. No need for you to have a face-to-face with the informant right now. Right now, only I need to meet him and speak with him directly. He doesn't need to know what you guys look like," Max said. "Make sense?"

Tan nodded.

"It does," Ashe replied. "Sounds good."

"So, this is how it'll work. I'll go with the techs to the outside of the first apartment door at two-fifteen a.m. Wei Ming's door on the twelfth. The tech gives us a reading. If the twelfth floor has a spike, we'll know there's something hot inside. Good to know and leave it at that. Then I'll go downstairs with the techs and do Jia Li's eighth floor apartment door and do the same. If there's no spike, then I'll take the chance of going inside and the tech can do a complete sweep just to be one hundred percent sure. Sound good?"

They all nodded.

"All right, so we'll get up there at two a.m. We'll take two cars. I'll ride with the techs; Teresa, Sam, you guys can drive up in one of our cars, and remember," Max said, with a half-grin, "we have to head out to Queens and come back over the bridge that gets you onto Roosevelt Island, the Thirty-Sixth Avenue Bridge. So, we have to give ourselves extra time."

After they planned for the tech team to show up at their Roosevelt Island apartment building at 2:15 a.m., Max cut Tan and Ashe and the techs loose until their plan to meet on the island at two a.m.

MAX WAS IN HIS CAR cruising up the FDR Drive when his phone rang on the dashboard. It was 5:52 p.m. according to the car's digital clock.

He could see the name 'Jack H.' in his caller ID displayed on the dashboard.

"Hey, Jack, what's going on?"

"This a good time, Max?"

"Yeah, yeah, I'm just heading home to get a few hours of sleep," Max said. "We're going to meet with the informant on Roosevelt Island about two a.m. tonight, do an electronics sweep, and do an interview."

"Oh, good, good to hear," Hunt said. "Listen, got some news on the tram homicide professor. Turns out the Eastern District had a case on him."

"What!"

"Yeah, I spoke to the prosecutor who's handling the case, close friend. He's a straight shooter; another CCIPS attorney. He's pissed big time about the homicide," Hunt said. "They had a sealed indictment on Dr. John Xu a.k.a. Zhang Kan for failure to disclose his participation in the Chinese Thousand Talents Program and our National Institute of Health. He'd been getting fifty grand a month for the seven-eight years from China. Plus, NIH had given him about fifteen million in grant funding."

"Whoa," Max said again.

"And there's something else."

"Okay."

"The professor was with the Chinese military and had been for the last thirteen years."

"Whoa. How about that," Max said, feeling his heart skip a beat. "The Nineteenth Squad detectives gave me a heads-up—the professor had a Chinese military-looking tattoo on his arm."

"No kidding," Hunt said. "Well, what the Eastern District has confirms it."

"Any details on the unit he was with?"

"Yeah. He was associated with the Fourth Military Medical University. They call it, FMMU. In their chain of command, FMMU falls under the air force component of the People's Liberation Army."

"Yeah, yeah," Max said, half in a daze with that news, letting it fully compute.

Max recalled from his master's thesis on the PRC's military and intelligence global IP theft strategies, FMMU sends military scientists—with bogus identities—into the U.S. and other countries to steal.

"How'd they find out?"

"They were watching the professor for a while and eventually got into his electronics," Hunt said. "The professor was sitting in one of those lecture classrooms observing another teacher give a talk, and the Eastern District had an agent pretending to be a student nearby who dropped an extra potent laxative into his tea. It hit him so fast, the professor left his laptop unattended. He didn't have time to grab it, so he left it on one of those small desks. It gave the agent time to download everything onto a flash drive, which included the names and backgrounds of other military scientists."

"No kidding. Darn good work. That must be why the assassins took off with his briefcase after they left him in the tram. The briefcase I bet had his laptop. The Chinese wanted to do damage control," Max said. "How'd they confirm the military angle?"

"From what our agent downloaded, they came up with photographs of him in military uniform, documents, emails, and other communications on his computer with the PLA," Hunt said. "He had everything backed up on the cloud. They subpoenaed Apple and got his CV and more."

"He backed up all this information on the cloud?"

"Yeah. Big mistake."

"Sloppy," Max said, convinced that's why the professor was dead.

"You're not kidding," Hunt said. "Anyway, no doubt he was active with them. He had the military rank of lieutenant colonel. His mission was to steal nanoscience research from the university and document the progressive layout and infrastructure of the university lab over the years and continue to replicate it in China."

Max inadvertently blew past his East Sixty-First Street exit, trying to absorb what he was now being told. He'd get off at the next exit, East Ninety-Sixth Street, and work his way back in the direction of his apartment on Eighty-Fifth Street.

Hunt continued, "Apparently, he was one of the senior guys of that PLA program. He served as the coordinator. They identified another sixteen Chinese military scientists of different ranks in different U.S. research labs and universities across the country, all with the same mission: steal research, observe and replicate the lab processes when they return to China."

"Whoa."

"And besides the massive research theft, it's got a visa fraud component too—all the military scientists had to lie, of course, about their being in the Chinese military."

"So, they had sealed indictments on the professor and the other scientists," Max said. "Were they planning a takedown?"

"They were. Eastern District was planning to do a GPS takedown in seventeen different states a week ago, but it went to crap when the professor showed up dead on the tram," Hunt said. "Not only is their lead suspect dead, but—"

Max interrupted, "All those other junior scientists are now sitting in various Chinese consulates or a safe house somewhere until they can sneak them back to China."

"That's about it," Hunt said. "All MIA Missing in action. A big flop."

"You tell him about the Delaware shell—Tech Dragon?"

"I did. They didn't have that, knew nothing about the twenty-six hundred Chinese national graduates floating around," Hunt said. "It just wasn't on their radar."

"So, that's the consensus," Max said. "They took out the colonel because he exposed the whole program?"

"That's one theory; the Eastern District is running on that right now," Hunt said. "But that's not what's driving them. They're not interested in nailing the assassins or looking to salvage the case. Right now, they know they have a mole and need to pick it out before they try to salvage anything or build another case. They've been shaking the tree hard, but the mole has not yet dropped on its traitor-shaped head."

"They've got to work through everybody that had access to the case."

"Exactly, no small job," Hunt said. "The FBI is handling the investigation. They've got to sift through every FBI agent and analyst and every assistant U.S. attorney and staff who had access."

"Who's overseeing the investigation for the Bureau?"

"Dick Roach."

"Ah ha. Okay, thanks, Jack," Max said. "Please keep me posted if you hear anything else."

"You know it."

MAX PULLED INTO A PARKING space on his block. He had to decide. Would he confirm for Ed Vance that the professor was Chinese military or stay silent? If he confirmed it, Vance would know he was likely working on a nation state-sanctioned assassination. It would move Vance to submit the tattoo information on the deceased through NYPD official channels to the FBI for confirmation. If Max didn't confirm it, Vance and his detectives would waste more time trying to find out who was behind the murders.

Was he killed because of something personal, as Vance wanted to learn from the start, such as the deceased professor was into the Chinese mob for thousands because of a drug or gambling addiction? That would lead the detectives down a whole different line of inquiry.

Max hit the name 'Eddie V' on his iPhone directory.

"Hey, Max," Vance picked up on the first ring.

"Hey, Ed," Max said and paused.

"What's up?"

"Did you put that tattoo through channels?"

"Not yet."

"I would."

Silence.

"Ten-four," was all Vance said and ended the call.

CHAPTER 10
Thursday, May 18

Max was in the stairwell on the twelfth floor of the Roosevelt Island apartment building at 2:15 a.m. sharp. Fortunately, the apartment door was directly opposite the stairwell door, which had a webbed glass window in which Max could watch the tech do her thing.

The tech stepped out of the stairwell, went right for the door and placed a suitcase-looking bag on the hallway floor in front of the apartment door and opened it. It had knobs and a screen like an EKG machine, and she also opened flaps to each side of the suitcase, put on a set of headphones, turned dials, and pushed buttons. Max could see the graph-like images as the tech monitored the different readings. He'd learned from prior experiences that the tech was trying to discern normal vibrations such as radio and Internet waves from surveillance-device type waves. Suddenly, the tech shot her hand, thumb up to the ceiling, quickly closed the flaps of the suitcase, grabbed it, and Max opened the door to the stairwell for her.

"That apartment's hot. Definitely something different inside."

Max nodded and led the way down the stairwell to the eighth-floor apartment. It was then 2:23 a.m.

This time the stairwell door was not in a position from which he could see the tech, so, he kept it open a few inches and watched her do what she'd done upstairs: Open the suitcase and flaps, put her headset on, fiddle with knobs, and listen. Within minutes, she was back in the stairwell.

"No spikes. My guess there's nothing in there."

Max took that in for a moment.

"All right, let's do a complete sweep of it then," Max said to the tech. "I'll go in first."

He didn't knock on the door or ring the bell. He'd texted Jia Li that he was outside her door, and she opened.

Max put his index finger up to his mouth to Jia Li and Wei Ming. It was no time for introductions, not that he had to remind Jia Li of that. They had to do a sweep of her apartment first before talking.

He took off his shoes and looked around. It looked like Japanese master-organizer, Marie Kondo, had organized it. Not one item was out of place, it seemed. The kitchenette area had a Taiwanese siphon coffee maker he'd noticed at a Taiwanese restaurant he enjoyed going to over the years on St. Mark's Place.

There was a Murphy bed up against the wall, a small table with a Mac on it and bookshelves above it. He wondered if that was an arrangement directed by the Taiwanese NSB, or was it her nature? He liked its simplicity.

Max, Jia Li, and Wei Ming sat in complete silence while the tech did the sweep. It took about fifteen minutes. Jia Li had pulled the single curtain down over her single window facing the East River, as Max had texted her to do.

Max then pulled out a sheet of paper in which he'd written something for them to read: *Did Wei Ming leave his iPhone in his apartment upstairs?*

Jia Lia and Wei Ming both nodded.

"Nothing here, Max," the tech said.

Max noticed the tech look at the single window with the curtain down and addressed Jia Li and Wei Ming, "That's good. Remember that laser technology can direct a beam at a window and capture conversations happening inside. Keep the curtain down when you're having a confidential conversation in here. It obstructs the laser."

"We understand," Jia Li said.

"Not that keeping the curtain down is total protection. There's technology out there today that can capture conversations from the sliver of an opening that sneaks out around the curtain. But it's not likely a foreign state intelligence service can pull it off here in the U.S. It would be a whole different story if this apartment was in China," the tech said and left the apartment with her gear.

As soon as the tech stepped out, Max greeted Wei Ming in customary greeting fashion by holding their hands together as if in prayer.

Max then explained that the tech had a very high spike outside Wei Ming's apartment door, so it was likely there was a recording device of some sort in his apartment. Max explained that Wei Ming absolutely could not have any conversations in his apartment that would compromise himself or the investigation. That no conversations or discussion of developments about the case or exchange of communications could take place in Wei Ming's apartment. It could only take place where they were all then standing   Jia Li's apartment.

"Do you understand?" Max asked.

"Yes," Wei Ming replied.

"Unless, of course, we want you to have a conversation that we want the listener to hear to throw them off or confirm something we want them to believe," Max said. "Disinformation."

"Disinformation?" Wei Ming asked.

"That's when we want to intentionally mislead the person listening."

Wei Ming nodded, "I see. I understand."

Jia Li and Wei Ming sat on the blue loveseat in front of a coffee table resting on a thin pink carpet, a single sunflower in a vase on the table's center. Jia Li had placed a foldout chair on the opposite side of the coffee table where Max sat.

Max presented Wei Ming with an affidavit that showed he was giving U.S. law enforcement permission to monitor his electronic devices and put him under audio and visual surveillance, just as they had done with Jia Li.

Wei Ming immediately signed the document.

"Okay," Max said. "So, had representatives of the Chinese government contacted you any other time?" Max asked. "Or was this the very first time?"

Wei Ming explained about first being approached by a Tongji University professor in Shanghai seven years earlier.

"Tongji University," Max repeated and thought: *The same university that tried to contract the PIs to put him under surveillance.* "Did you know who he was before he approached you?"

"No, I did not."

"Did you ever confirm he was with Tongji University?"

"I did," Wei Ming said. "They listed him on the website of the university."

"Did the website indicate what his area of study was?"

"Yes, he is a nanoscientist."

"Really?" Max said, holding his pen over his notepad. "His name?"

"Dr. Zhang Kan."

Zhang Kan. Whoa, Max thought: *That's the tram-murdered professor's alias.*

"I assume your education was financed by the Chinese government."

"Yes."

"What about USC?"

"No, I received a scholarship from USC to attend their master's program, as I have received a scholarship here from Manhattan University to attend the Schimmel Center."

Max was relieved to hear that. Not that it made a difference who financed his education. Chinese financing of his education did not entitle them to direct him to steal research. But no doubt they would use that as leverage to persuade an unwilling participant if needed.

Max just felt comforted knowing that Wei Ming did not receive his Schimmel Center PhD education through Chinese-state funding.

And if the Chinese had financed his PhD quantum studies, fortunately, at this final stage of his education, it would be too late for them to threaten cutting off his financing if he did not cooperate. Too late for that potential chess move to ensure he would do their bidding.

Wei Ming continued by saying it alarmed him when Professor Zhang asked about the quantum curriculum at the Schimmel Center just before he started the PhD program.

"Why did this alarm you?" Max asked. "You weren't alarmed while you were attending USC?"

"He never asked me anything specific in the past," Wei Ming said. "But this time he wanted me to give him specifics. It did not make me comfortable."

When Wei Ming said that Max thought of a conference he'd attended—as a representative of the NYPD—coordinated by the U.S. Office of National Intelligence in Washington, D.C. There, it was driven home again of the legal obligations all entities and people inside China (and ethnic Chinese outside of China) have to cooperate with PRC national intelligence services, spy services.

Of course, you couldn't legally obligate Americans to make that promise, nor would we want to. The spirit of being American would be inspiration enough for most Americans to protect their country's secrets.

Wei Ming continued, "After I received a text and then a call from a woman that night, she said she was interested in what I had learned in my quantum studies and wanted me to introduce her to others in the field. The next day I mailed my envelope to you and again at ten p.m. the same woman called and said I could continue research and development of a quantum project in China after I completed my studies in the U.S., but that I must bring information with me otherwise interested parties would be very disappointed."

"Wait a second. It was a woman's voice?" Max asked.

"Yes, oh, yes. It was now a woman."

"Okay. And after you spoke with the woman the first time, the Tongji professor has not been in contact with you again?" Max asked.

"No."

"Huh. All right," Max said. "How did you respond to the woman about her wanting you to bring information?"

"I reminded her she had said that she only wanted me to introduce her to others."

"What did she say to that?" Max asked.

"She said that I must remain flexible."

"I see."

"It was at that moment I knew with clarification that she wanted me to steal."

"And the next morning you recognized us on the river and gave us your message," Max said. "And that night, did you receive the call from the same female at ten p.m.?"

"I did."

Wei explained she said that there was a substantial financial reward associated with his cooperation, that they wanted to move on this quickly because the school year was coming to a close and reminded him that his family in Shenzhen would be very proud.

Just hearing that the recruiter mentioned his family hit Max's chest, and thought, *Jia Li nailed it.* Bird in the cage.

"And tonight. Did she call?" Max asked.

"She did," Wei Ming said, and shook his head. "She asked me if I had made a decision. And I replied I was considering it. She then replied that she would call me tomorrow night and expect to hear my decision."

"All right," Max started. "Tell her you will cooperate with her."

Wei Ming paused before speaking up again. "Mr. Valentin, I need to bring my family to the United States before I can continue on," he said. "I just cannot continue to help you if my family remains in China."

"Wei Ming, we understand your urgency to get your family out of China. But we need to develop this case more before we can make that kind of arrangement."

Wei Ming shook his head. "I cannot help if my family remains in China. I just cannot."

"I'm sorry, Wei Ming, but we can't do anything like that until we have more," Max said. "I'm sorry."

Wei Ming continued, "I am in a very disturbing situation now. If I had not notified U.S. authorities, I would not be in this position."

Max jumped right on that.

"If the Chinese bad actors had not contacted you, you would not be in this position," Max said. "Remember the truth here, Wei Ming. They want you to do something that is absolutely wrong, and you know it. That's why you reached out to us. You know that's true. You respect what others like yourself put into research and development to achieve something important. You just did not want to be part of something that has no integrity."

"But my family, Mr. Valentin," Wei Ming said. His voice trailed off, "My..."

"I know, Wei Ming. I know. It is a very tough situation. But consider this. Let's say you had not reached out to us right away. What if we found out you were stealing for them? How do you think that would've developed for you?"

Wei Ming didn't reply.

"You were on our radar before you reached out to us, Wei Ming," Max said, thinking it would help Wei Ming realize that the Chinese government or its proxies dropped him in the mix long before he thought to contact U.S. authorities.

Wei Ming stared at Max with wide eyes. Max sneaked a peek at Jia Li, whose eyes were wide too.

Max nodded. "We were informed that you'd stolen trade secrets from a Chinese university."

"That is a lie!" Wei Ming shouted. "That is a lie!"

"An alleged representative of Tongji University wanted you put under surveillance by private investigators here in New York," Max said. "They claimed you had stolen R & D from them."

"Not true, sir. I never stole from any university. Not true."

"I believe you, Wei Ming. But what if you had helped the Chinese spies here because of the pressure they could put on your family?" Max asked. "I'll tell you what is likely to have happened. We would build a case against you and the woman-recruiter. And could you blame us?"

After several more moments of silence, Wei Ming said, "No, Mr. Valentin, I could not."

"And what effect would that have had on your life and your family's life if you were to be arrested for trade secrets theft and sentenced to twenty-five years in a U.S. prison?"

Silence.

Max continued, "It would destroy all that your family worked so hard to give you, and it will destroy you."

"It would," Wei Ming said in a whisper. "It would destroy me and my family."

"And do you think that while you're wasting away in prison, the Chinese government will compensate your family for the sacrifice you've made?" Max asked. "I doubt it."

"I doubt it too, sir."

"I know this is difficult, Wei Ming. I am very sorry that you are in this situation. But think this through. We are your only way out."

There was an eternal silence.

"Jia Li, can you give Wei Ming something to drink?"

After a few minutes, Jia Li gave him a hot cup of green tea. Wei Ming sipped on it slowly. Hands trembling.

"Wei Ming, tell me about your family," Max asked.

Max learned that Wei Ming's only family were his parents in Shenzhen and his sister. His father's parents had already passed, and he had no other siblings, and his mother was an orphan.

Max looked at Wei Ming for a few long moments.

"Would they want to stay once they're here?" Max asked.

"I believe they would," Wei Ming said, "after I explain the situation. You see, Mr. Valentin, my father is a freethinker. He does not concern himself with government or politics. He does not belong to the Communist Party. He is apolitical. My mother will follow my father, of course. He often said he would like to visit me here and openly wondered what it would be like to live in a free country. And I think the opportunity for my sister to continue her education here will urge him to agree. There are more opportunities for the blind in the United States."

"I understand," Max said and remained silent. He wouldn't press him. At least not right away. But Max knew if Wei Ming didn't come around, they'd have to monitor him.

Max knew Wei Ming had a narrow set of options, and suddenly the following quotes from the Bible came to mind:

The way is straight and narrow and few there be that enter.

The way of truth is straight and narrow, Max thought. *No doubt about it.*

What was Wei Ming's option if he didn't help them? Max asked himself. Go back to the Chinese? Max knew they couldn't let that happen. And his family would still be in jeopardy even if he tried to help the Chinese. The Chinese would not stop using his family as leverage until they got the quantum data. His only choice was to stay committed to helping Max and his team. Max genuinely hoped Wei Ming could see that.

"Mr. Valentin?" Wei Ming finally spoke up.

"Yes, Wei Ming."

"Please, please, Mr. Valentin, please give me your assurance that you will do all you can to protect my family," Wei Ming said, reaching out to hold Max's hands. "I know your resources are limited in China, but please promise me you will do all you can."

"You have my word, Wei Ming," Max said, bracing Wei Ming's hands. "I will do all I can. I promise you that."

After several seconds Max released Wei Ming's hands.

There was a long silence

Max waited.

"Okay, I will cooperate with you. What do you want me to tell the woman when she calls?"

Hearing Wei Ming say those words, "I will cooperate with you," reminded Max that not only was it his and his American law enforcement team's responsibility to protect the science, but also the future of a seemingly honest and promising Chinese-born scientist, and the future of his family.

He could not help recall, at that moment, those prophetic words spoken by the police commissioner at his graduation from the New

York City Police Academy twelve years earlier, "Your mission is to protect life and property. Your mission is to put your own life at risk, when necessary, to protect the life and property of another."

Then the following Bible passage came to Max's mind:

Greater love has no one than this, to lie down one's life for his friends.

"Return to your apartment. We assume they are tracking your iPhone's GPS, so continue to always leave your iPhone in your apartment when you come down here," Max said. "It shouldn't come as a surprise to you that governments have the technical capability to penetrate your phone and look at you through the phone's camera and listen to you speak."

"Yes, of course," Wei Ming said. "I am not surprised."

"Tell the recruiter you will assist. Ask her exactly what she wants you to do, and what your compensation will be. Whatever it is, don't negotiate too hard, accept it. I'm sure it will be good. Then, again, leave your cell phone in your apartment, return to Jia Li's apartment and call me from Jia Li's cell phone and tell me what her instructions to you are."

Max then handed Wei Ming a couple of listening devices. "Put one near your window, another in the center of your living room. Do you have a bookcase?"

"I do."

"Put one on the bottom shelf of your bookcase."

"Yes, sir."

"Put the last device in a bowl in your kitchen."

"Yes, sir, I will."

"All right. I'm going to leave now," Max said. "Just one more thing. In the one year Zhao Hua has been in the program, did you ever see him do anything suspicious?"

"No, I cannot say that I have."

"Okay, thank you, I'll talk to you both later today." Max stood up and left.

IT WAS ALMOST 3:30 a.m. when Max jumped in the car with Tan and Ashe. Tan was sitting behind the wheel, wide awake, sipping on a Dunkin' coffee. Ashe was in the passenger seat, snoring, the seat reclined all the way back.

Max didn't have a problem with that at all. Tan and Ashe were pros. Never, ever, could both investigators be asleep, but they would whack up nap times between them when possible. As soon as Max slammed the car door shut, Ashe woke right up, brought his seat upright, rubbed his face, and gave Max his complete attention.

"How'd it go?" Tan asked and handed Max his cold cup of coffee.

Early morning hours brought Max an odd and sublime sense of comfort: hours when cops and bad guys and their victims are customarily the only ones on the street—easier for bad guys to pick their victims out, and easier for cops to pick the bad guys out.

"We're good," Max said. "Wei Ming pressed a bit about getting his family out of China right away, but he came around. Told him we need to develop this more before we can try to pull it off."

"That's good news," Ashe said. "But it'll be critical we find a way, otherwise his family will be toast."

Max nodded and sat quietly in thought for a few long moments, looking out the rear side window.

Tan looked back at him with one hand on the steering wheel. "Are we done here, Max? Can we take off?"

Max turned to face them. "Yeah."

Tan pulled out, and Max filled them in on Wei Ming's background and his initial interaction with the Tongji University professor, Dr. Zhang Kan.

"Another nanoscientist," Ashe said. "Interesting."

"It is," Max replied.

He would save what he learned the Eastern District had on the dead professor's Chinese military profile until later that day—after each of them had gotten a few hours of sleep and a shower.

BY NOON, MAX AND HIS team were back at 26 Federal Plaza sipping on the office coffee.

As soon as he had a couple of gulps, and watched his team settle into their seats and come to life, Max opened his mouth.

"The Eastern District had a case on the dead professor."

"What?" Tan blurted.

"Jack Hunt ran it down for me."

"No, shit!!" Tan screamed, almost losing a grip on her coffee and croissant. "No, shit!"

After he finished running it down for his team, he went for another cup of coffee himself.

"What name did they have?" Ashe asked.

"He went by the name Xu Nan," Max said. "Lieutenant Colonel Xu Nan."

"So," Ashe said. "The Eastern District had him running a program for Chinese military scientists, pretending they were just students, but in truth to infiltrate U.S. research universities and steal."

Max nodded.

"Now, that's a surprise," Tan said.

"Right, no surprise there," Ashe said and worked his way to the coffeepot for a refill.

"And the other young Chinese military scientists?" Tan asked. "I assume they're *hasta la vista* baby. Made it out of the country."

"Chinese consulate, either here in New York, or another Chinese consulate in the country, there's a few, or maybe a few are being stowed at the Chinese embassy in D.C." Max said. "They know we have them on a no-fly list."

"So, they'll be camping out until they can sneak them out," Ashe said rhetorically.

"Oh, man, what a disaster," Tan said, shaking her head.

"They must be reeling at the Eastern District," Ashe said. "They must have a mole."

Max nodded. He and his team were silent for a couple of moments, taking it all in.

"Roach is conducting the investigation to uncover the mole," Max said.

Tan and Ashe looked and nodded with wide eyes.

Max looked at Tan, Ashe, and Mehta and finally broke their silence. "So, getting back to our case. We don't want to settle just on getting the recruiter. We could have our guy cooperate with the ghost until we can identify and collar her. But that's jumping the gun. This is a whole different opportunity."

Tan jumped in, "And I think the ghost will eventually want him to recruit others, do the legwork for her."

"Why do you think that?" Ashe asked.

"I mean, why not?" Tan continued. "It makes perfect sense. Why would the ghost expose herself to other potential recruits if she didn't have to? She can have our guy make the offers for her. She can just handle him and let him manage the other potential recruits involved in that quantum stuff."

"But why recruit others if she gets what she needs from our guy?" Ashe asked.

"Because the more recruits she has on the hook, the better," Tan said. "She should know as well as we do that some of her recruits will be more effective in stealing what she wants than others."

"I agree. Standard tradecraft," Max said. "And if it comes up, we'll direct him to agree to do just that. Agree to approach other recruits because he's suddenly hungry for the money—or so the ghost thinks—and with the opportunity to score more points for himself, since she believes he's now come around to their side."

"All right, I see what you mean," Ashe said.

"Right," Tan said. "And we believe once they think they have our guy on the hook, they're going to want him to make offers to others for sure."

"Yes, makes sense," Ashe nodded.

"Well, the Chinese are going big, so the way you think it's going to go down makes sense," Mehta said. "We know quantum is one of the information technology areas the Chinese have their sights on, along with AI, cloud computing, information security, Internet of things infrastructure, robotics, semiconductor technology, telecom and 5G technology."

Max, Tan, and Ashe looked at Mehta for an extra second.

"You just do that off the top of your head, Parth?" Max asked with a grin. "Or did you use an acronym?"

Mehta smiled. "Still working on an acronym. Top of my head for now."

Max nodded with a grin and continued, "So, we have an opportunity to not only nail the ghost for buying our guy, or, believing she bought our guy, but to nail other recruits at Schimmel or other U.S. schools or even in private industry that sell out."

"Exactly," Tan said.

"All right, let me head over to Roach's office. Let him know where we're at."

"He's not in the office," Mehta said. "Hasn't been in all day."

Max looked up at the digital clock on the wall. It read 1:17 p.m.

"All right. Let's see if he can take a call," Max said. "I'll put it on speaker."

Max punched Roach's number on his ePhone.

"Special Agent in Charge Richard Roach," Roach answered.

Max, Tan, Ashe, and Mehta could not help looking at each other over how formally Roach answered his phone. Not SAC Roach, or S-A-C Roach, or Agent Roach or Mr. Roach or Dick Roach, or just Roach, but 'Special Agent in Charge Richard Roach.'

"Mr. Roach, it's Max Valentin. I'm in my office with Teresa, Sam, and Parth."

"Yes."

Max ran down what he and his team had just discussed.

"What about entrapment?" Roach asked. "Assuming the recruiter asks your informant to do that. Your informant would give the other theft candidates an opportunity to steal for compensation."

"We don't see it that way," Max said. "Jack Hunt can give a legal opinion on it, but we're not creating the opportunity for the other Chinese recruits to sell out. The Chinese created that opportunity. The ghost just doesn't know that her number one recruit did not cooperate and is working with us. We're not creating it, we're not financing it, we're just giving our informant the green light to work it."

"You think your guy will go for it?" Roach asked. "Agree to recruit others if asked to? These are people he would've hoped to develop a professional network with and maybe collaborate with."

Tan jumped in, "True, Mr. Roach, but would he want to work with those rotten apples? The ones who would steal IP from the institutions they're associated with for a buck and status?"

"We'll see if he sees it that way."

"Right, we can't be sure of that yet, but we can't get too ahead of ourselves," Max said. "What do you think so far, Mr. Roach?"

Roach remained silent.

"This has got tremendous potential, sir," Ashe jumped in. "If they're recruits in various universities around the country who sell out to the Chinese. Two, five, ten, twenty..."

Tan interjected again, "For crying out loud, every year there's three hundred and fifty thousand Chinese foreign students studying in the U.S. If only one percent sell out, that's 350 trade secrets bad actors."

"There's another thing that's critical we learn," Max said.

"What's that?" Roach asked.

"Is the Chinese state directly involved in this trade secrets recruitment/theft operation?"

"Go on."

"Is the ghost not just somebody working for the Chinese..."

"Like a subcontractor," Ashe interjected.

"Right. And the Chinese are using more and more subcontractors these days," Max said. "They picked that up from the Russians playbook, so they have plausible deniability."

"Yeah," Roach said.

"But if the ghost turns out to be an intelligence officer with the MSS or a military officer with the PLA like that spy—that Chinese MSS deputy director who was arrested in Belgium and extradited back here, convicted and sentenced to twenty years for recruiting insiders at GE Aviation and paying them off to steal trade secrets.

"Ministry of State Security," Ashe said.

"Right," Max said. "Or the PLA. And we also know that back in 2014, when we indicted a bunch of Chinese cyberhackers, they were attached to the PLA. And that was a big leap for us. It was a conventional law enforcement investigation—identify hackers and prosecute, but it had major national security implications because the hackers turned out to be Chinese military officers."

"Ah, huh," Roach said.

"And the way the PLA and MSS has been operating over the last couple of years—often through the Thousand Talents Program—to entice primarily Chinese nationals in the West to return to China with what they've stolen, it feels like it would be right up the Chinese state's direct control," Max said.

Silence.

"Get Hunt's opinion," Roach said and hung up.

Max looked at the others. "Was that casino bells and whistles in the background I heard?"

With raised eyebrows, Tan, Ashe, and Mehta slowly nodded.

BY LATE AFTERNOON, Max received Jack Hunt's legal opinion that there was no entrapment issue for the investigators to consider.

Hunt's view was that not only was there no potential entrapment, but the entrapment defense didn't apply in foreign intelligence cases the way it applied in domestic cases.

"So, do we have an entrapment problem?" Tan asked.

"No, according to Jack Hunt, we're good, but we'll see if any of the candidates go for it with no implied threat to their families," Max said. "That's really who we want to take down. We want to especially take down the ones who don't need to feel any heat to steal. Cash and prizes are all it takes."

ASHE WALKED INTO THE office. "You want to take a walk to Chinatown?"

"You hungry, Sam?" Max asked. "It's about that time."

"I can eat," Tan said, looking up from Max's desk.

Ashe shook his head. "Negative—the New York office executed a search warrant on a Chinese police station secreted in a building on East Broadway. They might have something for us."

Max stood up, grabbed his blue sports jacket from the coat tree and said, "Let's go."

"Chinese police station?" Tan asked with wide eyes, unable to take her legs off Max's desk.

"Yep," Max said looking down on Tan, and motioned toward her like he was pulling up a gate. "Up."

The Joint NYPD/FBI IP Crimes Strike Force was out the door.

WHEN THEY JUMPED ON the elevator, Tan asked again, "Did I hear that right? They executed a warrant on a Chinese police station?"

"That's it, Teresa. The Chinese government pretends they set up these overseas service centers to assist ethnic Chinese living outside of China," Max said. "But they do more than assist in administrative stuff. They act as law enforcement for communist China."

"What do they claim to assist with?" Tan asked as they walked through the vast lobby of 26 Federal Plaza.

"Like renewing a Chinese driver's license. Which is nonsense. Chinese consulates help ethnic Chinese with those administrative matters," Max said. "These so-called service centers are used to intimidate ethnic Chinese abroad. They want to control negative and truthful talk about China."

Ashe jumped in, "Chinese police stations are a relatively recent discovery for U.S. law enforcement. They've been harassing ethnic Chinese legal residents here for a while now. The diaspora. Chinese dissidents. Any ethnic Chinese who do not do the bidding of the Chinese Communist Party. We knew about that harassment and intimidation, but not about these police stations until recently."

"So, these police stations don't go through official channels, obviously?" Tan asked. "They don't request our assistance? They do this on their own? And we're kept in the dark about their actions on our soil?"

"That's about the size of it," Ashe said. "One of their more persistent activities is something we call Fox Hunt. The Eastern District have charged a bunch of folks—Chinese agents and American citizens—for going after Chinese dissidents here."

"They've indicted Americans helping communist China?" Tan asked.

Max nodded his head. "If you read the indictments on these cases—this will sound nuts, but the Chinese have recruited U.S. private investigators to do some of their dirty work for them. Just the way that Chinese university professor tried to recruit my ex-partner to put Wei Ming under surveillance. American PIs have done background checks and surveillance for these Chinese agents operating here."

"American PIs. Wow," Tan said and shook her head.

Max added a thought. "It wouldn't come as a shock to me if that Chinese university professor is associated with the Chinese officials harassing the diaspora here."

Ashe nodded. "Agreed. Whether it's trade secrets theft from U.S. universities or businesses, or harassment of Chinese diaspora legally living here, it is all directed by the Chinese Ministry of State Security."

"What makes it even more disturbing is that most of these PIs are prior law enforcement," Max said.

"Wait a minute, wait a minute. I did see something about this. My agency, Homeland, put out a press release on a recent case—retired Homeland Security agent now a private investigator—from what I understand, paid off by the Chinese, reached out to one of his former subordinates, an active HSI agent in our Austin office, and got him to do a federal database background check on a Chinese dissident," Tan said. "What a bunch of knuckleheads."

"How about this one," Max added. "A New Jersey PI, retired NYPD detective retained by a police official from one province in China. They got the PI to not only do proprietary database background checks and surveillance on a Chinese target, but to leave threatening notes on the door of the target's home that the target better return to China or else."

Ashe added, "In my view, most of these PIs are duped into believing they're assisting a legitimate law enforcement or other legal function."

"I agree," Max said. "These PIs just don't recognize what's cooking."

"Man, is that crazy or what," Tan said.

"And these bogus police stations are not just in New York," Max said.

"That's right," Ashe said. "The word is these unauthorized police stations are located in over a hundred countries worldwide: Ireland, Canada, the Netherlands and a bunch more."

When they got to the six-story office building on East Broadway, the intercom showed there was an acupuncturist on one floor, an accountant on another and an engineering firm on yet another. But, on the top floor, where the agents had seized documents, laptops, iPhones, etc., they omitted listing that office's business.

When they arrived at the doorway of the offices of a Chinese state police operation, they found every room wiped clean by the FBI. Nothing on the walls. Nothing in the file cabinets. No computers or laptops left. Not even a single notepad. Nothing. The only things left were the empty file cabinets, desks, and chairs. A female agent approached Ashe and gave him a big hug.

Ashe introduced Max and Tan to her. The agent showed them a document which she permitted Ashe to photograph with his ePhone. It was handwritten slip of paper in Mandarin. It had Wei

Ming's name, the name of the PI firm Max's former partner Sophie Morales worked for, and the name, "Zhang Kan."

THEY STEPPED DOWN INTO Wo Hop, one of hundreds of Chinese restaurants. Since it was open twenty-four hours, Max often found himself eating there after processing another arrest at Manhattan Central Booking.

"So, the dead professor went through this police station to get a PI contact to follow Wei Ming," Tan whispered to Max and Ashe. "Just like Sam said. Chinese intelligence work is all interconnected."

With that whisper they ordered.

"There must be other places like that ID'd here in NYC." Tan said.

Max and his team recognized the need to speak in code while sitting in a Chinatown restaurant.

"I don't know for sure," Ashe said. "But I have little doubt there are not one or two more in this city of eight million."

"Oh, yeah, there has to be," Tan said. "There's nine such communities in New York alone."

"That's a good bet. I'm sure there's one in Flushing. Big community out there," Max said. "They did a good job of embedding one of their people. Community affairs cop born in Jia Li's country. Marine reservist. An embarrassment for my job."

"Yeah, we've all had our share of embarrassments," Ashe said. "They're relentless."

Tan nodded.

Max added, "About ten years ago they pitched an idea to my job—wanted a memorandum of understanding—a cooperative program with my folks to train some of their folks and then let them assist us in that community."

"It wasn't approved, was it?" Tan asked.

"No, we declined," Max said. "Even though my job was in the dark about their true intentions, we had concerns it would be interpreted as inviting the long arm of those folks into our ranks. We didn't want to appear to be endorsing what they were doing."

CHAPTER 11
Friday, May 19

The next day they were on a Zoom-like encrypted meeting. There were seven squares on the screen: Max, Tan, Ashe, Roach, Mehta, the *OJO* team leader (without his face displayed), and Jia Li.

Max led the meeting and laid out the developments to the group from the previous forty-eight hours.

They designated the investigation: The Cage.

The Cage would operate primarily from one command center at 26 Federal Plaza.

Parth Mehta would be the sole analyst assigned to assess the information collected, enter the information into analysis software, and make connections between various pieces of information.

"Parth, can you explain a little bit about the software we're using?"

"Sure, we're using MBI i2 software. It's a link analysis and data visualization software. It can analyze massive amounts of information and make connections and show relationships that the human mind could not make. We often use this software in money laundering cases to make connections that appear to be separated by countless buffers."

"We also use such software," Jia Li said. "The graphic representation of the results always appeared like a spiderweb to me."

"Agreed. We're also using face recognition software," Mehta said. "With that continuous footage of faces we will be able use AI facial recognition software to compare those faces coming on and off the island with identified Chinese intelligence actors we already have in the DOJ, National Security database, and/or use the ID photographs on file of all school employees and students against footage of those observed coming and going from the school, or general area of the university, and pick out those faces not associated with the school."

Ashe jumped in, "Like what we often do with fingerprints. Identify all persons who are expected to be in a certain location, eliminate their fingerprints, then focus on the prints of persons who have no business being in that area, and attempt to put faces and IDs to those prints."

Max recognized that the ghost recruiter may have already infiltrated the school and could already be registered as a student, professor, in administration, maintenance, or a school security guard, but they had to gather data somewhere. They had to shake the tree; they couldn't only wait for bits and pieces from Wei Ming to trickle in.

Max directed a question to Jia Li. "Do you know anything about a fake Chinese tech start-up that claims to hire ethnic Chinese tech graduates?"

"You must mean a company named Tech Dragon?"

"Yes."

"My agency has been monitoring it for some time on LinkedIn. Co-owners Fang Yang and Xu Nan. There are hundreds and hundreds of Chinese nationals who claim to be employed by that firm. But we have very limited information. We do not have access to U.S. Immigration records and have had to rely on public information. We only know what is recorded in the State of Delaware public records, which, as you must know, are very limited," Jia Li said. "Why do you ask?"

"Homeland Security Investigations did a takedown of almost twenty-six hundred that publicized their employment with Tech Dragon."

"Really," Jia Li exclaimed.

"Yes," Max said. "Curious setup. We suspect the Chinese could pressure many, if not all, of the alleged Tech Dragon employees to steal if they found real employment with a tech company in the U.S."

"Yes, that makes entire sense," Jia Li said.

After a long pause, Roach said, "I think we're done here," and logged out. Max and the other remaining squares evaporated from the screen.

BY 3:30 P.M. MAX WAS in his car and on his way up to Riverdale in the Bronx to have dinner with his sister Maya and the twins, Ben and Jess.

As he was cruising up the Westside Highway in his black VW Tiguan, his ePhone, synced to the dashboard of his car, rang, and he hit the answer button on the steering wheel.

"Yep."

"It's Teresa, Max,"

"Hey, Teresa, what's up?"

"Can you talk for a bit?"

"Sure, go ahead," Max said. "I'm on the Westside Highway about a Hundred and Twenty-fifth Street. Another twenty minutes at least before I get to my sister's."

"Good, good, okay, so we're going to kick off on Monday."

"Looks that way," Max said with a half chuckle, hearing the excitement in Tan's voice.

"Anyway, this is big," Tan said.

"If we work it right."

"Are you nervous?"

"Excited," Max said, without hesitation. "And that's what you're feeling. There's real potential here. Up to this point, the U.S. has only made cases against individual IP thieves. With this informant, we got the chance to get into it deep, if we do it right. The chance to find out how far and deep it goes, the chance to dismantle a major Chinese state IP theft espionage operation, if that's how it ends up."

"Yes, yes, right, right," Tan said. "You're right, it's exciting."

"Yeah, it is," Max said. "Enjoy your weekend, Teresa. When this kicks off on Monday, there's no telling where it's going to lead, and what the pace will be for us."

"Okay, okay, Max, sounds good. See you in the command center on Monday at oh eight hundred," Teresa said, "right?"

"Yes, oh eight hundred. It'll give us all a chance to make sure everything is in place when it shifts into gear," Max said. "And just remember, we're going to do this like we've worked any investigation, building it from the ground up. The fundamentals don't change. One piece of information leads to another and another. We'll just be stringing the beads until we get to the bead maker."

"Right, right," Tan replied with a laugh. "You always have the right thing to say, Max. I always wanted to string beads because when I was ten years old at summer camp, I was sick the day they did the stringing beads thing."

Max laughed too, "See you Monday."

"See you Monday," Tan said. "And say hello to Maya and the twins for me."

"Will, do. Big hello to Denise."

⸻⧻⧻⧻⸻

WHEN MAX ARRIVED AT his sister's seventh floor apartment on the Henry Hudson Parkway that evening, and Maya opened the door, she tilted her head to the twins who were sitting on the balcony browsing their Catholic instruction books.

"They've been waiting for you," Maya said with a smile, then said, "Look who's here, guys."

With that, the twins looked over into the living room. "Uncle Max!" they shouted together, jumped up, and scooted to Max.

Each grabbed a leg and stood on his black running shoes. Max walked them back over to the balcony like he was walking on stilts.

"So, how you guys doing today? I see you've been studying?"

"Yeah," they both said.

"Yes," Max said to correct them.

"Yes, Uncle Max," they both replied.

Max smiled. "Okay, well, let me get my shoes off and I'll join you guys."

"Uncle Max I got an 'A' for my science project," Ben said. "Thank you for your help."

Max looked over to his sister who stepped out of the kitchen with a beaming smile. Max then rubbed Ben's head. "You're welcome, Ben. Very happy to hear that. We knew you could do it. Well, done."

Ben was glowing. And so was Jess. She was proud of her brother, too.

Max tossed his black Nikes back over by the front door, made it back to the balcony door and stood looking down on the twins.

"Anything to drink, Max?" Maya had to semi-shout from the kitchen over the twins' excited-to-see-Uncle-Max chatter as she brought a chair for Max to sit by the balcony door. He wouldn't step onto the balcony itself.

"Ahh, thanks, Maya," Max said, as he took the chair. "Ginger ale is good." He then looked down at their books. "Okay, so, what chapter are we up to here?"

"Chapter twenty-four," Jess said.

"We Share God's Love," Ben said, reading it with focus.

"Great topic. Who reads first?"

"You read first, Uncle Max," Jess said. Followed by Ben, "You are the leader."

"Okay, so, I say as the leader, 'After Jesus rose to new life, he visited his followers. Let us listen to Jesus's words when he first visited them,'" Max said. "Okay, who's the first reader?"

"I'll read," Ben said. "'Jesus came and stood near them. He said, Peace be with you.'"

And Jess followed with, "'Jesus, you gave us your gifts of peace and love.'"

"Very good," Max said. "I'll continue. 'Jesus told his followers that he wanted them to share God's love with everyone. We are followers of Jesus. He wants us to'... what?"

The twins recited, "'He wants us to share God's love, too.'"

"And what is the last prayer?" Max asked.

The twins recited, "'Jesus, help us to share your gifts of love and peace with everyone.'"

After Max and the twins read a few more pages, they all sat at the dining room table and devoured Maya's cooking of fried pork chops, rice and beans, avocado, and fried plantains. Max and Maya stayed at the dining room table as the kids relocated to the sofa, each with an iPad in their palms.

"They're doing good?" Max asked.

"Yes, yes. They're doing good. Just you know Ben sometimes still has dreams with Gus." she said, twisting her head to look at the kids, then back to Max.

Max nodded, "And you?"

Maya paused and looked at her brother, nodding with just a touch of moisture in her eyes. "You know, Max. It is what it is."

"I know, sis. I know."

A LITTLE AFTER 10:30 p.m., Max was home at his East Eighty-Fifth Street apartment, sipping on a glass of iced tea reading *Spies and Lies* by Alex Joske on his Kindle.

"... MSS officers were playing a different game to Western intelligence agencies, striking at unprotected parts of democratic systems. When the FBI was looking for sophisticated espionage operations or the theft of defense technology, China Reform Forum and other influence operations seemed insignificant.

"At the same time, China work was under-resourced across Western intelligence agencies, and there was scant political will to take a hard stance against Beijing, so MSS operations faced little opposition. Counterintelligence agencies were also lulled into a false sense of ease by the fact that these MSS officers usually weren't using the kinds of sophisticated tradecraft that might indicate they were engaging in high-risk operations."

"Fascinating," Max whispered, shook his head, and thought, *It's like a cancer.* You don't know it's consuming you until it's too late.

He continued reading, "...The MSS was taking the West's dream of a more free and open China and turning it into a weapon that gave China valuable time to build up its power and ability to challenge the existing world order."

Max's encrypted case phone buzzed, "Yes, Jia Li."

"Max, Wei Ming wants to speak with you."

"Okay," Max said. "Put it on speaker."

"Mr. Valentin?" said Wei Ming.

"Did you hear from the recruiter?"

"Yes, sir. She instructed me to look for an opportunity to invite Zhao Hua to join me at the café."

"The café?"

"Yes, the café at the Schimmel Center."

"The café," Max repeated. "Ah, huh? Is the café open to the public?"

Jia Li jumped in, "Yes. It's open to all visitors. Residents of the island are welcomed to use it. And with so much new construction occurring, the workers often have lunch in the café too. It gets most busy."

"Do you know Zhao Hua well?" Max asked.

"Not too well. He is a first-year student," Wei Ming said. "Very intelligent and very industrious. But it is not like Jia Li and I."

Thanks to the preliminary background research, they knew what year of study each of the Schimmel PhD students were in.

"Do you know if he has family in China?" Max asked.

"He does not," Wei Ming said. "He's an orphan."

"Okay."

"Mr. Valentin. If he accepts the offer, he will be in trouble, won't he?"

"Yes, Wei Ming," Max said. "But try not to project at how he'll react. He may do what you did or notify the school administration."

"But how can he? If he doesn't cooperate with them, they could make trouble for him in so many ways."

"Maybe so," Max said. "But they don't have the leverage on him they have on you, right? You said he's an orphan."

Wei Ming remained silent.

Max recognized that there was only so much he could do to help Wei Ming accept what needed to be done. Max felt Wei knew it was the right thing to do, to expose others that would steal the hard-earned R & D work he was doing with Professor Kleinheidt, Jia Li and the others, whether it felt good or not.

"Okay, what else did she say, Wei Ming?"

"She advised me to keep my first conversation with my colleague simple and mention that I am doing my best to contribute to our country. If he asks for more information, she said to give it to him.

She said that if he asks what my compensation and arrangement is with her to tell him. And she said that if he asks if he could have the same arrangement, she said that I should just tell him I would ask."

"Very good," Max said. "Anything else?"

"When I told her we have our lunch break between twelve-thirty and two, she said that she knew that."

"She did. Okay," Max said. "Listen, I'm just curious. Does she ever speak to you in English?"

"Yes, sometimes she does, and her English is very good, much better than mine. But I can detect a Chinese accent."

"Did her phone number appear on your ePhone caller ID?"

"No, no," Wei Ming said. "It always says 'NO ID'"

"Well, we put a trap on your phone to capture her phone number," Max said. "If our technicians get the number, we'll see where it leads. But it wouldn't surprise us if she's using a burner phone."

"Burner phone?" Wei Ming asked.

"A phone that can't be traced," Max said. "The smart ones pay for the phone in cash or a stolen credit card, so it's not traced back to them. But Chinese intelligence services have a supply of burner phones as we do."

"I see."

"Have you ever met Zhao Hua in the café before?" Max asked.

"Yes, but only once, when he started last September," Wei Ming said. "But I do sometimes speak with him in our lab."

"Okay, Wei, just do as she wants," Max said. "Please make sure that your bracelet is on. We'll be there. You won't see us, but we'll be around. But, let me just say this so that you remember. This is very important. Simple but important."

"Yes, Mr. Valentin?"

"If you ever see me, you must ignore me. You *must* ignore me. That's critical. If they have you under surveillance, and they see you respond to seeing me with any reaction at all that you recognize me, they will pick up on it. They'll become suspicious and it'll jeopardize our investigation."

"I understand, sir."

"Do you understand that Jia Li?" Max asked. He knew she must as a trained agent but wanted to be consistent by treating both as inexperienced equals.

"Wei Ming, please call me Max, as well."

"If you do not mind, Mr. Valentin, I will continue to call you Mr. Valentin," Wei Ming said. "It reminds me that this is formal, important collaboration."

"No worries. I understand. That's very smart," Max said. "We'll be monitoring you Monday."

CHAPTER 12
Saturday, May 20

Max had just returned from a morning run and was walking the East River promenade when his ePhone buzzed. It was a text from the tech team, "Negative results on the trap. Burner phone. No follow-up on the phone."

Max forwarded the email to his team, including Jia Li.

Soon after, Max received a text from Jia Li. "Can you speak?"

Max called her. "Everything okay?"

"Yes, yes," Jia Li said. "The technical section of my agency could detect a use location of the disposable phone used by the recruiter to call Wei Ming last night."

"No kidding," Max said. "And?"

"GPS analysis revealed it was located at West One Hundred Twenty-Second Street and Riverside Drive."

"One Twenty-Second and Riverside," Max repeated. "That's where Grant's Tomb is located."

"Yes, that is what Google Maps indicates."

"Grant's Tomb," Max whispered, but it was loud enough for Jia Li to hear. "The ghost is here in New York City."

"So, it seems."

Max's next thought was why was the ghost hanging around Grant's Tomb?

This again reinforced for Max that the ghost rarely wanted to give up her identity through a trap-and-trace, but she had to know that she was taking the chance of giving up her location. It was hard for Max to conclude that the ghost didn't realize the burner phone sometimes gave up GPS information within six feet of where she was making the call, but stranger things had happened.

This got Max's juices flowing. It opened the possibility of tracking her location at the time she'd be on the phone with Wei Ming. Would she make the call from the same location? Not likely, Max figured. But Max would notify the *OJO* team leader anyway, and he would sit on West 122nd Street and Riverside Drive that night as well, with Tan and Ashe if they wanted to join, in case she made the call from there again.

"Will your tech team be monitoring the burner phone tonight?" Max asked.

"Yes, I am certain they will," Jia Li said. "Will it be your intention to observe that location tonight?"

"I sure will," Max said. "Let us know if your techs pick up the call and location again."

"I certainly will."

"Thank you, Jia Li."

"Of course."

━━━━✕━━━━

MAX THEN EMAILED THE entire team as he stood there on the promenade taking in the East River breeze at East Eighty-First Street.

From: MValentinGroup23(at)fbi.gov

To: Group 23

Subject: Operation "THE CAGE"

WM directed to invite potential recruit to Café at Schimmel Center. Meeting will occur between 12:30 p.m. and 2 p.m. on Monday.

The Café is a public place. It is possible the Ghost and/or associates will watch the meeting.

Request OJO team visit Café prior to Monday, 9:30 a.m.

Request OJO team be in place by 11 a.m. Monday—outside and inside the cafeteria.

Agents Tan, Ashe and the undersigned will be inside.

Request all access points into and outside the café and Roosevelt Island itself be manned from 11 a.m. until 3 p.m.

Request continuous filming and recording of the café area inside and outside.

Command Center to assign radio frequency in which all members can receive real-time encrypted point-to-point communication.

DEVELOPMENT: Communications techs report no follow-up ID possible with incoming call to WM from burner phone. However, Taiwan NSB able to determine location of target through GPS— cell tower —tracking of burner phone. Call to WM at 10 p.m. previous night made from W. 122nd Street and Riverside Drive.

Recommend Surveillance Team set up on Grant's Tomb from 2100 to 2300 hours tonight.

Max's ePhone buzzed again.

It was Roach.

Max walked north when he punched 'accept.'

"So the recruiter was supposedly calling from Grant's Tomb," Roach said. "Well, if that was her, she won't be out there again."

"We'll see," Max said. "I'm going to notify *OJO* to cover it."

"Don't waste *OJO's* time."

Here we go again, Max thought.

"All right. I'll be out there."

"Suit yourself," Roach said.

Max found it curious that Roach wasn't wondering why the ghost was calling from Grant's Tomb—the Upper Westside of Manhattan. Was she living up there? Visiting friends up there? Just passing by?

"What about extra coverage on Monday?" Max said. "We can use a few more hands and eyes out there or at least more video."

"What are you looking for?"

"Continuous video surveillance/CCTV set-ups at the different ways to access and leave Roosevelt Island as well as inside the café as I requested in the email."

"I'm not authorizing that. You've got Tan, Ashe, one analyst, Mehta, and *OJO* on Monday," Roach said and hung up.

Within minutes of that conversation, Roach email-approved Max's request with an amendment that excluded video surveillance of any kind beyond what Max, his immediate team, *OJO*, and the video footage from Wei Ming and Jia Li's Fitbits would provide. No additional video surveillance. No CCTV.

Within seconds of Roach's limited approval, the email acknowledgements came in from Tan, Ashe, Mehta and *OJO*: RECEIVED, RECEIVED, RECEIVED, RECEIVED...

MAX MADE IT TO EAST Ninety-Sixth Street when his ePhone buzzed again. He stopped and started to walk back south down the FDR Drive.

"Yes, Teresa."

"So, Jia Li's NSB came up with a fix on where the recruiter called Wei Ming," Tan said. "That's pretty impressive."

"It is."

"How come our folks didn't come up with that?"

"Good question," Max said. "But I wouldn't be too hard on our guys. You know it's tough nailing down the pings from all those cell towers out there to come up with a definite location."

"True enough," Tan said. "So, the ghost is definitely here in the city. And we have a shot at getting a look at her and maybe ID her if we can get to her before she makes a move."

"Right."

"But what the heck is she doing up on the Upper Westside anyway?"

Max smiled. "Good question?"

"Yeah," Tan said. "Yeah."

"We'll give that some thought, but I hope you didn't interrupt a beautiful Saturday morning with your better half to call?" Max said, as he walked over to the wrought-iron fence overlooking the East River, put his hands-free into his ears, and stretched his calf muscles.

"Hah. Don't worry about Denise. She knows the deal."

Max laughed, "Well, that's good."

"So, this is important. We got a shot at seeing her and IDing her."

"It is, if she's in the city. But she could be anywhere else in the country or out of the country when she makes her next call," Max said. "But if she makes the call from there again, we got a shot."

"Good."

"If she does show up, we don't want to alert her when we do. If we can identify her, then track her for a while, that would be ideal," Max said. "See who she meets with, develop more and more information on her..."

"Right. As we talked about. We're not looking to collar her out of the gate," Tan said. "We want to take this as far as it goes."

"Exactly, but if we do identify her, we need to stay real sensitive to any sign that she's looking to take off."

"Especially mainland China."

"Exactly," Max said. "Until we identify her, she can skip anytime she picks up on our scent. Until we ID her, we don't have a name to even put on a no-fly list."

"Right, right, okay," Tan said. "So, we're going out to Grant's Tomb tonight?"

"I'm going to be there, Teresa," Max said. "But I got no problem with you passing on this one."

"Are you kidding, Max? Of course, I'm going to be there," Tan said. "You heading over to take a look at the café this weekend?"

Again, Max had every intention of grabbing a shower and taking the ferry over to Roosevelt Island and making a quick visit at the café. He'd Googled that the café was open seven days a week, eight a.m. to five p.m. And on weekends eleven to five. He was looking forward to treating himself to a cappuccino in the Schimmel Center café.

"Yes, this afternoon, but..."

"See you there," Tan said. "You want me to let Sam know?"

"No need, Teresa. Let the guy enjoy his weekend."

"Ah, huh," Tan said. "Okay. See you later."

He waited for the light to change on York Avenue and East Eighty-Sixth Street, watching traffic zip down the hill from Eighty-Fifth Street like it was a NASCAR race.

HE JUMPED ON THE EAST Ninetieth Street New York Waterway Ferry and across the river to Roosevelt Island, descended the ramp onto the sidewalk, and strolled under the shadow of the Ed Koch Queensboro Bridge on the way to the Schimmel Center café. He could not help taking in the spectacular Manhattan skyline.

THE CAFÉ WAS WELL LIT. Plenty of natural light spreading through the wide and high glass windows that wrapped the south and east sides of the L-shaped café. They spread out a variety of white tables and chairs in an assortment of arrangements. Single tables, with two chairs, or group of two to eight tables pressed together to accommodate the size of the party. A layout of hot food and sandwiches with servers at the ready to put a plate together, or a sandwich from behind a counter that spread in the same L shape.

At the southern tip of the café was a counter with coffee, tea, and other drinks, pastries, and a register with the cashier standing at the ready. Max ordered his cappuccino, selected a lemon-flavored biscotti, and made himself comfortable at the southwest corner table of the café. His back was to the river. He could see in both directions of the L from that vantage point. That spot is where he would recommend at least one of the *OJO* surveillance team members to plant him or herself. The others, he'd recommend they set up at each tip of the L.

The café looked to accommodate about 250 people, but there were only about twenty-five of an eclectic weekend group present. Parents making a visit with their kids to see the cherry blossoms, some of whom were in strollers, senior citizens who Max assumed were also visiting or residents of the island, and some Gen-Z and Millennials who may have been a mix of tourists too, with a sprinkling of students. He knew that Monday afternoon, café attendance would quadruple at least.

He took a long sip of his cappuccino and when he looked back over in one direction where he thought another surveillance operative should sit, he saw Teresa Tan sitting there sipping on a bottle of ice tea, and when he looked at the other corner that would also be ideal for another operative, Sam Ashe was sitting there.

Not even for a tenth of a second did they acknowledge each other, but he was driven to look down at the cappuccino in his hand, and the biscotti on the paper plate on the table, not to give away the pang in his heart over such a minor gesture.

They were saying, *"We're a team, Max Valentin. We got your back."*

Max and his team remained in the café for almost three hours taking in all the ways in and out, where the restrooms were located, and not only where they would conduct the surveillance but also where their adversaries could conduct their surveillance. There was also an outside seating area which made it possible to watch the activity inside the café. Which meant not only could Max and his team watch the activity from the outside but so could the ghost and her operatives, if any.

BY NINE P.M., MAX HAD been sitting in his VW Tiguan parked on West 122nd Street, facing west with Grant's Tomb in his direct line of vision; Tan was parked north of the tomb on West 123rd Street, and Ashe was parked on West 121st Street.

If the ghost made the call from the area of Grant's Tomb, they wouldn't miss it. The tomb looked to Max like a miniature cathedral with Doric columns and a dome that resembled a top. Immediately west of the tomb was the rest of Riverside Park, followed by the Hudson River. To the east of Grant's Tomb was Sakura Public Park.

Max fixed his eyes on the tomb. He'd learned from experience that you couldn't look away for even one second. If you looked away or down for one instant, your target could be gone.

He was conditioned to not drift away from his fixed view for anything; not for his invariably cold coffee sitting in the center compartment of the car; not to jot a note down on his legal pad resting wide open on the front passenger seat. He'd learned to pick up his coffee without looking down; to scribble notes onto his legal pad without looking down. Nothing would drive him to look away. Nothing!

Ironically, the training he'd received at the NYPD shooting range when reloading your gun came in handy with surveillance. They trained police officers to reload without looking down at their weapon. The obvious complication with looking down to reload is that during the one to two seconds you're reloading, the shooter could stand over you and deliver a bullet to your head. Which, regrettably, had happened more than once. Over and over again, the NYPD drilled all officers on reloading their gun by feel, as if they were blind.

The same principle applied to surveillance.

At precisely ten p.m. Max saw a tiny figure come out from the west side of Grant's Tomb and meander to the front entrance and stand between two of the columns with a phone up to its ear, like it was Grant himself giving a speech.

"I got a figure top landing front doors of the tomb between the columns, on the phone," Max announced into the radio.

"Ten-four," Ashe replied. "I can see it."

Tan replied, "I don't have an eyeball on it."

With Tan's reply, vicious screams screeched from Sakura Park. Max twisted his head north into the park but could see nothing. It was too dark. Then twisted his view back to the front of the tomb. He could see that the figure had lowered its phone arm down to its side and appeared to be looking in the park's direction. The screams bellowed.

"Fuck," Max whispered and jumped out of his car and ran into the park as he picked up speed in the direction of the screams. He could then see a woman with a chihuahua being attacked. The assailant had a knife to the victim's neck as he was trying to tear down her shorts.

The bad guy never saw Max coming. Max cracked the guy across his head with his Glock. The guy went down with a thud, and the knife bounced on the cement walkway a few feet before it stopped. Tan and Ashe both descended on the guy too and handcuffed him.

"Stay with them," Max said, and ran back to West 122nd Street to within viewing range of the front of Grant's Tomb. The figure who had been on the phone was gone.

A few minutes later one NYPD radio car took the bad guy into custody and to the precinct, and another radio car, with two female officers, transported the victim back to the precinct to be interviewed by Special Victims detectives.

They then went right to Grant's Tomb and did a 360-degree inspection of it, expecting to find no one and nothing of any value, and, in fact, found no one or nothing of any value, but went through the motions anyway. Max directed Tan and Ashe back to their vehicles and he went back to his Tiguan.

Max had not yet received an update call from Wei Ming.

AT 10:45 P.M., HE COMMUNICATED by radio to Tan and Ashe that he would text Jia Li to see if she'd heard from Wei Ming.

"Have you communicated with WM tonight?"

"Yes... we studied together in my apt... he went upstairs @ 9:35..."

"I have not heard from him."

"I cannot go up to check... they may record me."

"Correct... do not go up."

Max wondered if that, in fact, was the ghost at Grant's Tomb, and if she had tried to call Wei Ming at ten p.m. If so, maybe she got spooked, which would explain why Max had not yet heard from him.

"And Grant's Tomb???" Jia Li texted.

Max called Jia Li and explained what had happened.

"Are you well, Max?"

It was the first time Jia Li used his first name.

Max paused for a moment. "Yes, I'm fine, and my team is fine."

"Good. Very good."

"Thanks," Max said. "Unfortunately, a missed opportunity."

"Do you think she would think that you were all there for her?"

"There's no reason to think so. We cannot rule it out. But it wouldn't be unusual for a couple of plainclothes cops to be sitting near a park waiting for any assortment of knuckleheads to strike. But if that were her, and I were her, it would make me a lot more cautious. She may just blow it off, thinking if we were there for her, we wouldn't have dropped her."

"Agreed," Jia Li said. "She might find it inconceivable that if she was being watched that surveillance operatives would have dropped her to respond to an assault in a public park."

"Maybe."

"But she may instinctively be more cautious going forward."

"Yes."

"Okay."

"That's it for now. We'll talk tomorrow."

"Okay, Mr. Valentin. Good night."

Back to Mr. Valentin, Max thought. *Good.*

"Good night."

MAX RADIOED TO TAN and Ashe that the surveillance was terminated and to meet him in front of Tom's Diner on Broadway and West 119th Street. Tom's Diner was the facade used in the hit comedy series *Seinfeld* during the 1990s. Grant's Tomb was only a few blocks from it.

THE THREE FEDERAL STRIKE force investigators doubled parked in front of the brightly lit diner. Tan and Ashe jumped into the back of Max's Tiguan to review the evening's events.

"Wonder if that was our girl," Tan said before she fully closed the car door.

"Yeah," Max said. "Looks like Wei Ming didn't get a call from her."

"Otherwise, you would've heard from him," Ashe added.

"Exactly."

Max didn't think Wei Ming would be in any danger so early in the investigation, but he had some concern. Hopefully Wei Ming was wearing the bracelet and would push the alert button if he needed to.

"All right, it's a quarter after eleven. Let's wrap it up for tonight," Max said. "I'll see you guys at zero-six hundred on Monday. Maybe will have more luck then. Enjoy your day off tomorrow."

"Ten-four, boss," Tan said with a big smile, and jumped out.

"See you then, Max," Ashe said and did the same.

Max took a slow ride down Broadway toward his apartment in deep thought.

Driving down Broadway from the upper 100s was a joy. Max always thought it should be called Broadway-Boulevard, since a park-like strip divided the northbound side of Broadway from the southbound with park benches and all. He always found it curious that Park Avenue on the East Side had the same park strip, but no benches to relax and take in the sights and sounds.

But there was more on Max's mind as he traveled down the southbound side of Broadway. Again, he wanted to know why the ghost—if that's who it was at Grant's Tomb—why she made a call from there. Why was she in that area? Was she just driving by and decided to pull over and make the call? Two consecutive nights? Was she living or working in the area and stepped outdoors on a beautiful spring night at ten p.m. to make the call?

Max knew it was something they had to find out.

CHAPTER 13
Sunday, May 21

Max was sound asleep when his ePhone vibrated.

He squinted with one eye closed, backing away from the glare as he tried to read the message.

"Please call me," the text read. It was from Jia Li. The screen read 3:33 a.m.

He sat up immediately, stretched over to switch on his nightstand light that then illuminated the cover of Alex Joske's *Spies and Lies*, and punched her contact-name 'JLM-PhD.'

He'd decided to also order the print edition of the Joske book. Amazon delivered it the same day. He wanted to keep it for his bookcase. Couldn't do that with a Kindle.

"Max?"

"Yes, Jia Li. What's wrong?"

"Wei Ming is here in my apartment. He just received a call from that woman. He wants to talk to you."

"Okay, put him on speaker," Max said, and rubbed his eyes.

"Mr. Valentin?"

"Yes, Wei Ming."

"That woman just called me. She said the first thing she wants me to do is attempt to download as much information on our research as possible onto a USB drive. I told her it would be very difficult. I told her I am never alone in the lab. But she said that she wanted me to go this morning before anybody else is in and download the information. I told her that was impossible."

Wei Ming sounded out of breath, and Max felt he could practically hear his heartbeat.

"Okay, Wei Ming, you're doing good. Just slow down a bit," Max said.

"Okay, okay, I am so sorry."

Max listened to him take a deep breath and continue.

"I told her I would need a reason to be in the lab at such an early hour, and not only that, but I don't know when the professor is there. If I was in the lab and he walked in, he would want to know why I didn't tell him I planned to be there so early. I reminded her that the CCTV cameras would see me going in and out."

"Good, good," Max said. "How did she respond?"

"There was a change in her tone. She said she was just kidding. She said that she knew I would need time to prepare; that I would need to find the right time to do it. Then she said that I can pull up the data on the screen of my computer and take photographs with my iPhone. I told her again that I am never alone. Then she said again, she was just kidding, that she knew I needed to find the right time. Then she just said, 'Good night.'"

"But when I said, 'Good night,' I could just hear her call out my name, as if from a distance, before hanging up and saying, 'One more thing,' then her voice was loud and clear again.

"She said that she knew I have the passcode to the lab door. I didn't know if I should deny it or not, so I just admitted that I did. But I explained they change the passcode every day and we only receive the new code at six o'clock each morning. I told her nobody can enter the lab until then. She then said goodnight and that time the phone went silent."

"You did good, Wei Ming," Max said. "Remember that you are working with us. If the recruiter asks you something that you know to be true, admit to it. Don't hesitate. We want her to feel confident that you're working with her now. The only thing we will not give her under any circumstances is actual trade secrets."

"Okay, thank you for telling me, but why did she call me at this hour?"

"This is standard tradecraft," Max said.

Jia Li jumped in, "This is her way of keeping you off balance, Wei. And her way of letting you know she will call you at any time."

"Jia Li is right," Max said, and shook his head, wondering if Jia Li just could not help sometimes displaying her agent training. Wei Ming did not know she was a Taiwanese agent.

"I see," Wei Ming said. "But what about this research information she wants? What am I to do?"

"Don't worry. We have time to decide how to handle that. You did an excellent job of putting her off, and she knows what you're telling her is true. We'll be in touch tomorrow with instructions. We will give her something eventually, but it won't be the true research," Max said. "Does she still want you to approach Zhao Hua?"

"Yes, she does," Wei Ming said. "And she gave me an email address that she said she will sometimes use to communicate with me."

"What is it?" Max asked.

"Seizetheday2025(at)CCPmail.gov."

"How did you receive it? Did she email it to you?" Max asked.

"No, she told me to write it down."

"Did she say when she would contact you next?"

"No, she did not."

"Okay. Get some rest, Wei Ming. You're doing excellent work. Just continue to keep us informed of when she contacts you."

"Okay, Mr. Valentin."

"By the way, did you put the recording devices out?"

"He did," Jia Li said. "Just as you suggested."

"Yes, sir," Wei Ming added. "I placed one by my window and one by my bookcase."

"Good," Max said, and thought about letting him know they had more information that advanced the notion that the woman made her call to him from somewhere in New York City, but there was no need to mention it then. More information that she may in fact be here might alarm him.

"We'll be in touch with both of you tomorrow sometime," Max said. "And thank you both for contacting me right away."

"Not at all, Mr. Valentin," Wei Ming said. "I am so sorry we woke you. Her call just made me so nervous I needed to tell you right away."

"I'm glad you did," Max said. "What we're doing is very important. No time, day or night is a problem."

"Very important indeed," Jia Li repeated, playing up her role as PhD student assisting a government investigation.

"Yes, it is," Max said. "Wei Ming, one last question."

"Yes, sir."

"I know you didn't hear from the woman at ten p.m. this evening," Max said. "But did your phone ring at that time?"

There was a pause. "Yes, yes," Wei Ming said with a touch of anxiety in his voice. "It did ring. After the second ring, I picked up the phone, but when I said hello, it sounded like I could hear screams in the background. Then the connection ended abruptly. Very strange."

"Yes, very strange," Max said. "Okay, thank you, both. Good night."

"Goodnight," they both replied.

CHAPTER 14
Monday, May 22

It was six a.m. sharp when Max, Tan, and Ashe made it into the office and were working on the bagels Max had picked up from B & B on East Seventy-Third Street and First Avenue on his way down. After his conversation with Wei Ming and Jia Li, he jumped out of bed, grabbed a shower and shave, and was out of his apartment by five a.m. He'd only had about two hours of sleep.

Max's bagel of choice was cinnamon raisin, toasted, with plain cream cheese, but his colleagues were polar opposites. Ashe opted for a plain bagel, not toasted, with plain cream cheese, and Tan's bagel of choice was an assemblage of poppy seeds, sesame seeds, onion flakes, garlic flakes, pretzel salt, and pepper, a.k.a. "everything bagel," with a thick spread of peanut butter and granola and toasted. Max felt bloated just ordering.

Their coffees of choice, Max knew very well. Ashe always had his black. For Ashe, adding milk and sugar or anything else was an exercise in the destruction of a wholesome cup of coffee. If he wanted a coffee shake—as he would say—he'd go to a Shake Shack. Tan opted for a latte that morning. Max tried to stay neutral on the coffee issue. He settled for a little cream and half a sugar, and, on rare occasions, treated himself to a cappuccino as he had snuck in at the Schimmel Center cafeteria, but would never admit that to Tan or Ashe.

Tan had taken Max's desk, which was fine with him. She needed a lot more room to navigate her bagel, anyway. He was on the small sofa as usual, and Ashe sat on a chair. They were chewing in silence when Max got a call from the command center.

"Max, it's Parth Mehta."

"You're up early, Parth," Max said, as he wiped his mouth.

"I'm doing a six to two."

"Instead of an eight by four."

"Yeah, it's better for travel," Mehta said. "Beats the rush."

"Good. Okay, listen," Max said, knowing that Mehta would work overtime as needed and gave him the details of their sighting of somebody at Grant's Tomb the night before.

"Wow, too, bad."

"Yeah, close," Max said. "So, what do you have for us?"

"We got a notification from the communication techs. You know your guy got a call this morning about three-fifteen from that burner phone?"

"I do. I got a call from him about three-thirty."

THE ENTIRE TEAM WAS present in the command center at 7:30 a.m., including Roach. The *OJO* team leader was on Zoom.

Max briefly updated everybody on the developments at Grant's Tomb the night before.

Roach rubbed his forehead and moaned. Max couldn't blame him. They were so close to getting a fix on the ghost.

"We hope the National Park Service has cameras running 24/7 at the Tomb," Max said. "Parth is working on it."

Max then updated everybody on the status of the burner phone and GPS information, and the unusual hour that their informant had received a call from the ghost which surprised no one. He then asked Mehta to send everyone The Cage investigation update electronically, which was now up to about 100 pages. It contained everything they had on the case up to that point: statements, photographs, background screening synopsis on each character, embedded video, the works, including photographs of Wei Ming, Jia Li and Zhao Hua.

They were all eager to get out there and observe the informant, communicate with another potential Chinese recruit, and—if the ghost recruiter was present—to identify her. The ghost had already made one mistake with the burner phone, giving up her location at Grant's Tomb. Max knew that that was information she didn't want them to have. He hoped nobody in her circle would bring it to her attention.

Roach blurted, "Are you only going to target Asians in the café?"

"Yes," Max answered. "Mostly Asians, yes."

"Ethnicity is not a risk factor," Roach continued. "You can either target everybody or nobody. You cannot single out persons who look Chinese."

"But this is an urgent scientific espionage case, Mr. Roach," Max answered. "This is different."

Roach spat out, "It's not different."

Everyone in the room took Roach in for an extra moment.

"It is different," Max said calmly. "We can't chase everybody around regardless of ethnicity. We can't pretend that we won't be looking especially at Asians under the circumstances."

"That's profiling," Roach shouted.

"That's right, it is, and it has to be done. We have to assume that the ghost is Asian, and that the people assisting her are Asian. Therefore, we need to vet the Asians we see during the surveillance," Max said. "Twenty years ago, after 9/11, out of necessity, we targeted Saudis and Muslims. We can't pretend that we didn't. Fifty years ago, when my father was an NYPD detective and a radical Puerto Rican domestic terrorism group, the FALN, was planting bombs around the city, law enforcement wasn't looking for them in Knights of Columbus clubs, they were looking for them in the Puerto Rican social clubs in East Harlem and the South Bronx. And where was law enforcement tracking the Black Liberation Army? They were looking for those domestic terrorists in Harlem."

"But terrorists sometimes come from other ethnic and racial groups that sympathize and take part in the terrorists' cause."

"I agree, Mr. Roach, but proportionately it's very small. We need to use common sense here. This is a Chinese trade secrets espionage operation. We need to target those who appear to be Chinese."

Max then paused, looked at Roach and again wondered if he'd just picked up a smirk or another grin from him.

"Everybody okay with that?" Max then asked.

"Absolutely," Teresa Tan announced. "Damn right."

BY 10:30 A.M. MAX, Tan, and Ashe were sitting on Roosevelt Island in a surveillance van with the markings, "East Side Electricians," a short distance from the Schimmel Center and café. They watched the screens being fed video and audio from the Fitbits Jia Li and Wei Ming were wearing.

There were several real-time video feeds coming into the van—albeit with frequent movement—as their arms swayed and swung. Except the pin Jia Li was wearing provided a semi-steady stream of whatever she was facing. At that point in real time, the teacher at the bottom of the semi-amphitheater classroom was droning on about QED. Max theorized it was quantum something, but that's as far as it went for him.

"Any idea what QED is, Sam?" Tan asked.

"Quantum Electro Dynamics," he replied without hesitation.

"Now, how the heck did you know that?" Tan asked.

"ChatGPT."

"Thank God," Tan said. "You were about to frighten me."

Eventually, they observed the class break up and watched Wei Ming approach Zhao Hua as he was still closing down his laptop. Audio was as important to Max as video.

"Would you join me for lunch, Zhao?" Wei Ming asked in Mandarin. "I would like to hear how you have found your first year of study."

"Yes, of course, Wei," he replied. "Thank you."

Max and the team watched the bouncing images as they left the classroom, through the hallways, onto the elevator, down the elevator, off the elevator, and into the café from the video vantage point of Wei Ming's swinging arm.

IT WAS ABOUT 12:40 p.m. when Wei Ming and Zhao Hua arrived in the café. Both had the soup of the day: green pea with ham.

Max and his team listened to their conversation. They continued to speak in Mandarin. The translator continued to translate from the command center like it was the annual meeting of the United Nations General Assembly. It would require the translator to create a written transcript of all video recorded conversations, including the conversations picked up from the listening devices placed around Wei Ming's apartment. Teresa Tan and/or Max could add nuance.

"Only two weeks before completion of your first year, Zhao," Wei Ming said, as he took a sip of his green tea.

"Yes, it has gone fast," Zhao said. "And you are graduating in two weeks. You must be very excited."

Max adjusted in his swiveling pilot's seat, eyes focused on the three screens that were capturing the exchange. One screen was feed from Wei Ming's Fitbit, the other two screens were feed from the two surveillance operatives inside the café that the *OJO* leader had assigned.

"Yes," Wei Ming said, then there was a pause. "When I graduate, I plan to help our country. I plan to bring some information back with me."

Zhao Hua's head came up from his soup like he'd just got a disturbing whiff of the Wuhan wet market.

"I thought you would stay here and work for one of the U.S. firms," Zhao Hua said. "Google, IBM. They are doing much work on quantum here, too."

"I changed my mind," Wei Ming said. "The motherland has made me an excellent offer."

There was a long pause.

"May I ask, what is the offer?"

"He just asked Wei Ming what he was being offered," Tan interjected abruptly over the translator's translation, as if Max was not also fluent in Mandarin and the others listening in would not understand the translator's clear translation.

Max recognized Tan was feeling the enormity of the question, nodded in silence and kept his eyes fixed on the landscape-size CCTV screen containing the three views of the exchange, consciously aware that everything transmitting to their screens in the van was simultaneously being viewed by anyone in the 26 Federal Plaza command center, including Roach being baby sat by Mehta.

"Ten thousand initially, then five thousand U.S. dollars per week while I am here, with a promised increase when I return. And promised I can work in our same science."

Zhao gasped, "Ten thousand to then five thousand per week?"

Wei Ming nodded.

There was another long pause.

"You know, Wei Ming, I do not have a family back home. I am an orphan. I have no resources," Zhao Hua said and looked down at his soup, and slowly stirred.

Wei Ming remained silent.

Zhao Hua looked up from his bowl, looked around, then at Wei Ming, and said, "May I have the same arrangement?"

"You must withdraw proprietary data from your research here and pass it onto our motherland."

"I understand."

Wei Ming paused for a long time too, then nodded. "I think so. I will ask."

Tan whispered, "He took the offer."

"All right, they're getting up," Max said. "We have to assume the ghost and any associates are in the café," Max said. "*OJO*, track anybody getting up to leave as soon as our informant and the other student leave the café."

"Ten-four," *OJO* replied.

Ashe then said, "Male, white, mid-fifties bald, gray polo shirt, kakis, light blue waist-length jacket, heading to the exit on the north end."

"We got him," one of the surveillance operatives inside the café said.

Everybody could then hear the *OJO* leader direct the surveillance op to stay with him.

"Ten-four," the op replied.

Tan then said, "Male, Asian, gray jacket, forties, black pants, leaving solo."

"*OJO*, you got that?"

A few seconds passed. "We got him."

Wei Ming and Zhao Hua departed the café and walked back to the main part of the building and through the turnstiles into the school, which the public did not have access to.

"Elderly female Asian just finished her beverage, getting up now," Tan announced. "Female, looks to be in her seventies, with a shopping cart leaving through the westside entrance."

Max said, "You got that, *OJO*?"

"Got her," *OJO* said. Then a few minutes later he said, "She's waiting at the Roosevelt bus line stop, not the city bus stop."

Max and others immediately recognized that the bus she'd gotten on would not leave the island. They sat in the surveillance van in silence and waited for *OJO* to give an update.

About five minutes later, the *OJO* leader came over the radio, "Asian senior with a shopping cart just entered Roosevelt Island Seniors Association. Four five six Main Street."

"Seniors Association," Max repeated under his breath, nodded, and looked at Tan and Ashe, who nodded as well.

"Status on the male, white, light blue jacket?" Max asked.

The operative that was on him replied, "Just got into a red Ford Escape, New York plates, prelim data screen, retired NYC firefighter, lives in Long Island City."

"Retired firefighter probably enjoys the café for a change of pace," Max said rhetorically, then said into the radio, "*OJO*, your op can break it off. Thanks for the ID on him."

"Ten-four," *OJO* replied. "Anybody else?"

Max got on the radio. "No, but the target that took the offer, 24/7 surveillance on him. Let us know if he meets with anyone on or off the Roosevelt Island."

"Ten-four. Will do."

THEY WATCHED WEI MING and Zhao Hua walk down a few hallways on screen until they arrived in an area that must be the lab, Max figured. It was a much larger room than he had expected. It was half the size of a football field. He immediately noticed a large gold and copper container with countless wires in the center of the room that could be mistaken for a metal wine vat.

Except, in a winery, there would be a series of vats lined up like prison jail cells, but they isolated this gold and copper vat. Max intuitively felt that that baby must be a quantum computer.

"Wow," was what he felt, and thought about what David Sanger's *The Perfect Weapon* claimed; that quantum could one day break any kind of encryption.

The huge vat was not one of many; it was the principal attraction. It was the heart of the operation, in a large white room with multiple wide screen computers spread out with graphics and charts and a rainbow of colors, and tall file cabinet-size machines lined up around it with dials, and screens, and switches that must be an assortment of hard drives, Max thought, presenting the sense that every lever, every shelf, every wire was there to support that one huge isolated copper vat.

"Look at that," Tan said, slightly out of breath. "That monster must be a quantum computer."

Max nodded, then jumped on the mic to the command center. "Parth, terminate all recording, video, and audio while our operatives are inside the lab. And erase whatever we have recorded inside the lab up to this point. And document that we did that."

"Got it," Mehta replied immediately.

The last thing Max wanted to do was record the research and development process taking place in the lab, especially since the Schimmel Center had not given them permission to do so, and as yet was not even aware of their investigation.

They sat in silence in the van for a minute and sipped on their cold Dunkin' coffees.

"We need that Grant's Tomb CCTV," Max said. "Where's that stand, Sam?'

"I'll call Parth. See if he's been able to get it."

Max then sent Jia Li a text: "...tell WM to call me after he hears from the recruiter."

Within seconds, he received a return text, "OK. Good."

"All right, we can take off," Max said.

MAX, TAN, ASHE AND Mehta walked into Roach's office. Roach did not stop tapping on his computer. Again, they were not invited to sit down.

Max went over the results of the Schimmel Center surveillance, then he brought up the exfiltration of Wei Ming's family.

"We need to try and get the informant's family out of China," Max said.

Roach did not respond or stop tapping.

Max continued, "It looks certain that we're dealing with an active Chinese spy operation. It's time to give it a shot."

"Did the informant bring it up again?" Roach asked over his shoulder.

"No," Max said. "I'm bringing it up. I told him we needed more before we would try it. I understood your pushback. But now we need to try. This is the real thing."

"Let me know when he brings it up again."

"No," Max shut back. Tan, Ashe and Mehta kept their eyes focused on Roach.

Roach turned to face Max.

"Mr. Roach," Max said. "We must deal with this informant in good faith. Everything up to this point appears to be legit. He's put himself at risk and now his family is at risk."

Silence.

Roach then turned to Ashe. "What do you think, Sam?"

"We have to try, sir," Ashe replied. "That's what'll take to maintain his cooperation."

"There's one pitfall," Max said. "But we still need to give it a shot."

"What's that?" Roach asked.

"If the Chinese block their leaving," Tan said.

"That's a big pitfall. Especially if we jump through a bunch of hoops for them," Roach said. "A colossal waste of time and resources."

"Yes," Max said. "Hopefully, we can get it done under Chinese radar."

Roach turned his back to Max and his team, once again tapping on his computer and said over his shoulder, "All right. Set it up."

MAX MADE IT HOME BY about seven p.m. He picked up a veal parmesan dinner from the pizza shop on York Avenue across the street from his building. Perfect time to catch the twins on FaceTime, he thought. They should've just had dinner and settled down. He jumped onto his Mac on his home/office desk and pulled up their contact info.

"Hey, Uncle Max," Jess said first, then Ben leaned his face into view. Max never knew which of the twins would answer first, even though they each had their own iPads.

"Hey, guys, I see you got a haircut today."

"Yeah," the twins both said together.

"Your hair is as short as Ben's, Jess."

"I like it short," Jess said. "I don't want to look like a girl. I'm a boy."

"Okay, well, it looks like you both have high-and-tights."

"What's that?" they both asked.

"That's what marines call a very close-cropped haircut."

"Did Papa have a haircut like that?" Ben asked.

"Yes, he sure did," Max said, feeling a twist to his heart. "Your papa was a United States Marine, too. He sure did have a high-and-tight haircut."

"Good," seven-year-old Ben said. "I always wanted a high-and-tight."

Max nodded. "And what about you, Jess?"

"High-and-tight, okay for me, too."

Max could then hear his sister Maya swiftly moving toward the twins and their iPads. "Who are you talking to?" Then she leaned into view.

"Oh, hi, Max," Maya said, with a smile from ear to ear, "What are you up to?"

The twins had drifted away.

"Just made it home. I see the twins' got haircuts."

"Yeaaaah," Maya said, then descended into a whisper. "Jess likes it just as short. And she refuses to wear the underwear I get her. She wears Ben's jockeys."

Max smiled, "God's hands, sis."

"True enough. So, how about you? How was your day?" Maya asked. "Working on anything juicy?"

"Yeah, I think so. We'll see where it leads. Can't say much," Max replied. The same reply he'd been giving his sister for the last twelve years he'd been in law enforcement. "But I'll say this..." Max stopped. He was about to bring up Jia Li but thought better of it.

"What?" Maya asked, with that woman's sixth sense. "A girl?"

"No, no, not really," Max said. "I think my dinner's getting cold."

"Ahh huh," Maya laughed. "You okay?"

"Good," Max said. "You?"

"Good, Max. Thanks for calling."

"Of course."

"We'll be talking."

"You know it."

AT 10:16 P.M., HE RECEIVED a group text from the tech team: "Burner phone call from E. 42nd Street between south side, closer to 5th Avenue."

"Hmmm," Max could not help murmuring. The Taiwanese Consulate was on that street. Then his ePhone rang.

"You see that, Max," Tan said. "You see that. The ghost was hovering around the Taiwanese consulate. Her signal was picked up opposite the Taiwanese consulate."

"Yeah, yeah, I see it," Max said, somewhat absentmindedly, absorbing that bit of information.

"Looks like the ghost's monitoring whatever's cooking with Taiwan," Max said and wondered if the ghost was on to Jia Li.

"We must have permanent cameras on the Taiwanese consulate," Tan said.

"I'm sure we do."

Max was relieved the call had not been made from inside the Taiwanese consulate, just as he'd been relieved Jia Li had not walked into the Chinese consulate days earlier.

For an extra moment, Max pondered what the intel was telling them: that all the players in the case were so far staying in their lane.

"Max, I'm going to give Parth a call. We need film around the Taiwanese consulate from the last few days, too. Maybe we can pick up the ghost making the call," Tan said. "You okay with that?"

"Yeah, sure, good idea."

"Okay," Tan said, and the phone went dead.

AT 10:31 P.M., MAX received a text from Jia Li asking to do a Zoom call with her and Wei Ming. Max went to his kitchen table where his laptop was set up, logged in, and texted Tan Ashe Mehta to log on if they could.

Four squares appeared on Max's laptop. Wei Ming and Jia Li were sitting in front of her computer at her desk. Tan and Ashe also appeared, but only their names displayed.

"Good evening, Mr. Valentin," Wei Ming said. "Sorry to contact you so late."

"No worries at all. Did you hear from the woman?"

"Yes, I did. She said she was very pleased with how everything went today."

"Wait a minute, Wei Ming," Max said. "Did you have to explain how it went? Or did she already know how it went?"

"Oh, oh, no, she knew what happened. She told me she liked how I presented myself to Zhao and how I presented what she wanted me to do."

"Ahh, huh? Did she say how she knew?" Max asked. "Did she say she was in the café?"

"No, no, she did not say."

"So, she could hear your conversation? She said that she could see you and hear you?"

"Yes, I believe so."

"How do you know, Wei Ming?" Max asked. "Did she say specifically that she watched you do something, anything, that would show she was there?"

"Ohhh, I see, okay, yes. She told me, for example, that when she heard Zhao ask me if he could have the same arrangement, she said she found it funny the way he instinctively looked around."

"I see," Max said. "Okay."

The recruiter was there in the café or watching and listening from another location as Max and his team had done. Since it wasn't likely they planted a video or audio in the café, that meant that either the recruiter or one or more of members of the recruiter's team were in the café.

"What does she want you to do now?" Max asked.

"She wants me to tell Zhao that he could have the same arrangement," Wei Ming said. "She told me to call him and tell him."

"Call him yourself," Max said rhetorically. "Do you have his number?"

"I do."

"Did she mention if she had his number?"

"Well, yes, she did. When she asked me to call him, she offered to give me his number if I did not have it."

"Ahh huh," Max said.

"And, Mr. Valentin, she said she wants me to communicate with him for her from now on. And I agreed," Wei Ming said. "Should I have agreed?"

"Yes, Wei Ming. That's good."

Just what Teresa had predicted the recruiter would do—use Wei Ming to be her liaison since she believed she now owned him.

"Anything else?" Max asked.

"She said that she has a list of others who are working on the same research at different labs and universities in the U.S. and she wants me to tell her who I know."

"Do you know many people around the U.S. or other parts of the world also working on quantum?"

"I do," Wei Ming said. "Jia Li and I, and all of us, are in an organization of quantum students and professors and scientists in labs."

"Did you tell the recruiter that?"

"No."

Tan jumped in, "What's the organization called?"

Jia Li answered, "IBM Q Network. It's a collection of over a hundred organizations. Schools and labs around the globe that are working on quantum mechanics. IBM calls this organization and its pursuits Quantaneo Q."

"And are you guys communicating with any of them directly?" Ashe asked.

"We do," Jia Li said. "Regularly."

"I assume some are ethnic Chinese?" Max asked.

"Yes, many of them," Wei Ming said, and Max noticed Wei Ming's voice drop. "Many of them."

"Okay. We'll see who's on her list and how she wants you to approach them," Max said. "Also, Wei Ming, when she contacts you next, ask her when you'll receive your initial ten thousand."

Max knew it was only a formality for the recruiter to make the payoff for the charge of economic espionage to stick. Just her recruitment effort was enough. But tangible proof of money being exchanged between the Chinese spy and the student she's trying to recruit would be very convincing to a potential jury.

"I will, sir."

"Okay, before I let you go..."

Max explained they would plan for his family to receive visas for their immediate entry into the United States and that the U.S. government would finance their travel. He continued that after they'd safely arrived in the U.S., they would make living arrangements for them. They'd be under protection throughout the investigation, and for some time thereafter.

"Thank you so much, Mr. Valentin. Thank you."

"Okay. It's eleven p.m.," Max said to Wei Ming, looking down at the time on his ePhone and looked back up into the computer screen. "So, it's about noon in China, right?"

"Do you want me to call them now and prepare them?" Wei Ming asked.

"Yes," Max said. "Use Jia Li's phone. Tell them they have an opportunity to visit you, but they need to leave within twenty-four hours. Tell him that three visas have become available through your school. And put the call on speaker."

Wei Ming made the call and conversed with his father in Mandarin. Max and Tan followed the conversation.

Wei Ming explained to his father what Max had instructed him to say, that there was a once in a lifetime opportunity for his family to come and visit him, but it would need to be in the next twenty-four hours. He explained that three other family members of a fellow student at his university in New York City had received U.S. visas, but because of a sudden death in their family in Beijing they could not leave, so, the school arranged for the visas to be used by Wei's family. He explained to his father there are a certain number of visas allowed to the school for the family of their students to visit the campus. But they must make the trip within the next twenty-four hours, otherwise the visas would expire.

Wei Ming's father said they would pack and be ready within three hours, China time.

Tan punched a thumbs-up emoji into her box on the screen, and Max nodded.

Wei Ming got more information from the family while he still had them on the phone and passed it on to Max: names, dates of birth, passport numbers for each of Wei's family.

During the next ninety minutes Max and his team arranged for the family's exfiltration.

Max directed Tan to fire off an email to Homeland Security Investigations with the information. HSI sent Tan an email stating they had been cleared for use and that an approval record was embedded in the reply from Homeland Security, and that the visas would be ready in thirty minutes.

In the meantime, Max had directed Ashe to put through an urgent request for three tickets from Shenzhen to New York City through the FBI clandestine emergency traveling system. Ashe forwarded a copy of the Homeland Security visa approvals along with the other documentation to the travel system.

Wei Ming's family had a booking for a flight that was scheduled to leave Shenzhen International Airport at 9:30 p.m. to New York City on United Airlines flight 664 with an arrival time the next day, 5:30 p.m., JFK International Airport.

Tan then fired off an email to the exfiltration coordinator (XCoor) in Singapore who would deploy operatives to monitor the family's transport from their home in Shenzhen to the airport, remain and report back when the flight took off.

"Okay," Max said. "It's in motion, Wei Ming."

"I am grateful, sir. Thank you all," Wei Ming said, and momentarily bowed his head to them in the Zoom squares. "Thank you so much."

After Max and the others logged off, he picked up the Alex Joske's *Spies and Lies* and read a few more sentences:

"Over decades, the MSS has deployed these techniques to mislead world leaders about the CCP's ambitions, lulling them into the comfortable belief that China would rise peacefully—maybe even democratically—and slot itself into the existing international order. Its targets have included former presidents and prime ministers, multinational corporations, business leaders, Buddhist monks, influential think tanks and respected China scholars. It's an influence operation that continues to this day."

Max flipped to the inside back cover of the book and wrote this thought, *We had been blind to it for decades. But that has now changed. We are no longer blind to China's ambitions and the means they continue to use to achieve it. We will no longer permit China to advance on the backs of U.S.-funded research—on the backs of U.S. creators. NO FUCKING WAY!* – Max slammed the book closed and turned off his nightlight.

CHAPTER 15
Tuesday, May 23

By 7:45 a.m. Max, Tan, and Ashe were in the command center. Parth Mehta was working another six to two shift.

"What's the story with Grant's Tomb?" Max asked.

"If you can believe this," Mehta said. "Their CCTV has been out of commission for a week; they put in a repair request but they're still waiting."

"So, we got big zip there," Max shook his head, then suddenly got a text from the XCoor, "problem… uniforms took family off line."

"Crap," Max said out loud as he sat in his office with Tan and Ashe.

"What's up?" Tan asked.

"They pulled the family off the boarding line," Max said, still looking at the text.

"Will advise…" the text continued.

"We knew that could happen," Tan said, and stood up, hands on her hips, and circled the office.

Max slid down on the small sofa, leaned back, looked up at the ceiling, and remained silent. Tan then slipped into Max's chair behind his desk, put her legs up on it, as usual, and rotated a stretched rubber band around her hands, and interlaced through her fingers, again, and again, and again. Ashe leaned up against the office doorframe and practiced with his yo-yo. Something he'd recently picked up on YouTube.

" 'Ideal for such situations,' " he'd once said. " 'Helps me ride the tsunami.' "

MAX TOOK A SWIG FROM his FBI National Academy coffee cup.

"National Academy," Tan said, with a furrowed brow and smile. "You get the cup as a gift?"

"No, no, I attended the program a couple of years back."

"No kidding, I didn't know that," Tan said. "What was that like?"

Ashe stood up. "It's a great program, Teresa. Let me follow up on a few things," Ashe said and walked out.

Sam Ashe knew Max had attended the FBI National Academy program and was very familiar with it. As a Homeland Security agent, Teresa Tan took her new agent training at the Federal Law Enforcement Center in Glynco, Georgia.

Most of the public, even those in law enforcement, knew little about the FBI National Academy that started in 1935.

"The idea behind it was to bring local and state and federal law enforcement (not in the FBI) to Quantico for three intense months of academic and physical training, not unlike any police academy. Except, the real purpose of the NA program was to foster a spirit of cooperation between all American law enforcement," Max explained. "Eventually, they expanded the program to include senior law enforcement officials from all around the world."

"Interesting," Tan said.

In Max's class of 250 attendees, it included male and female police executives from Scotland Yard, the Czech Republic, Australia, Canada, Saudi Arabia, Israel, and on and on. Every continent was represented in the FBI National Academy program. And because of the global nature of fentanyl cases, Max had already benefited from having reached out to fellow NA graduates and getting their help on a few cases. As they had reached out to him for assistance in New York City.

Without NA contacts, whenever any NYPD detective needed to be in touch with law enforcement outside of the country to follow up on an investigation, you'd either make a request that went through department channels to an NYPD detective assigned to one of 104 foreign countries around the world, or you could start with the FBI legat in that country. But, as a graduate of the NA program—and lifetime member of that worldwide network—he had access to 16,000 senior law enforcement graduates from agencies and departments around the globe.

"That's quite a network," Tan said.

"The thing to keep in mind about the FBI Academy at Quantico, Virginia, is that there are three major training programs going on simultaneously throughout the year," Max said. "The new FBI agents and new DEA agents training, along with the NA program. And, of course, the NA program differed completely in that they are not new to law enforcement."

"And they're all in the same classes?" Tan asked. "Correct?"

"No, we crossed paths in those tube-like hallways connecting the different buildings on the grounds."

"Tube-like?"

"Yes, you felt a bit like a gerbil, going through those connecting tubes," Max said with a laugh. "Everybody ate in the same cafeteria, but we were all in classes that were exclusive to the program you were in, for good reason. There were things that needed to be taught to new DEA and FBI agents that we in the NA program didn't need to hear. And we had our own uniforms."

"Are you kidding me?" Tan said. "You had to wear a uniform?"

"We did. But we each had our own. The FBI new agents' classes wore khakis with a blue polo shirt, DEA was all in black."

"Black?"

"Yes, black polos, black cargo pants, and black combat boots."

"And your group, the NA group?"

"NA, we wore khakis with green polo shirts, each with a nice FBI National Academy logo."

"What's the FBI motto again?" Tan asked.

"Fidelity, Bravery, Integrity."

"And the NA program," Tan said. "Do they use the same motto?"

"No, they do not," Max said. "The motto for the FBI National Academy is, KCI. Knowledge, Courage, Integrity. Doesn't rhyme as well as FBI, but that's what it is. What can you do?"

"Interesting," Tan said with genuine fascination.

MAX'S CELL PHONE BUZZED on his desk, and he straightened up from the sofa and lunged for it like it was an escaping pair of dice.

"Flight took off... family didn't make it."

Max texted, "Still held? Or cut loose?"

"Cut loose... cab back home."

"Crap," Max expelled.

MAX SENT A TEXT TO Jia Li immediately.

"Family stopped at airport. Did not make flight. Let him know."

Jia Li returned Max's text about ten minutes later.

"He's very upset. We need to meet," Jia Li texted back.

Max texted back, "Manhattan side of tram, walking/bike path park pavilion... enter at 60th St and York... red pavilion in the park."

"Okay."

Max looked up from Jia Li's text. "Wei Ming is very upset. I'm going to meet Jia Li up at the pavilion on the Manhattan side," Max said. "See if you can find out from the XCoor what happened. Text me as soon as you hear that the family is back home. I'll get the details after I meet with her."

"You want me to go with you, Max?" Tan asked.

"No, I want you both to head up to Roosevelt Island as soon as you hear from the XCoor. We don't know the reason for their being turned away. Did the visa cause the problem? Was it Chinese intel that put the family on a no-fly list? Was it because they picked up on our electronics sweep?" Max asked. "I just want you to hover around the school and the apartment building. I don't want you guys all the way down here if something develops up there."

"Got it, I'll let Sam know."

"I'm going to take the subway up. You guys take a car," Max said. "I'll meet you on the island after I talk to Jia Li."

MAX TOOK THE Q SUBWAY line up to Lexington Avenue and East Sixty-Third Street. He worked his way to the East Sixtieth Street entryway to the Andrew Haswell Park Green off the FDR Drive and York Avenue, almost directly under the Ed Koch Queensboro Bridge and the Roosevelt Island tram. It had just drizzled, and he yanked the black Metropolitan Museum cap he'd picked up at a recent Caravaggio exhibition from his pocket and put it on.

He went up the hill to the pavilion. It was built on top of an old, decommissioned NYC sanitation structure by the architect Nicholas Quennel, with a massive sculpture resting on it created by Alice Aycock. It always looked to Max like a roller coaster swirling around a series of red beams with no apparent end point, but eventually, abruptly concluding. The sculpture was called "East River Roundabout." A lot like investigations, Max thought, swirling around with no apparent end point for a bit. Then finally it ends in a smash.

Max scanned the pavilion to see if Jia Li had arrived. She hadn't and there were only a few stragglers working their way out as the rain started to pick up. He sat himself at the northern most metal bench overlooking the East River, in good position to see her as soon as she entered.

She arrived a few minutes later wearing a black thigh length trench coat, black slacks, red shoes, carrying a red umbrella and marched directly to him, sitting next to him, thrusting out her umbrella to share with him.

"I'm fine, thank you."

The pavilion had cleared. They were alone.

"How's he doing?"

"Not well," Jia Li said. "He had not considered the possibility of his parents being unable to leave. He wonders if something was wrong with the visas or has it anything to do with the woman who has been calling him. He suspects that their intention is to ensure his family's confinement until he cooperates."

"That's what we want to know. As we said, we were afraid of that," Max said. "We'll get a better idea in the next few hours after our representative in China speaks with the family. Assuming our agent can without raising suspicions."

Max then watched her look away from him and across the river toward the Schimmel Center and the apartment buildings.

Max turned to look out over the river for a moment too.

"Jia Li," Max then said, and she turned to look at him again. "What's he saying? He knows he's got to work with us despite his family situation, right?"

"Not yet," Jia Li said, and shook her head. "Regrettably, he said he just could not. If he helped U.S. authorities, it would put his family into jeopardy."

"I was afraid of that," Max said. The increasing drizzle and fog partially obscured the view of the Schimmel Center.

"Jia Li, Wei Ming is in a tough position. He has no choice but to continue with us."

Jia Li raised her voice. "What do you mean?"

"I mean, he has no choice than to help us. It's too late for him to back out."

"Do you mean you will force him to help you? That's terrible. He came forward to help you, but you couldn't get his family out of China."

Now, Max's eyebrows raised high. What's up with this Taiwanese agent?

"This is terrible."

Max looked at Jia Li as the drizzle turned into solid drops of rain.

"This is just terrible," Jia Li said again. "He is now cornered by America and the Chinese."

Max was stunned by Jia Li's reaction. She may be a Taiwanese agent, but when it comes to making the best of only bad options to nail the Chinese state, she was not yet up to it.

Then it hit him. It hit him hard when he realized what was going on. He'd neglected to consider the fact that although she was an undercover Taiwanese agent, she had been with Wei Ming for almost three years in their PhD program and had gotten too close to him.

Max realized that he'd neglected to factor in Jia Li's reaction to hearing it was Wei Ming who the Chinese were trying to recruit when they'd first met, *"Wei Ming, oh my goodness, he is my friend,"* *and overlapped her hands to her heart. "He is brilliant. He is my friend."*

And now she couldn't pull the trigger. She'd had come to overly identify with Wei Ming. She had come to the point of wanting to protect Wei Ming more than she wanted the investigation to advance.

Max had seen this behavior come up with deep undercover detectives before. He'd seen some undercovers completely unable to witness the takedown of the bad guy that they'd come to be trusted by when it was time. And some undercovers vehemently objected to their targets being taken down at all, as bizarre as that was. That's why the NYPD had the policy of pulling the undercover at one year—no exceptions. Make the case, if there's a case to be made, and pull the undercover out.

Now all Max could do was manage it and try to reel her back.

"We're not cornering him, Jia Li. It's the predicament he finds himself in. We did not put him there. The Chinese put him there. His only choice now is for him to help us identify this ghost recruiter and make a case against them," Max said. "In the meantime, we will look into unorthodox ways to get his parents out of China when the time is right."

Jia Li shook her head and walked to the fence overlooking the East River as raindrops pounded them and the pavilion and turned back to Max. "What does that mean? When the time is right? This is terrible."

Max got up and walked over to her, bent down, and got under her umbrella, inches away from her face. "Jia Li, listen to me. You're a Taiwanese security agent. Help him see what he now needs to do."

Max took in the hard look she turned to give him.

"He made a mistake by coming to U.S. authorities for help," Jia Li said. "Now his family will be harmed if he doesn't help the PRC. And because he told you, you can't let him work his way out of his commitment without taking action."

"No, of course we can't," Max said. "Remember what the Chinese want here. They want to steal scientific research: quantum research, semiconductor research, IP of the university, critical research that has national security implications for my country and yours. That is the bottom line here. We cannot just let him walk away now. Of course not."

"And if he helps you, and the Chinese learn of it, his family will still be harmed," Jia Li said. "Isn't that so?"

"He'll be helping both of our countries, right? Isn't that so? Our two governments are secret partners in this. We're supposed to be partners, right?" Max asked. "So, he'll be helping both our countries. Right?"

Jia Li did not reply.

"Listen. We will do all that we can to keep it completely quiet as he helps us, and we'll try to get his family out of there at the right time."

"What if Wei Ming tells that woman that he made a mistake because he was so nervous and contacted U.S. authorities, and I just monitor him to make sure he steals nothing?" Jia Li said. "Maybe his family won't be punished, and they won't want to pursue further action now that they know U.S. authorities have been alerted."

Max remained bent under her umbrella, looking into her eyes, hoping she would recognize the absurdity of that idea, as a sheet of rain spread across the oil tanker trudging up the East River. That she would eventually recognize Wei Ming's only option was to help them. Keep the quantum computing research and development of her university program from being stolen.

"This is espionage, Jia Li," Max said, held her by both arms. "This is a wicked game. How could you not understand that in your position? Remember who you are. It's a wicked game."

Max watched her hold his eyes for a few long moments, turn in the river's direction and the Schimmel Center, then back to him and said, "I can no longer help you," and walked away.

She tramped through the puddles that had accumulated during the downpour, apparently oblivious to its impact on her stylish ankle-high red boots.

"What the fuck?" Max said under his breath.

MAX CALLED TAN AND Ashe to find out if the exfiltration coordinator had called and to let them know that he'd just finished with Jia Li and that she was on her way back on the Roosevelt Tram.

"All right, no worries. He'll contact us when he can. Anyway, keep track of Jia Li when she gets off," Max told them, and gave them a description of what she was wearing and the red boots. "See where she goes. They're both very upset. I'm going to pick up the F at Sixty-Third Street to Roosevelt Island. I'll call you when I'm there."

"Jump on the tram too, Max," Tan said. "You're right there."

"The F is faster."

"What are you talking about? Who knows how long you'll be waiting on the subway platform, and you're right under the tram," Tan said. "You're going to get soaked. You have an umbrella?"

"No, Teresa, I don't," Max said. "I'll let you know when I get there."

"All right, all right," Tan said. "I'm not judging, I'm just saying."

MAX WALKED THROUGH the rain to the F train, knowing that Teresa Tan was completely right. It would make more sense for him to take the tram across the river instead of wasting time with the subway. As he approached Second Avenue, he could see the tram Jia Li must have been on heading back over the river to Roosevelt Island, and the tram coming from Roosevelt Island pulling into the dock. If he jumped on it, he would be on the other side of the river in ten minutes. If he went for the subway, it would take at least a half hour to forty-five minutes, and this was no time to be wasting time.

He went up the stairs to the tram platform, swiped his NYPD Metro Card through the turnstile, and waited for the doors to open with the others. As soon as he got onto the cable car, he went directly for one of the center poles and closed his eyes. The doors closed, and it started to ascend. Max kept his eyes closed. He could feel the rumble as the car climbed up the cable.

"Don't look, Max. Don't look, Max," he repeated to himself.

The ascending car rattled him as it rumbled over the different markers. Sweat dripped from his forehead into his eyes. The rain had consumed the tram. With his head on the pole, he prayed. He started to again recall that day in Afghanistan when he and his platoon had to slide across a cable from one side of a river gorge to the other. He was a second lieutenant and only six months out of officer candidates' school.

He sent his marines first; he was the last one on the cable when it began to fray; it left him dangling over the river when Taliban fighters started to unceasingly fire at him. Within seconds of those repetitive shots, a marine Apache helicopter—coming seemingly from nowhere—lit up the Taliban fighters and rescued Max.

"Are you okay, Mr. Valentin?" It was a soft female Asian voice.

Without lifting his forehead from the pole, Max barely squinted open one eye to look at the voice. It was Jia Li.

"Not really."

Without hesitation, Jia Li wrapped her arms around him, her face pressed against his back, her hands over his hands gripped to the pole, pulled herself tightly against him, and said, "It is okay. I will not let you go."

When the doors to the cable car opened on the Roosevelt Island side, she walked him onto the platform and helped him get oriented again.

"Will you be okay?"

Max looked like he'd just come out of a sauna. "Yes, thanks. How did you come to be on the same tram I got on?" Max asked, as he pulled a handkerchief from his back pocket and slowly wiped his face. "I saw the one before this one pulled out. I would've thought you'd be on it. You left me in a hurry."

"I felt the need to think. I took a few minutes to sit in the small park under the tram. I missed it."

"I see," Max said, looked at her.

AFTER SEVERAL LONG moments, Jia Li spoke up again, "I want to ask you something. Mr. Valentin?"

Max looked over at her for an extra moment before answering and looked back at the tram that was ascending again, "Okay."

"Is Max your true first name?"

Max turned to Jia Li. "No, my name is Maximo."

"Maximo," Jia Li repeated softly. "You are part Asian, aren't you?"

"Why do you ask?"

"You appear to have some Asian features," Jia Li said. "Your dark eyes, your complexion."

"You're the first person in my life that ever picked up on that," Max said with raised eyebrows. "Yes. My great-great-grandmother was Chinese."

"Really. I could tell," Jia Li said with a broad smile. "What is her story?"

"Why don't we grab a seat," Max said and drifted over to a bench on the platform. Jia Li followed.

"My great-great-grandmother immigrated to Puerto Rico in 1883 from Shanghai. The family story that was passed down to all of us is that she wanted to immigrate to the U.S., but in 1882 the U.S. Congress had enacted the Chinese Exclusion Act which prevented Chinese nationals from immigrating, and it wasn't repealed until 1943."

"And why were they excluded?"

"Historians say the Chinese were originally welcomed to immigrate to the States to work on the railroad. After the railroad was finished the immigrants stayed to become U.S citizens. Except, since railroad employment dried up, other kinds of work became scarce and as a result Chinese immigrants became a threat to white immigrants also looking for employment. So, for sixty years from 1882 until 1943, the Chinese Exclusion Act was the law of the land until China and the United States came together in their fight against Japan during World War II."

"But Puerto Rico was a U.S. possession, was it not?" Jia Li asked. "Why would the United States not permit the Chinese to immigrate to mainland United States and, yet permit them to immigrate to one of their possessions?"

"Puerto Rico didn't become a U.S. possession until 1898."

"Ahh, so Spain still possessed Puerto Rico in 1883 when your great-great-grandmother arrived there," Jia Li said. "And the Spanish were accepting of immigrants from China, I presume."

"Yes. But it was conditional," Max said. "The Spanish had issued a decree in 1815 called the Royal Decree of Graces. In Spanish, it's the *Real Cedula de Gracias*, which said that foreigners could immigrate to Puerto Rico, but they had to become Catholic. So, when my great-grandmother arrived in Puerto Rico in 1883, she became Catholic."

"How interesting. And are you a practicing Catholic?"

"I am. And so is my family," Max said, "since my great-great-grandmother arrived."

"That is so fascinating," Jia Li said. "I presume you do not speak Chinese."

Max looked at her with a grin, then back out to the descending tram that was approaching Manhattan Island. "Well, actually, I speak Mandarin."

"Is that true?" Jia Li asked, with a combined expression of being intrigued and shocked. "No?"

Max nodded and recited the following poem in Mandarin:

> *I live upstream and you downstream,*
> *From night to night of you I dream.*
> *Unlike the stream you are not in view,*
> *Though both we drink from River Blue.*
> *When will the river no more flow?*
> *When will my grief no more grow?*
> *I wish your heart will be like mine,*
> *Then not in vain for you I pine.*

There were a few moments of silence before Jia Li spoke up. "That was beautiful," she said. "What is its title?"

"It's titled, 'Song of Divination' by Li Zhiyi," Max said. "Nice poem for someone whose name means good and beautiful."

Jia Li turned to Max and smiled, then continued, "So, generations since your great-great-grandmother arrived in Puerto Rico, you know how to speak Mandarin," Jia Li said. "How fascinating that you acquired it from so long ago."

"Actually, my great-great-grandmother did not pass down Mandarin to me," Max said. "The last person who learned to speak Chinese in my family was my great-grandfather, my great-great-grandmother's only son. I learned Mandarin in the marine corps. They trained me as a Mandarin cryptologic linguist. But my great-great-grandmother was the inspiration for me to learn Mandarin in the marines."

"You are fluent?"

Max smiled. "Yes, speak, read, and write."

Jia Li was silent for a moment, then asked, "And are you likewise fluent in Spanish?"

"I am," and Max recited a poem in Spanish:

Por una mirada, un mundo, Por una sonrisa, un cielo, Por un beso... ¡yo no sé

Que te diera por un beso!

Max could feel the heat of Jia Li smiling at him. "How fascinating," she said. "What does it mean?"

Max then translated it into English, *"For a look, a world, for a smile, a sky and heaven, For a kiss... I do not know. What you give for a kiss!* That poem is titled 'Sonnet XXIII' by Gustavo Adolfo Becquer."

Jia Li suddenly looked away, and Max thought her ears had turned a little red.

Max could not help but sense that the inside of Jia Li's legs had become suddenly moist. And he had more than a sense that the inside of his legs had suddenly hardened.

They sat in silence.

"I assume you practice either Shinto or Buddhism," Max said, finally speaking up again.

Jia Li did not respond right away, then turned to look at Max and said, "I am Catholic too."

Max could not help turning to look at her with a furrowed, intrigued, brow, "Really?"

Jia Li nodded her head, smiled at him.

"Northern Taiwan became a Spanish Colony in the seventeenth century. A Dominican friar built a Catholic church, and the church has been in Taiwan ever since. My mother is Taiwanese and Catholic. My father is African American, and also raised Catholic. In fact, my father's upbringing took place here in New York City."

"No kidding," Max said, "No kidding."

They looked at each other for several long moments. Then Jia Li leaned in and kissed him.

After two or three soft seconds, Max leaned back and stood up. Silence.

What could he say? He wanted to kiss her since the moment they'd met. Apparently, that's what all that poetry was about. But what does it mean that she would lean into him and kiss him then and there? Was she working him? Taking advantage of an opportunity. Trying to manipulate him? Was she deliberately trying to use that romantic lapse to divert his attention from her reaction earlier to abandon what needed to be done with Wei Ming? Or is it simply that she just could not help herself as he was barely resisting her? He didn't know how to respond so he pretended it hadn't happened and carried on.

"Help Wei Ming see what he must do."

"Mr. Valentin," Jia Li stood up too. "I owe you a sincere apology. My recent behavior was entirely unprofessional. I don't know what had come over me. I had clearly forgotten the significance of the investigation we are conducting. I clearly had a lapse in judgment."

"You are very close to Wei Ming."

"Perhaps," Jia Li nodded. "But I want to assure you it will not happen again. I am again clear on our priorities. My fondness for Wei Ming will not interfere with my future objectivity. I hope you can have confidence in me?"

Max held Jia Li's eyes for an extra moment and repeated, "Help Wei Ming see what he must do."

SOON AFTER MAX HAD jumped into the back seat of the SUV with Tan and Ashe, he'd gotten the call he was expecting from the exfiltration coordinator in Singapore. Tan and Ashe were seated up front. They were parked between the school and apartment building where both Wei Ming and Jia Li lived.

"Thanks for calling. Listen, I'm going to put you on speaker. I'm sitting in a Bureau car with two other agents."

"Sam Ashe here."

"Teresa Tan."

"Hey guys," the coordinator said.

"So, what did it look like over there?" Max asked.

"It was going smooth for a while until they got on the line for boarding and a uniform approached them and took them down a hallway to Chinese customs until our operative lost sight of them. About fifty minutes later, they came out and took a cab home. We had to assume they were being watched, so we didn't pick them up and take them back. They had enough sense to grab a cab."

"Right, smart," Max said. "Did your op tail the cab back home?"

"Yes, all the way back. When she felt the time was right, she snuck into their home and spoke to the family. The sister did most of the talking. She said customs asked them why they were going to the U.S., and she explained they were going to visit her brother who was studying at an American university. The sister said that she asked why they were being detained, but they didn't even attempt to offer an explanation. The sister also asked if they could fly soon, but they didn't answer her and told them they could return home."

"Not exactly a democratic approach," Tan said.

"Who interviewed them in the room?" Max asked?

"Two uniforms who claimed to be customs officers," the coordinator said. "The sister, you know, is blind. But we asked the father to describe the interior of the room. He said there was a big mirror embedded into one wall."

"Of course. Two-way mirror," Ashe said. "It would be interesting to know who was watching and listening on the other side."

"Listen, the family thinks our operative is associated with your guy's school, and we reimbursed them for the cab fare. It doesn't look like they're a family of means," the coordinator said. "Oh, and by the way, our op told them we would let your informant know they didn't make the flight."

"Great, thanks," Max said. "I'll give you a shout if we need any follow-up."

"Sounds good," the coordinator said. "Whatever you need."

"Oh, one last thing. Did they let them leave with the visas?" Max asked.

"No, no. Forgot to mention that," the coordinator said. "No, they kept the visas. Returned their passports but kept the visas."

"Okay, I'm not surprised. Thanks."

"You bet, brother," the coordinator said. "Good luck, guys."

"Thanks," Max said, and punched off his ePhone.

They sat in silence for a few moments.

"So, Chinese customs stopped the family, offered no explanation, took their visas, and sent them on their way," Max said.

"That sounds about right," Tan said with a sigh.

Max started to slowly sip from the lukewarm Dunkin' coffee they'd picked up for him.

AT ABOUT 6:40 P.M., they watched Jia Li leave the Schimmel Center and take a vigorous walk back to her apartment building. The rain had stopped. About ten minutes later, Wei Ming did the same. They were both back home.

"What are you thinking, Max?" Tan asked.

Max thought they were both in Jia Li's apartment and she would do her job and try to help Wei Ming decide what he should do. Jia Li was a Taiwanese intelligence agent. He was relieved that she soon recognized that Wei Ming had no real choice than to cooperate with U.S. authorities. But there was no guarantee it would go that way. Max had been in law enforcement long enough to witness people do things that were clearly not the better option, but they just couldn't see it, and sabotaged themselves. He regretted that Wei Ming was boxed in. He liked Wei Ming. He seemed, up to that point, to be a sincere young scientist.

"I think we'll be getting a call before ten p.m.," Max said, and took another sip from his cold coffee. "Let's head over to the Commencement Hotel. See what the eating options are there."

Both Tan and Ashe twisted back and looked at Max sitting in the back seat and nodded, jumped out of the SUV, and took a walk to the only hotel on Roosevelt Island.

AT 9:23 P.M., THEY were all back in the government SUV in position to see the front door of Wei Ming and Jia Li's building when Max's mobile phone buzzed.

"Yes, Jia Li."

"I will put Wei Ming on. He wishes to speak with you."

"Okay," Max said. "Put it on speaker."

"Mr. Valentin."

"Yes, Wei Ming."

"Mr. Valentin, this is very difficult for me. I am heartbroken that my parents were stopped. What do you think that means? Does that mean that they know I am cooperating with you?"

"No, of course not, Wei Ming," Max said. "It may just be that the woman put your family on a no-fly list 'cause that's what they always do. They always do that when they approach a student to cooperate with them. For them, it is a routine precaution."

Wei Ming did not respond.

"Wei Ming, this is a difficult situation. We promised you we would try and we have," Max said. "Isn't that true?"

"Yes, sir."

"We went through a lot to try and get your parents out of China as soon as possible."

"Yes, sir, that is true, and I am very grateful."

"We'll try again when the time is right and we have a plan to do it without the Chinese knowing about it," Max said. "Do you believe we want to get your parents and sister out of China?"

"Yes, sir, I do."

"All right," Max said. "Your family is safe right now. Let's keep focused on what we're trying to do here. Okay?"

"Okay, Mr. Valentin. I will try."

"We'll talk again after you hear from that woman tonight."

"Okay, sir."

"Okay," Max said, hit end on his phone and sat quietly as he looked out at their apartment building.

Teresa Tan and Sam Ashe had faced the windshield throughout Max's brief conversation with Wei Ming and Jia Li, but as soon as the call ended, Max watched them twist around from their front seat again to face him.

"Good job, Max," Ashe said.

"Yeah, good job," Tan said. "Dicey stuff."

"It sure is," Max said. "Let's get out of here."

IT WAS 10:40 P.M. WHEN Max received another call from Wei Ming.

"You there, Jia Li?" Max asked.

"Yes, I am here. It is on the speaker."

"How'd it go, Wei Ming?" Max asked, as they cruised down the FDR Drive back to 26 Federal Plaza.

"The woman said that she was sorry my parents and sister couldn't fly to visit me."

"Geez," Max thought. This ghost recruiter is darn close to the Chinese nation state, or dead center in it, to have been notified so damn fast after the parents' attempt to leave, and then choosing to put it right into Wei Ming's face. As if she's telling him, *We got you, and we want you to know it. But we'll play along with you some.*

"That's consistent with what we were told, Wei Ming," Max said. "Our rep in China spoke to your sister, and she said they took the visas without explanation. They said nothing was out of order, just took the visas and let them go."

"The woman said that after she and I finish their work together, my parents will be permitted to come visit me."

Max asked, "She said, 'come' to the United States, not, 'go' to the United States?"

Wei Ming was silent for a moment. "No, she said, 'come,'" Wei Ming answered. "Is that important, Mr. Valentin?"

"Maybe not," Max said, but 'come' implies that the recruiter was physically in the U.S. Maybe in New York, not directing him from outside the U.S. "Did she seem suspicious? Did she give any impression she wondered about your family's planned visit so soon after she'd first been in contact with you?"

"Not that I could recognize."

Max figured the visas sufficiently convinced the Chinese that the school arranged it with no U.S. government involvement, but he also figured they would still be a bit suspicious of that sudden effort and more attentive, as he would be.

CHAPTER 16
Wednesday, May 24

Max got a text from Jia Li at 6:45 a.m.

"Wei received email fr recruiter. List of names. I took photo. Will send."

The next text from Jia Li was a photo of the email Wei Ming opened on his personal iPhone that Jia Li took a picture of.

It was a list of eight typical Chinese sounding first and last names associated with eight separate U.S. universities:

Wanli Ma, MIT
Wenjing Zhang, UC Berkeley
Shushi Long, University of Maryland
Ying Ji, University of Chicago
Bin Sun, Harvard University
Ye Ding, Princeton University
Zili Cai, University of Colorado
Meng Cheng, Stanford University

"You know these students?" The ghost asked.

Wei Ming replied, "Yes, I know them."

To which the ghost replied, "You have their contact information?"

"Yes. I have their email addresses."

MAX MADE IT INTO THE command center by 7:20 a.m. Parth Mehta was already in.

"The ghost wants to know if Wei Ming knows these students," Max said and looked at Mehta, who was sitting in front of his Mac. "Let's find out if any of their names come up anywhere in our case or any federal investigation."

Mehta got right on it and within minutes answered as he pulled up their records.

"Wanli Ma, no."

"Wenjing Zhang, no."

"Shushi Long, no."

"Ying Ji, no."

"Bin Sun, no."

"Ye Ding, no."

"Zili Cai, no."

"Meng Cheng, no."

Max nodded again, then received another text coming in from Jia Li with another text photo of Wei Ming's reply to the ghost.

The ghost replied, "You, of course, plan to attend the Q conference this weekend?"

Wei Ming replied, "Yes."

The ghost replied, "Determine if they attending."

"Q conference?" Max said out loud.

Mehta went onto the Quantaneo site and the Manhattan University Schimmel Center site and searched for upcoming events, and there it was: Friday, May 26 until Sunday, May 28.

THEY LEARNED THAT THERE was a Quantum Industry conference planned for the approaching weekend at the Schimmel Center. Quantum students and scientists from around the world would be in attendance.

Mehta pulled up the flyer on the big screen.

The IBM Q Network in cooperation with Manhattan University's Schimmel Science Center in New York City.

It will take place on Roosevelt Island, New York City.

The IBM Q Network, & Schimmel Science Center, Manhattan University, Roosevelt Island, New York City, will organize it in collaboration with other local colleagues.

Scope of the conference:

* *Quantum Communications and Quantum Cryptography*

* *Quantum Sensing and Quantum Metrology*

* *Quantum Computing and Quantum Simulation*

* *Quantum Networks*

* *Quantum Information Theory*

* *Quantum Control and Quantum Engineering*

* *Foundations of Quantum Physics*

Latest news:

The nominations for the International Quantum Award "for outstanding achievements in quantum science research" are open until Friday, April 7.

In 2000, scientists and engineers established the International Conference on Quantum Computing (QC) to encourage and bring together individuals working in the interdisciplinary field of quantum information science and technology.

Max texted Jia Li, "Can you meet me at the Ninetieth Street ferry? We need to find out about the Q Conference this weekend."

Within minutes, Jia Li replied, "Yes. I can be there by 3:30."

Max replied, "Ok, c u then."

MAX TOOK HIS STRIKE force car up to the Upper East Side to meet Jia Li, recognizing that as the case picked up momentum, he could not rely on mass transportation to get him where he needed to be in a hurry.

He parked it a couple of blocks away. He could've pulled the car right up onto the promenade and walkway that led to the Ninetieth Street ferry and toss an official law enforcement police business plaque onto the dashboard, but that would have made it too easy for anyone enjoying the walkway or going to or from the ferry to notice him and the vehicle, and wonder what law enforcement was doing there. And of course, not only would that draw attention to him, but it would draw attention to Jia Li when she arrived. So, he parked on a police only parking space, with other police vehicles, on East End Avenue in front of Gracie Mansion.

As usual, he'd arrived before she did, and looked at his ePhone to see the GPS tracking on her Fitbit and her ePhone as the ferry traveled across the East River from Roosevelt Island to East Ninetieth Street.

The sky was a rich blue, not a cloud to be seen up and down the river. It was in the low sixties. The navy blue and gold City of New York flagpole under Gracie Mansion on the promenade rhythmically lifted and waved as he walked by it on his way to the ferry.

Max took a seat on a bench nearby and immediately stood up when he spotted Jia Li just coming off the ramp of the boat. She waved at him, wearing a jean jacket, black leotards, and white running shoes. She was a dancer indeed. It seemed her heels never touched the ground, as if she was walking over air vents that lifted her up just a touch above. All toes. Swinging her arms with perfect precision. He couldn't help breaking into a grin. Her grace reminded him of the marine corps silent drill team. Absolute precision.

When she approached him, he said, "Thanks for sending me that photo of the email he received. You recognize any of the names?"

She nodded. "Oh yes. I have often seen their names come up in the organization's newsletter about different issues relating to quantum that they may have been involved in at their university. Wei Ming and my name have also been sometimes mentioned in the newsletter. I have met all of them, in fact."

"You've had direct contact with all of them?" Max asked to be sure he heard her right.

"Yes. All of us in the Schimmel Quantum program attend the four Q conferences each year: there are two each semester. We all attended the quantum conference last in January at the University of Southern California. All those eight students were in attendance, too. I had the opportunity to meet them all over that weekend."

Max took that in for a minute. "Who's tracking them?" he asked. "You're here. Is your NSB tracking them at those other schools?"

Jia Li nodded. "Yes, but I have not been given information. I do not know what the status of their situation is."

"If we need to find out, can you do that?"

"Yes, of course."

All Max could think was that the Taiwanese NSB was proving to be a very sharp intelligence outfit.

Jia Li went on to explain that they have held the spring conference every year for the last few years during the Cherry Blossom Festival weekend on Roosevelt Island.

"Yes, I noticed the cherry blossoms," Max said, feeling the need to make small talk, if only for a moment. The immensity of what was at stake in this investigation was bearing down on him. "I guess you're also familiar with the cherry blossoms in Washington D.C. that open up every year. It's a big event. Are you familiar with that?"

Jia Li smiled her radiant smile and said, "Yes. I am."

"The cherry blossoms originated in China, didn't they?" Max couldn't help smiling to himself for having Googled it the night before.

Jia Li, still smiling, "Yes, the cherry blossoms are very popular in my country as well, and, you know, you may find this silly, but one reason I chose to attend the Schimmel Center was because of the annual Cherry Blossom Festival here."

"Is that right?" Max asked. "The NSB gave you a choice of where you wanted to attend?"

"Yes. They did. I had been offered the opportunity to attend several schools to pursue my PhD and keep my eye on a Chinese student or two also registered. The Schimmel Center was on their list," Jia Li said. "But when I learned of the annual Cherry Blossom Festival that takes place here, I thought, I will attend the Schimmel Center. It is a good sign. Don't you agree?"

"Yes, I suppose so," Max said, and felt his face heat up a bit as she held his gaze.

Jia Li provided Max with more information about how they organized the conference, explaining that they followed the usual weekend format for setting it up.

"Most of the attendees stay at the Commencement Hotel here on Roosevelt Island," Jia Li said. "Essentially, attendees occupy the entire hotel for the weekend, and as the hosting school, we make all the arrangements. However, some visitors may choose to stay at the homes of friends, family, or with students or faculty of our school."

"What about transportation for those not staying on the island?" Max asked. "Does the school arrange for buses to get the guests to the school?"

"Other conferences, yes, sometimes, but not here. The Schimmel Center feels if you're not staying on the island, there are enough ways to get to the center through mass transportation. Either the tram or the subway or the ferry," Jia Li said. "And using a bus to transport visitors to the center is not practical since the only way to travel onto the island by motor vehicle is to go over the Thirty-Sixth Avenue Bridge from the Borough of Queens. As you know."

Max nodded.

Jia Li went on to explain that the conference would start on Friday with a cocktail period and dinner, then Professor Kleinheidt, as the Director of the Schimmel Science Center's Quantum Program, would welcome everyone to the conference, acknowledge the schools and companies represented in attendance, some other scientists by name, and summarize what would take place over the weekend.

Then the next day the conference would begin with different presentations going on simultaneously in different classrooms or in one or more of the auditoriums throughout the day, which would include bagels and muffins and coffee and tea in the morning, lunch in the afternoon in the café, and after the presentations of the day on Saturday, there would be a formal dinner, with several keynote speakers, and Sunday more presentations until 12:30 in the afternoon, after which visitors were welcome to stay for lunch or travel home.

"Are you directly involved in any of the preparations?"

"Oh, yes. They directly involve all the students in the quantum program. Even some other PhD students in different programs will assist, because it is a big event. But we, Wei Ming and I, and the others are directly involved."

"Do you know which of the presentations each of the visitors has chosen to attend?"

"Yes. We must know, otherwise we don't know what size room to assign for the lecture or presentation."

"Do you have that information?"

"I do."

Max nodded and knew that having that information would be a very useful. Knowing beforehand what presentations the eight targeted by the ghost planned to attend would be good to know.

"I assume Wei Ming also has access to it."

Jia Li nodded. "Yes, he does. And there can be little doubt that the woman will ask for it."

"We need a copy."

"Of course."

"Thank you," Max said and drifted into thought.

He wondered why the ghost was targeting those eight? There were hundreds if not more students working on quantum at universities all over the country, many more who were ethnic Chinese. So, what was it about those eight that particularly interested the Chinese?

He looked away from Jia Li and across the East River. It was not the eight students who were the targets, Max thought. It was the university research, of course. The students were just their passkeys in, or so the Chinese spy recruiter hoped. But then why target those eight research schools?

"Jia Li," Max looked over at her. "Let me ask you something?"

She immediately turned to Max.

"There are many universities working on quantum in the United States, and many more students than just those eight working on quantum, right?"

"Yes, over one thousand I would estimate."

"So, why do you think they would select those eight?"

"Well, those universities are the finest," Jia Li said. "They are most advanced in their research."

"Who says?" Max asked. "Does the quantum research community have that opinion?"

Jia Li took a moment before answering. Max could see a light go on in her eyes.

"Well, yes. How could I not think of this? Those universities are of particular interest because they are actively working on algorithms to resist quantum computing capacity when it is fully developed."

"What?"

"Besides working on the development of a fully operational quantum computer, we are working on algorithms to resist quantum."

"Wait a second, wait a second," Max said. "Are you saying that even though quantum is not developed enough to speed up solving anything right now, there are scientists working on ways to resist it—with algorithms, you say—when people start using it?"

"Yes."

Max looked at Jia Li in a daze, then paused and thought about it. This development blew him away.

"Jia Li," Max started, "the quantum science community and our governments are thinking so far ahead that not only are we working on getting a quantum computer up and running, but we recognize that once it is up and running, that our adversaries around the world will eventually have access to its power too, and it will then be used against us to decrypt the encryptions protecting our data today?"

"Yes," Jia Li said again. "That is exactly so. The United States National Quantum Initiative has awarded each of our universities the opportunity to compete to discover these resistant algorithms.

Our universities have been selected to be National Quantum Initiative Post Quantum Cryptography research centers."

Max sat there without a word for several moments, looked away from her again, and then had a moment of remembrance that the National Quantum Initiative Act had been signed into law a couple of years earlier. That's it. That's why the ghost was interested in those students at those universities.

Max then looked back at Jia Li. "And the Schimmel Center is tasked with not only getting a quantum computer up and running, but tasked with finding algorithms that quantum cannot break when it is discovered?"

"Exactly," Jia Li said. "We know China is currently stealing data from countless companies and governments institutions around the world that they cannot read because they cannot break the encryption but are storing it with the hopes to decrypt the protections and read everyone's secrets when quantum computers can. The strategy is called Store Now—Decrypt Later."

"Did you say steal now—decrypt later?"

Jia Li smiled. "No, I said 'store' not 'steal,' but that is truly what is taking place. They are stealing now and storing what they are stealing with plans to decrypt later."

"Steal now decrypt later, hmm," Max repeated, then pulled out his ePhone and called the command center. Sam Ashe answered.

"Yeah, Max."

"Sam, listen, that National Quantum Initiative Act you mentioned..."

"Yeah, signed into law a couple years ago—2020."

"Sam, reach out to somebody coordinating that program. I just found out from Jia Li that each of the eight students the ghost is targeting are attending university research centers—including Schimmel—that are working on discovering algorithms that will resist quantum."

"Wait a second, Max," Ashe said. "You're saying these eight—plus Schimmel—are working on algorithms to resist quantum even though it's not developed yet?"

"Yes."

"Wow, wow."

Max continued, "These nine centers have been designated by that initiative to work on this quantum resistance research."

"Wow," Ashe said again.

"Here's what I want you to look into," Max said. "See if you can find out from the program coordinator if any recent attempts were made to hack any of the algorithm research at those universities?"

There was silence again.

"Sam, you still there?"

"Oh, yeah, I'm still here, Max," Ashe said.

"I know. It's darn intriguing, isn't it?" Max said. "Listen, maybe the Chinese tried to do a smash-and-grab, and they couldn't get access."

"Oh, yeah, that's excellent," Ashe said. "You're thinking the ghost maybe tried to hack those research centers for quantum algorithm resistance data and couldn't break in, and that's why they're chasing those students, including Wei Ming."

"Exactly," Max said.

"I'm on it," Ashe said, and hung up.

After punching the red end button on his ePhone, Max was lost in thought for a few moments, then he looked up at Jia Li.

"That was quite impressive."

"What?" Max asked.

"You're jumping to the hypothesis that the Chinese have targeted Wei Ming and the others. The possibility that they attempted to hack into those research centers, including The Schimmel Center, and were unsuccessful."

Max smiled and could feel his face heat up a bit again.

"Well, I don't know about impressive," Max said. "It's just a logical possibility."

"That is abductive reasoning you just exhibited," Jia Li said with excitement. "We learned about that investigative approach in training. Deduction comes from facts. But abductive reasoning comes from experience. In abduction you arrive at a hypothesis and see if the seemingly unrelated piece of information could fit."

Max smiled over Jia Li's observation and thought somebody should tell Roach about abductive reasoning and continued, "The Chinese often look for other ways to get the data they want before they commit to recruiting people. Cyber hacks of universities' databases are the ideal place to start. If they can get the data from the hack, there's no urgency to recruit. And it's been our experience that universities are a little easier to hack than private companies. All the Chinese need to do is drop a phishing communication to somebody with a link. Usually, a professor who believes it's a legitimate link and opens it, and they're in the school's computer network or they use social engineering to get in by impersonating a professor who asks the university IT person to reset their password."

"Of course, that makes entire sense the Chinese would do that," Jia Li said. "Try to get what they want through digital intrusion first."

"And not just the Chinese. There's another three major theft/disruption players in that game too," Max said. "Iran, Russia, and North Korea. There was a huge hack by Iran a couple of years ago. Hackers hacked over three hundred universities in the U.S. and universities in twenty-one other countries after professors all over the world opened the compromised link."

"Including my country," Jia Li said, cutting in.

"That's right," Max said. "Over a hundred thousand professor accounts worldwide were compromised, including Taiwan, along with five U.S. government agencies."

"Staggering."

"It is," Max said. "The estimated value of IP lost was three to four billion."

"Staggering," Jia Li repeated.

Max nodded, then felt the vibration of a text from his personal iPhone. The text read, "Max... any chance you can pick up twins @ jiujitsu ... I can't get out of hospital in time... babysitter in car accident... she's ok... but delayed."

Max jumped up from the bench. "I have to go, Jia Li, I'm sorry. I'll be in touch."

"Is there something wrong?" she asked, looking up at Max.

"No, well, it's family."

"Can I help?"

Max shook his head. "My sister can't get out of work to pick up my niece and nephew from jiujitsu, so I need to get them."

"Jiujitsu?" Jia Li asked with a smile.

"Ahh, yes, jiujitsu."

Jia Li reached for Max's hand and held his eyes. "Let me go with you. We can talk more about the conference and the eight students on the way."

Max froze, taking that in. Knowing, absolutely knowing, it was just not a good idea. Not a good idea at all. But, he thought, Jia Li is not a target or suspect. She's a colleague, a fellow government espionage investigative agent, she was part of their team. It was not unusual to become friendlier with a fellow agent. No? Not unusual to have a fellow agent in your vehicle to discuss a case. Right? Of course, not.

They could use the ride up and back to talk about the targeted eight, like she said. He could live with that. But he also could not deny that if he'd been having that conversation with Tan or Ashe or just about any other agent, he would insist they get back to work, (and in Jia Li's case back to school and work) and he would get on with that personal family issue.

"They're in the Bronx," Max blurted. "Riverdale."

Jia Li let go of Max's hand, stood up, and said, "Okay, let us go." With a smile that made it feel like all the walkers and ferry travelers had gone silent, the jet skis cruising north on the East River had put on their brakes, and the City of New York's flag suddenly fell dormant.

Max finally broke out in language again. "Okay, me follow. I mean, I mean, follow me. Nearby car parked." *What the fuck?* He thought. *What was that?*

As they strutted to his car, one thing he was clear about—he was clear about omitting from his notes any reference to her joining him to pick up his sister's twins. With that thought, he shook his head with a sinking feeling.

MAX OPENED THE PASSENGER front door for Jia Li, and she got in. He jogged around the front of the car, jumped in himself, whipped out of the parking space outside Gracie Mansion, jumped on the northbound entrance of the FDR Drive at East Ninety-Sixth Street and zigged and zagged his way up. No lights or siren. He wouldn't even think of doing that on a personal errand. Not a chance. But it didn't mean he was going to drive like grandpa. He needed to get up to the twins' jiujitsu school quickly.

They were now going under the entrance of the George Washington Bridge lower level, heading west, grabbing the exit to the Henry Hudson Parkway northbound and cruised up.

They rode in complete silence. Not so much as glancing at each other. Eyes fixed on the windshield. What happened to furthering their discussion, he wondered.

Max pulled into a space directly in front of the Jiujitsu Warriors storefront on Riverdale Avenue. They were ten minutes early. Max was relieved. By the time he came around the car to open the door for Jia Li, she was already out.

As soon as they stepped in, the owner of the school, Steve Dahut, a retired NYPD sergeant, instructor, and owner of the school, attired in his white jiujitsu outfit, a black belt around his waist, gave Max a simulated fist bump and nodded to the twins in the opposite corner. Jia Li bowed to Dahut, one fist cupped in her other hand, as if in prayer, which he returned with a grin from ear to ear.

Each of the twins were paired off with two other seven-year-olds of the opposite sex as they practiced grabbing the garment of their opponent, twisting the other kid over their hip, and awkwardly flipping them down to the mat. In each case, Jess and Ben were doing the flipping. After the twins straightened up, pressed down on their white outfits with yellow belts, they got ready to be flipped by their opponents. Max and Jia Li slid over to the bench up against a mirror on the west wall of the studio and sat with the other adults, watching the action.

There were about eight kids working on their technique. The instructor, a teenage girl with a brown belt, and her opponent, a teenage boy also with a brown belt, were in the center of the mat, surrounded by four couples of seven-to ten-year-olds. After the unsynchronized flips, the teenage instructors went to each of the coupled-off kids and reminded them of how the flip was executed. The kids worked at it. It was tough for them to get the hang of maneuvering their hips under their opponent.

"My goodness, they are cute," Jia Li said.

"Yeah," Max said, with an uncle-love grin.

"Have they been doing this long?" Jia Li asked. "They are very good."

Max hesitated before answering.

"They started last year, right after their father died."

Jia Li's head twisted to look at Max with a snap. After several moments Max could feel Jia Li's gaze, turned to her, and nodded.

"I am so sorry to hear this, Max," Jia Li said, and looked back at the twins twisting and flipping. "So sorry to hear this."

"Yeah, too young to not have a father," Max said, also focused on the twins.

Jia Li turned to Max again and put her two hands over his and said, "But they have you."

Max nodded but did not look at her. He could feel her eyes reaching out to him.

At that moment, he couldn't turn.

The seven-year-old girl Ben was practicing with was having some trouble flipping him, so he whispered to her, trying to explain how it's done. Eventually, she got it and flipped Ben down to the mat. Ben didn't give away at all that he'd really flipped himself.

"That was great, Maryann," Ben said. "Really great."

Jess had no trouble at all getting her hip under the overweight little boy they matched her against and flipped him fast but pulled back to break his fall.

"Okay, kids, that was great. That's all for this afternoon. See you all ncxt Thursday," the female teenage instructor announced.

After the four coupled-off group of kids stood at attention, faced the center where the two instructors were standing and bowed, Max noticed Jia Li quickly wipe a tear from her eye.

As soon as the twins looked around for their babysitter, they spotted their Uncle Max sitting on the bench, raced over and crashed into him. All motion and sound.

"Did you see us, Uncle Max?" Jess asked. "Did you see us?"

"We've been practicing." Ben then said again, "We've been practicing."

"I saw you guys. You both looked great."

The twins each grabbed one of Max's arms and pulled him to the mat. "Come, we want to show you how it's done."

"Whoa, wait a minute, guys, I want to introduce you to somebody," Max said and looked at Jia Li. "This is my friend, Jia Li."

"Hi, Jia Li," Jess immediately extended her hand to shake hers. "My pleasure to meet you."

"My pleasure to meet you, Jess," Jia Li said. "You are very good."

"Thank you," Jess said with a heart-melting smile.

Max looked at Ben, who was silent. "Introduce yourself to Jia Li, Ben."

Words finally came from Ben's lips. "Wow, you're pretty."

Max let out a laugh.

"Thank you, Ben, that's very kind of you to say."

Ben then extended his hand and shook hers with a blush.

"Okay, Uncle Max," the twins said and picked up where they'd left off, each grabbing a hand and pulled him in the mat's direction.

Max looked to the jiujitsu studio owner to make sure that was okay, who gave Max an enthusiastic thumbs-up.

"Okay, guys, show me how it's done."

The kids each took a shot at bringing Max down to the mat, which he submitted to with a flourish. "Wow, you guys are excellent."

As Max stood up, the twins ran over to Jia Li, each grabbing a hand and dragged her to the mat.

"Try to do that to Uncle Max, Jia Li," Jess said with a resonating joy.

"Yeah, you try it," Ben followed up with. "But you can't. He's too big."

"Are you sure you want me to try that with your Uncle Max?"

The twins screamed with excitement, "Yes!"

"You okay with this?" Max said in a whisper. "I'll just let you flip me over."

"I'm okay. Are you ready?"

Max nodded with a confident smile. Then his view of the universe changed in an instant.

Jia Li grabbed his jacket, twisted into Max, and flipped him up and around like he was a geisha girl, landing him on the mat with a thump.

The studio went silent.

He couldn't move. The last thing he remembered seeing was a flash of the fluorescent light in the ceiling before he landed on his back.

Max moved. And the entire studio erupted into applause. The kids were beside themselves in laughter, having just witnessed a beautiful young woman flip a full-size man who had at least 100 pounds on her on to his back with ease.

"Oh, my goodness, Max," Jia Li said, leaning down to him, touching his face. Her face inches from his. "Was that too hard? I'm so sorry."

Max smiled. "I'll live."

With that, the twins were on top of their Uncle Max and helped him get up from the mat. Max exaggerated his rising a bit, more or less. Looked like martial arts was also taught to NSB agents—scientists or not.

"How about ice cream?" Max said.

"Yeah," the twins said simultaneously as they put their little backpacks on, each plastered with male and female images of ninjas. "Can we have strawberry sundaes, Uncle Max?"

"You bet."

AFTER MAX BROUGHT THE twins up to their mom who had made it home by then—leaving Jia Li in the car to wait for him—he was back in the car with her, heading south on the Henry Hudson

Parkway when his ePhone rang on the dashboard. He could see it was Teresa Tan.

He hit the button on his steering wheel and answered, "Hey, Teresa, what's up?"

Teresa's voice circled around the interior of his car. He wondered if he should tell Teresa that Jia Li was sitting right next to him. Of course, he should. Jia Li was an agent. But why did he even hesitate? He knew why.

"Hey, Max, did..."

"Teresa, I'm not alone," Max said, cutting her off.

He hated when calling somebody in their vehicle and they didn't have the courtesy of telling him up front there was somebody else in the car with them.

"Oh, I'm sorry Max, call me when you can. We got something."

Now he was up against his decision of letting Jia Li take the ride with him to pick up the twins. It's always the little things that catch up with you. Teresa had something to say about the case, but should he tell her to continue?

Or, tell Tan that he would call her back, so he could filter whatever that something was before sharing it with Jia Li, which would show Jia Li that, although she was part of the team, apparently not enough a part of the team to listen to Tan's information unfiltered.

Max took a shot. He would tell Tan to continue, but secretly hoped she would have the wherewithal to know this was not the time. In fact, he then recognized he shouldn't have answered at all, but that would have been just as bad. Jia Li would see Tan's name on the dashboard-caller ID and wonder why he would not answer.

"No worries, go right ahead. Jia Li's in the car with me."

There was a long pause.

"Teresa?" Max said.

"Oh, hey, hi Jia Li."

"Hi, Teresa."

"Listen, Max, it can wait. Call me when you can."

"Where are you?" Max asked.

"Command center."

"Okay. We're just heading back into the city from my sister's."

There was another long pause.

Max continued, "While I was talking to Jia Li about the Q conference, I got a text from Maya who was at work that the twins' babysitter was in a car accident and couldn't pick the kids up from jiujitsu."

Man did Max hate having to explain himself.

"Babysitter okay?"

"Yeah, no injuries but delayed," Max said. "The twins are back home."

"Good, okay, call me when you can," Tan said. "Bye, Jia Li."

"Bye Teresa," Jia Li said, and the call went dead.

Max then flipped the siren on and put the red misery lights (as Richard Price described it in his terrific novel, *Lush Life*) on the dashboard and flew down the Henry Hudson Parkway, under the George Washington Bridge, down the FDR Drive, off on East Sixty-Second Street exit, west to Second Avenue, south on Second Avenue, cut the lights and siren and pulled up on the corner of East Sixtieth Street.

They were silent the rest of the ride back.

"Okay, I hope you don't mind taking the tram across," Max said, jumped out of the car to come around, but Jia Li again was already out of the car.

"Will you update me later?"

"I will," Max said, as he jogged back around to the driver's side. "Thanks for taking the ride up with me. We'll be talking."

Max pulled out without looking back.

AS SOON AS HE DROVE a few blocks away from the Roosevelt Tram station, he pulled over again and called Teresa. What was that all about? Why didn't he insist Tan tell him what she had in Jia Li's presence?

Again, if it had been any other colleague he was working the same case with, he would not have hesitated to have Tan detail what she had in that colleague's presence, but because of what was stirring in him with Jia Li, he hesitated, even though one thing had nothing to do with the other. Max shook his head. Funny how the mind works, he thought. He didn't want to reveal anything about his feelings and ended up giving himself up about it.

"Hey," Teresa answered.

"Hi, sorry I couldn't speak with you before," Max said. "What's up?"

There was another long pause.

"Listen, Max, I don't want to be out of line here," Teresa said, "but what's up with you and this Taiwanese agent?"

There it was—Teresa picked up on it, making clear Jia Li was strictly business—a foreign agent, strictly business. And she was absolutely right. And he would not try to waltz around it. This case was too damn important to complicate business with private stuff, and that's just what he'd done by bringing her up to the Bronx to meet the twins.

"Nothing's up, Teresa," Max said. "Lapse in judgment. I got caught off guard when I got that urgent babysitter text from my sister while I was talking to Jia Li."

Max waited for Tan to say something else. He knew she wasn't done.

"Max, I got to ask you if you've been with her?"

Now it was Max's turn to pause.

"No, Teresa," Max said, but knew that if there had been a follow-up question along the lines of "do you want to be with her," well...

"Listen, you're a great boss, and I know she's a looker," Teresa said. "I'd probably give her a toss myself if I didn't have Denise."

Max let out a laugh. "That's comforting to hear."

"You know I'm kidding, but are you okay continuing to be in such direct contact with her?" Teresa asked. "Has she touched you, Max? You know what mean? In that way?"

Max remained silent and shook his head. If Teresa only knew. Here Teresa was trying to protect him from himself.

"You want me to run interference for you, Max?" Tan asked. "I can be her direct contact going forward?"

It would've made good sense for Teresa to handle Jia Li from here on out, and if the circumstances were different, he would've done just that, but he was now married to Jia Li, so to speak. He had to handle her directly and, not only that, just the thought of no longer being in direct contact with her brought an immediate ache to his chest. *For crying out loud,* he thought. It felt a bit like flying a kite without a string.

But he couldn't let this take him out. He had one minor overt lapse in judgment in bringing her up to Riverdale and couldn't change that. Time would tell if collaborating with Jia Li would turn into a major covert lapse in judgment.

But, in what Teresa Tan was raising, nothing happened, nothing really, he thought, and nothing was going to happen, he asserted. He would stay focused. No more leaks into his personal life. And no more damn poetry!

"Not necessary, Teresa," Max said. "I can handle it."

Silence.

"That's that then," Tan said. "You coming back downtown?"

"Yeah. I'll be there in about twenty minutes," Max said into the car dashboard as he jumped on the FDR south to 26 Federal Plaza.

"Great. Sam said he has something for you."

WHEN MAX RETURNED TO the command center, Tan, Ashe, and Mehta were there.

"Max, I spoke to the administrator of the Quantum Initiative in D.C.," Ashe said.

"Okay."

"Well," Ashe said with a big smile, "you nailed it. The administrator operates out of the National Institute of Standards and Technology. NIST. A Dr. Araceli Venegas-Gomez."

"Quantum Initiative. What's that again?" Tan asked. "Why's that familiar?"

Mehta jumped in, "National Quantum Initiative Act. Legislation that funds quantum research."

"Except, I just learned from Jia Li that even though quantum is still in development," Max said, "China and our other adversaries are doing what is called Steal Now Decrypt Later aka SNDL."

"Excuse me," Tan said.

"The Chinese know quantum computing is coming, and they will eventually have access to it, like most of the tech world," Max said.

Ashe jumped in, "True. We may develop it enough first, but eventually everyone will have it. It'll be like the Internet. It started here, but the world now has it."

"Right," Max said. "So, the Chinese know once they have quantum, they'll be able to decrypt the cryptography protecting all our secrets."

Tan jumped back in, "Let me get this. You're saying with that 'steal now decrypt later' thing the Chinese are stealing data now and saving it because they know quantum is coming and they'll then be able to decrypt it."

"That's it," Max said. "They're stealing and storing now, then in ten, twenty years down the road when quantum is fully developed, they'll crack the encryption and get access to our stuff."

"That's darn intriguing," Mehta said.

"Yeah, the breach is being compared to a submarine that dives deep and collects your data, but they can't yet read it because it's encrypted," Max said. "But when quantum arrives and they decrypt the data, the submarine will resurface with all your stuff. Imagine any heavy R & D industry like aviation, medicine, military data. They will then have access to the designs and formulas that they stole ten to twenty years earlier."

"So, what the hell are we doing about it?" Tan practically shouted.

"The word is scientists are working on something called post quantum cryptography a.k.a. PQC. Quantum cryptography schemes that will resist being cracked by quantum when it lands," Max said.

"Oh, man," Tan said. "This is giving me a headache."

Ashe continued. "The way it works is they, NIST, in collaboration with the Energy Department and the National Science Foundation, select the research centers they will fund. There are currently nine, as Jia Li said. Five are what they call National QIS Research Centers, and four are what they call Multidisciplinary Centers for Quantum Research and Education," Ashe looked at his notes. "Schimmel is recognized as a QIS Research Center, and the other eight are one or the other. But they are all detailed to work on post quantum cryptography algorithms."

"So, was there a hack attempt at any of them?" Max asked.

"All of them, Max," Ashe said. "All of them. Since early January some unidentified bad actor has been spear phishing the professors at each of the research centers and reported it to NIST right away, but none of them took the bait. Dr. Gomez said they have schooled the researchers to not open links they're not one hundred percent certain are legit."

"So, the phishing attempts weren't made at the same time, but spread out since January?" Max asked.

"Exactly."

"When was the last attempt and what research center?" Tan asked.

"Ironically, the last phishing attempt was the Schimmel Center. They emailed Professor Kleinheidt. The sender pretended to be another university professor at a university in the Netherlands and suggested the professor open the link. The email message alleged it would provide some valuable quantum research that can speed up the semiconductor lithography process," Ashe said. "But Kleinheidt Googled the name of the alleged professor who sent the email and then reached out to that professor directly."

"And the Dutch professor never sent it," Max said.

"Exactly."

"I assume NIST reported it to DOJ," Max said. "Do we know who was doing the phishing?"

"We do, indeed," Ashe said. "People's Liberation Army Unit: 61398."

"Bingo!" Tan said again.

"61398," Mehta repeated. "The PLA unit that dumped malware into Google back in oh nine?"

"The very same," Ashe said. "The second bureau of the PLA's general staff department's Third Department."

Max could not help but blink when Sam Ashe rattled off the official name of the PLA unit. "So, that's got to be what's driving this recruitment effort," Max said. "And NIST said they're each working on an algorithm?"

"Oh yeah. He said that each of the nine research centers is working on a separate algorithm."

Max nodded. "Designed to protect the integrity of the research. Separate compartments."

"That's exactly right," Ashe said.

"Did he mention at all if any of the research centers have come up with an algorithm, so to speak?" Max asked. "I assume each research center is at various stages of their contribution to coming up with one?"

"Yes, all eight centers, plus Schimmel, have completed their work on separate PQC algorithms that are being reviewed now."

IT WAS 9:25 P.M. WHEN Max made it to his apartment; dropped a brown bag of sushi and his keys and Glock onto his dining room table, pulled off his blue blazer, dropped it on the back of one of the dining room chairs, stepped over to his refrigerator, came back to the table with a bottle of Snapple ice tea, twisted off the cap, turned the cap over and looked down to read the "Real Facts" inscription inside: *The smallest county in America is New York County, better known as Manhattan.*

He pulled his miso soup out of the brown paper bag, placed it on the table mat, and pulled out his sushi platter with its assortment of colors and shapes. Max sometimes wondered if he ate sushi for its taste, or more for the aesthetic effects of all those colors. It did not have an aroma that would make your mouth water, and without the soy sauce, he'd have to admit the sushi was pretty bland. Maybe he ate sushi because it was a fish. "Healthy, after all."

Max shook his head with that thought, pulled out a couple tubes of soy sauce, ripped off the tops, two at a time, and poured them into one corner of the clear plastic covering that came with the platter, mixed a little wasabi into it with one chopstick, grabbed the other chopstick, picked up a spicy tuna roll, dunked it into the sauce, raised it to his mouth when his ePhone rang.

He lowered the tuna roll—a brown, white, green work of art—back down, and answered. It was Wei Ming.

"Good evening, Wei Ming," Max answered.

"Good evening, Mr. Valentin. I just got off the phone with the woman."

"Is Jia Li there?"

"I am here.".

"Good. What did she have to say?" Max asked, as he wiped his hands with a napkin. Not that they'd gotten dirty.

"She asked me many, many questions about the arrangement for the quantum conference. Many questions. She wants me to find out what lectures the eight students have registered to attend. She wants me to find that out and give her that information," Wei Ming said. "What should I do?"

"Give her the information, Wei Ming. It's confidential information, but it's not R & D," Max said.

"That makes excellent sense," Jia Li reinforced.

"Yes, of course, thank you," Wei Ming said and fell into silence.

"Did you ask her about receiving your compensation?" Max asked.

"Oh, oh, she gave me a password and the twelve-word recovery phrase for a cryptocurrency account."

"No kidding, they're using the blockchain to pay you," Max said. "What wallet service?"

"Inframax," Wei Ming said.

"Really, very good," Max said, and immediately he could feel his heart rate picking up the pace. He drifted over to his night table in his bedroom to retrieve the oximeter and returned to the dining room table.

A couple of weeks earlier, he'd had a FaceTime conversation with an old high school buddy of his who had attended NYU Medical School, fell in love with another medical school student from Prince George, British Columbia, moved to Canada after medical school with her, and started a family practice.

His friend had recommended he pick up an oximeter to monitor his heart rate. Why? Because his buddy said that when the right girl comes into his life, and he's in her presence, or had just been in her presence, he should check his heart rate, and if it's over ninety beats per minutes, she's the one. He ordered one from Amazon as a gag, but he could sense that the oximeter might come in handy for other reasons.

"And you asked her about it?"

"I did not have to. She brought it up and said that my first payment of ten thousand dollars was in the account and that I could draw from it whenever I liked."

Max put his index finger into the oximeter. His resting heart rate was normally about sixty. His heart was beating sixty-eight beats per minute.

"Okay, Wei Ming, go into the Inframax wallet and see if you have access to the funds," Max said. "We'll talk tomorrow. Have a good night."

"I will sir, good night," Wei Ming said.

"Good night," Jia Li said as well.

Right after Max got off the phone with Wei Ming and Jia Li, he emailed a message to Parth Mehta for him to follow up on the Inframax password and recovery phrase first thing in the morning, and finally put a piece of sushi in his mouth.

As he slowly chewed, pondering the ghost's use of cryptocurrency to pay off Wei Ming, he realized he'd never told Jia Li what he learned from Jack Hunt about the tram-murdered professor and his association with the Chinese military.

He again had a flickering thought, like he'd had earlier when Hunt told him Professor John Xu's alias was Zhang Kan, only this time it was more intense. The name sounded familiar.

But why, he wondered. Where had he heard that name before?

Then it hit him. He grabbed his ePhone and poked Jia Li's name.

"Do you know if Wei Ming knew about the professor's murder?" Max asked.

"I do not know. We never discussed it," Jia Li said. "I would not be surprised if he never knew about it. He was always very deep in his studies. I never once saw him watch or read the news online or otherwise. We never discussed the news. And if it was not for my government position, my attention would not have been drawn to a murder occurring in a global city like New York, either."

"Even though it happened on the Roosevelt Island tram?"

"Yes, I think so," Jia Li said. "The tram is public transportation. I would not have immediately known how unusual an event such as that would have been in this city. Additionally, I was completely absorbed in our studies too."

"All right, show Wei Ming the *New York Times* article that covered the homicide. There's a website university photo of the dead professor in the paper. Ask him if he's ever seen that professor before." Max said. "Should I send you the link?"

"No, no, unnecessary. I can retrieve it. I will bring him back down and show it to him immediately. Very important to do," Jia Li said, and Max could hear her then clear her throat. "Ahh, Max..."

"Yes."

"I just want to tell you how much I enjoyed spending time with you today and with Ben and Jess. They are beautiful children. Thank you for inviting me to Riverdale. It was so much fun."

It was now time to get into what he had to get into with Jia Li.

He cleared his throat too, his heart rate had risen, Teresa Tan's concerns on his mind. He knew he had to lower the temperature on this simmering stew.

"Are you still there, Max?"

"Ahh, yes, I'm here."

He placed his index finger back in the oximeter. It had risen to seventy-seven. He shook his head.

"Ahh, Jia Li, in the future, if what you need to tell me is not directly related to our investigation, please don't share it with me, and that goes the same for me. When I reach out to you for any reason, it will be strictly directed to our investigation."

Consummate and screeching silence followed.

"Do you understand?"

"I am sorry if anything I did has created a problem for you."

"Jia Li, what we're working on is too important to let anything distract us."

"I do not feel distracted."

"Good, let's keep it that way," Max said. "When friendships develop between colleagues, it can taint one's judgment if things get dicey."

"Do not colleagues often get to know more about each other's personal lives?"

"Yes, but this is different."

"How is it different?" Jia Li asked. "Surely you must know much about Teresa and Sam's private lives."

"Some, but this is different."

"How is it different?"

Max was at a loss for words. He checked his pulse on the oximeter. It now registered at ninety-two beats per minute.

"You know it is, Jia Li."

Jia Li did not respond.

"Call me back as soon as Wei Ming sees the photo, please," Max said and hung up.

WITHIN MINUTES, HE received Jia Li's reply.

"Yes. He is in shock and frightened... the murdered man is the Chinese contact who approached him in China."

Max could hardly believe it. The Chinese contact who had approached Wei Ming in China before he came to the States and stayed in touch with him until he was passed on to the ghost recruiter was tram-murdered Professor John Xu.

Then Max got a text from *OJO*. "Target Zhao Hua moved off Roosevelt Island to one- hundred-twenty-second and Broadway this afternoon. A/O Kings University. Has not departed location since. Will advise."

"Kings University," Max whispered, then thought, *that was sudden.*

CHAPTER 17
Thursday, May 25

After Max parked in the underground garage at 26 Federal Plaza, he popped over to a *Pret a Manger* and picked up a half dozen coffees with cream and sugar on the side and a bag of heated butter croissants, jumped on the elevator up to his office, launched his blue blazer onto the coat tree, pulled out his notepad from his black backpack, stuffed it into his back pocket, dropped the backpack on his desk chair, grabbed the coffees and bag of croissants, and got back on the elevator down to the command center.

Only Parth Mehta was in. Max knew Tan and Ashe would float in soon enough and placed the coffees and croissants on the coffee table over by the side of the center.

"Ahh, thanks, Max," Mehta said as he got up from facing his Mac and walked directly to the coffee table. "No time to pick up anything on the way in. Sanjay kept us up all night. When I finally fell asleep, it was time to get up, and I was running late."

"What is Sanjay, now?' Max asked. "He must be at least six, seven months already?"

"Eight," Mehta said, with the traditional young father smile.

"That's great, Parth."

"I shot that password and recovery phrase for the crypto account over to Trailalysis to track it for us," Mehta said, as he worked his way back to his Mac with coffee and croissant in tow.

"Good, Parth." Max was familiar with Trailalysis. It was a company that provides blockchain analysis and cryptocurrency investigation services to government agencies and businesses especially financial institutions. It specializes in tracking blockchain networks like Bitcoin and Ethereum to catch illicit activities like money laundering and ransomware attacks.

"Should have something by this afternoon," Parth added.

"Great."

"And we got some CCTV footage from Wilmington that's darn interesting," Mehta added.

"Oh, yeah," Max said with wide eager-to-see eyes when the door to the command center suddenly opened and Tan and Ashe walked in.

"We thought we'd beat you in, Max," Tan said, as she put her jean jacket on the back of one chair and went right for the coffee table herself and sniffed. "Something smells good."

"Fresh coffee and croissants," Mehta said. "Max brought it."

"Great, great," Tan said. "Thanks, Max." And went right for it.

"Thanks, Max," Ashe said too, as he dropped his gray blazer on the back of another chair.

"Spoke with Wei Ming last night," Max said. "He received an email from the ghost with a password and recovery phrase for an Inframax wallet..."

Tan jumped in with excitement in her voice, "To collect his payoff?"

"Yep," Max said.

"The ghost is using the blockchain to pay him off," Ashe said. "Now, that's interesting."

Max nodded. "Parth sent the info to Trailalysis?"

"Good," Tan and Ashe said together.

"Why don't you guys grab a seat? I've got something else to tell you, and I don't want you to spill your coffee."

Max watched Ashe keep his eyes on him as he slowly reached back blindly for a seat. Tan remained standing, but also focused on Max.

"I asked Jia Li to show Wei Ming a photograph of the tram-murdered professor."

Tan and Ashe nodded.

Even Mehta turned away from setting up for the big screen to look at Max.

"You know the Chinese professor who approached Wei Ming in China and stayed in touch with him until he was passed on to the ghost."

There was a long pause, then Sam Ashe spoke up. "Yeah, wasn't it... last name Zhang?"

"Yes, Zhang Kan." Max nodded, and said, "Well, Zhang is Xu and Xu is Zhang."

Tan and Ashe were silent and looked at Max for several long moments.

"Whoa! Wait a minute," Tan blurted. "The tram-murdered BIT professor who turns out to be a Chinese military scientist coordinating that U.S. lab infiltration program that the Eastern District was about to nail is the same Chinese professor who approached Wei Ming in China?"

Max nodded. "And as it turns out, his specialty is nanoscience, too. Which makes sense, since it's the same guy."

"Holy shittttttt!" Tan squealed.

"And this dead professor, along with the other Chinese principal, have a connection to Tech Dragon," Ashe rhetorically stated. "Whoa."

"Yeah, whoa," Mehta said.

"So, the ghost must be military too!" Tan blurted.

"Maybe," Max replied, and looked at Ashe, who had his elbows on the chair arms, hands closed and up against his mouth as if he was in prayer, nodding.

Teresa Tan was still standing.

"All right. Let's take that in for a while. Parth's going to bring us up to date on some other stuff," Max said. "What do you have for us, Parth?"

"CCTV from Wilmington."

Max, Tan, and Ashe swiveled their chairs to face the big screen as Mehta presented from the podium behind them.

"CCTV from Wilmington," Tan said, looking back at Mehta with a big smile. "Let's see it."

"The agent pulled the CCTV from the two intersections on the corners at opposite ends of the parking lot to the UPS store," Mehta said. "Apparently, there're cameras on those two corners. Directly across from that parking lot is an elementary school. The corners are camera'd-up because of all the kids."

"Terrific," Max said.

Mehta pulled up the CCTV onto the big screen.

The cameras were fixed on the two intersections, giving them footage shortly before the female Asian was at the UPS store, according to the manager, and after she'd left. They watched several cars traveling through the intersections driven by all races and genders.

Parth then stopped the CCTV footage on a BMW going through the intersection near the UPS store with New York license plate DPL-671 and magnified the image of the Asian male driver and a person in the passenger seat that only showed the passenger's left arm and hand—but they were unable to determine gender or race.

"DPL," Max said. "Is that a diplomat's plate?"

"It sure is, Max," Mehta answered. "Registered to the Chinese Consulate on West Forty-Second Street."

"Bingo!" Tan shouted.

Max looked at Mehta in thought, then said, "All right, throw this diplomat plate into the plate tracking database."

"Yeah, yeah," Tan said as she rocked in her swivel chair like she was seated on a stool in the corner of a boxing ring eager to get at her opponent.

"Will do," Mehta said, and jumped into the database that contained a collection of hundreds of thousands of vehicle images and license plates from CCTV cameras throughout the country that law enforcement used to identify targets of their investigations and their movements.

"Did we ever get that report from the Wilmington agent?" Max asked Ashe. "The interview with the manager of the UPS store?"

"I didn't see it in my inbox. Let me check again," Ashe said, and pulled out his ePhone. "Yes, just came in. I'll send it to you, Parth. Pull it up on the screen."

Parth opened it up on the big screen and they read through it until Max, Ashe, Tan, and Mehta stopped and looked at each other simultaneously.

Max then read out loud, "'The elderly woman appeared to have two thumbs on her left hand.'"

"Holt shit," Tan then blurted. "Two thumbs!"

"Yeah, holy shit," Ashe whispered. "Great physical identifying characteristic."

"Parth, blow up the car photo," Max said. "Focus on the passenger's hand."

Mehta blew up the photo of the driver and the passenger's left hand, but the hand was not close enough to see.

"Can you blow it up more, Parth?" Max said.

Mehta blew it up to more, but it was still blurry.

"Can you improve the resolution?" Max said.

Mehta did just that. And there it was. The left hand of the passenger had two thumbs.

"Wow! Wow!" rang out from Tan.

Max and his team looked at the hand in silence for several seconds.

Mehta then pulled something else up about the BMW onto the big screen.

Max picked up on Mehta's eager tapping and mouse surfing on his computer.

"What do you got there, Parth?"

Mehta pulled up several dozen photos of the same BMW parked at different locations throughout the city including around the corner from the Chinese Consulate on West Forty-Second Street.

"Whoa," Tan said.

"Last location?" Max asked.

"Around the area of Kings University," Mehta answered. "West One Hundred and Twenty-Second Street between—"

Tan cut him off, "No kidding, no kidding," she said, and jumped up from her swivel chair. "That's near Grant's Tomb!"

"Please continue, Parth," Max said, with a wink at Teresa Tan in appreciation of her excitement.

"Over the last ninety days, the Beamer has been parked up and down and between blocks around Kings University a Hundred and Nineteenth Street and Broadway— Hundred and Eighteenth Street between Broadway and Amsterdam, etcetera, seven times," Mehta said.

"So, that's why she made the call from Grant's Tomb," Ashe said. "She's pitched her tent in the university area."

"Looks that way," Max said, staring hard at the map with all the digital, red-pinned BMW sightings around Kings University.

"She may be associated with the university in some way," Ashe said.

"Could be," Max said. "Anything on tracking the ghost through her cell call from Grant's Tomb?"

"Unproductive so far," Mehta said.

"Zhao Hua now lives near Kings University by the way?" Max said.

"I thought he lives on Roosevelt Island," Ashe said.

"Got a text from *OJO* yesterday afternoon. They observed Zhao Hua move off Roosevelt Island into a building on West One-Two-Two and Broadway," Max said. "Notify *OJO*, Parth. They're already sitting on Zhao Hua's new building. Let them know about the Beamer."

"Got it," Mehta said, and fired off an email to the *OJO* leader with the make, model, and plate number of the vehicle and photo of the male Asian driver which included the left arm view of the passenger with two thumbs.

Max then put in a call to Jack Hunt and told him about the murdered tram professor being the same professor who approached Wei Ming in China and stayed in touch with him until the ghost reached out to him.

"No kidding," Hunt blurted. "The guy the Eastern District had a sealed indictment on?"

"The same," Max said. "Do you know if the Eastern District had any financial information on the dead professor, Jack? He had to have received funding from the Chinese state somehow, plus he had to finance the sixteen scientists he was supervising."

"Huh, yeah, right."

"Our informant was given a crypto account password and recovery phrase to draw his payoff from."

"No kidding," Hunt said. "You got Trailalysis working on it?"

"We do," Max said. "Did the Eastern District put any financial info into the sealed indictment?"

"Didn't mention it, but I have a copy, haven't read it yet, I'll email it to you. It might have something. It'll be good for you to have, anyway."

"Okay, thanks, Jack. Talk to you later." Max said and pressed 'end' on his phone.

"Hunt know if the Eastern District had any financials on the professor, Max?" Tan asked.

Max didn't answer right away. He'd poked the email icon on his ePhone and was staring at it, waiting for Hunt's email with the indictment to drop.

"He didn't know," Max answered without peeling his eyes away from his ePhone. "But he's sending a copy of the sealed indictment."

After two to three minutes, Hunt's email landed, and Max forwarded it to Parth Mehta. "Put it up on one of your screens, Parth."

The indictment popped up onto the screen and they all browsed it together.

UNITED STATES DISTRICT COURT
EASTERN DISTRICT OF NEW YORK
UNITED STATES OF AMERICA, CASE NO. 10-MJ-07623 DAG
Plaintiff,
V.
NAN 'John' XU, a.k.a. Zhang Kan
Defendant.
Defendant Nan Xu has been charged on a complaint alleging a violation of 18 U.S. 1832 "Theft of Trade Secrets and 18 U.S.C. 1546, Visa Fraud."
Defendant is an active-duty People's Liberation Army ("PLA") military scientist who lied to get into the United States and remain,

stole intellectual property at the Brooklyn Institute of Technology (B.I.T.) and coordinated other PLA military scientists across other United States research institutions to do the same.

FACTUAL BACKGROUND

The government proffers the below information to provide a fuller record to the Court of the relevant facts in a future filing.

Mehta continued to scroll through the document as Max and his team kept an eye out for any crypto account information.

"*Skilling Crypto Exchange* is in the indictment, account number 9052150120."

"Skilling," Ashe said. "That's one of the largest crypto exchanges in China."

"Yeah," Tan shouted.

"Interesting," Max said. "Anything from Trailalysis, Parth?"

Mehta worked his computer mouse. "Yes, it's back. I'll open it up on the screen."

Mehta pulled up the report, and they collectively focused on the screen, trying to take it in.

Mehta explained, "So, if you look at the mapping they did with the password and recovery phrase we gave them—"

Ashe jumped in, "They're trying to disguise the wallets. Typical strategy in NFT rug pulls and money laundering."

"What the heck is an NFT?" Tan asked.

"Non-fungible token," Ashe replied. "It's a digital asset that uses blockchain technology to transform it into something immutable—cannot be changed or tampered with."

Max added, "Yeah, it links to the media it represents to provide an irrefutable certificate of ownership for a digital work of art like a photograph, cartoon, written work, anything like that."

"Huh. Interesting," Tan said. "So, five years ago, bad guys all over the world started to use crypto to hide their IDs, and we couldn't nail them."

"Yeah, we'd subpoena these different wallets, and we'd get things back like Mickey Mouse at 123 Main Street," Ashe said.

"We had the same problem in the DEA task force. But with Trailalysis, we tracked a major Chinese fentanyl manufacturer. Up to that point, we were firing blanks," Max said. "What else you got there, Parth?"

Mehta continued, "You can see on the mapping they did, they could take the Inframax wallet creds we gave them and connect it with—"

Tan jumped in, "Whoa! Must be over a hundred other different wallets. How could they track that many wallets?"

Mehta explained that there was a forensic tool called "reactor" that could cluster wallets and trace them back to one entity.

"And the ID of the entity?" Max asked.

"Yep," Mehta said, and expanded the mapping. "It looks like it's in Chinese."

Niǔyuē zhēnzhèng de yàzhōu yánjiū

"It's in Mandarin," Max said, and Teresa Tan translated, "True Asian Studies of NYC."

Ashe jumped in, "This is how they gave themselves up. To open a Inframax account, somebody has to provide government-issued ID with a photo."

"Know your customer requirements," Mehta said.

"Exactly," Ashe said.

"What's the exact address on that?" Max asked.

Mehta entered 'True Asian Studies of NYC' into Google.

"3078B Broadway," he answered.

"Cross streets?" Max asked.

Mehta threw it into Google Maps, "West One Hundred and Twenty-Second Street."

"Whoa. West One Hundred and Twenty-Second Street," Tan blurted. "Where the Beamer's been spotted."

Max nodded.

"Oh, yeah," Ashe whispered.

"3078B Broadway," Mehta said. "Morningside Heights area."

"Pull up the photo of the address, Parth," Max said.

Mehta pulled it up onto another screen.

"3078B… what the hell is that?" Tan blurted, squinting at the screen. "Is that a basement address?"

It was a six-story red brick residential building. Except, on the ground floor corner of the building with steps that led down to the basement, the door of the location was obscured by the street.

"What the hell is that?" Tan repeated.

"Good question," Max said. "What's Zhao Hua's new address according to school records?"

"Hopefully he's notified the school," Ashe said. "He just moved."

Max nodded and looked at Mehta as he pulled up Zhao Hua's student record.

"Up to yesterday, it was a building on Roosevelt Island," Mehta said. "Now, it's 3078 Broadway."

"Whoa," Tan whispered.

Max nodded again. "So, looks like the ghost is associated with that Asian Studies office."

"She didn't waste any time relocating her convert," Tan added.

"What kind of Asian Studies are they doing?" Max asked.

"Could be a Ministry of State Security United Front operation," Ashe said.

"Could be, could be," Max said. "All right. Plug that Skilling account number in the indictment into the Trailalysis Reactor program, Parth."

Max and the others held their breath as Mehta tapped away, then hit enter.

"It's a hit," Mehta said. "They link the Skilling account number in the indictment to the password and recovery phrase Wei Ming gave us for the Inframax wallet."

"Yeah!" Tan shrilled with a pumping of her arms like she was now calling a runner out at home plate over and over and over again.

"Parth, what about the source of funding to Skilling?" Max said. "Does the mapping extend that far?"

Mehta widened the mapping to its final destination, and the big bold letters CHINA DEVELOPMENT BANK appeared on the screen.

"Whoa," Ashe said.

"That's a Chinese state-owned bank," Max whispered.

"It sure is," Ashe said.

"Yeah!" Tan expelled again.

They then all sat in silence, staring up at the screen

Tan spoke up, "Crypto uses the blockchain and we all know the blockchain is on a public ledger, right? Why would the Chinese keep using it?"

"It's the most efficient way to fund illegal and clandestine operations, except for paying in cash, but the logistics of doing it with cash have its own problems," Max said. "But you can see with all the wallets Tech Dragon is using, they're trying to hide its originating source like any typical money launderer would do."

"Even though they used a bulletproof hosting service," Ashe said rhetorically. "Interesting."

"Bulletproof hosting?" Tan asked.

"Bullet hosting companies are set up in countries that have lenient or non-existent Internet laws and just ignore requests from law enforcement," Ashe said.

"Of course," Tan said and shook her head. "Like what countries? Russia?"

Ashe nodded. "You got it. Russia, China, Bulgaria, Belize, Panama… and more."

"All right, that's enough on that for now. I'll run it all down for Roach. But before that," Max said and looked back at Parth, "please throw the Roosevelt Island map onto another screen. I want to run something else by you guys."

Max pointed at the Schimmel Center to start.

"Roosevelt Island is a two-mile-long self-sufficient island," Max said, and pointed out different locations as he spoke. "It has a supermarket, a couple restaurants, post office, countless high-rises—"

"That look like a series of Legos," Tan said. "If you ask me."

Max let out a laugh, "Yeah, I agree. Anyway, the island has ball fields, tennis courts, the island even has a brand-new high-rise hotel, appropriately named the Commencement Hotel, as we know, and a Starbucks."

"And tram service that started on the island in Seventy-Six," Ashe threw in. "Subway service began in Eighty-Nine and regular ferry service in 2017."

"In other words," Tan said, "anyone can live and commute to and from the island with no problem."

"Exactly," Max said. "And that means our ghost can do the same. Live here or easily commute to and from here. Anybody can fade into the day-to-day traffic on that island without being noticed."

Max watched the faces of Tan and Ashe compute what he was trying to get at.

"So, what are you saying, Max?" Ashe asked. "That we need to spend more time on this island because the ghost is possibly spending most, if not all, of her time on the island coordinating things?"

"Yes. But I'm saying we do more than just spend more time there. I'm saying we need to move in. We need to set up shop there on the island. We need to move our command center to the island, move our investigation operation to that island. It gives us a better shot to pick out the ghost when she shows up on the set."

"You mean to work out of the public safety building?" Tan asked. "You think they can handle all of us?"

"Or you mean we should rent a couple apartments to work from—" Ashe started to say.

Tan jumped in, "which we, of course, do a lot with long-term surveillance investigations?"

"No, I mean we move into one or more of the historical buildings on the island."

Tan and Ashe looked at Max in silence again.

"Do either of you doubt the ghost will physically be on this island this weekend? I don't. She'll be here. And we're going to flush her out," Max said. "The quantum conference this weekend is what we're moving in for."

"Ahh," Ashe said with a smile. "Of course."

"Have you guys explored some of the historical buildings on this island?" Max asked. "There's a house, a lab, a former hospital, a church, and a lighthouse, for crying out loud."

"You want us to work out of a lighthouse?" Tan asked with a wink.

Max shook his head and laughed. "No. We can work out of the house, but all those locations give us broad coverage over this island; the opportunity to set up monitoring posts throughout the island."

Tan and Ashe continued to listen.

"The techs can set up equipment for the drones inside each of those buildings, including the lighthouse, and launch drones from there," Max said. "Parth can operate the drones from the Blackwell House, and we'll have the whole island covered."

"Roach give the green light on drones?" Ashe asked with a grin of curiosity.

"Not yet," Max said. "But it's the ideal way to cover the island. Don't you think? If Roach doesn't give us more people..."

"I do," Ashe said. "Absolutely, but..."

"I'm going to ask for NSA's surveillance assistance, which he'll shoot down out of the gate," Max said. "Maybe that will divert his automatic urge to say no again right away."

Ashe laughed. "It's worth a try."

Tan jumped in, "I think using drones is a great idea. We use drones all the time in Homeland."

"All right. So, we set up the command center in the historical house you mentioned?" Ashe asked. "That's what you saying, Max?"

"Yes, the Blackwell House, colonial architecture, built in 1796."

Tan's eyebrows raised. "No joke, there's a colonial house on that island?"

"Yep," Ashe interjected. "Built twenty years after the Declaration of Independence was signed."

"Who the heck was Blackwell?" Tan asked.

Mehta answered, "James Blackwell. First owner of the house. Blackwell inherited Roosevelt Island, which was then Blackwell Island, from his stepfather, and built the house in 1796. The city bought the island, which included the house from the family, for thirty thousand dollars in 1823. It's the sixth oldest piece of architecture in the city."

"And, I just found out, that after the city bought it," Max said, "it built different institutions, the lab I mentioned, an asylum for the emotionally disturbed, even a prison."

"A prison," Tan said. "No shit."

Ashe nodded and said, "True enough. It was the New York City penitentiary from 1832 until the 1930s when Riker's Island opened for business."

"How ironic is that?" Tan said. "All right, so I guess that Blackwell House could work. It has a few rooms? I mean, it's not a shack, is it?"

"No, it's not a shack," Max said, knowing that Tan was just having some fun. "It's got a bunch of rooms as far as I can tell and two floors, but we can set up in the main room, the ground floor, I bet."

"Speaking of operating with the best vantage point," Ashe said. "Too bad that new proposed construction for the island isn't up and running."

"What's that's, Sam?" Tan asked.

Parth Mehta answered, "A French architecture firm has proposed to build a two thousand, four-hundred-foot-tall futuristic building that looks like a Mandrake plant on Roosevelt Island. It's designed to have sixteen hundred trees, eighty thousand feet of plant walls, and eighty-three hundred shrubs. It's supposed to absorb carbon and hopefully create a less polluting ecosystem."

"How the heck would that work?" Tan asked.

"Supposedly, all that green traps the carbon and turns it into something healthier," Ashe said.

"Is it part of Manhattan University?" Tan asked.

"No, residential building with one hundred and sixty floors, three thousand feet of solar panels and thirty-six wind turbines will partly power it," Mehta said.

"A hundred and sixty stories?" Tan asked with more than a little excitement.

"That's what's been reported," Ashe said. "It'll be the tallest building in New York."

Max listened to Ashe explain to the genuinely intrigued Teresa Tan about the proposed construction, even though it had nothing to do with their current situation.

"You hear about this, Max?" Tan asked.

"I did. Caught it on Apple News a couple days ago," Max said. "So, questions or concerns about our working off the island?"

"If we did that, Max, what would be our cover?" Tan asked. "I mean, we'll be going in and out of that house and maybe some other buildings, including the lighthouse. People will become suspicious?"

"When necessary, we can dress like maintenance people or other employees. I've already discussed it with my old boss."

Former Deputy Chief Manley was more than happy to have NYPD/FBI Strike Force investigators continuously traveling through and around the island, giving Max and the strike force access to not only the observation booths on both ends of the tram, and access to their public safety building, if needed for any reason, including bathroom and chow breaks, and offered the use of their marked public safety vehicles to conduct surveillance. A Chinese intelligence agent would not expect to be under observation by Roosevelt Island Public Safety.

Since Max gave assurances that the Roosevelt Island Operating Corporation itself was not under investigation, Max had the run of the island, and all their buildings. Max was convinced that the ghost was local. Maybe even lived on the island. In this day and age of technology she could coordinate the operation from the moon, but Max's gut told him that the ghost was hands on, and with school ending in days, she had to be on the ground, present.

That's why it was also critical that Max and his team and the other members of the surveillance team fade into the scenery of the island. They could not risk the ghost—or others working with her—to recognize their surveillance. This needed to be invisible.

Max continued. "They have all the uniforms we need to fade in. Shirts, pants, jackets. The whole bit. Plus, we can use some of their vehicles or we can put Roosevelt Island decals on a few of our vehicles. But most people won't notice or care."

Tan nodded. "I guess we could even stay overnight during the weekend."

"Just what I was thinking," Max said. "No problem getting a few cots into a few rooms and the house was just renovated, so everything is working good."

Max then looked at Mehta. "What do you think about setting up in a house on Roosevelt Island for a few days, Parth?"

"Works for me. I live out on Long Island. It'll be nice not to have to commute all the way down here. It'll probably take forty-five minutes off my commute."

"Great," Max said. "Let me run it by Roach."

MAX KNOCKED ON ROACH'S office door and stepped in without waiting for a reply. Roach was turned to one angle of his desk on his Mac, as usual. Roach didn't tell Max to leave his office or stop whatever he was working on, so Max spoke up.

"We have a link between the crypto account the ghost gave Wei Ming and the dead tram professor."

Roach kept working his computer.

"We have CCTV of a BMW in the area of the Wilmington Tech Dragon UPS PO box with New York plates registered to the Chinese consulate," Max said. "The passenger has a birth defect. Two thumbs."

Roach stopped typing and looked at Max for a few seconds, then returned to typing.

"The same BMW that has been spotted parked about West One Hundred and Twenty-Second Street and Broadway," Max said. "Not far from Kings University and Grant's Tomb."

Roach kept typing.

"The address to the crypto account is a building on West One Hundred and Twenty-Second Street and Broadway," Max said. "And the other Chinese national student in the quantum program, Zhao Hua, the one the ghost had Wei Ming pitch, now lives in that building. Moved in one day ago. Right after he was bought by the Chinese spy through our informant.

Roach finally turned to look at Max again, this time like a deer frozen by the sight of headlights, then returned to working on his computer.

Max stood there for a few seconds before speaking up again.

"I want to move my team onto Roosevelt Island. We'll work on the island. Roosevelt Island Authority has given us access to all their buildings. We're going to work out of the Blackwell House and stay overnight for the quantum conference weekend."

Without looking away from his computer, Roach said, "Approved."

Happy to get him out of 26 Federal Plaza, Max thought. *Works for me.*

"Also, I want to get NSA's satellites to help with monitoring people's movements on the island this weekend. With their help, we have a better shot at nailing down the ghost's location."

Roach replied without turning to face Max and said, "Denied. We don't want other agencies involved in our case. Valentin, the FBI enforces domestic laws while the NSA focuses on international intelligence."

"It could help us identify Two-Thumbs."

"Denied."

"Mr. Roach. You and I both know getting the assistance of other agencies is often done to get the job done," Max said. "And this case is a Chinese espionage operation."

Without looking back at Max, again Roach repeated, "Denied."

"What about drones?"

"The FBI does not make a lot of use of drones," Roach said. "No need."

"The NYPD uses drones all the time," Max said. "Our Technical Assistance Response Unit—TARU—has made real good use of drones over the last couple of years with surveillance when necessary. I'll call them in to give us a hand."

"No, this is a federal operation, Valentin. We don't want local law enforcement involved."

"What are you talking about? You say the FBI doesn't much use drones," Max said. "I don't know how that's possible, but that's what you're saying. And the NYPD can help us out. We should ask them to give us a hand. I know my chief of detectives would be happy to help us out."

"Denied," Roach said again, and continued tapping away on his Mac.

"Then I need additional people to cover Roosevelt Island properly during the conference," Max said. "*OJO* is monitoring that other student who accepted the ghost's pitch, living near Kings University now plus canvassing the Chinese consulate area and Kings University area for the Beamer."

"Denied," Roach said yet again. "What you have is all you're getting."

"So much for a joint local and federal strike force," Max said and stood there staring down at Roach's back for several long moments. Roach did not stop working his mouse and typing.

MAX MADE IT BACK TO the command center.

"Roach gave moving the operation out to Roosevelt Island the green light."

"Really," Ashe said. "That easy?"

Max nodded. "I won't be having many face-to-face meetings with him for a while."

"Huh," Tan let out. "Just as well. What about drones?"

"Negative," Max said.

"Extra people?" Ashe asked.

"Denied."

Tan and Ashe shook their heads.

After they stood quietly for a couple of seconds, Max then looked over to Mehta working his computer.

"What do you got on that Asian Studies address, Parth?" Max asked. "Do we have any names yet?"

"There's a few on the website," Mehta said. "Working on their backgrounds."

"Good," Max said.

"Max," Tan said, and he turned to her quickly, "Weren't you planning to take the twins to the Met-Yankee game tonight?"

Max suddenly looked up at the digital wall clock above the widescreen.

"For crying out loud," Max said as he grabbed his blazer. "I got to take off."

"We got a face recognition hit on the Wilmington Beamer driver." Mehta's head lifted with a snap.

Everybody turned their heads to Mehta, who blurted, "He was not in the café," with a huge grin.

Max, Tan, and Ashe looked at Mehta and waited.

"The Wilmington Beamer driver with the tattoos on his neck was on the tram."

"On the tram," Ashe said. "One of the two guys who got off the tram and left the professor dead?"

"Yep," Mehta said with enthusiasm.

"Oh, shit," Tan slipped.

The command center was quiet for a few moments.

Then Max spoke slowly and deliberately.

Tan, Ashe, and Mehta focused on him like the point of a diamond.

"So, the Beamer driver and two-thumbed passenger—the Beamer registered to the Chinese consulate—is now linked to the tram homicide; the tram homicide victim who was Chinese military is linked to the Tech Dragon shell; the sixteen other Chinese scientists missing in action and the crypto account they were using, and the same crypto account given to Wei Ming by the ghost is linked to the Asian Studies office near Kings University. Huh."

"Yes!" Tan blurted.

"All right," Max said, feeling his breath get a little shallow from all the interconnections. "Parth, let *OJO* know. Text them photos of the Beamer assassin and the matches with the tram homicide. And the two-thumbed passenger. All right?"

"On it."

"And the two-thumb passenger in the Beamer we still can't make out?" Max asked. "Right?"

"Right," Mehta said. "We can't see who that two-thumbed person is."

"Max, you got to get out of here," Tan said. "The twins."

"I know, I know," Max said as he raced to the door. "I bought the tickets a month ago, figuring we'd be wrapping up our day by now, but here we are."

"We got this covered," Tan said. "We got plenty to do getting set up at the Blackwell House and following up on the latest."

"All right. I'll give Roach a call in the car. Let him know about this new connection," Max said.

"Get out of here!" Tan shouted with a big smile. "Their first major league baseball game. They're going to love it."

"Okay, thanks," Max said, with that uncle-love grin again. "Call me if something urgent comes up. Game starts at seven, I'll be dropping off the twins and my sister by eleven, eleven-thirty. But you can reach me anytime."

MAX JUMPED INTO HIS VW Tiguan, headed for the Queens Midtown Tunnel en route to Citi Field, and gave Roach a call. Max kept it brief. He told Roach the Chinese consulate Beamer driver spotted in Wilmington was on the tram with the murdered professor.

Roach's two-word reply was, "All right," and hung up.

AS SOON AS HE GOT OFF the phone with Dick Roach, he put in a call to Chief of Detectives, Delia Mannix.

"How's the case looking, Max?"

"Progress, Chief," Max said. "We think the Chinese recruiter's going to be on Roosevelt Island this weekend."

"During that quantum conference and Cherry Blossom Festival?"

"Yes, ma'am," Max said. "We think the recruiter has a birth defect. Two thumbs on one hand."

"Two thumbs, interesting."

"I think it would help if we had a bunch of drones circling around."

"See if they pick up Two-Thumbs?"

"Right," Max said. "Except Roach doesn't think that's necessary and doesn't want to devote any resources to it or give us extra people to pick her out and cover all the ways the target could get away."

"Like the Thirty-Sixth Avenue Bridge, subway, tram station, and the ferry landings?"

"Exactly."

Silence.

"Sounds like that convergence of young scientists traveling to and from Roosevelt Island by land, sea and tram plus the crowds and families that will visit with friends and kids for the annual Cherry Blossom Festival is a public safety issue for the City of New York," Mannix said. "I'll notify TARU to cover it all with drones. If they happen to see somebody with two thumbs, they'll give you shout."

"Thanks, Chief."

"You got it, Max," Chief Mannix said. "Reel that spy in."

MAX FLASHED HIS GOLD lieutenant's shield at the NYPD uniforms at the gate to police parking at Citi Field, who saluted him and waved him through. On the way out to the stadium, he was listening to the game. It was already a 4–3 game with the Mets ahead by one run against the Yankees. Max had purchased tickets for him, Maya, and the twins. It was the subway series season-opener game.

As soon as he jumped out of his VW Tiguan, he looked up at the massive illumination coming from inside the stadium walls like a spaceship was about to fly out of it, and suddenly he heard the roar of the crowd. He semi-jogged. It was already the bottom of the third inning. It was a beautiful spring evening for a baseball game. A nice Flushing Bay breeze lifted his blue blazer like he was a superhero.

The twins and Maya were on the third base line at the mezzanine level. As he went up the narrow staircase to their section, the twins stood up and waved when they spotted him. He always reserved the aisle seat. He didn't want to climb over others if he could help it. Except for Jess's New York Mets baseball cap, the seat was empty. She had placed it there to ensure that nobody sat in her Uncle Max's seat, even though the seats were reserved.

"Hey, Uncle Max," the twins said together, and Jess grabbed her cap from the seat. Maya waved at him too with a big sisterly smile, "Hey, Uncle Max."

"Hey, guys," he said to the twins and kissed them both on the top of their heads; then he stretched over the twins, leaned down to his sister and gave her a kiss on the cheek. Maya held his arm for an extra second and whispered, "So, the twins approve of the pretty woman who laid you out on the mat."

Max nodded, winked at his sister with a smile, and asked out loud, "So, what's the score?"

"Four to four, Uncle Max," Ben said. "Aaron Judge just hit a home run."

Max and Jess were both Met fans. Maya and Ben were Yankee fans. Maya was actually a Met fan, too. Maya and Max were both lifetime Met fans because their father had been a Met fan. But her deceased husband, Gus, had been a Yankee fan, and since Ben adopted his father's team, she did the same.

"Did you guys eat?" Max asked, looking at the kids at first, but deftly shifting up to their mom for a more accurate reply.

"We were waiting for you, Uncle Max," his sister replied.

And Jess followed up with, "Yeah, we were waiting for you."

"Yes," Max said, and gave Jess that warm uncle-teaching-moment look.

"Yes, Uncle Max. We were waiting for you."

Max looked over at Maya, and they smiled at each other. That was how their deceased detective father had corrected Maya and Max when they were kids.

Max headed back down the staircase and put in their order when his ePhone buzzed. He could see it was Ed Vance.

Max stood at the counter of the concession and answered. "Hey, Ed."

"Max, you got a minute."

"Yeah, sure. I'm at the Met-Yankee game with my sister and the twins, just ordered a couple dogs."

"Hey, that's great. Wish I was there with you," Vance said. "Listen, on the tram homicide. A couple of things might interest you."

"Okay. I'm listening," Max said, when there was another roar of the crowd. Max could see from one of the many screens televising the game above the concession stand and intermittently hanging from the walls of the cavernous passageway to the seats, that Pete Alonso hit a triple that drove the runner on second base home.

"Sorry, Ed, say that last part again?" Max asked with a shout to be heard over the roar of the crowd.

"FBI confirmed our murdered tram professor was Chinese military with the name Xu Nan a.k.a. Zhang Khan. We ran both names and came up with a New York driver's license address of 3078B Broadway for Xu Nan. Address is curious. Says it's an Asian Studies office but not associated with the university. According to property records website search, the leaseholder is an LLC called Tech Dragon, but no names recorded."

"Can you hold on a minute? Gotta pay."

The counterman announced it was $102 for four hotdogs, one order of fries, one pretzel, two boxes of Cracker Jack, and four Cokes. Max paid, then shuffled over to the counter with the mustard and ketchup pumps, placed down the two packed cardboard boxes he was now carrying, and got back on with Ed.

"Sorry, Ed, go ahead."

"One of my detectives is dating the property records lady down on Centre Street. She said the name of the leaseholder is a Fang Yang."

"Holy shit," Max whispered. That was the same name associated with Tech Dragon in the Delaware LLC documents. He paused and smiled. Ed Vance and his NYPD detectives came up with a connection to the NYC Asian Studies office and Tech Dragon and the name Fang Yang.

"You there, Max?"

He then thought, *Fuck it,* and slowly said, "D-P-L-6-7-1."

The more eyes looking for the Beamer the better, Max reasoned.

Now Ed Vance paused for a second and repeated, "D-P-L-6-7-1. Enjoy the rest of the game."

"Thanks, Ed," Max said, and hit end on his ePhone. Before he picked up the two boxes of stadium food and headed back to his family, he put in a call to Tan.

"How's the game, Max?"

"Good, the Mets just went ahead five–four," Max said, and explained what Ed Vance had just given him.

"No, kidding," Tan replied. "Tech Dragon Fang Yang is now also connected to the Asian Studies office. Wow."

"Yeah, it is. Listen, ask Parth to screen all the names associated with the Chinese consulate. Don't expect the name Fang Yang to be listed. If she's attached to the consulate, she'd be using an alias for the Tech Dragon and Asian Studies operation, but it's important we check."

"Absolutely."

"Also, ask Parth to do a social media search of all photos associated with the consulate," Max said. "Maybe Two-Thumbs will pop up."

"Will do, Max. Good idea."

WHEN MAX GOT BACK TO the twins and his sister and distributed the food and snacks, Maya slid down from being on the other side of the twins to where Jess was sitting and put her hand on her daughter's shoulder.

"Jess, you mind if I sit next to Uncle Max for a minute?"

"No, Mommy," Jess said, motioned for her brother to get out of his seat, which Ben slowly did as he kept his focus on the field of play while munching on his hotdog, like he was sleepwalking.

"So, Jia Li joined you and the twins at jiujitsu," Maya said, looking at Max's profile. "What does she do?"

Max smiled with the mix of a grin and a cringe. "She's a scientist."

He sure would not add that Jia Li was also a secret agent for the Taiwanese government.

"A scientist. Really?" Maya said, smiling from ear to ear.

"Yes."

"Ben says she's very pretty," Maya said and gave Max a sisterly nudge with her shoulder.

"She is," Max said, and hesitated to continue, but did. "Actually, she's beautiful."

"Ohhhh. Beautiful and smart," Maya said. "She's Asian?"

"She's Taiwanese," Max said. "Her mother is Taiwanese; her father is African American."

"What's she doing here?" Curiosity plastered across his sister's face.

"I really can't say," Max said. "But I don't have any illusions there, sis. First, we've got important work to do. Very important work to do together. And she's really out of my league."

Maya's eyes opened wide. "Out of your league? Why? Because she's beautiful and a scientist? Oh, no, no, no, little brother. You are a handsome, intelligent, athletic, six-foot tall thirty-three-year-old," Maya said and nudged her brother again, "... accomplished man. A police lieutenant with a graduate degree and speaks three languages. Do not sell yourself short. You are a class act. And I know you could be the police commissioner or director of the FBI one day, if that's what you want."

Max had that smile from ear to ear now too. He was accustomed to his sister's unconditional love and confidence in him.

"And most important, little brother, you are a good man, just like Dad, a good man. Any woman would be blessed to land a man like you," Maya said. "Scientist or not."

Max grinned at his sister. "Thanks, sis. You're my biggest fan. No pun intended."

"Well, somebody's got to root for the home team. Pun intended," Maya said with a big smile. Then put her hand over her brother's hand. "But it's true."

Max nodded.

"Butterflies?"

Max paused, still not looking at Maya. "Maybe."

"Uh-oh," Maya said. "Houston, we have liftoff."

The Mets beat the Yankees by one run in the bottom of the ninth inning: 9–8.

ON THE WAY TO DROPPING off the twins and their mom from Citi Field in Queens to Riverdale in the Bronx, they were singing—at the top of their lungs—"Beautiful" by Christina Aguilera. Max joined in—he knew the lyrics too—word for word. He'd introduced the twins to that song when their father died.

After the twins and Maya jumped out in front of their building and exchanged hugs, he worked his way to Roosevelt Island, cruising back down the Henry Hudson Parkway.

There was no simple way to get to Roosevelt Island from the Northwest Bronx. When he merged into the Cross-Bronx Expressway, it was a slog of traffic heading east.

It was a little after midnight.

He pulled up his ePhone directory on the dashboard screen, scrolled down names and punched 'TT.'

"How was the game?" Teresa Tan answered.

"Good, the Mets won, nine–eight. It was a good time; the twins had a ball. Ben was a little disappointed since his Yankees lost, but we solved that with Carvel and singing."

"Beautiful?" Tan asked.

"You got it," Max said. "Are you guys set up in the Blackwell House?"

"We're all here," Tan said. "It's a terrific space. We're all set up in the main room. There's a bunch of rooms upstairs on the second floor. There's a back door to this place too and a large window facing a nice view of Long Island City. Your TARU guys set up the launch pads for the drones at the different buildings, including the lighthouse, and set up one big screen inside the house, with over thirty viewing-screens for all the different real-time drone footage. Plus, they left one van with the same number of monitors so we can still watch the action and coordinate the drones and two unmarked cars if we need to go mobile in a hurry."

"Terrific," Max said. "Is *OJO* cruising the island, too? Has the Beamer been spotted anywhere?"

"They're out there, but no Beamer yet."

"And the area of Kings University and the consulate?"

"You got it. They have a surveillance team circling all three areas."

"Good," Max said. "Any Fang Yangs at the consulate?"

"Negative," Tan said. "No Two-Thumbs spotted on social media yet either."

"Yeah, that would be too easy."

"Parth threw the CCTV at the bridge and all available footage for the last couple weeks into the MBI i2 software for analysis—no sight of the Beamer coming or going."

"All right."

"You heading here or heading home?"

"Heading your way," Max said. "I want to get a look at how all the drones are set up."

"Sounds good. I checked them all out. Looks good. And the techs put out a set of binoculars and a Mac to see all the footage and hear the radio transmissions in the lighthouse and a couple of the other buildings if any of us want to catch things from there."

"Great, I'll see you when I get there."

After he got off the call with Tan, he was already on the FDR Drive approaching the Ed Koch Queensboro Bridge. He went over the East River that overshot Roosevelt Island, landing on Queens, then the Thirty-Sixth Avenue Bridge and the East River to double back onto the island.

HE DIDN'T MAKE IT TO the Blackwell House until almost one a.m.

He entered through the back door and could hear that familiar command center sound. Radio communications, laptop Mac tapping, conversation between Teresa Tan and Parth Mehta, and the aroma of coffee. A real-time, temporary command center. He was home.

He had to walk through the kitchen to get to the main room when Teresa spotted him first.

"Hey, Max," Tan said, sweeping her arm around like she was a real estate agent. "What do you think?"

"Hi, Max," Mehta greeted him too and gave him a backhand wave from his seat in front of the big screen with multiple monitors.

"Hey, guys," Max said, and looked around the room. "Sweet. Where's Sam?"

"He's walking the island," Tan said. "Wanted to get a better feel for the roads, buildings, alleyways, the ways to get through and around things here. And the ferry landing."

"All right," Max said. "Everybody knows there's no need to stay over tonight. Only *OJO* needs to stay out there. The tech team, you, Sam and Parth, can head home and get a few ZZs. We'll meet back here at ten-hundred tomorrow and stay over through the weekend, or until we nail the ghost."

"The tech team and your TARU guys are gone, but Parth, me, and Sam are staying. This place is very comfortable, Max. Plenty of rooms and single beds, chairs and a few sofas,"

"All right," Max nodded, feeling that 'We're a team thing' again. "I'm going to start with the lighthouse. See the setup there."

MAX WORKED HIS WAY up the spiral staircase of the lighthouse on the northernmost tip of Roosevelt Island. It provided the perfect panoramic view of the East River from the shore of Manhattan to the shore of Long Island. There was no rotating light reflecting off the glass of the observation deck as he imagined it would have almost 150 years earlier to warn ships of the island's presence in the treacherous waters of Hell's Gate and provide warning to islanders of approaching ships.

Max figured the then rotating lighthouse light was like the rotating light atop the roof of a police car when they were first introduced in the 1930s. He wondered if that rotating lighthouse light was, in fact, the inspiration for the first police light. Except, it was illuminated in a purple glow from the surrounding lights implanted in the ground, firing its rays up against its nineteenth century stone façade like a pole dancer's pole.

Max grabbed the binoculars placed on the table of the lantern deck by the tech team earlier and took in the island when he heard the door to the lighthouse below open.

"Is that you, Sam?" Max semi-shouted down the spiraling staircase, without pulling the binoculars from his eyes.

"No," a female voice answered.

Max moved the binoculars from his eyes and listened to that female voice ascend the spiral steps. "Teresa?"

"No. It is not Teresa," the female voice echoed up to him.

Max looked at the entrance to the observation deck where the female voice was then standing.

"Jia Li. What are you doing up here?" Max asked, his heartbeat picking up. "Teresa tell you I was here?"

She stood there in her body-fitted jeans, white V-cut T-shirt, jean jacket and white running shoes. Max's breath became a little labored. *My God, what a beauty.*

"I stopped by the Blackwell House. Teresa informed me you were here."

"It's very late. I planned to brief you in the morning, but I'm glad you're here," Max said, and wished Teresa had not mentioned it. "You okay?"

"Yes, course," Jia Li said, as she moved closer to Max. "And no need to wait until the morning with such news. We are agents of our governments in collaboration. No?"

"Yes, of course," Max said, wondering if she was really okay.

"Like you said, it is a wicked game," Jia Li said, and scanned the lighthouse again. "I see you have set up the entire investigative operation on this island. That you are using the Blackwell House as your command center. That's what it's called, correct? A command center?"

"Yes, that's what it's called," Max said, and scrutinized her.

"I suspect we hope to identify the woman during the Q Conference," Jia Li said. "That it is believed she will be present."

"That is what we hope."

"Teresa informed me about the recent developments. Most interesting about the Wilmington Delaware BMW motor vehicle associated with the Chinese consulate and the so-called Asian Studies office near Kings University," Jia Li said. "Is this deceased Brooklyn Institute of Technology professor Dr. Xu the same Nan Xu that is associated with Tech Dragon?"

"We cannot be sure yet," Max said, "but it appears so. Registering a company in most states, including Delaware, does not currently require a photo ID. So, we don't have a photo to compare with the DOA on the tram."

"Very, very, intriguing development," Jia Li said. "So, there is a possible connection between Tech Dragon and the recruiter."

"Maybe."

"And how interesting about the two thumbs passenger in the BMW," Jia Li said. "It would certainly assist with a positive identification when that time comes."

"Yes."

"How intriguing," Jia Li said. "Is there any way I can help right now?"

The nightlights reflected off their faces through the elongated glass of the lighthouse. Jia Li's radiance in those lights was breathtaking.

Max had not realized he still had the binoculars in his right hand. Like a birdwatcher waiting for another sighting, his other hand rested on the counter.

"Tell me something," Max said, in an effort to shift the energy in their space. "What are some jobs Schimmel students will do over the weekend?"

"Dr. Kleinheidt has given us a choice of what we'd like to do, as long as all the duties are covered."

"All right," Max said. "Like what?"

"Of course, there will be several in the main lobby of the Schimmel Center for reception as others arrive. There will be a student assistant in each of the classrooms or lecture halls to assist the lecturer and respond to any of their needs. Visitors will be assisted by students on each floor to navigate the center, including the lecture hall, classrooms, café, elevators, and restrooms."

"What about the hotel?"

"Yes, there will be several students assigned to the lobby of the Commencement Hotel to assist visitors there. Professor Kleinheidt has put out an assignment sheet. We can fill in our names with our preference for duties to perform."

"Okay, good."

"We, of course, will have badges that will distinguish us from the visitors," Jia Li said. "Our badges will have a blue background with white letters. The visitors will have badges with a white background and blue letters, the lecturers will have white badges with red letters."

"I want you to spend the weekend in the lobby of the Commencement Hotel," Max said. "You'll see everybody checking in before they head to the Schimmel Center."

Max paused for several moments. Jia Li looked at him with a curious smile that silently seemed to telegraph the question: *Is there something else?*

"Yes," Jia Li said, moving closer to Max.

What was going on? Max could not help wondering. *What was this sudden shift in behavior Jia Li was now exhibiting? Is she seducing me?*

"I need your help with exfiltrating Wei Ming's family when the time is right. Our FBI boss—Roach—is not going for it again after it fell through the last time."

"Of course, how can I help?"

"I can get his family to the Macau coastline, off the South China Sea. But we could run into problems getting them across the South China Sea to Taiwan. The Chinese military or coast guard could intercept them."

"Of course," Jia Li nodded. "That's quite possible."

"Can I confide in you about something?" Max said, as if asking that of Jia Li or anyone else guaranteed they wouldn't divulge what they'd been told, but he just had to take that leap of faith with Jia Li.

"Yes, of course."

Max then went into some detail about the twins' father being killed with countless others through exposure or overdose on counterfeit fentanyl manufactured in China.

"Oh, my goodness. That's how the twins' father died?" Jia Li said and shook her head. "That is horrible. Just horrible."

"Yes. It is," Max said and continued.

Then he got into the next part, again, hoping that telling her would not bite him on the ass. He explained the problem he ran into in his attempt to kidnap Mr. Fentanyl and get him across the South China Sea, about a month ago, when they were hit by a Chinese missile and had to abort.

MAX SLID OUT OF THE Macau International Airport and spotted Min Wu with her wave. She jumped behind the wheel while he threw his backpack in the trunk and jumped in with her. They took off down the Macau streets wickedly fast.

"Min Wu, I presume," Max could not help asking.

"Yes, Mr. Valentin," Min Wu said, smiling as she wheeled the car through traffic like she was born attached to it.

They pulled up in an alleyway next to the fentanyl manufacturer's family home. Min Wu and Max went to the side of the house. Max's Chinese operative was holding "Mr. Fentanyl", or Xhinghi Pa, the deliberately drugged, communist party, fentanyl manufacturer with a black hood over his head.

They slipped out the front door, spun to the left, then another left into the narrow alleyway, moving like a military column. Min Wu immediately jumped behind the wheel; the operative put the owner in the backseat, jumped in with him, and slammed the door closed.

Max spotted a car's headlights suddenly flip on, and light up that previously pitch-dark alleyway and come in their direction, blocking the way straight out. The chemical manufacturer had security watching his home.

Suddenly, rotating lights flashed on, making the compact alleyway now look like a Lunar New Year fireworks display. Max dove into the front seat.

Min Wu put the car in reverse and tore out like Jason Bourne as a staggeringly loud siren joined all the flashing lights.

"They watching his house!" Min Wu yelled as she wheeled the vehicle on to the narrow street and took off, heading toward the airport.

"We got to lose them," Max shouted rhetorically. That was exactly what Min Wu was doing. "They can't tail us to the coast."

"I going to lead them to airport. They will think you are trying to take him to plane," Min Wu yelled as she bobbed and weaved through traffic. "When I lose them, I swing around and get to coastline."

In no time at all, Max could hear vehicles chasing them, breaking and screeching to keep up. Min Wu swung around two corners with such speed and precision, balanced on two wheels on the passenger side of the car for seconds, then swung the steering wheel in the opposite direction, angling them onto the driver's side on two wheels. The security vehicles could not keep up.

The sound of the siren became fainter and fainter. Min Wu kept up her acceleration. Then the collision. Max looked back; the two pursuit vehicles folded up into each other like puppies.

Forty minutes later they pulled up on the dark and quiet eastern coastline of the South China Sea.

The operative yanked out the fentanyl manufacturer. Max pulled his backpack from the trunk, strapped it to his back, and pulled the black hood off the big shot's head. The manufacturer looked like a typical drunk.

"Thank you, Min Wu." Max turned back to shake Min Wu's hand. "You're the best."

"My pleasure, Mr. Valentin. Good luck," Min Wu said, giving him a military salute with a big smile.

They needed the fastest boat they could get their hands on to fire them across the Taiwan Strait. Waiting for them was the *Spirit of Australia*, the fastest speedboat in the world, capable of traveling at 318 mph. They needed to cover almost 435 miles to get to Taiwan and get there in a hurry. Max's clandestine exfiltration coordinator had gained one for this operation. The Chinese operative helped Max get Mr. Fentanyl on the speedboat.

"We're getting recent reports that the Communist Chinese Coast Guard has been chasing down boats trying to make it to Taiwan," the pilot said.

Max lifted his chin in acknowledgment. "Anything recent?"

"About a dozen young Hong Kong activists tried to make it across. They didn't. For starters, they're being charged with illegal border crossing. The charges are certain to ratchet up before they have their day in a PRC court," she said.

"Of course."

"You hear about the arrest warrants and bounties issued for eight Hong Kong activists now living in the West for protesting against the Chinese state?"

"No," Max said and shook his head. "Relentless."

The consensus was that although getting to the Macau coastline would work—as it had—getting the fentanyl hotshot from Macau to Taiwan would prove a whole distinct challenge especially with the new Hong Kong Chinese Security Law.

The Chinese had extra boat patrols in the South China Sea to keep Hong Kong citizens or anyone else from attempting an escape to Taiwan.

As soon as Max got himself and the criminal buckled in, the speedboat revved up like the launch of the space shuttle. There was a lot of noise and smoke, but no significant movement.

It should take them about two hours to get to Taiwan across the South China Sea.

"Is this baby going to take off anytime soon?" Max shouted at the pilot over the noise.

"Standby," she replied with an unconcerned smile.

The speedboat eased away from the shoreline like it was giving birth; the noise increased, and the smoke increased, inching its way forward when it suddenly took off like a shot. They were all plastered against the back of their seats. It didn't seem possible a boat could move at such a speed, but it did.

Ninety minutes into their escape they spotted several Chinese Coast Guard boats racing in their direction from about ten miles away.

The Chinese Coast Guard made an ill-conceived attempt to block the speedboat's way by spreading out, but the Spirit of Australia zigged and zagged between them. The fastest Chinese Coast Guard boats were no match for the *Spirit of Australia*. It was like a bulldog trying to chase a Jack Russell terrier. Not a chance.

"One minute away," the pilot announced. "The Chinese Coast Guard is about three miles behind us."

"You think the Chinese Navy's out here too?" Max yelled.

With that, there was then a sudden loud explosion, and the roar of the *Spirit of Australia* came to a deafening quiet, like the sound of a charging grizzly suddenly shot in the head.

"What the hell was that?" Max shouted.

Smoke filled the cabin where he and Mr. Fentanyl were strapped in. The pilot was unconscious, leaning over to one side.

Max knew just what it must've been. The *Spirit of Australia* could outrun the Chinese Coast Guard, but it couldn't outrun a Chinese Navy missile.

Water was pouring into the boat. Max yanked the life preservers from the boat's wall. Strapped one on, then unbuckled the still-drugged Mr. Fentanyl and put one on him. He then unbuckled the pilot and put one on her. There was no bleeding. The blast must've knocked her out, Max thought. He pulled Mr. Fentanyl off the boat and into the water, then went back for the pilot and pulled her out. Max could see they were less than 1,000 feet from the coast of Taipei.

He had to leave Mr. Fentanyl, floating in his life preserver, for the Chinese to pick up. He then swam furiously, dragging the pilot to the Taiwanese shoreline.

"THAT WAS YOU!" JIA Li said with wide eyes. "That was you! My goodness, that was so courageous. We heard about an American swimming on our shoreline with somebody he had saved. And left a Chinese national with a life preserver to be rescued by the Chinese minutes after the interception. I could not know who it was. That was you!"

Max nodded and looked away from her gaze.

With that, Jia Li slid to within inches of Max, pulled his face down with one hand, her brown eyes glowing into his, put her other hand over his resting on the counter, leaned up into Max and kissed him long and deep. Max leaned back like he was preparing to edge himself under an imaginary horizontal pole that was three feet off the ground.

He lost all sense of time and place.

Jia Li then spoke up, breaking his trance.

"So, you need assistance transporting Wei Ming's family across the South China Sea. We can help."

Max took a few moments to become alert and stuttered, "... they... they used a missile to intercept us."

"No worries," Jia Li said. "If your team can get Wei's family to the Hong Kong coastline, we'll get them to Taiwan. We have anti-missile defense capability, of course."

Jia Li then kissed Max again.

The next thing he could recall, Jia Li was pulling her lips from his, nodded at him with another heart-melting smile, turned around and walked out of the observation deck, then turned back and asked, "Is there anything else?"

"What?" he asked again in his foggy state.

Jia Li smiled, turned, and stepped down into the spiral staircase.

Max listened to each step like it was a metronome and wondered if she'd learned that approach from the Taiwan National Security Bureau. *Very effective*, he thought.

MAX WAS SITTING ON the cot in one bedroom on the second floor of the Blackwell House, having just opened his Mac laptop and checked to see Wei Ming's location. From the video transmitting from the Fitbit on his wrist, Max could see that he was talking to somebody on the phone at his tiny dining room table. He figured Wei Ming was talking to the ghost, and he would hear from him shortly.

With no capacity to resist, he checked to see what Jia Li was up to. She was sitting at her desk, wearing that same V-cut white T-shirt, the blue of the computer screen reflecting off her intelligent eyes. His heartbeat rose again as she suddenly stood and headed for her apartment door. Then his ePhone rang. It was Wei Ming.

"Hello, Wei Ming."

"Good evening, Mr. Valentin. Is it okay to talk right now?" Wei Ming asked. "You sound out of breath?"

"Ahh, no, yes, this is fine," Max said, shaking his head. "You're in Jia Li's apartment?"

"Yes, yes, I just came running down," Wei Ming said. "She is right here."

"I am here, Mr. Valentin," Jia Li said as if nothing had occurred in the lighthouse minutes before.

"Okay. Did the recruiter call?"

Wei Ming explained she had, and he gave her the itinerary of lectures the eight targeted students had signed up to attend, including all the locations and times of the social events.

"She took all the information over the phone. She didn't want to give me an email address in which I could forward it," Wei Ming said. "But I have, of course, emailed it to you."

"Thank you," Max said, recognizing the ghost continued to not leave any electronic trail.

"Did she give you any instructions on how, when and where she wanted you to approach them?"

"Yes," Wei Ming said. "She wants me to, one by one, approach each of them immediately following any lecture and invite them to have a cup of tea or something to eat in the café to chat. She said that they would watch me throughout the entire weekend."

"Only the café?" Max asked. "She didn't give you the option of chatting with them outside of the café. Lecture hall or in one of the seating areas in the corridors?"

"No, Mr. Valentin. I asked. She said she wanted me to speak to them only in the café."

Max took that in for a moment. He was certain the ghost would be on the island. But he wondered if the recruiter would do the observing herself, or would it be one or more of her operatives? If the first café pitch Wei Ming made to Zhao Hua days earlier was any indication, she would be in the café herself or close by.

"Okay," Max said, wondering when she would again bring up her wanting him to steal actual quantum data. "Was there anything else?"

Wei Ming let out a sigh before he spoke. "She directed me to extract quantum research data. She wants me to devise a plan to extract specific quantum data by tomorrow and commence to conduct the extraction the day after tomorrow—Saturday morning. She is aware of our research on post quantum cryptography. Her demand is for me to take it without permission. She anticipates that nobody will be in the lab because they will all be busy assisting with the conference. She doesn't believe Professor Kleinheidt will be there at that time, and even if he is, she doesn't mind. If anyone is there and interferes, she said she will have associates nearby. She does not care that I will be on CCTV. She said that as soon as I steal the formula, she will arrange for my transport to a safe location.

"She's given you until tomorrow to devise a plan?" Max asked.

"Yes, tomorrow. She expects me to provide her with my plan and how I intend to execute it. She will call me tomorrow at ten o'clock as usual and expect to hear my plan. She insisted that Saturday I must find an opportunity to sneak into the lab while everyone is at either a lecture or social event and take the data."

"Okay," Max said in acknowledgment, feeling Wei Ming's palpable anxiety.

"This is becoming more and more disturbing, Mr. Valentin."

"You are doing very good, Wei," Jia Li said.

Max appreciated Jia Li's efforts to calm him down.

"Remember, you are not doing this alone," said Max. "We are with you and around you. Give some thought tonight to when you think you can get away to the lab when nobody is there, as she suggests. We'll be monitoring you when you do it. You won't be taking anything. We'll give you something to give her, some authentic-seeming quantum research, but it won't be."

"Really?" Wei Ming said.

"Yes, we'll come up with something," Max said. "But we hope to identify and have the recruiter in custody before you need to give or transfer anything to her. But we'll have something authentic looking to give you just in case we need to buy some time."

"But, if the time comes for me to give her the unauthentic data and she has it evaluated," said Wei Ming, "she will know immediately that I am not cooperating and suspect I have other allegiances."

"I understand your concern, Wei Ming, but we're not there yet," Max said.

"But, Mr. Valentin, I am anxious. I am anxious for my family. That professor that was killed on the tram is very disturbing. Someone murdered him, and it cannot be just a coincidence that he was communicating with me before the woman contacted me. The Chinese officials must think there is something going terribly wrong. Do you think they know I am cooperating with you?"

Jia Li jumped in again, "No, Wei, it is obvious they do not."

"I agree with Jia Li," Max said. "But as I told you from the beginning, we would do all we can to protect your family when we reached the last stage of this investigation. Before there's any chance the Chinese officials know about you, we will do all we can to remove your family. I will let you know when I want you to let your family know that somebody will pay them a visit to escort them out of China. Okay? It will be within the next forty-eight to seventy-two hours. Do you understand?"

"Yes, Mr. Valentin. Thank you. Thank you."

CHAPTER 18
Friday, May 26

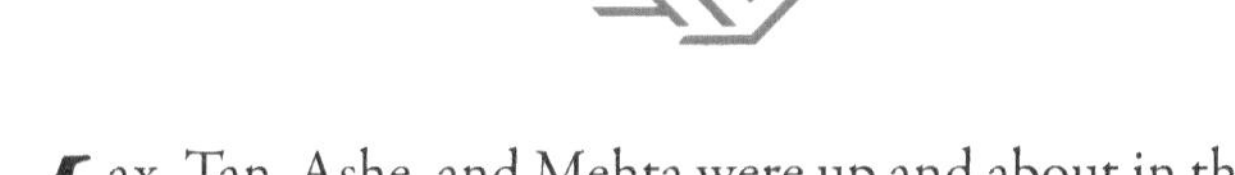

Max, Tan, Ashe, and Mehta were up and about in the Blackwell House at six a.m. and by 6:30 they were on a Zoom call with Jia Li and Wei Ming, who logged in from Jia Li's apartment.

The instructions were straightforward. Jia Li was to assume her position in the lobby of the Commencement Hotel by early afternoon. Tan and Ashe would secretly film Wei Ming's interactions with the targeted eight in the café and lobby of the Schimmel Center.

Max would stay in the Blackwell House with Mehta, coordinating all developments with the help of the NYPD drones.

As it turned out, there were no opportunities for Wei Ming to meet with any of the targeted eight during the late afternoon conference registration and hotel checking in process.

After all the visitors got settled and were greeted by Professor Kleinheidt in the massive Schimmel Center auditorium, by evening everyone separated to make their own arrangements for dinner. Some ate at the Commencement Hotel restaurant; others took the tram across to Manhattan and had dinner in midtown or the Upper Eastside.

The only thing accomplished was the accumulation of video footage from Tan and Ashe, and from Wei Ming's and Jia Li's body camera and Fitbit, and the outdoor footage provided by the drones.

Then his phone buzzed. It was Ed Vance.

MAX AND TAN WALKED into the Nineteenth Precinct detective squad interview room, designed like every other interview room in every precinct in the city built or renovated after 1970. Two-way mirror, gunmetal table with three chairs like a triangle; two chairs for detectives facing a seated suspect.

The BMW driver with the tattoos was already sitting at the table.

When Max gave Ed Vance the plate number to the BMW without further comment, Max knew Ed would know that if his detectives spotted it, it was okay to not just observe and report, but—if occupied—to bring it in. There were two thoughts Max had when he made that spontaneous decision to offer Vance the DPL plate.

First, the occupant(s) could be one or more of the assassins, including the ghost recruiter. But if only the assassin(s) were present—and taken in—it could unsettle the ghost and lead her to make mistakes.

"DO YOU SPEAK ENGLISH?" Max asked.

The tattooed assassin, handcuffed hands in his lap, did not respond, nor did he make eye contact with Max or Teresa Tan, looking down into the center of the table as if he was trying to decide his next chess move.

Max spoke in Mandarin, "My name is Lieutenant Valentin. This is Special Agent Tan."

Still no response.

Max then used a standard approach to interviewing suspects. Give them the feeling that you understand their situation. Start with empathy.

"We know you're Chinese military. We know you were carrying out orders. We know you did not decide on your own to do what you did. You were ordered to kill the professor on the tram, and you carried out your orders. No different from the orders of my colleague and me. We are carrying out our orders."

The tattooed suspect looked up at Max briefly, then back down into the center of the table. So much for empathy.

"I want to cut to the chase," Max said. "We have you on video tape getting on the Roosevelt Island tram with Professor Xu and getting off with your colleague where the professor was left dead. We know Nan Xu—also known as Lieutenant Colonel Zhang Kan—is Chinese military too."

The tattooed suspect again looked up at Max briefly, then back down into the center of the table.

"At trial we will convict you of his murder."

The assassin kept his view on the table.

Tan jumped in, "The question as to whether your last breath will be expelled in a U.S. prison is up to you."

Max detected a slight twitch from the assassin's eyebrow and a tenth of an inch move in his seat to make the metaphorical noose around his neck a bit more comfortable. But he remained silent.

Max recognized they would need to ratchet up the interview. They could not waste time. They needed to present the tattooed suspect with imagery of what life would be like for him in a U.S. prison for twenty-five years. Max needed the suspect to apply his five senses to the imagery he would present to help him have a tangible experience of his future.

"You will be in solitary confinement. You will not be with the general prison population," Max said. "The prison staff will serve your meals through a slot in your cell door. You will be on twenty-four-hour watch. You will spend twenty-three hours a day in the cell, and one hour for exercise."

Max thought he could detect another eyebrow adjustment.

Tan interjected, "Do you know what a four-by-four cell smells like for someone who eats, shits, and pisses in that cozy space?"

Silence.

"I respect you are a trained military man. I know as trained military; you are conditioned to take horrible discomfort. I know. I am a former United States Marine. Much of Marine Corps training prepares the marine to tolerate horrendous discomfort. All the extremes. Extreme heat. Extreme cold. Extreme noise. Sleep deprivation. You understand?" Max said. "But the worse is isolation. It drives any person to madness."

The suspect looked up from the table.

"But over time, it becomes impossible to live like that. Maybe the first five or six years of confinement you will manage," Max said. "Maybe a little longer or a little less. But eventually it will become impossible to live another second in such misery. You will wish for the end."

They still had his attention.

Tan jumped in, "And there'll be no opportunity to take your life in a U.S. prison. Not that it doesn't sometimes happen," she said, and shook her head from side to side. "But somebody like you, oh, no. The U.S. government does not want to report that a Chinese spy and murderer committed suicide in a U.S. jail."

The suspect looked back down at the table.

Tan continued, "As a member of the People's Liberation Army, the last thing the U.S. would want is to explain that you died by suicide; that your death was self-inflicted. Nobody will believe that. Your country and its allies will assert that someone murdered you. As a guest of the U.S. prison system, the U.S. will not let you die in any other way but natural causes. And you're only in your thirties."

There was a long silence.

The suspect finally spoke up in accented English, "I cannot help you."

Max took the Chinese assassin in for an extra moment then replied, "I understand."

"May I have a Coke?"

"Of course," Max said.

MAX WAS ON THE MAIN floor of the Blackwell House in semidarkness watching the seemingly endless collection of videos taken inside the Schimmel Center café, registration area in the lobby, and the lobby of the Commencement Hotel.

Amid the quantum students and lecturers, he was desperately seeking any sign of an Asian woman with two thumbs. He looked at each of the video files carefully. Countless Asian females ranging from ages twenty to seventy traveled throughout the conference areas. He magnified the left hands of each. None had two thumbs.

By 3:30 a.m., as he neared completion of his review of all the surveillance footage, Max saw something that made the hairs on the back of his neck stand up. He then rushed back to two other files where he seemed to recall having seen the same peculiar looking, lean, elderly bearded man and fast-forwarded to that spot.

The man appeared on three separate occasions: once walking through the registration area, then in the lobby of the Commencement Hotel and by early evening in the café.

The elderly, bearded Asian man wore a dark gray suit and blue shirt with an open collar. The man had a visitor's nametag around his neck. White background with blue letters, but Max could not make out the name on the tag. In each of the recordings, the man appeared to be paying no mind to the targeted students. Just traveling through. Except, in the café, he appeared to be holding a book or writing in a notebook or reading his iPhone.

Max zoomed in on the left hand of the bearded man—then stopped cold. He had two thumbs.

CHAPTER 19

Saturday, May 27

By five a.m., Max, Tan, Ashe, and Mehta were all showered and in the main room of the Blackwell House, sucking down their first cup of coffee, ready to go.

Max briefed his team on the appearance of the elderly bearded man showing up several times during the previous afternoon and evening. He had Mehta freeze the images of the man, focus on his two-thumbed left hand, magnify it, and put it up on the big screen.

Max then pulled out his ePhone and punched in Jia Li's name.

"Yes, Max."

"It's possible the recruiter was in the Schimmel Center at different times yesterday afternoon and evening," Max said. "But she's disguised as a bearded man."

"Is that true?"

"Yes, he has two thumbs," Max said. "He mingled with the crowd in the café, the Commencement Hotel, and the registration area in the Schimmel Center."

"Are you certain?"

"Yes, no problem magnifying the video," Max said. "It's the same hand that was in the BMW."

"My goodness," Jia Li said. "I didn't notice in all that time I was in the hotel's lobby."

"Don't worry about it," Max said. "We didn't catch him either and we had all those areas covered."

"One moment, Max, there is knocking on my door. It must be Wei Ming."

Suddenly Wei Ming's voice came over the phone.

"Mr. Valentin, the woman called me moments ago. She has demanded I enter the lab this morning very early and extract the quantum data," Wei Ming said. "What am I to do?"

IT WAS 6:30 A.M.

Max watched Wei Ming from the Blackwell House in real-time video feed from his body camera as he approached the lab door. Tan and Ashe were sitting in the van parked behind the Schimmel Center looking at the same video. They watched Wei Ming's hand punch in the code to unlock it.

Max and his team followed Wei Ming's view entering the lab, his hand turning the florescent lights on and closing the door behind him.

The ghost had yet to tell Wei Ming what to do with the flash drive once he downloaded the data.

"How long will this take him?" Tan asked over the secure point-to-point radio from the van.

"About ten minutes," Max answered. "Wei Ming estimated it would take him about ten minutes to turn on the computer, enter his username and password, locate and download the bogus quantum-resistant data Professor Kleinheidt had put on a file for Wei Ming to download onto a flash drive, shut everything down and get out of there."

"Got it," Tan replied.

Suddenly the lights went out in the lab—pitch black. Because of the sensitive nature of their research, there were no windows in the lab for even a thread of light to slip in. Only solid white walls from floor to ceiling.

Then, within only a few seconds of the lights going out, they all heard a voice.

"Let me have it," the male voice said to Wei Ming in Mandarin.

"Who are you?" Wei Ming asked.

"I am with your employer," the voice said. "Give me the flash drive."

Max could not see a thing. Then they heard what sounded like the lab door slamming.

Tan and Ashe bolted out of the van and raced to the quantum lab.

When they arrived, Tan flipped the lights back on. It was too late. The voice had escaped.

"YOU, OKAY?" ASHE ASKED, as Max watched on the live feed.

"Yes, yes, sir," he replied.

"Who was that?" Tan interjected. "Could you see him at all?"

"No, no," Wei Ming said. "He had a mask over his face. He was entirely in black. I could only see his eyes. He was dressed like a ninja."

Max then recognized there was one probable explanation.

"Would Zhao Hua have received the code for the lab door too this morning?" Max asked over the radio.

"Yes, Mr. Valentin," Wei Ming said. "He would not have access to our quantum resistance research, but, yes, he would have received the code at six a.m."

"The ninja must've been here waiting for him inside the lab, Max," Tan said.

"Yes, I think so," Max said. "But Zhao Hua did not have access to the quantum-resistant research."

"No, sir," Wei Ming said. "Only Dr. Kleinheidt, Jia Li and I have the password to that data."

"All right," Max said over the mic, "bring Wei Ming here to the Blackwell House. We'll keep him here until you guys follow him back into the building to continue his pitch to the rest of the targeted eight."

Max knew now that the ghost had the bogus post quantum cryptography (PQC) algorithm, it was just a matter of time before she would recognize that what her ninja operative gave her on the flash drive was useless and put the stop on Wei Ming's family in China.

Max poked the exfiltration coordinator's number on his ePhone.

"Listening," the XCoor answered.

"It's Max Valentin. Get the family out of there," Max said. "Do it now."

"Got it."

Max then texted Jia Li, "Just activated exfiltration of Wei's family. Notify your team. Shenzhen coast. South China Sea is their pickup spot."

"Okay."

The same strategy Max had used in attempting to kidnap Mr. Fentanyl from China and transport him to Taiwan would be used to exfiltrate Wei Ming's family. He hoped a Chinese missile would not neutralize the NSB team arranged by Jia Li to get them across the South China Sea as he had been.

As soon as Tan and Ashe returned to the Blackwell House with Wei Ming, Max said, "We have to find this damn recruiter. Once she figures out we've given her a bogus formula, she's going to take off."

"And my family, sir?"

"There's a team exfiltrating them now."

MAX WAS STILL SITTING with Parth Mehta in the Blackwell House. Mehta launched drones from various locations on Roosevelt Island to capture video of vehicles and people, particularly within 500 feet of the Schimmel Center.

Tan and Ashe were inside the center, mingling. Everything was proceeding as one would expect at a research university conference. No one had spotted Two-Thumbs.

BY THREE P.M., IT OCCURRED to Max he hadn't seen Professor Kleinheidt in any of the live video feeds since early that morning. He had spoken to the professor after Wei Ming was accosted in the lab to give him a heads-up.

Max pulled out his ePhone and called the professor's cell number. No answer. It went right to voicemail.

"Parth," Max said. "You see Professor Kleinheidt around?"

"No, haven't seen him floating around since this morning."

Max then got on the radio. "Teresa, Sam… have you seen Professor Kleinheidt around?"

"Negative, Max," Teresa immediately replied.

"Not since this morning, Max," Ashe responded.

Then a thought fired a freezing rod up his spine. Was the Chinese spy so desperate to get that PQC algorithm that she or he would go after an American university professor and researcher on U.S. soil?

With that thought, he jumped up from the captain's chair and shouted, "Sam, Teresa, I'm heading to the lab. Meet me there."

"Ten-four," they both replied simultaneously.

They converged on the lab door at the same time. Max punched in the code, threw the door open so hard it slammed against the wall. The three of them tumbled in.

"Professor Kleinheidt, Professor Kleinheidt, Professor!" Max shouted as they dashed in and out of all the desks, tables, computers, and quantum computer in the football field size lab. There was no answer.

They stopped. Looked at each other from different ends in that eerie humming of an unoccupied state-of-the-art technology lab. Panting, sweat dripping down their faces.

"He's not here," Tan said rhetorically

Then they suddenly heard a moan coming from the storage room and Max took off for it like he'd just heard the gun go off at a track race.

He slammed into that door too and there was Professor Kleinheidt, tied up like he was cattle. Masking tape wrapped around his mouth and head. Max removed the tape as carefully as he could without wasting time. It was a good thing the professor was bald and clean-shaven.

"They have the algorithm!" Kleinheidt said. "The PQC algorithm!"

They learned that the same ninja-outfitted spy had accosted Professor Kleinheidt in the lab and at gunpoint forced him to download the authentic quantum-resistant formula onto a flash drive.

AT THAT MOMENT, JIA Li had been standing inside the lobby of the Commencement Hotel as she continued to assist guests as a representative of the quantum conference.

She heard a female voice, seemingly come from right alongside her, speaking in Mandarin, but there was nobody within twenty feet of where she was standing.

She scanned the room and could see people grouped off, milling around speaking to each other, but this voice was a one-sided conversation. As she listened to this female apparently talking on the phone, she wondered where the distressed-sounding conversation was happening.

She then heard the female urgently repeat, "Wei Ming, Wei Ming, are you there? Where are you?"

"Wei Ming," Jia Li whispered, continuing to scan the area. *Who is asking for Wei Ming?*

It seemed to Jia Li that the voice had dialed Wei Ming, and may have gotten his voicemail. "Call me at once!"

She again looked around, turning 360 degrees, like the twirling ballerina she was, but still could not identify where the voice could be coming from. It then dawned on her that the acoustics of an indoor space could make it seem like a voice was coming from the opposite corner of the room.

The best example she knew of was New York's Grand Central Station on East Forty-Second Street. During her first semester at the Schimmel Center, she and Wei Ming explored New York City landmarks like the Metropolitan Museum of Art, the Museum of Modern Art, Central Park, the United Nations, and Grand Central Station.

Wei Ming introduced her to the Whispering Gallery, which was named for certain corners of the station. You could whisper in one corner and the person in the opposite corner could hear and whisper back. The domed ceiling was the explanation. The sound traveled over the ceiling from one whisperer to the other.

It was at that moment that Jia Li looked up and noticed that the hotel lobby had a dome ceiling, too. She strolled across the lobby, looking up occasionally, as if reading the message on the ceiling that demanded Wei Ming to respond.

When she got to the other end, she saw an elderly bearded man in a dark gray suit and blue shirt with an open collar. Fitting the same description and attire of the two-thumbed man Max had spotted in the videos.

He was sitting in a red cushioned chair with his face buried in a cell phone. He had wedged himself in the corner, away from anyone within earshot, or so he apparently thought. It struck Jia Li as so strange that the elderly man sounded so much like a woman. As if he were a castrato.

One hand holding a cell phone to his ear, and the other hand over his other ear.

His hand had two thumbs! She screamed in silence.

Jia Li then watched another Asian man approach the two-thumbed elderly man and hand him something.

Jia Li stood there watching the two men in conversation for a few moments.

She then moved away to the opposite corner of the lobby, and whispered into her earpiece, "There are two men in the hotel lobby. One has two thumbs."

Max heard Jia Li's transmission. He was still in the storage room of the lab with Tan, Ashe, and Professor Kleinheidt. "Did you hear that?"

Then they all heard Jia Li's voice again, only louder, "Two-thumbed man in hotel lobby. Two-thumbed man in hotel lobby."

In her rush to notify Max about her sudden sighting of that two-thumbed odd sounding man, she'd entirely forgotten about the whispering acoustics.

The man had apparently heard what Jia Li was then saying and took off with that associate toward the tram. The Chinese agents were out the door before Jia Li realized they were fleeing. When she recognized it, they were almost halfway to the tram.

As she bolted out the hotel lobby door and gave chase, she lost her communication earpiece not having a chance to alert Max and the others.

Max shouted Jia Li's last transmission as he, Tan, and Ashe raced to the hotel lobby.

"Ghost in lobby of hotel! Ghost in lobby of hotel!"

MAX YANKED THE SIDE door of the air-conditioned Commencement Hotel, just as Tan and Ashe were doing the same at the opposite side door, neither waiting for the sliding doors to open.

They all stopped dead and scanned the lobby. There was no sight of Jia Li amongst the twenty or so guests at the hotel milling around, walking through the lobby to elevators up to their rooms, or coming off the elevators and heading to either the bar or the hotel restaurant.

Max shouted into his ear-mic, "Jia Li, Jia Li. You on the air? Jia Li, can you hear me?" No response.

They looked around. Was she still in the hotel? It needed to be searched, Max knew. But he couldn't stay. Jia Li could've left the hotel. Was she already off the island? Was she following them?

Max then looked at Ashe. "Stay here, Sam. Search for her, start with this floor first, hit every way in and out, hit the back alley, then hit the roof, do a vertical, come down from the top and work your way down, every stairwell, scan every floor."

"Got it," Ashe said, and took off.

Tan then handed Max an earpiece she'd found on the marble lobby floor, in a corner by the front doors.

"This has got to be Jia Li's."

"Damn it," Max said, then directed Tan to notify Mehta using all the real-time surveillance drones in the air set up by TARU to keep an eye out for the Beamer leaving over the Thirty-Sixth Avenue Bridge and especially the Roosevelt Island ferry and tram terminals.

He then blew out of the lobby and stood momentarily looking out at the turbulent river; looked north and south. Then looked down at the tram station just as a cable car was pulling in from Manhattan.

"I'm heading for the tram. They may head that way," Max said, and jogged in that direction when Parth Mehta's voice came into his earpiece.

"Yeah!"

"Max, it's Parth. Jia Li's Fitbit shows she racing to the tram."

Max yelled into his mic, "Jia Li's running to the tram. Jia Li's running to the tram!"

"Max," Mehta came through his earpiece again. "One drone has picked up Jia Li. She's chasing two Asian males in the direction of the tram. The tram just pulled in."

His jogging pace turned into a race that Tan did not have a prayer of keeping up with.

All that running over his lifetime—high school and college football, marine boot camp, miles of leading his police academy platoon on runs up and down the FDR Drive, the FBI Academy obstacle course at Quantico, and chasing bad guys through the back alleys and rooftops of New York City tenement buildings—came together in that moment of propulsion that led him to the Roosevelt Island tram, up the stairs, and across the ramp. He could see Jia Li fighting one assassin as the two-thumbed elderly bearded Asian looked on.

"Jia Li!" Max shouted as he watched Jia Li use jiujitsu moves on the assassin like Bruce Lee, but the recruiter's associate also had martial arts training and knocked her down onto the platform while jumping into the cable car. Jia Li bolted up suddenly and dove into the tram before the doors could close.

The tram started to pull out. Max raced across the ramp, landing at the edge of the platform, and leaped over six feet, just grabbing a bar under the tram with one arm as the tram ascended into the sky.

Max could not look down. He had a split-second thought to let go, but he just could not. Not with Jia Li on that tram with those Chinese spies and killers, one of which was the ghost-recruiter.

The tram continued to rise. He got his second arm up and was dangling from the rising Roosevelt tram with both arms, but could he continue to hold on? Could he last until the tram reached the Manhattan side? He knew he could not. The tram was still on the ascent and his arms were already giving out.

He swung one leg up and over the rod he was hanging from, then his other leg. He held there for a moment, wrapped around the rod like he was holding Jia Li herself.

"Don't look down, don't look down," he whispered to himself, but felt compelled to take a peek, "Ahh, Christ."

The tram still had not reached the top; he knew he needed to somehow climb up on the side of the tram. The thought of their killing Jia Li the way they'd stabbed their colleague with an ice pick and broke his arms drove him to climb up.

He was soon hanging from the floor of the tram door and managed to pull himself up and was facing the bad guys through the glass of the tram. Jia Li was lying on the floor of the tram, either knocked unconscious or dead.

Max slammed on the glass door with one hand as he held onto the corner of the door with the other. One assassin fired a shot at Max point blank, but the bullet could not completely penetrate the glass.

Max knew another shot at that same spot would go right through his eye. He pulled himself up by reaching to the top of the door. Just as the tram started going down, he successfully climbed onto its roof. He slammed open the hatch on the roof of the tram.

The assassin fired another shot at Max but missed then forced the tram door open, and the Chinese spies leaped out.

They went down like missiles.

"For crying out loud," Max whispered as he jumped down through the hatch onto the cable car floor, dashed to the door, and peered down just as the two spies plummeted into the river with a vicious splash.

Max promptly dropped to the floor beside Jia Li and shook her. "Jia Li, Jia Li."

She gradually opened her eyes, then snapped to attention, as if emerging from a trance. Her gaze fixed on Max, and she demanded to know where the Chinese spies had gone.

"They jumped out," Max explained, kneeling beside her. "They landed in the river."

With that, Jia Li sprung to her feet, as if propelled by a trampoline, and leapt out of the cable car too.

"For crying out loud," Max said, still kneeling where Jia Li had lain unconscious one moment ago.

He dashed to the door and watched Jia Li's body plunge into the river, too.

Max gazed upward, closed his eyes, crossed himself, and jumped out as well, shouting, "Marine Corps!" as he plunged into the depths of the East River.

He resurfaced; his vision revealed a speedboat heading southward down the river. The spies were prepared for an interception, having arranged for transportation in the middle of the East River.

When the wake from the speedboat settled, Max spotted Jia Li's head bobbing in the water, her waving arms a signal. He swam toward her with remarkable speed, reminiscent of a stingray. As he reached her, she commented,

"You are an excellent swimmer, Max."

Max leaned in after a moment, capturing her wet face in his hands and kissed her. In the midst of their kiss, he felt Jia Li embrace the connection, then lift her arms to encircle Max's head, her warmth pressing against his chest. Max felt a ripple of love's laughter reverberating through her.

Within minutes, a NYPD Harbor speedboat arrived, swooping in as if they'd hailed a cab, and yanked Max and Ji Li aboard.

Handcuffed and faced down on the floor of the NYPD speedboat was the ghost's associate and the pilot. Apparently, they'd been ejected and picked up by Harbor as they frantically tried to reach the Manhattan shoreline.

The ghost was now traveling alone, and the pursuit was on.

Max jumped to the bow of the boat, and the pilot handed him the police radio's mic to communicate with the Citywide dispatcher coordinating communications between the various NYPD units about to join the chase.

"How the hell did you guys know we might need help in a hurry?" Max yelled over the roar of the engine and the blaring siren."

"Chief Mannix sent us," the female pilot shouted as she skillfully maneuvered the boat.

"Yeah, Loo, the chief was following the real-time video our TARU drones were spitting out," the co-pilot chimed in.

Max shook his head, feeling that heart pang thing again, "we got your back."

The ghost sped southward down the East River. The NYPD boat was hot on its tail.

"Citywide, this is NYPD/FBI Strike Force Lieutenant," Max shouted into the mic. "We've been picked up by a NYPD Harbor Speed Unit and now in pursuit of one Chinese national on a black speedboat with a red trim wrapped around the center of the boat."

The dispatcher's voice crackled in response. "What is the suspect wanted for, Lieutenant?"

Max's reply was swift and to the point, "Homicide and other crimes."

"Ten-four, Lieutenant," the dispatcher acknowledged. "All Citywide units be advised NYPD/FBI Strike Force lieutenant is in pursuit of a murder suspect in a black speedboat with red wrap-around trim heading south down the East River area of Fortieth Street. Units responding?"

"Harbor Two-Three responding, Central, heading north on the East River adjacent to Wall Street."

"Aviation Seven-Two responding, Central." The chopper's blades could be heard over the radio. "Three-minute ETA to East River."

"Ten-four, Aviation Seven-Two and Harbor Two-Three," the dispatcher acknowledged.

"Harbor Five-Four responding, Central, heading south from Hell's Gate."

"Ten-four, Harbor Five-Four."

"Where could she be going?" Jia Li yelled above the noise. "There seems nowhere to run."

Max nodded, keeping his eyes fixed on the speedboat as it cut through the river, bouncing hard on the swells.

"She is gaining distance from us," Jia Li shouted.

The ghost appeared to be making a beeline for the Thirty-Fourth Street ferry landing. Max, Jia Li, and NYPD harbor speed boat had just reached the mid-forties by the United Nations.

"She's heading for the ferry landing," Max observed. He then transmitted to the dispatcher, "Central, notify the Seventeenth Precinct to send a radio car to the East Thirty-Fourth Street ferry terminal. The speedboat appears to be heading that way."

The Seventeenth Precinct covered Sutton Place, Turtle Bay, Tudor City, Murray Hill, and the East River coastline from East Fifty-Ninth Street to East Thirtieth Street.

"Ten-four, Lieutenant."

The spy's speedboat closed in within 100 yards of the ferry landing, the flashing lights of a marked police car arrived at the landing. The speedboat abruptly shifted course, veering away from Thirty-Fourth Street.

"Where is she now going?" Jia Li shouted.

"The Wall Street Ferry landing, it looks like," Max said. "Central, notify the First Precinct to dispatch a radio car to the Wall Street ferry terminal."

The First Precinct covered the southern tip of Manhattan that included the Financial District, Battery Park City, and Tribeca as well as the East River and Hudson River coastlines from Dover Street on the East River side to West Houston Street on the Hudson River side.

"Ten-four, Lieutenant."

The speedboat tried to make a mad dash across the East River toward Brooklyn, just missing several sailboats drifting up the river and a few NYC Ferry boats.

"She's going to get some person killed," Jia Li shouted. "Where is she going now?"

"Looks like she's targeting the Brooklyn Terminal ferry landing," Max shouted amidst the clamor. "She's just trying to escape. She doesn't care where she docks, she wants to vanish in a New York City maze."

Max radioed the dispatcher again. "Central, alert the Nine-Four Precinct to have a radio car respond to the Brooklyn Terminal ferry landing."

The Ninety-Four Precinct covered the Greenpoint area as well as the westside coastline of the East River north up to the Newtown Creek.

"Ten-four, Lieutenant."

"Aviation, Seven-Two to Central."

"Go ahead, Aviation," the dispatcher replied.

The sound of the chopper was audible.

"Be advised we have a visual of the black speedboat heading east toward Brooklyn."

"Ten-four, Aviation."

The ghost's speedboat shifted course once again, crossing the East River and heading eastward in the direction of the Wall Street ferry landing.

"She is headed back to the Wall Street ferry landing it seems," Jia Li shouted.

"We'll see," Max whispered.

The ghost's speedboat raced around the tip of Manhattan, bypassing Wall Street, and turned north. The vessel soon disappeared from view.

"Strike Force Lieutenant to Central," Max said. "Does Aviation have an eyeball on the speedboat?"

"Aviation Seven-Two, affirmative. The speed boat is approximately West Fourteenth Street, weaving in and out of other boats, headed north up the Hudson."

"Ten-four, Aviation Seven-Two," Max acknowledged.

The NYPD Harbor boat Max and Jia Li were on completed its circuit around the southern tip of Manhattan. The ghost's speedboat came into view once more, weaving between other vessels as the helicopter's report had indicated.

"What is she doing?" Jia Li rhetorically asked.

Then, the ghost executed a maneuver that genuinely startled Max. Recognizing the risk of landing without being spotted, Max figured, the ghost made a calculated move.

Max noticed two Circle Line boats, distinctive tour vessels that couldn't be missed. One headed north, while the other traveled south. They would pass each other in their respective directions. The implications sent a shiver down Max's spine.

The spy raced up the center of the Hudson River and sandwiched itself between the two Circle Line boats as they crossed parallel to each other.

"My goodness," Jia Li shouted. "Those big boats could crush her."

"Aviation Seven-Two," Max called into the radio. "This is the strike force lieutenant."

"Go ahead, Loo."

"You still have the speedboat in view?

"Lost sight of it, Loo, sandwiched between the Circle Lines," the Aviation chopper replied. "Standby."

Max waited.

"It's empty, Loo. Dead in the water. Floating unattended."

"Any bodies in the water?" Max asked.

"Negative, Loo."

"Damn," Max shouted. "The ghost jumped off the speedboat—she must be on one of the Circle Lines."

"Damn," Jia Li repeated.

Max could not help glancing at Jia Li.

With that expletive, the southbound Circle Line boat continued to pass them as it headed south.

"Aviation, is the northbound Circle Line heading for its landing on Forty-Second Street?"

"Yes, sir."

"What's the approximate passenger count on the Circle Line?"

"Packed, lieutenant on both levels," the NYPD chopper pilot replied. "Must be over five hundred tourists on board. Numerous Asians."

"Crap," Max muttered again.

"Central, notify Circle Line not to allow anyone off the vessel when it docks."

"Ten-four, Lieutenant."

"Central, direct several units to respond to the Circle Line landing," Max said. "Nobody gets off the boat without NYPD/FBI Strike Force clearance."

"Ten-four, Lieutenant."

"Harbor Five-Four on the air."

"On the air, Loo."

"Your location?"

"Just coming around the southern tip of Manhattan, Loo."

"There's a Circle Line boat heading your way. Track it until I tell you to break it off," Max said. "If it docks anywhere, don't let anyone off the boat until you hear from me."

"Ten-four, Loo."

"Harbor Two-Three?"

"Go ahead, Loo."

"Harbor Two-Three, after the Circle Line pulls into the landing, keep an eye on it—make sure nobody tries to sneak off. You need to cover both sides of the boat."

"All right," Max told the boat's pilot. "Drop us off at the Forty-Second Street landing."

Max and Jia Li disembarked the boat onto the West Forty-Second Street landing. Tan and Ashe were already waiting there, having listened to the chase transmissions over the radio.

Max approached them, joined by the uniformed police sergeant on the platform, along with the Circle Line boat's pilot and facility manager. He quickly briefed them on the situation.

Max organized two columns for the passengers to be screened before disembarking. Tan and Ashe were at the head of each column with a uniformed police officer announcing the same instruction repeatedly.

"Show us your hands, please."

Max and Jia Li closely monitored each column as Tan and Ashe did the screening.

Max couldn't limit the search to only women, given that they believed the ghost had disguised herself as a bearded man when Jia Li had spotted Two-Thumbs in the hotel lobby.

After screening over 400 passengers for an hour, they were left with just 100 more.

Max radioed the two NYPD Harbor boats to keep watch for anyone trying to jump ship.

"Strike Force Lieutenant to NYPD Harbor units. Everything quiet?"

"Nothing, Loo," Harbor responded.

"Maybe she is on the other boat," Jia Li suggested.

"Maybe," Max responded thoughtfully.

After completing the screening of the remaining 100 passengers and with the boat now empty, Max decided, "We need to search the boat." He directed the uniformed sergeant to have his team of twelve officers conduct a thorough search.

"Go through every nook in that boat," Max ordered.

The sergeant directed four of his officers to search each of the boat's three levels. Max, Tan, Ashe, and Jia Li stood by on the landing, waiting.

A few minutes into the search, Max noticed the Circle Line crew standing around, watching and waiting. They were each dressed in black pants, beige polo shirts with "Marine Crew" printed across their backs and beige baseball caps.

Then, a shout from the officers on the middle level, "We got an unconscious, stripped female in the bathroom!"

With that information, Max instinctively turned away from the boat and saw a petite Asian woman dressed in a Circle Line Marine Crew uniform racing across Twelfth Avenue toward the Chinese consulate on the opposite corner.

"The ghost is going for the consulate!" Max shouted, pointed, and took off after her. "She's going for the consulate!"

The ghost's agility thoroughly impressed Max as she dodged traffic and police officers, maneuvering like NFL Kansas City Chiefs championship quarterback Patrick Mahomes.

But Max was on her. When she cut away from the last police officer between her and the entrance to the Chinese consulate, Max dove at her, catching her blindside. He hooked her left ankle with his outstretched arm; she landed on the pavement hard.

Tan, Ashe, and Jia Li descended on the ghost.

"Search her for the flash drive," Max directed Teresa Tan as Ashe helped him off the ground.

Tan went through all her pockets like she was a starving cat searching for a meal, then yanked the flash drive out holding it up like it was a diamond. "Here it is!"

It was over.

LATER THAT NIGHT, MAX, Tan, Ashe, Mehta, Jia Li, and Wei Ming sat in the main room of the Blackwell House, their attention fixed on Jia Li's ePhone lying still on the desk.

The ghost, the two assassins, Zhao Hua, and—as it turned out—three other of the targeted-eight Chinese quantum students, those who had succumbed to Wei Ming's proposal to steal on behalf of the Chinese spy recruiter, had been processed at the Manhattan federal correctional facility. There, they would remain throughout the weekend, awaiting their arraignment scheduled for Monday morning before a United States magistrate judge.

Jia Li's ePhone buzzed and vibrated on the desk. She snatched it and brought it up to her ear, choosing not to put it on speaker.

"Yes," she answered in Mandarin, and listened. A visible sigh of relief escaped her; her head dipped, misty eyes turned to Wei Ming, broke into a smile, and nodded.

Wei Ming's family had safely made it to Taiwan.

Their excitement erupted, and they all leapt to their feet, converging in a jubilant embrace, akin to a team that had just secured the winning goal at the World Cup.

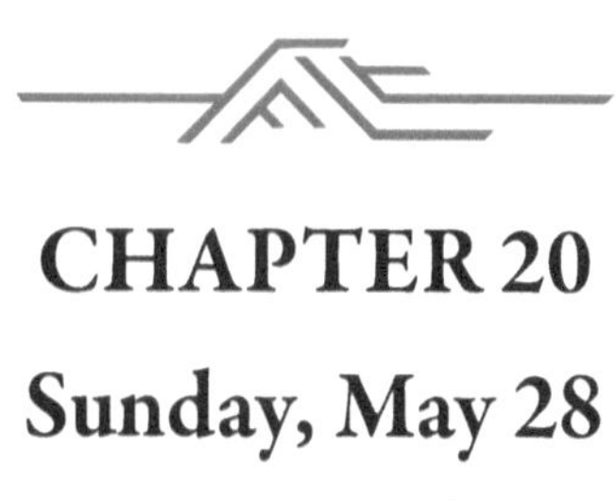

CHAPTER 20
Sunday, May 28

Max and Jia Li were sitting across from each other at the small table in her Roosevelt Island apartment, each eating a slice of toasted raisin bread with butter and strawberry jam. It was a favorite of Max's. Breaking the silence, Jia Li spoke up.

"Tell me about this communist Chinese fentanyl manufacturer responsible for the twins' father's death."

CHAPTER 21
Wednesday, June 7 –
Saturday, June 10

Max and Jia Li, along with other NSB members, were waiting at Taiwan's Taoyuan International Airport for flight 335 from Beijing. They were expecting a person of interest.

The passenger's name was Xingshi Pa. Taiwan's NSB had lured Mr. Fentanyl to Taipei to establish a few fentanyl labs—or so he thought. All along, the Chinese fentanyl manufacturer had been communicating with Taiwan's intelligence and law enforcement services.

As soon as Mr. Fentanyl entered the arrivals area, Taiwanese authorities approached him, put him in handcuffs, and escorted him on a long walk through the corridors of the airport for the next flight to Fiji. Max and Jia Li followed them to the plane, boarded the plane with them and flew to Fiji, unbeknownst to the criminal.

When the plane landed in Fiji, the NSB agents turned Mr. Fentanyl over to the Fiji Police Force Narcotics Bureau, who then walked through more long corridors of Fiji's Nadi International Airport and boarded a plane to New York City.

Max and Jia Li again followed them to the plane and boarded the flight to New York, too.

Twenty hours later, they landed at JFK International Airport and the Fiji Police Force Narcotics Bureau escorted the criminal off the plane to the arrivals area. Waiting were Teresa Tan and Sam Ashe.

The Fiji police officers then turned to Max and said, "On behalf of the Republic of Fiji, we are turning custody of the accused over to you," and removed their handcuffs.

"On behalf of the United States of America, I accept custody of the accused," Max replied, then turned to face Mr. Fentanyl and said, "You are under arrest for murder," put his handcuffs on him and listened to the satisfying clicks of justice close in around his wrists.

Max, Jia Li, Tan, and Ashe walked the fentanyl killer to the black SUV waiting for them.

CHAPTER 22
Sunday, June 11

Max and Jia Li had just finished having dinner with Maya and the twins at their Riverdale apartment.

The kids drifted away to the balcony and descended into their iPads.

Max watched them settle in.

"You have beautiful children, Maya," Jia Li said.

"Thank you, Jia Li," Maya said and held her hand across the dining room table.

Max then whispered to his sister, "We got him, Maya."

Maya looked at Max with wide intense eyes. Looked to Jia Li then back to Max.

Max nodded and whispered, "We got the Chinese fentanyl dealer. Jia Li helped lure him to U.S. soil. He's here in a federal jail. He's going to trial for Gus's murder and for the murder of many other Americans."

After a few extra moments of increasing comprehension, Maya stood up, stepped around the dining room table and hugged Max and Jia Li releasing a deluge of tears.

CHAPTER 23
Monday, June 12

Max was home when he read the following passage from the *Art of War* by Sun Tzu (504-496 B.C.):

Having inward spies means making use of officials of the enemy. Worthy men who have been degraded from office, criminals who have undergone punishment; also... men who are aggrieved at being in subordinate positions, or who have been passed over in the distribution of posts... fickle turncoats who always want to have a foot in each boat. Officials of these several kinds should be secretly approached and bound to one's interests by means of rich presents.

"Secretly approached... means of rich presents," Max whispered, when his ePhone buzzed. He could see it was Jia Li.

"Max, I have learned something from my agency that will be very important to you."

"You're at your consulate, Jia Li?"

"Yes."

"Okay, what do you have?"

"I was not aware of this. I do not know all the intelligence gathering operations of my agency in America, but I have now been told that my agency routinely observes Chinese consulate officials coming and going from their consulate."

"Okay," Max said again. Now that they'd identified the ghost recruiter he immediately assumed if they had captured footage of the recruiter coming and going from their consulate at some point.

"I asked if they had occasion to put the recruiter under surveillance and my colleagues replied that they had. As they explained it to me, they had occasion to sometimes follow the recruiter from the Chinse consulate to a gambling establishment, the Empire City Casino, to meet with people," Jia Li said. "Are you familiar with it? It in the City of Yonkers, which is in Westchester County, New York."

"I am," Max said, and recalled the casino-sounding bells and whistles he and his team had heard in the background during one phone conversation with Dick Roach days earlier.

"Well, she met with someone who may be of interest to you," Jia Li said. "I have been given video of who she would meet which I can send to you."

"Yes, please send the video," Max said. "I'll be waiting."

Max slid over to his kitchen table and opened his MacBook.

Within seconds he received an email from Jia Li with one video attachment.

The video showed the backs of two people sitting adjacent to each other at slot machines, pulling on the one-arm bandits, without appearing to converse at all. One was a petite female with short dark hair; the other was a bald middle age appearing male.

Max felt a cold chill ripple up his back to his head giving him a stinging sensation, like a thousand needles stabbing at his skull.

Neither turned to the other as they pulled on the slots handle, but then the petite woman slid her hand to the male's thigh and the male slid his hand down and appeared to take what she had slid to him as he continued to pull on the one-arm bandit. The female soon swiveled around—unbeknownst to her—to then face the surveillance camera. It was indeed the ghost recruiter.

The male remained pulling down on the bandit's arm for another fifteen minutes or so, then swiveled around too, stood up and left.

"Geez," Max whispered, slowly leaned back and vigorously rubbed his face and head. He leaned into the screen and stared at the frozen video image. "Geez," Max repeated.

It was FBI Special Agent in Charge Richard "Dick" Roach.

ONE HOUR LATER, MAX trudged into the Blackwell House to the main floor as Tan, Ashe, and Parth Mehta were breaking the temporary command center down.

"I've got something to show you all," Max said as he worked his way to the empty table that had just been occupied by two of Parth Mehta's huge Mac computers and placed his MacBook laptop down.

Both Sam Ashe and Parth Mehta stopped what they were doing and looked at Max. Teresa Tan continued to pack things up and said, "Go ahead," without looking at Max.

"Teresa," Max said. "Please come over here and grab a seat."

He then looked at Ashe and Mehta and waved them over too.

They each approached Max with furrowed brows and puzzled looking grins, grabbed one of the rolling chairs, and sat down. Max was not grinning.

Tan, Ashe, and Mehta were no longer grinning either.

Max opened his laptop and started the Empire City Casino video.

They sat in silent focus; eyes fixed on the video until Max stopped it.

Silence.

"Holy shit!" Tan finally said, as Ashe and Mehta shook their heads. "Where did you get this?"

"Jia Li."

After several moments of silence and shaking heads, Max jumped on the phone with Jack Hunt and told him what he had and sent him the video.

"Call me back after you've watched it," Max said.

A couple a minutes later the call came in.

"Are you fucking kidding me?" Hunt said.

Max could not remember a day ever when Jack Hunt used expletives.

"Yeah, it doesn't look good."

"No, no, it doesn't," Hunt said. "He could be the Eastern District's mole."

"Yeah," Max said, "Could be. I assume at Roach's level he'd been briefed on the progress of their investigation."

"He sure was," Hunt said.

THAT EVENING MAX WAS waiting for Jia Li in front of her building on Roosevelt Island. She had something special she wanted to share with him, she had said. They took the Roosevelt Tram over the East River without incident. Max then whistled for a cab on Second Avenue at Jia Li's request. She'd written the address she was taking him onto a piece of paper and handed it to the driver. The driver nodded and smiled.

"Any idea where I am taking you?" Jia Li asked, as the driver made a right turn on East Fifty-Ninth Street.

"Not yet," Max said. "But I see we're heading west."

It was a cool spring evening. They'd opened the cab's windows. The Central Park south wind blew past his face. When they arrived at Columbus Circle, Max started to get an inkling of where they were going, and he was right. The driver swung north on Broadway a few blocks then over to Columbus Avenue, turned south and pulled up in front the New York City Ballet at Lincoln Center.

She squeezed his hand as he was paying the driver and jumped out. She looked like she'd just landed home after being away for years.

"My former ballet company is performing *Swan Lake* here tonight," Jia Li said with such a radiance that Max's heart ached in joy for her.

"Really," Max said. "The Taiwan Ballet Company?"

Jia Li nodded and delivered Max a beaming smile, took his hand and pulled him to the theater doors practically at a jog.

AS MAX AND JIA LI TRAVELED back to the Roosevelt Tram from Lincoln Center in a yellow cab, Max's ePhone vibrated; he could see it was Jack Hunt.

"Yeah, Jack."

"Sorry to bother you, Max," Hunt said. "You have a minute?"

"Yeah, sure, go ahead."

"Max, the FBI director sent the calvary up to Roach's house to bring him in. The agents hit the house, not realizing he was in his garage gym. When they went to the gym, it was too late."

"Too late?"

"He was DOA," Hunt said. "Suicide."

"Mercy," Max whispered.

"Yeah."

"He ate his gun?"

"No, all his weapons were inside the house," Hunt said. "They found him in the garage. The garage had a bench press. Theory is he deliberately dropped four hundred pounds of barbell onto his neck."

"Mercy," Max whispered again.

"Max. He left a very short, scribbled note," Hunt said. "It had today's date and time just before his body was found. It read, '*So sorry. So sorry.*' signed Dick Roach."

Max closed his ePhone.

"Is everything all right, Max?" Jia Li asked, twisting almost entirely around in the cab seat to face him.

"Dick Roach took his life."

Jia Li pulled Max into her and held him.

Max stared out into the swiftly passing trees as their cab breezed through the West Sixty-Sixth Street Central Park transverse to the East Side of Manhattan.

They traveled in silence.

CHAPTER 24
Wednesday, June 14

"The Select Committee on communist China will come to order," Chairman Mike Gordon said. "Will the witnesses before us today please stand to the take oath."

With that, Lieutenant Max Valentin, NYPD; Special Agent Teresa Tan, Homeland Security Investigations; Special Agent Sam Ashe, FBI; Senior Analyst Parth Mehta, U.S. Marshals Service; and Security Agent Jia Li May, National Security Bureau, Republic of China, (Taiwan) stood up and raised their hands.

"Do you swear and affirm under the penalty of perjury that the testimony you are about to give is true and correct to the best of your knowledge, information and belief so help you God."

A chorus of "I do's" followed.

CHAPTER 25
Friday, June 16

Max's ePhone alarm chimed first. He reached over Jia Li to silence it. The time was four a.m. She stirred, turned toward him, drew him closer, and planted a lingering kiss. He went for the shower first.

Two hours later as the sun rose over the East River, Max and Jia Li stood on the walkway opposite her Roosevelt Island apartment building, waiting for an Uber. A whirling breeze carried cherry blossoms away, creating an illusion of springtime snowfall to Max.

Jia Li turned and looked up at Max, gently touching his face.

"Why won't you promise to visit me?"

Max shook his head. "Jia Li, you know I have my work and I have my sister's twins. I can't promise you that. Taipei is on the other side of the world. It's just not that simple. I don't want to promise something I cannot be sure will happen. But I'll be here."

Max absorbed her gaze. His heart had been beating steadily at eighty-five beats per minute since the alarm went off.

"It's very exciting, the work you'll be doing, Doctor," Max said. He held her hand that rested against his face, leaned down, and kissed her. "I am relieved you have put NSB work behind you. The quantum research you'll be continuing is groundbreaking and exciting. Very important work. The future of our democracies depends on it. Right?"

They stood quietly, locked in each other's eyes.

Jia Li then rose onto her toes, reaching up to hold Max's face with both hands. She whispered, "You are in my heart, Maximo Valentin."

They kissed long and hard. Max could feel Jia Li's tears streaming down his face. Cherry blossoms landed on their heads like delicate blessings.

They both turned to the sound of a car coming to a stop in front of her building. Max swiped away the flowers from his hair, and gently removed the cherry blossoms that had nestled in Jia Li's hair, picked up her two bags and placed them in the trunk that the driver had popped open. The driver opened the rear door for Jia Li and got back into the car to wait until they were ready.

Jia Li nodded, squeezed Max's hand, got into the car, and it pulled away. Max watched the car's taillights head toward the Thirty-Sixth Avenue Bridge. She did not look back.

THE END

... the ongoing theft of IP is...
"the greatest transfer of wealth in history."
Commander of the United States Cyber Command
and Director of the National Security Agency, General Keith
Alexander

Don't miss out!

Visit the website below and you can sign up to receive emails whenever RONALD JAY ALVAREZ publishes a new book. There's no charge and no obligation.

https://books2read.com/r/B-A-GFMT-UDFJD

BOOKS2READ

Connecting independent readers to independent writers.

Also by RONALD JAY ALVAREZ

Detective Toni Santiago
Pilgrimage to Ruin

Standalone
Bird in the Cage

Watch for more at https://ipprobe.global/about-ron/.

About the Author

Ron Alvarez is a blog writer and novelist based in New York City and South Florida, exploring the captivating worlds of intellectual property (IP) investigations and protection. As a former NYPD police lieutenant, he spent years unraveling mysteries and solving cases ranging from robbery to fine art theft.

In 2021, Ron embarked on the exciting journey of publishing with the release of his first non-fiction book, "The World of Intellectual Property (IP) Protection and Investigations: An Overview." Building on this momentum, he released the revised edition of his first murder/mystery novel, "Pilgrimage to Ruin," in 2022.

Join Ron as he continues to delve into the intricate realms of IP investigations, protection, and fiction writing. With Ron, you'll unravel mysteries, ignite imaginations, and embark on thrilling adventures between the pages of his novels.

Read more at https://ipprobe.global/about-ron/.